Katy Jordan was born and raised in Stirling, Scotland. Since an early age she has dreamed of becoming a writer and/or actress, and for the last six years she has been pursuing both. Official website: www.katyjordan.net

Katy Jordan

COLOUR CODED:
THE BLACK BULLET

AUSTIN MACAULEY PUBLISHERS™

LONDON • CAMBRIDGE • NEW YORK • SHARJAH

A CIP catalogue record for this title is available from the British Library.

ISBN 9781528907330 (Paperback)
ISBN 9781528958547 (ePub e-book)

www.austinmacauley.com

First Published (2019)
Austin Macauley Publishers Ltd
25 Canada Square
Canary Wharf
London
E14 5LQ

E.D.M

I'm the most powerful woman I know because of you. I miss you, and you'll always have a place in my heart.

J.P.H

My favourite little superhero. This book exists thanks to you. You are loved endlessly and unconditionally.

Lesley and Philip

I told you about a story I had in my head, and you weren't so sure about it. I decided to have a go, see how things went, and you still weren't so sure… and then I wasn't so sure. I let you read the first draft, I asked for your honest opinion, and you said: "Go for it!" So, I did. And here I am thanking you in my first-published novel. Two people who have never wavered under my weight, never faltered in supporting me, and always believed in me, even when I didn't believe in myself. My heart and my soul swell with the longing to repay you while knowing I'll never be able to. Thank you.

Prologue
Monumental Murder

It was a cloudy Saturday afternoon over the city of Stirling in central Scotland, as Chief Inspector, Claire Marshall admired the scenery of the Ochil hills that towered over them while they travelled along Hillfoots Road. Marshall was in her early forties, her long dark brown hair clipped up into a bun.

The car journey was silent as she had to look past Inspector Matthew Ingram, who drove at top speed to their destination to see the hillside. Marshall decided to look out her own window, houses flying behind them in a blur, and views over open fields welcoming her.

"So, what plans did you have this weekend?" Ingram asked.

"When you work in the Specialist Crime Division for as long as I have, you learn not to make plans on your on-call days," she replied smugly, not once pulling her gaze away from the scenery.

"Yeah, I'm learning that the hard way; I planned to go see my nephew's football game. My sister was livid when I told her this morning that I couldn't go."

"How old is your nephew?" Marshall pried.

"He's twelve," said Ingram, "but, he's more like a son than a nephew. I tried to stay close after my brother-in-law died two years ago." Marshall stayed quiet, not knowing what to say.

She wasn't a family woman.

Marshall grew up as an only child, and she didn't really understand all the hype of family outings and get-togethers.

"I'm sorry," she forced out, awkwardly.

A horrid silence ensued.

After their unresolved fight a couple of days ago, meeting up for this case was the first time they had spoken since.

As they passed by the tiny village of Blair Logie, Ingram, a tall, thin man in his late thirties, noticed two helicopters circling the ever famous Wallace Monument.

"Ma'am."

Marshall leaned forward to look up at the scene of the monument that stretched high above the trees grazing the overcast sky.

"Step on it," she ordered, leaning back in her seat.

Ingram planted his foot heavily on the accelerator, the sirens wailing loudly, as they continued along their route towards the monument. Ingram turned into the visitor's car park and pulled in to the side.

"What're you doing?" Marshall asked judgementally.

"Stopping to go up," said Ingram.

"I am not climbing that hill in these heels. This is a murder investigation; we're investigators, not tourists. Drive the road," she ordered.

"Yes, ma'am," Ingram replied, rolling his eyes at her.

Marshall gave him a deadly stare.

"I saw that."

Ingram said nothing, turning on to the narrow slope and crawling carefully up the Abbey Craig.

As they reached the top, the nosey crowds had already gathered. Ingram honked his horn for them to step aside, with uniformed officers assisting them in getting through. They reached the peak of the hill, the monument cordoned off with blue and white police tape.

Marshall and Ingram exited the car, and a police constable greeted them.

"Officer, what have we got?" Marshall enquired.

"One body, unidentified male, looks to be mid-to-late thirties according to the medical examiner," the constable replied, walking them to the entrance of the monument.

"Dr Munro?" asked Marshall.

"No, it's Dr Prim today, ma'am."

"Where's the body?" Ingram asked.

The young constable gave them a rather sheepish smile.

"Right at the top, sir," he said, as he lifted the tape for them to duck under. They began to climb the stairs, Marshall leading the way.

"Well, this is cosy," Ingram joked.

"Yeah, you're not lying there."

"You ever been here before?"

"Oh, when I was about nine or ten. You?"

"Never. So, this is an interesting first visit for me."

"It'll be interesting to see if you'll 'visit' again once this case is over with," Marshall scoffed.

Ingram smiled at the comment as they reached the top of the monument, the wind taking them by surprise.

The medical examiner, Dr Leanne Prim, awaited them at the centre of the top platform. Marshall looked rather confused as she scanned the platform to see no male victim.

"Have you moved the body already?" she shouted to Prim over the noise of the helicopters.

"Didn't one of the constables tell you about the body?" Prim asked, walking past them and down the steps to the edge of the monument.

"Aye, he said it was right at the top," Ingram shouted to her.

"Yeah... right at the very very top," Prim replied, pointing upwards.

A look of horror filled Marshall's face, as she went to join Prim at the edge of the platform.

"What... the hell?"

As Ingram joined the ladies at the edge of the top level of the monument, they were all looking up to see an arm and a leg dangling over the top of the monument, impaled on the topmost spike of the landmark.

"How the hell do you know he's in his mid-to-late thirties from down here?" Marshall probed. "You can't even see his face."

"My assistant's in one of those helicopters. He sent me this," Prim replied, holding her phone up to the two inspectors. A zoomed-in photograph of the victim was displayed on Prim's screen.

"May I?" Ingram offered, holding out his hand.

Prim gave him her phone, and he looked closely at the picture.

"You know him?" Marshall asked, studying him.

"No, I don't recognise him, but I do recognise that tattoo on the underside of his forearm," Ingram explained. "That's an identifying tattoo for a gang in Glasgow called the Lion's Den. No one's ever been able to convict them of anything criminal."

"Well, we can get back to the office and look into them," Marshall stated. "Good luck getting him back to the morgue, Doctor."

"Yeah, thanks, it'll be so much fun," Prim replied sarcastically as she took her phone from Ingram and walked away to make a call.

"If this is a gang killing, that's one hell of a way to make a statement," Marshall said, as they headed back towards the stairs. "Do you think they were trying to send a message?"

"I don't know, but I doubt he feels on top of the world right now," he replied, extremely content with his pun.

They pulled into the Randolphfield headquarters in Stirling, and Ingram swung the car into a space. The pair made their way into the building and climbed the stairs to the third floor.

"How sure are you about that tattoo?" Marshall asked him, breaking the silence.

She passed through the door that he was holding open for her.

"One hundred per cent. I was chasing that gang for years as a sergeant," he assured her, "I'd recognise that tattoo with a blindfold on."

"That's all I wanted to hear," she replied. "Well, we're not going to get an I.D. until Prim gets him down from there, so, for now, we'll start working on how our John Doe actually got up there."

They entered a very plainly designed room which was surrounded with whiteboards and corkboards, a group of tables pushed together in the centre of the room. Two officers in uniform stood in front of a television, watching the news discussing the case they were about to work on.

"Hi," said Marshall.

"Hi there. You must be Chief Inspector Marshall and Inspector Ingram?" The young man enquired, pointing to them the wrong way round.

"As much as he would relish in that state, I'm the Chief Inspector, Claire Marshall, and this is Inspector Matthew Ingram," Marshall corrected him.

"Oh sorry... I just assumed... you know..." the officer stuttered.

"No, I don't know, why don't you explain that... "

"It's an easy mistake to make, officer," Ingram interjected, clearly annoying his superior officer. "And you are?"

"I'm Officer Tucker, and this is Officer Jamieson," Tucker shook Marshall and Ingram's hand.

"We're here to assist you in any way we can," Jamieson said.

"Thank you very much," said Marshall, trying to ignore the clear stereotyping of Officer Tucker, "we're most likely going to need as much assistance as you can muster up."

"Do you have anything so far?" Ingram probed.

"We've left word with the RAF to see if they had any planes or choppers in the air over the last twenty-four hours, but we haven't heard back yet," Jamieson offered.

"Good," Marshall replied with a smile, "check with any pilot schools nearby as well, see if any of their crafts were missing or checked out for any period of time. But, check for the last forty-eight hours, rather than twenty-four," Marshall headed for a computer at the front of the room, as Jamieson and Tucker looked at one another, confused.

"They'd have needed to plan their route. Did you not take that into account, Officers?" Marshall clarified in a snide manner.

She typed on the keyboard rapidly, watching the screen intently.

Ingram went over to join her, making the smart decision to keep out of this one.

"Okay, there's a fair few nearby," Ingram began, looking over Marshall's shoulder. "Pegasus in Kinross, Border Air in Cumbernauld, Air Service Training in Perth, Fife Flying Club in Glenrothes, and a couple more in Glasgow and Edinburgh."

"Printing... Now," Marshall announced.

The printer behind the office door sprung to life, as paper started being pulled in blank and spat out with information. Tucker lifted the two sheets with the different schools and clubs on it.

"We'll get started with that now, ma'am," he said.

Tucker and Jamieson left with the list.

"I like it when people assume I'm beneath you because I'm a woman," said Marshall, who began typing again.

"No, you don't," Ingram jabbed.

"Sarcasm really sinks in well with you, doesn't it, Matt?"

"Can we not do this now? They're away doing their job, let's just do ours."

"Well, I'm trying to," she retorted, "I don't see you doing much." Marshall was never considered unable to hold her own.

For the few times that she got along with Ingram, she disagreed and argued with him two times that. But, he was her partner, and they were a team.

He was good to work with. Sometimes.

The television announcing a breaking news report regarding the deceased at the Wallace Monument caught Ingram's attention, and he took position in front of the TV to listen in.

"They're getting the body off the top of the monument... That's never something I thought I'd hear myself say," he revealed, and Marshall joined him to watch the report.

The helicopter had lowered two rescue team members down to strap up the body, and John Doe was now being carefully lifted into the helicopter.

A knock at the door interrupted them.

"Ma'am, Margaret Peters from Stirling District Tourism is here," announced Tucker.

"Great, put her in the interview room. We'll be there in two," Marshall instructed. Tucker left them once again.

"Do you think she'll know anything?" Ingram asked.

"Probably not," Marshall admitted, "but she can maybe shed some light on any suspicious behaviour."

The interview room was cramped and plain.

A small window caused a glare against the polished wooden table in the centre of the room that a small middle-aged woman sat at.

Margaret Peters was a short, stout woman with neat grey hair that reached just above her shoulders. Her eyes met theirs through her small spectacles, as Ingram and Marshall closed the door behind them.

"Sorry to keep you waiting, Mrs Peters," said Marshall.

"Please, call me Margaret. This situation is serious enough as it is, so I hope you don't mind skipping the formalities," she replied.

"That's absolutely fine, Margaret," Marshall confirmed, as she and Ingram sat down in front of her.

"So, we just have a few basic questions for you, just to give us a general idea of the monument and how it's run."

"Absolutely," Margaret nodded, keen to get going.

"Okay. First of all, Margaret, do you recognise this man?" asked Marshall, holding up the picture that Prim had sent to her in the car.

She had zoomed in on the man's face to avoid the disturbing view of the rest of his body.

Margaret closed her eyes in discomfort.

"No, I don't quite honestly."

Marshall put her phone back in her pocket and scribbled on a notepad.

"Can you tell us how many volunteers you have working for you at the moment?"

"At the moment, we have twenty-two," she answered.

"And how many were working at the monument yesterday and today?"

"Six yesterday, and eight today," she said, going into her briefcase that sat at her feet, "I brought a list with me."

"Thank you very much, Margaret," said Ingram with a smile, taking the sheet of paper and scanning it over. "Who found the body?"

"It was the minibus driver, Stan Parker. Lovely man. He was getting ready for the morning crowds and he spotted it," Margaret announced.

"He noticed it from the ground?" Marshall asked, stunned.

"He said he thought something looked weird, and he radioed one of my volunteers, Emma Hainey, who confirmed it. Such a shame, she's only nineteen, and it was her first time volunteering for us," she said.

"So, Mr Parker noticed something weird but couldn't make it out, and it was Miss Hainey who found the body?" Marshall clarified.

"Yes."

"Do you do any criminal background checks on people wanting to volunteer?" Marshall enquired.

"We get them to get a certificate from Discovery Scotland and bring it with them," Margaret answered. "But, Emma is a good girl."

"We're not implying that she's not, Margaret, but we need to know: does anyone on this list have a record?" Ingram asked.

"No, they don't, I checked before I came down," she answered, "there's two volunteers that do have a record, but not to the nature of what's happened at the monument."

"I understand you might believe that, but I think we should decide, Margaret. Could we get the names of those two volunteers?" Marshall probed.

Margaret took yet another sheet of paper out of her briefcase and put it down to face them.

"This is a list of all of our volunteers, along with their address. I've notified them to let them know this would be happening," she claimed, her hands visibly shaking. "There's two with an asterisk next to their names; they're the ones that have a criminal record."

Marshall took the small stack of paper that was put down in front of her and handed it to Ingram.

"In the last week, have any fights broken out at the monument? Either between staff or visitors?" Marshall asked.

"No, there has been no report of that. All our staff are required to take a note of any skirmishes or trouble that occurs at the monument," Margaret replied.

"Is there anyone there at night time? Like security or maintenance?" Ingram interjected.

"The monument gets locked at finishing time and that's the end of it," Margaret admitted.

"Okay," Marshall replied, scribbling notes, "if you have any security cameras, we're going to need a copy from the last forty-eight hours."

"I can get that to you as early as this afternoon," said Margaret, proudly.

"That would be great," Marshall said, "thank you very much for coming in, Margaret. If we need anything else, we'll be in touch."

"Anything I can do," she replied as they all got up and headed to the door. "Please find whoever did this. Visitor counts could drop drastically if we don't know what to tell our tourists, and all of my staff are extremely on edge."

"As soon as we know something, you will, Mrs Peters," Ingram assured her.

Margaret flashed them both a forced smile before walking down the corridor and through the doors.

"I don't think she knows anything," Marshall offered.

"Neither do I," Ingram agreed, "she would have too much to lose. But, I think we should talk to Emma Hainey."

"Yeah," Marshall agreed, "have Tucker and Jamieson go and question her. I want to talk to Stan Parker."

"I'll go make some calls," Ingram announced and walked in the opposite direction that Margaret did.

The breeze that the fire exit door let in was nippy and forceful, as Marshall stood outside and sparked up a cigarette.

She felt the rush as the nicotine made its way through her.

Her phone started ringing in her pocket, and upon pulling it out, she saw it was Dr Prim.

"How's my favourite medical examiner? ... You do? Fantastic! Okay, I'll be right there," Marshall hung up the phone and threw her cigarette away. She came inside and bumped into Ingram.

"Oh jeez, sorry! I was just coming to find you," she said.

"And I was just coming to find you," he panted, "no schools or clubs have had anything in the air since Tuesday because of the weather, and the RAF have been doing training courses at the borders. There have been no planes anywhere across the central belt."

"Damn," Marshall barked, annoyed, "well, that just makes our job a little bit harder, doesn't it?"

Ingram and Marshall put on the medical aprons and latex gloves and entered the morgue to meet Prim.

"Well?" Marshall asked. "Who's the unfortunate tourist today?"

"His name is David Watt, thirty-eight years old."

"Ditch," Ingram muttered.

"Who's a bitch?" asked Marshall, stunned.

"No, Ditch," he clarified, "David 'Ditch' Watt. I was right, he was a member of the Lion's Den. I tried to pin a drug deal on him,

14

but he got out of it on a technicality. He was called Ditch because of the kinds of places he did drug deals."

"Well, he's been a very busy man over the last year or so," said Prim in a very unimpressed manner. "I had to excuse my assistant from this particular case."

"Why?" Marshall pried.

"Because a friend of his is connected to Watt. And that friend of his committed suicide," Prim explained. "David Watt was accused of raping a twenty-three-year-old girl called Jenna Harvey. Midway through the trial, Harvey committed suicide, and Watt was found not guilty."

"How long ago was this?" Ingram asked.

"The trial ended three months ago. My assistant gave testimony on Jenna's behalf. Her death was really hard on him," she continued, "it was such a frenzied and strange case."

"What makes you say that?" Marshall probed.

"Because they had this man every which way. Whether Jenna committed suicide or not, he should have gone to jail. But, another witness went missing right after the trial ended."

"What was her name?" Ingram enquired.

Prim checked the report she took for excusing her assistant from this case file.

"My assistant Martin said it was another young girl called Wells. Georgina Wells."

Within less than a day of the body being discovered, the murder case just turned into a possible conspiracy.

Chief Inspector Marshall and Inspector Ingram most definitely had their work cut out for them.

Chapter One

The dank, musty basement reeked of stale body odour as Jack slowly paced the length of the room. Sweat dripped carefully down his forehead, creating a steady course across the bridge of his nose as it came to a stop at the tip.

"Tell me what you know," he said to the bruised, beaten girl. "Tell me what you know, and I might just let you live."

"I don't know anything," she whimpered, her long blond hair, damp with sweat, dangled down either side of her face as her head slouched forward. "But, even if I did… I wouldn't tell you,"

A swift, hard blow struck her face, as Jack took a back-handed swing to her moist cheek.

"Are you sure?" He warned.

"Positive."

The man smacked her again, this time much harder than the last.

He stared at her arduously, bending down so that his face was level with hers. Grabbing a clump of her wavy hair, he pulled her head back with much power, forcing her to look him in the eye.

"I don't want to hurt you, Flare," he said, "I really don't. But, I will go through all means necessary to make you talk to me."

"You do that… it'll be a complete waste of your time," Flare replied before spitting in his face.

Angered, Jack threw her backwards, the chair tipping, her head smacking against the concrete floor.

He stormed away, and reaching on to a shelf behind him, he took a small jar from it and opened it. It rattled as he emptied the contents into his hand.

Small rings, some with spikes and some with oddly shaped ridges fell on to his palm, and he turned to Flare while he slowly slid them on to his fingers.

"Did you think this was merely going to be a batting session?" He teased. "I did warn you… whatever means necessary."

Jack prowled toward his prey, wiggling his fingers to show off his new accessories for torture.

Flare's breathing drastically sped up as he towered over her with intimidating height and mass in comparison to her small, weakened form lying sideways on the cold, dewed floor.

Feeling a possible broken arm trapped between the chair and the ground, Flare fought through the incessant ringing in her head and fumbled around with her hands, strapped tight behind her at the wrist, trying frantically to break free.

"Tell me who's hiding her. Tell me where she is. Tell me what she's planning."

A shard of wood from the chair pricked her finger, and Flare grabbed it.

"I don't know where she is!"

In a frenzy, she tried with all her might to stop the tiny piece of wood from sticking to her clammy, shaky hands and started to jab at the duct tape around her wrists, the muscle in her forearm stretching like old elastic as though it may snap any second. Flare could smell the metal from the tips of Jack's shoes as he stood centimetres away from her face.

Briskly, he grabbed her elbow in a tight lock and yanked her and her chair upright, so forcefully that the chair screeched across the concrete floor. She could feel the burning heat from the light that hung directly above her head.

Almost consumed with fear and anticipation, she continued to stab and poke and swipe at the duct tape with the small shard, not for one second taking her eyes off of her attacker.

"Tell me even one of those things, Flare, and then we're one step closer to this all being over," Jack offered.

Flare's lungs were working overtime, every intake of breath was sharp and sore as she painfully shook her head. A tear fell down the side of her cheek and met the ends of her lips as she braced herself for Jack's next clear move.

The rings of his right hand tore across the side of Flare's face, and she cried out in pain. She could taste the blood in her mouth as it streamed from the newly formed wounds on her cheek.

Flare took deep breaths in an attempt to steady her breathing

The sight of the wooden door loaded with locks and bolts started to blacken in her throbbing daze. Unfazed, Jack sauntered away from her and sat in his own chair in the corner of the room.

On the floor next to his feet stood a bottle of vodka, which he picked up and took a large gulp from. He grimaced at the nipping in the back of his throat as he felt the alcohol wash through him.

The bottle was almost empty.

"That hurt me more than it hurt you," Jack claimed, "I really didn't want to resort to these methods, especially on the one and only Fuschia Flare, but you're leaving me with no option."

Flare said nothing.

She gave no reaction as she continued to tremble and the tears continued to flow. Jack was suddenly up and with her, his face in hers, as quick as though it were supernatural. His horrid, beady eyes bore through her.

Flare did not blink.

She kept his gaze.

It felt like hours until finally, he looked away to the deep, ragged cuts on her face.

"Ouch, don't want them to get infected..." he taunted, and all of a sudden, a searing pain hit Flare's face as Jack splashed the rest of his vodka into her fresh wounds.

Flare screamed.

She didn't care anymore.

She could no longer bear to try and hide how he affected her. She crazily shook her head and stamped her feet, all the while scraping at the duct tape with the small shard that she could feel breaking between her fingers.

Flare openly sobbed.

"Kill me," she pleaded, "just kill me because I will never give her up and I can't take this anymore..."

"No, no, no. That would be too easy. If you want to make this game hard, you're going to suffer for it," he informed her, punching three finely round holes into her abdomen with his rings. Flare folded fast like paper, gasping for breath like it was rationed.

No air would come to her.

Her pink T-shirt began to mat to her wounded belly as she tried to sit back.

She longed for the duct tape to snap.

She prayed for a miracle that that tiny little piece of wood that slithered in her hand like a worm would break through her restraints, that she would have a chance to free herself, but she couldn't tell how much more she had to go, or if she had broken through any of the tape at all. Jack gazed deep into her eyes again, his stubble glistening with sweat.

He stared intently, as though he could see right through her.

"Where is she, Flare?" he asked again.

"I don't know!"

"Don't lie to me!"

"I'm not lying! I don't know where she is!"

18

Jack turned away and began to pace again.

He lifted his black jacket slightly and pulled a small revolver from the back of his trousers.

Flare gasped in horror, her eyes closing, her mind willing this to end.

She couldn't decide at that moment if she was more terrified of the pain to come, or more relieved that he may kill her, and thus, this would be over.

Dauntingly, he checked the cylinder to see how many rounds he had.

He smiled, menacingly, slowly drawing his eyes up to meet Flare's exhausted gaze.

"How about a game of Russian Roulette?"

Without even needing to think about it, Flare shook her head.

"Aw, why not? It'll be fun!"

"No," she begged, "please don't."

Jack spun the cylinder before slotting it back into the base of the barrel. He slowly and threateningly slid back the hammer and held the gun to his temple.

Flare shut her eyes and held her breath.

Click.

Her eyes batted open.

The noise of Jack's revolver coincided with the sound of the duct tape snapping behind her.

"Oh well, looks like it's your turn," Jack announced.

He made his way towards her, Flare feeling the confidence return to her now that she knew the element of surprise was on her side. He reached out his arm to continue his game, but Flare grabbed the gun with both hands and forced it back hard into his face.

Jack stumbled backwards and fell, stunned.

He scrambled to get more bullets from his pocket and load the gun, while Flare, in the same frenzy, clawed at the duct tape around her ankles.

She burst one free, as Jack slapped the loaded cylinder into the gun.

Flare didn't hesitate.

She swung her leg and the chair attached at Jack, knocking him over once more. The chair, as though in its own attempts to break free, separated from Flare's leg and hurled across the floor. She lunged.

Landing square on top of him, Flare aimed for the gun.

Four hands were grasping it as the pair rolled along the floor.

She tried to lock her leg underneath his knee, but Jack was anticipating everything.

He was trained.

Both her hands were in full grip of the gun, just like Jack's.

Their legs flailed around aimlessly as they tried to get the better of one another. There was nothing else for it.

Flare opened her mouth and latched on to Jack's shoulder.

He yelled and squirmed in pain, his blood filling her mouth, his skin tearing away between her teeth.

One hand came off the gun and crashed through Flare's hair.

She grabbed his arm, keeping the other firmly on the gun, and rolled forwards, flipping Jack over the top of her. As he sprawled across the floor and landed on his back, Flare stood up.

She tried to ignore the pain that tore through her entire body.

Flare gripped the revolver as tight as she could while it shook in her weak and trembling grasp, as she aimed it straight at Jack's head.

Jack flipped on to his front and stopped dead at the sight before him. He looked up at her, his eyes filled with hatred.

"How long have you worked for him?" Flare demanded.

Jack did nothing. Said nothing.

She forced back the hammer.

"HOW LONG HAVE YOU WORKED FOR HIM?"

Silence ensued until finally he replied.

"Why does it matter?"

"It matters to me," she hissed at him.

"Just over two years."

Flare felt her grasp on the gun loosen.

Numbness consumed her from her feet upwards as she heard the words uttered from his bloody mouth.

He's bluffing she told herself, and quickly regained focus on her target.

"You're lying," she said.

"Am I?" he asked. "You were stolen from him. You all were. He wants revenge."

"Shut up."

"He's after you all…"

"Stop."

"…he's after all of you, and your new boss."

"STOP!" Flare screamed.

Jack began to laugh mockingly.

He had her.

He knew he was there, in her thoughts, penetrating everything she had ever believed.

"Did you think you would all just leave him and that would be the end of it?" He asked, amused by her naivety. "He taught you all everything you know. He trained you to do what you do. And you left him 'to do better things'. He's pissed. But, he knows Bullet led the way and the rest of you followed suit. So, either you go back to him, or you go to the afterlife. His words, not mine."

Flare stared at Jack, silent, unbelieving.

"Stand up."

Jack fumbled to his feet, grimacing with every move, holding his hands up as he stood upright.

Keeping the gun pointed in his direction, Flare edged back towards the toppled chair and grabbed it. She dragged it behind her and slid it over to him, feeling her left knee about to buckle underneath her own weight.

"Sit down."

Jack sat down, his hands still in the air. Flare picked up the duct tape from the shelf and threw it at him, hard. It slammed into Jack's chest and landed on his lap.

"Tape your ankles to the chair legs."

He glared at her, annoyed that she now had the upper hand.

"NOW!" She shouted, angry.

Reluctantly, Jack began taping his legs to that of the chair he sat on.

Flare approached him, shoving the muzzle of the revolver on to his forehead.

She picked up the duct tape and gnawed at the end with her teeth and it came away easily

She pulled the gun away from his face.

"Put your hands behind your back. If you try anything, I'll make abstract art with your brain matter."

Flare taped his hands together around the back of the chair.

Learning from her own actions, she covered his fingers as well, being generous to herself with the amount of duct tape she used. She walked round to face him, gun still aimed in his direction.

"I implore you to not try anything," she warned.

"I'm pretty certain you're not the one trained with guns, Flare. What you gonna do?"

"Just because this isn't my primary skill, doesn't mean I don't know how, nor does it mean I've never done it before. Don't try me, Jack," she retorted.

Flare limped to the only door in and out of the basement.

Three bolts, two chains, and four locks secured it shut.

She unbolted and unchained it, and skilfully held the gun flat against the door and fired, breaking through all four locks. An irritated look of surprise hit Jack's face as Flare held the gun out in front of her.

Turning the handle slowly, Flare flung the door open, ready for anyone else who may be on the premises. She walked up the dark stairway and into a small hallway.

Carefully, she proceeded through the downstairs of a house, ignoring the shocks of pain shooting through her body, clearing all the rooms. The detail was modern but basic; all white walls, all grey carpets, no pictures, no personal detail to anything.

A safe house.

Flare passed through the living room, edging her way around the dark brown leather sofa, and jumped at the sight of someone. The sight of her own reflection.

Stunned, she limped closer to the mirror.

She resembled a victim in a horror movie; a bloody face, an eight ball for an eye, her hair matted and unwashed hung like rats' tails on to her pink T-shirt which was ripped and smeared with a mix of blood and sweat. Flare touched lightly at the cuts forced on to her face by Jack's rings of torture and winced.

She ran her fingers delicately over the three puncture wounds to her stomach, which bled steadily, causing a river across the waistband of her pink jeans. Her fingers scraped and bloody, her thighs lashed and bloody, her legs beaten and bloody.

The only thing untouched were the feet on which she stood so weakly, her fuchsia trainers now a shade of deep pink with the blood that stained them.

Flare sighed, choking back the tears that she was now out of the torture chamber in the basement.

She was safe.

For now, anyway.

Her security check ended in the kitchen, and quickly, she clocked the phone hanging on the wall. Flare flung it to her ear, thrilled to hear a dialling tone. She punched the numbers like her life depended on it and waited for an answer.

"Yellow Youth," said a voice.

"Youth, it's Flare."

"FLARE! What the hell happened? Are you okay?"

"I'm fine… sort of. I have no idea where I am. Can you trace this call?"

"Of course!" said Youth, almost insulted at the question. "I'll get Gecko to come and bring you home."

"Not just Gecko, Youth. It was Jack."

"JACK? Holy shit… where is he?"

"He's a little tied up at the moment," Flare said, enjoying her pun.

"Okay. Well, you've been held for three days. Surely there's food there?"

"There will be, somewhere," Flare considered, "I'll find something. But, this needs Colour Coded. So, send everyone."

"I will. Just hang tight, okay? I've got your location, everyone's on their way."

"Thanks, Youth."

Flare hung the phone back on the wall. She limped carefully over to the small, bland kitchen table and slumped into one of the seats. Her head fell backwards as she stared at the white ceiling, exhausted, in pain, longing for a long hot bath and a rested night's sleep.

All that could be done now was to wait.

Colour Coded were on their way.

Chapter Two

In a grey room, all on his own, Jack squirmed in his restraints that ensured his attachment to the table at which he was seated. The handcuffs scored his wrists as he struggled while knowing all his attempts would inevitably fail. His black shirt crunched with every move, as the sweat which soaked him in the basement had dried into the material.

He couldn't decide if he was in jail or in interrogation, but either way, he did not like his situation.

If Colour Coded didn't kill him, Neon sure as hell would.

A camera situated in the corner of the room glared his way, the little red light winking at him mockingly. Jack was agitated.

How long was this going to take?

Was anyone ever going to talk to him?

What the hell were they doing?

With the tension building inside of him, he let out a roar and came close to a frenzied psychotic break as he swung his arms so much that the metal table nearly separated from the attachments to the floor like Velcro. He could feel the blood rushing to his face.

This was their plan.

They wanted him panicked, worried and anxious so that he would talk.

Instantly, Jack obstructed his urges to let his anger out.

He steadied his breathing.

He relaxed into the chair.

Closed his eyes.

Keep the upper hand, he told himself.

"Alright then. I'm sure your tea party that I wasn't invited to is over, so why don't you come in here and talk to me? I might have something interesting to say," Jack announced loudly, knowing someone was watching him, and therefore, would hear him.

Moments later, the sound of keys jangling nearby could be heard.

Jack's head bounced up like a dog being offered a bone at the thought that someone was finally coming in. The thick iron door opened, squeaking loudly before it hit against the wall. It revealed a young woman in her mid-twenties, her long brunette hair swept neatly into a bun.

Like him, she too was dressed all in black.

The sound of her knee-high heeled boots against the floor bounced off of every stone wall as she entered the room, closing the door behind her.

She stood.

The silence was insufferable.

Jack's mind was racing.

Should he say something?

What should he say?

Something smart?

Something insulting?

Charming, petty, funny, enlightening? Should he even speak at all?

Finally, the woman walked towards the table, never for a second taking her eyes off of him and sat in front of him. She seemed strong, able and independent while contributing sheens of elegance and love when she needed or wanted to.

"Do you know who I am?"

Jack did not respond as he continued to look at her, evaluating every slight detail that was on show to him.

"Do you know who I am, Jack Burns?" she forced, placing her elbows gently on to the cold metallic table and clasping her fingers calmly.

Jack chuckled.

"Smooth. Letting me know that you know who I am," he mocked. "No, I don't know who you are. Should I?"

"If you work for Neon now, as you so claim, then yes, I'd imagine you would know who I am."

"Well, I don't. Neon only tells me what I need to know," Jack explained, trying to keep his cool. "I'd formally introduce myself, but you already know who I am. So, who do I have the pleasure of speaking to right now?" The girl sat back in her chair and crossed her arms in front of her chest.

She gave him a continuous calculating stare, as if unsure whether to believe his formality was just who he was, or forced out to influence her reaction.

"I'm the hidden gem," she stated.

"That means nothing to me."

"Oh really? Well, what about the Black Bullet, does that mean anything to you? It should, you battered my colleague enough trying to find me!"

Jack's jaw almost hit the shiny silver surface of the table as her words registered with him. Surely, she must be lying.

This girl's capabilities are legendary!

He leaned forward, intrigued and not afraid to show it.

"The Black Bullet?" he asked in awe.

"That's right," she confirmed, "so, you know what I'm capable of, I'm sure. Your reaction tells me that my instincts are right."

"Yeah, you're right in saying that. I know what you're capable of. You were Neon's pride and joy."

"I was Neon's go-to to sort out all his problems, only to get nothing in return like he promised me. I was sick of it," she exclaimed.

"So, you left him," Jack affirmed.

"Yes."

"And took another three members of the team with you."

"Yes."

"And started yourselves as Colour Coded instead of Prismatic and began taking on new recruits to broaden your team's capabilities, like the Lavender Lab, for instance," Bullet is suddenly filled with an immense perplexity.

"You know... you sure do know a lot for a man who claims to not know a lot," she said, but Jack was too taken by her to even arrange words into the form of a sentence.

Bullet continued to gaze at him for a little bit, studying him, and decided to go straight to the issue at hand.

"The Fuschia Flare is in the hospital ward, Jack," Bullet explained. "She's in a rather bad way; malnourishment, blunt and sharp force trauma, a severe concussion. Our on-site doctor is having a field day trying to keep her on bed rest. Why did you want to find me? Or should I say, why does Neon want to find me?"

Jack considered what Bullet was saying.

He knew immediately that how she worded her last comment there was a threat. If he didn't say what he needed to, Flare would 'die', and he would go to prison for the rest of his life, if not worse. If he told them what they wanted to know, Flare would live, and he would continue on as a free man.

He felt every part of him shake as he jiggled his foot nervously on the ground.

Neon would kill him either way.

"Jack… I don't want to hurt you. But Neon? He's a snake. You have to understand that we are a team. We protect our own, no matter what. He hurt one of us, and in doing so he hurt all of us. You were his weapon. Talk to us and we will help you. Why did Neon have you kidnap and torture the Fuchsia Flare? Why does he want my whereabouts known?" Bullet pleaded.

Jack sat rigid, having an argument with himself in his head.

He needed to know they were legit.

He needed information before he potentially opened a can of worms that he would probably later regret.

"Are there still only eight of you?"

"Answer the question, Jack,"

Jack and Bullet had what felt like the longest ever staring competition.

Finally, Bullet broke the trance and stood up.

"Fine. We tried. You've made your bed, you can lie in it."

She headed for the door.

"No, wait, wait…" Jack persisted, frantically.

Bullet stopped as soon as Jack's worried voice reached her ears.

She turned to face him impatiently.

"Look, I just want to know more about you. I need to know who I'm relaying information to and why before I divulge. It's only fair," Jack stated, hoping that she would return to her seat across from him.

Bullet held his pleading gaze. A part of her felt sorry for him.

This man was terrified.

"What are you scared of, Jack?"

"NEON! You worked for him! You know what he's like, he's ruthless," Jack cried. "People are dying. People are dying all because he wants you lot either back or dead!"

Bullet returned to her seat.

She reached over and held Jack's bound hands.

"We won't let anything happen to you, Jack. Talk to us. Talk to me. Why does he want to know where I am?"

"Prove to me that you really are the Black Bullet," Jack requested.

Bullet sighed with irritation, coldly letting go of his restrained hands.

This was ridiculous!

He kidnapped her friend, the girl that was as good as a sister to her, and he wanted proof that they weren't dangerous?

Bullet caved.

"See over on that wall there, that little spider crawling up towards the ceiling?"

Jack looked over his shoulder and squinted to focus his sights on the spider in question.

"Yeah," he said, turning back to face her, "yeah, what about…"

BANG!

Jack almost created an outline of himself on the ceiling as he jumped with fright. Out of nowhere, Bullet had pulled a gun and shot the spider dead-on, without turning her sights from Jack.

She was swift, she was confident, and she was precise.

She was everything Neon described.

She was the Black Bullet.

"It really is you," Jack said, almost hypnotised by her.

As if nothing ever happened, Bullet placed her gun back inside her holster, which lay conveniently hidden under her leather jacket.

"Satisfied?"

Jack nodded slowly, as if under a spell.

"Now, tell me why he had you kidnap Flare."

Jack tilted his head forward and strained to run his fingers through his hair. The smell of the smoke from the gunshot still lingered in the air, reminding him that she really was who she claimed to be.

He looked at her, confidence filling him.

"He told me to take her to one of our safe houses and question her using whatever means necessary. I was to find out where you were."

"But, why?" questioned Bullet impatiently.

"Because he wanted confirmation about the talk on the streets."

"The talk on the streets? I have no idea what you're talking about."

"Neither do I. That's all he told me," Jack confessed. "He only tells me…"

"…what you need to know. Yeah," Bullet cut in.

She slouched back in her chair, annoyed at not having an answer.

"Is there still only eight of you," asked Jack again, "or is there seven?"

"What is your obsession with that question?" Bullet snapped.

"I'm glad you asked. Means I didn't volunteer the information."

"What are you talking about?" she asked, eagerly.

"When Neon finds out I spoke to Colour Coded, I can't tell him that I openly disclosed topics of discussions that he had with me in confidence," Jack explained.

"Well, then, say we tortured you," suggested Bullet.

"He won't believe that," Jack assured her.

"Look, what is it about how many of us there are that you're so interested in?"

"How many of you are there? Eight or seven?"

"EIGHT! Now, tell me why you're… "

"So, your team haven't lost or exiled anyone since your last run-in with Neon?" Jack butted in.

Bullet growled, her teeth grinding against one another in agonising annoyance.

"Will you just tell me why you're asking please, before you drive me up the wall and round the bend to where my gun lives!" she yelled, ushering down to her jacket, trying desperately to hold herself back from shooting him in between the eyes.

"Because Neon told everyone at his agency that there were only seven of you," Jack stated, ignoring her outburst.

The confusion from Jack's words oozed from Bullet freely, as she looked at him like a dumb school kid.

"There's been eight of us for the last two years. He knows that fine well,"

"Bullet… Neon told everyone that you were dead," Jack declared.

Confusion turned suddenly to fear, and then steadily to nervousness in Bullet.

Dead?

She tried to think of the man she once knew. She strived to enter his mind, to anticipate his next move, to understand why he would make such a bold, yet false, statement.

"I don't understand…" she uttered, "what does he have to gain from saying I'm dead? I am not dead, and well he knows it!"

"Hey, I only just found out about two minutes ago that he's been lying for almost a year. Don't ask me," Jack replied, helpless. "But, I can tell you that he's very convincing when he says it. Like he believes it's true."

Someone banged on the window.

Without another word being spoken, Bullet got up and headed outside.

As soon as the door was closed behind her, she entered another room to her right where she was greeted by Tide, Gecko, and Rocket.

"He said I was dead!" Bullet panicked.

"Calm down, Bullet," said Rocket, placidly. "Neon will be up to one of his usual tricks. Which means he'll fail."

"I want to know why."

"So do I," Tide agreed. "It could be a hoax to confuse us to the point that, whatever he tries, we'll never see it coming."

"How could it be a hoax?" Rocket questioned. "Jack was torturing Flare to find out if it was true or not. I don't think we were supposed to catch him. We need a plan."

"Well, what do you suggest?" asked Gecko.

"How about, rather than continuing to hide from him like we've been doing for the past year, we send Bullet out into the open for his men to spot her and report back to him?" Rocket offered.

"Are you kidding? They'll kill her for real, then!" Tide pointed out.

"Well, maybe not…" said Gecko, walking over to Rocket.

The three of them began to argue, while Bullet merely observed.

An older man entered the room amid the feud, with grey receding hair and small spectacles balancing skilfully on the tip of his nose. His flashy suit fit snug around his round belly.

He smiled at Bullet encouragingly. She knew what to do. He told her with his eyes.

Bullet broke through the noise.

"Guys! Guys! All fabulous suggestions. But, there's only one clear option here…" she stated to the team. "We act as though what Neon is saying is true."

Rocket, Tide and Gecko looked at Bullet as though she grew horns out of her head.

"But, you're not dead, Bullet," said Tide, "and we need Neon to know that you're still a threat to him. You're by far the most dangerous one when on your own than any of us are."

The others nodded in agreement.

"The thing is, children, that if Neon is spreading rumours of the Black Bullet's downfall, then he will have a reason. Until we know what that is, we shall keep up the pretence. Or he genuinely believes, by whatever manner of means, that she really is dead, and so, we will have the element of surprise when his next attempt to take revenge for the loss he has suffered arrives," The Spectrum explained.

His words of authority carried across everyone's ears like an old, beautiful melody.

When The Spectrum spoke, no one else did.

Not out of discipline or fear; out of nothing but respect.

Bullet looked through the window in the room that looked like a mirror on Jack's side. She watched him display nothing but fear and anxiety.

"Cut him loose," she demanded.

"What?!" Gecko screeched.

"But, Flare…" Tide began.

"What he did to Flare was atrocious," Bullet finished, "and condoning it is something I will never do. But, we need him to keep up the charade. I'm going to see Flare and tell her what's happening."

Bullet headed out, confidence consuming her again, allowing her to feel content in her own skin once more.

"Let him go, guys!" she shouted back as she passed the door that led to Jack.

She heard the echo fall back down the corridor, knowing that Jack would hear it, knowing that it would confuse him, knowing that he would panic.

Knowing that he would do whatever they asked him to.

It was official.

The Black Bullet was dead.

Chapter Three

The hospital ward had no colour mixed in with the lilac, other than the blue sky that could be seen through the windows.

Everything was cleaned to a pristine condition.

Bullet walked down the centre aisle past multiple empty beds until she stopped stunned as she reached Flare, who lay still in her bed, eyes closed, a drip attached to her arm, looking extremely worse for wear.

Bullet approached her and gently sat on the side of the bed. She eyed her friend who lay weak and sore on her hospital bed.

Bruised. Beaten. Pained.

Bandages covered the most part of Flare's arms and body.

Her face had stitches holding three horrid looking cuts closed near to her eye, her other eye black as night with bruising. She gently stroked Flare's arm with the back of her fingers. Her friend stirred, showing a sheepish smile as she acknowledged Bullet beside her.

"Hi."

"Hey you," Bullet replied, "how do you feel?"

"Like I've been hit by a spiky bus," she flinched and winced, groaning in pain, as she tried to sit up in bed.

Bullet grabbed at the pillows to help her be more comfortable.

"Thanks," said Flare.

"I'm sorry we couldn't find you sooner. We tried everything."

"It's fine. You got me home in the end," Flare reassured her.

A moment of silence passed, as Flare took a gulp of water from the glass that sat on the gleaming lavender-coloured table next to her. Bullet fiddled with one of the bandages on Flare's arm, trying to work out how to break the news of their plans to her.

"What's going on?" Flare asked, suspicious.

Bullet looked as guilty as sin while she prepared to tell Flare all that was discussed.

"We spoke to Jack," she began, "and we're letting him go."

"You're letting him go? Why? The guy tried to kill me!" Flare cried with rage.

"I know. I know he did, and believe me, he will be punished for that," Bullet informed her, trying to calm her friend. "But, we believe he can help us stop Neon. The only way to do that is to have him playing for our team. He's going to be our man on the inside."

Flare thumped her glass on the table, frustrated, angry, facing herself away from Bullet who merely looked at her showing nothing, but love and concern for her friend.

"Tell me what happened," Bullet requested.

"You already know," Flare snapped, "he put on crazy rings, smacked me around, and started to play Russian Roulette. I freed myself, got hold of the gun and called for help. How many times do you want me to say it?"

"You know that's not what I'm talking about. You said nothing about the first two days. What did he do to you?"

Flare began to well up as she recalled the first two days in her mind's eye.

Her bottom lip started to quiver, and she looked up at Bullet.

"I kept calling for you," she sobbed, "I was screaming your name, I was calling for you but you didn't come," she cried freely to Bullet, who looked nothing but guilt-stricken at Flare's words.

"I'm sorry," Bullet too began to cry.

"I thought he was going to kill me. I honestly thought that was the last place I was going to see. He'd be the last person I ever spoke to," she explained, "I don't know how he got me at my last mission location, or even how he knew where I'd be. I put out the fire, I was heading down the stairs, and everything went black."

"He hit you from behind?" Bullet clarified.

"Must have done. Anyway, when I came to, I was duct-taped to a chair, and he was sitting in front of me drinking vodka... or maybe gin. He started asking me about you. The Spectrum. Everyone. He said I could tell him because he was 'one of the good guys'. But, I refused. So, he said he would start at the bottom and work his way up... and that's when he pulled out the bat."

Bullet closed her eyes in horror, as Flare continued to explain the series of events to her for the first time through her voice choking up and breaking, her sniffling, and her squirming uncomfortably. The brutality that Flare described had Bullet regretting her decision to let Jack go. That they should have come up with a different way.

But, it was too late now.

He was probably already getting geared up and briefed.

"This is... that's horrible. Flare, I'm so so sorry. I tried everything I could to find you. We've never heard of that safe house before. It must be new."

"Why did he want to find you so bad?" Flare asked, dismissing Bullet's last comment.

"It's a really complicated situation," she replied, "and that's before we even know the whole story."

"Well, what did you get out of Jack?"

"Apparently, I'm dead," Bullet mocked.

"What's that now?" asked Flare, baffled.

"Neon's been telling people I'm dead. Jack's not sure if it's some kind of trick, or if Neon actually believes it. So, we're sending him back to find out, and see what else he can dig up," said Bullet. "In the meantime, you get some rest. And remember, you can talk to me about anything, any time, you hear?"

Flare nodded as Bullet got up off the bed.

She turned to face her again before she left.

"I know you're upset about us letting him go, but it was the best plan we had at the time. This is going to work."

"I hope you're right," said Flare. "But, Bullet… if it doesn't? If he betrays us? I'm just letting you know I'm unleashing my flame thrower on him."

"I may be good with a gun, but I would never step in the road of the Fuchsia Flare. Especially when she's getting down to business with the flames," Bullet smiled at Flare, who returned the loving gesture.

Flare relaxed back into her pillow as she watched Bullet walk out, her heels clicking against the tiled flooring, her hips swinging from side to side with authority and confidence. Bullet left the hospital ward and headed to the conservatory, never for a moment reducing her speed to get there.

A small, elegant seating area resided there, with eight different chairs; one pink, one green, one yellow, one blue, one purple, one grey, one red and one black.

She settled herself on to the black chair; her chair.

Bullet looked out the window that stretched from ceiling to floor at the other side of the room. The conservatory was also known as the upper foyer, as it rested on a balcony above the main entrance area to the building.

Light flooded in from the afternoon sun burning high in the sky through the glass wall ahead of her as Bullet took a moment to herself and admired the always beautiful view of the countryside.

"How did she take the news?"

Bullet barely even flinched when The Spectrum's low and respectful tones penetrated the quiet air.

He walked right past her before she even answered, and he too looked out over the balcony at the view.

"She took it as well as you'd expect," Bullet replied, resting back into her chair, worried about her friend. "She's anxious. Not that I can blame her."

"Nor can anyone else," The Spectrum replied considerately, "what she has gone through is an ordeal that can only be experienced, yet no one should ever have to. But, the Fuchsia Flare is strong of will and of mind, much like the Black Bullet, and much like the rest of the team. Because that's how you were trained. With time and support, she will find a way to make this part of who she is and use it to her advantage, rather than think of it as something that happened to her that holds her back."

Bullet hung on every word her boss let out aloud, all the while with him never turning to face her. She viewed him with much love and regard, and the loyalty she felt for him was something she had never felt before.

She knew he was right about Flare.

Bullet knew that with time and patience from the rest of Colour Coded, Flare would plough her way through all her fears and anxieties and come out the other side even stronger than she was before.

There was nothing but silence between Bullet and The Spectrum. It was peaceful, calming, and both were no less than content with it.

He stood like a statue, staring out to the world which was displayed to him, hands clasped behind his back.

"This view has always taken my breath away," he said, "I feel it puts things into perspective. That the world is so big, and yet, we only play a small part in it. Thus, we must do what we have to to make our presence known," The Spectrum spun around to face her, his hazel eyes beaming at her gladly. "Jack will need to be briefed on what is to be done, and to do this you will all need to come up with a plan of action," he stated, as he held his silver, glimmering cuff link up to his face.

"This is The Spectrum. A discussion needs Colour Coded. Make your way to the conservatory immediately, please."

Bullet heard her mentor's voice both in person and through her own earpiece that they all wore from awakening in the morning to going to sleep at night. Voices niggled in her ear as they confirmed The Spectrum's requirements and made their way to where they stood.

No more than five minutes later, Tide, Lab, Gecko, Youth, Sparrow and Rocket joined them on the balcony, taking their designated seats. The Spectrum, without releasing his clasped hands, began to pace the length of the sitting area.

"So, we start how we always start. What do we know?" He began. "Is Jack on board with our plans for him to be our man on the inside?"

"Yeah. He took a little convincing though, but he's good to go now," Gecko replied.

"Good," The Spectrum exclaimed. "Now, what are the specifics? What are his main objectives?"

"To eavesdrop on Neon?" Tide offered. "Isn't that all he's doing?"

"Yes, Tide, it is. But, what specifically is he listening for? What information should he be aiming to seek out as his first priority?"

"Any information on Bullet," Rocket piped up.

"Indeed," The Spectrum beamed at him, "and?"

"Any information on Colour Coded," Bullet added.

"Precisely! Any content on Colour Coded that comes up in discussions or conversations must be reiterated to us," he clarified. "And now, method of communication. Youth?"

"Well, obviously giving him high-tech equipment from here would make him stick out like a sore thumb. Neon doesn't have that kind of technology…"

"…that we know of…" Lab cut in.

"…Yeah. That we know of. So, it'll need to be sleek and easily concealed and not too difficult to work, because Jack's skills are rather limited in that area. But, I think I have a plan."

"Let us hear it, boy," The Spectrum requested, as everyone listened intently.

"Well…" Youth began, as he took his phone out of his pocket and fiddled with it, "it's not quite finished yet, but I've been working on a new earpiece. It was meant to be for all of us, but I can give him the prototype after I tweak it a little," he stated.

As he held his phone out on the palm of his hand, a hologram elegantly rose from the screen, revealing his latest project.

"It looks like goop," Gecko said, scrunching his face up at the image.

"I suppose it sort of is, in a way," Youth continued. "Basically, it's a long-lasting gel that moulds to the shape of the inside of your ear. I saw something similar on an advert as a treatment for people with tinnitus – I thought it would make for a good cover story. There are small chips in the mould that, when communicated with, change the frequencies to… "

"Cut to the chase, Youth," Sparrow said boldly, displaying his boredom by slouching on his chair and squashing his face on his hand.

"Uhh… right… so, it moulds to the shape of your ear, it won't show up in metal detection, it comes fitted with a cover story, and it's almost finished," Youth concluded.

As his phone sucked in the hologram, he folded his arms and relaxed into his chair, pride oozing from him.

"That sounds perfect to me," Bullet stated.

"I guess it's okay," Sparrow unenthusiastically waved, still bored.

"I suppose it'll be fine," Tide reluctantly agreed, looking confused.

Bullet leaned over and took her hand.

"Don't try and understand how he does it, honey," she giggled.

"But… it's gel. How can you hear through gel?"

"Because… "

"DON'T!" Sparrow cut Youth off again. "Don't even start. You'll give us all a headache."

Silence slowly lulled over Colour Coded, and they turned to look at The Spectrum, who merely raised his eyebrows.

"Visuals?" He said, implying that they should have thought about that.

"Oh, I can give him five small cameras that will be attached to his clothes, and that way we can follow him around Neon's premises. They have Wi-Fi attached so I can access them, and we can watch him from the comfort of our own home," Youth stated, continuing to feel immensely proud of himself.

"What if five cameras isn't enough?" Tide asked anxiously.

"I can go in with a disguise and supply him with more," Gecko said.

"I can also use one of my drones to do occasional perimeter checks of the premises," Sparrow volunteered.

"What the hell is this?" Jack's voice rang out over their discussion.

Nobody had noticed that the whole time Jack had stood by listening to the entire conversation they had about him and his 'objectives'.

Nobody apart from The Spectrum.

"Why do you need all of this? Can't I just go and ask him?"

"No," Bullet replied.

"Why not?" Jack barked, angry.

"Because, young man, Neon set you a task to capture and question the Fuchsia Flare with whatever means necessary, did he not?" The Spectrum stepped in, revealing his authority within the building.

"Yes," Jack confirmed.

"And you had a deadline, I assume. Correct?"

"Yes."

"But, Flare overpowered you, and called us to the scene, thus, I continue my assumption that you missed your deadline. Correct?"

"Yeah."

"And you think after all of that, Neon doesn't know that we have you? Do you think he ponders if your good self and the Fuchsia Flare fell madly in love and ran off into the sunset together?"

"Obviously not," Jack retorted, agitated.

"Well, m'boy, if it is so obvious, then clearly the reason you cannot 'just ask him' is also obvious, no?"

Jack said nothing as he felt belittled by the man that they all called their boss.

"If he knows you have me… how am I going to convince him I'm on his side?" Jack asked nervously.

"That's what we are trying to figure out," The Spectrum replied softly.

He looked at Jack standing far away by the back wall, his hands stuffed so far into his pockets his knuckles almost burst through the seams, his tense and stiff posture beginning to tremor with nerves.

"My dear boy, come over here, please."

Jack edged closer to The Spectrum, who had his arm extended warmly. Jack walked past the chairs and stood by him in front of everyone, curious.

"Introductions are in order," The Spectrum clarified, reading his expression. "You have met the Black Bullet. She specialises in guns as well as other weaponry. Her key weapon is her beloved sniper rifle."

Bullet smiled gracefully.

"Over here we have the Yellow Youth. Youth is our expert in all things technological and manufactures gadgets and other helpful items for any missions we embark on. If you are James Bond, he is your Q. On his left, is the Green Gecko. Gecko can blend in anywhere, much like a gecko, with the exception that he uses backstories, costumes, wigs, accents, etc. when clearly that is something a gecko cannot do. The Fuchsia Flare you are aware of as you spent some time with her for a period of three days, but as I predict that your meeting wasn't for a catch-up; she specialises in all things to do with fire, starting them, containing them and putting them out. Here, we have the Red Rocket. Rocket not only fixes our vehicles, but if you're late for an appointment… he'll have you there before you've even shut the door. To his right is the lovely Lavender Lab, who deals with all narcotics and is also our lead first aider. The Silver Sparrow is not only a registered pilot, but is also a stealthy drone operator. Lastly, meet the Teal Tide. She is an Olympic level swimmer, as well as someone knowing all sorts of things about water you never thought could be possible. And I am The Spectrum; I hold all the colours together. I tell them when to shine, when to mix together and with what other colours, or to merely use shades of their own. When we are together, Jack… we are Colour Coded."

Jack stood in awe, suffering severely from information overload, as he tried to process what he had just heard.

"And you, my boy, are going to help us stop Neon once and for all."

Chapter Four

The yellow room was bright and vibrant, somehow having a positive vibe. Monitors, keyboards, computers and small gadgets sat everywhere in disarray like a storage room for a computer lab. At the back, there was a single curtain pulled to the side with a small bedroom area behind it.

The Yellow Youth followed Jack and Bullet into his lair.

"Welcome to my humble abode!" he announced, proudly.

"Wait… you all live here?" Jack probed in shock.

"Yes, Jack, we do. Now, let's get you set up," Bullet confirmed, and walked past him into the room and stood by Youth.

"So, what do I call you?"

"Youth."

"No, but, what's your name?" Jack clarified.

Youth looked at Bullet with an expression of confusion.

"Youth," he reiterated.

"We give up our identities when we become Colour Coded," Bullet explained.

"Seriously? Why would he make you do that?"

"The Spectrum doesn't make us do anything. Back when we were Prismatic, run by Neon, as you know, it was recommended that we give up our real identities if they were blackened in any way," said Bullet.

"Blackened?"

"Criminal record, bad background, stuff like that. Or if we just wanted a fresh start," Youth explained.

"You guys have criminal records?"

Youth was about to answer until Bullet walked over to Jack and pulled his jacket from his back, startling him.

"What the…?"

"Youth's going to fit a camera into your jacket, so we need to leave it here with him," Bullet explained as she handed the jacket to Youth.

"Does that mean I have to wear that jacket all the time?" Jack enquired.

"No. I'll give you another couple of jackets with cameras in them. You'll also be wearing my gel earpiece so that you can communicate with us 24/7," said Youth.

"Right... cool," Jack replied, nervously.

Bullet clocked his newly acquired posture and the worried look on his face.

"Hey... you're going to be fine, okay? While we're getting your surveillance ready, you're going to be officially briefed by The Spectrum. Then we'll be dropping you off at Neon's."

"I get briefed? Why?"

"Because you need to know precise things to look out for. If you find evidence, where to hide it. If things go wrong, say the safe word. Things like that," Bullet explained.

Jack nodded nervously.

Bullet and Youth shared a look between them before she walked Jack out of Youth's room.

The walk to The Spectrum's headquarters seemed like an eternity to Jack. A long, wide corridor, a few turns and the enormous doors had him admire just how grand their premises was, and how hard they must have worked to get a building of this scale. Bullet walked slightly ahead as Jack followed.

He admired her.

Immensely.

She had a walk of complete confidence, which he liked.

Her brown hair bounced on her shoulders as she marched down the concrete corridor, the click of her heels rebounded off of every surface and echoed down the hall. Her hips swung with every step she took.

For a girl so petite, she moved with an impressive pace as Jack felt the strain in his ankles become very real during his long strides to keep up with her. After a final left turn, they came to a large oak door, where Bullet abruptly stopped, almost causing Jack to walk into the back of her.

Quietly, Bullet knocked on the door and waited patiently for a response.

"Come in," The Spectrum's muffled voice was heard from the other side.

Bullet swung both doors open with zest, revealing what looked like the presidential suite of a five-star hotel.

The Spectrum sat at a desk at the back of the room up some small marble steps, as though he sat on a podium. His elbows leaned on the desktop, with his fingers clasped between the other in front of his face as he observed them over the top of his spectacles.

Bullet, without hesitating, headed straight for The Spectrum and his desk, while Jack wandered slowly through the large room in awe.

Three ample sized windows evenly positioned down the right-hand wall had red floor-length curtains tied back with gold rope at each side. The view that The Spectrum got to behold every day was incredible. The mountains, a patch of water dripping off into the distance, they seemed to be literally in the middle of nowhere. Two gold-coloured sofas sat facing each other, and Jack couldn't help but think how comfortable they looked.

It was only then that it occurred to him how long it had been since he last slept.

Days, maybe even a week.

On the left was a fireplace fitted halfway up the wall, and further down, an aquarium, also fitted into the wall. Six tropical fish swam happily around one another.

From the ceiling hung one of the most beautiful chandeliers Jack had ever seen. He'd never been anywhere to see many chandeliers, but he was certain that this one was the most spectacular. Around it was a Victorian-style border, with pictures of clouds and cherubs, like the ceiling of a cathedral.

He glanced ahead of him to see Bullet and The Spectrum merely staring at him in amusement.

"Quite nice, isn't it?" said The Spectrum sarcastically.

"Yeah, it's okay."

"Come here, boy. Take a seat."

Jack made his way up the steps and sat in one of the two seats positioned opposite The Spectrum at his desk. Bullet sat down beside him.

"Now, how much about your mission do you know?" Asked The Spectrum.

"My mission?" Jack asked, astounded.

"Yes. You're proceeding into an enemy lair to retrieve information on our behalf, preferably undetected and preferably without you receiving any harm by said enemy. We consider this type of thing to be a mission. Do you not agree?" The Spectrum quizzed Jack, lowering his hands down to the desk to look at him more closely.

Jack felt extremely uncomfortable as he began to squirm in his seat.

He glanced over to Bullet hoping she'd throw him a lifeline, but she merely stared at him awaiting an answer.

"I guess."

"Good," said The Spectrum, "now, if you could get me up to speed with your know-how, what information do you have so far about your mission?"

"I've to… umm… I've to go back to Neon and find out information about you guys. And Bullet. And… uhh… I think that's it?"

"No. It's not," The Spectrum confirmed.

"No, of course it isn't," Jack scoffed.

"You are right in the two things you stated, yes. But, we also need information on anything that he's planning. We also want to know if he sets you any other tasks. Anything at all, you tell us. Bullet."

"The gel earpiece that Youth is sorting for you just now," she began confidently, "is a device ideal for us due to the reasons that Youth listed, however, we can't hear any third parties."

"So, what does that mean?" Jack enquired.

"It means that you'll need to find a way of telling us important things that Neon, or any of his minions, says without getting made," said Bullet. "So, for instance, if he asks you to rob a bank, you just repeat it: 'You want me to rob a bank?'. It keeps us in the loop while keeping your cover secure. You with me?"

"Does the camera thing that Youth is fitting on to my jacket not record sound?" Jack pondered out loud.

"No. For us to have something that small and inconspicuous attached to your clothing, it isn't possible for it to record sound over and above capturing footage. Unfortunate, but nevertheless, fact," said Bullet.

"We're also looking for any electronics that Neon might have, especially if it's regarding Colour Coded. Anything from flash drives to desktop computers. You'll have a compartment in your case containing gear, one of which will be a portable drive. If you could copy any information that would be splendid."

"I'll try."

"Son… that's all we're asking of you," The Spectrum reassured Jack.

"Now, Sparrow will continually have an eye on the perimeter with his drone that he and Youth made. If you need anything that you don't already have, Gecko can suit up with some kind of disguise and get it to you. If you're handed a weapon you haven't seen before, ask me. Any technology you're unsure of, ask Youth…"

"So, you guys can also talk to me on those gel things?"

"Yes, as I said, we'll be right there with you, every step of the way."

"In spirit," Jack muttered.

Bullet looked at him sympathetically.

"We'll be closer than you think," she assured him. "Okay, so, if you feel like you've got everything you could possibly get, or, God forbid, you really just don't want to do it anymore and want out of there, then you say: 'I feel homesick'."

Suddenly, Jack was up out of the chair, and wandering over to the window, staring out into the highlands.

The Spectrum merely viewed his movements naturally, while Bullet looked perplexed as to the precipitant way he dismissed himself from their company.

"Something wrong?" asked Bullet.

"You're being nice to me," Jack stated.

"You want me to be mean to you?"

"No, I don't but… don't I deserve that?" he asked, turning to face them. "I hurt your friend. Badly. All because I was scared of what Neon would do if I didn't. I hurt her, and you're being nice to me."

Jack turned back to stare out of the window.

"Jack, with all due respect, we're asking you to risk your life to help us get one up on Neon," said Bullet.

"I'm only doing it because I hate what I did to Flare!" Jack snapped.

"We know why you're doing it, Jack!" Bullet forced. "It's only human, you don't have to explain that to us, we get it."

"Do you?" Jack grilled. "Do you really? So, you understand what it feels like to break someone's kneecaps with a bat? To rip their face open with spiky rings?"

"Jack…"

"To put a cloth over their face and tip water on it?"

"Jack, listen…"

"You ever played Russian roulette with someone? Or flung a chair around a room while someone was strapped to it?"

"Jack!"

"I HATE MYSELF!" Jack began to sob uncontrollably.

In a daze, he staggered and thumped his back against the wall, running his fingers through his sandy blond hair, his breathing getting out of control as he started to hyperventilate.

"I hate what I did. I didn't want to do it. I'm sorry, I don't think I can do this," Jack stormed out of The Spectrum's headquarters, the echoes of his footsteps slowly following him down the corridor.

Bullet turned back to The Spectrum completely dumbfounded by what just happened.

"We just lost our only option."

"No, we haven't," The Spectrum assured her. "We have, however, just witnessed our only option have a nervous breakdown. What does that show?"

"That he's not competent enough to do this."

"On the contrary, Bullet. He has just displayed precisely how competent enough he is to do this. His guilt and want for forgiveness and redemption will drive him to do everything he can to make sure we have what we need."

"But, he just said… "

"He just acted irrationally. As have you in the time that I've known you, have you not?" The Spectrum looked at Bullet waiting for her to confirm that he was right.

Sheepishly, she nodded.

"Well, that's all that Jack has done. He's walking it off. Taking some time to himself. You should talk to him. Alone. You both have something in common after all."

"Like what?" Bullet asked, almost offended.

"Neon," The Spectrum replied, as he ushered her to the still open door to his quarters.

Bullet got up, considering everything The Spectrum had just said as she headed for the door and turned right as had Jack upon his exit.

She tried to think of where he would go, taking into account he didn't know his way around. He enjoyed the view from The Spectrum's window, and the best view you could find was from the conservatory, so she headed there.

Sure enough, Jack was leaning on the railing over the foyer, rubbing hard at his eyes with his palms. Slowly, Bullet approached him and leaned on the railing next to him. He saw her but did not acknowledge her presence.

As a matter of fact, he made a point of looking anywhere but at Bullet.

"Don't be embarrassed, Jack," Bullet pleaded.

"Well, I'm hardly proud of myself, am I?"

Bullet turned to face him. She studied his mortified and uncomfortable stature.

"You're right. You hurt my friend, and a huge part of me really hates you for that. But, another part of me gets it."

Jack faced her, stunned by her words.

45

"Think about it Jack; I used to work for Neon. I left. It wasn't over a little disagreement. I left because of him; who he was and the fact that he wouldn't change. He's a very twisted man who gets easily obsessed with something, and right now his obsession seems to be us. He's apparently hearing rumours that I'm dead, and he ordered you to grab Flare to find out if it was true or not, with any means necessary. You did what you had to do to stay alive. So, I get it, and I'm sure Flare does too, in some way."

Jack shuffled around uncomfortably before dropping his head into his hands.

"Don't give up on us, Jack. Help us. Please."

Bullet rested her hand on his arm. Jack perked up and looked at her.

Into her deep blue eyes. Those eyes that swallowed him whole while they pleaded with him to do what he was being asked.

He nodded.

Bullet beamed an ecstatic smile at him as her eyes lit up.

"Thank you!"

Both of them continued to admire the view from the balcony as the sun began to make its way to bed behind the hills.

"Where exactly are we?" Jack asked.

"Oh… if I told you that, I'd have to kill you," she smiled.

Bullet was visibly happy when Jack chuckled back.

"Fair enough," he muttered. "Before I get geared up there's something I want to do, if I may?"

"Which is?" Bullet asked.

"Flare…" he murmured.

Jack was mesmerised by the pristine condition of the hospital wing as he followed Bullet through an empty ward. He found it weird to see it in a shade of purple rather than white like every other hospital. It wasn't long before they were at Flare's bedside, who was awake and just finished eating when they arrived.

"Oh, my God, you've got to be kidding me," she snarled.

"Flare, let him say what he needs to say."

Flare folded her good arm underneath the other that remained in a sling due to ripped tissue in her forearm, and stared anywhere but at Jack or Bullet, saying nothing.

"Flare…" Jack started, "I'm not trying to excuse my actions when I say that Neon had me at every turn when it came down to his orders regarding you, but I do want to apologise for them. He threatened my life, which really didn't bother me… but… he threatened the life of my family. That was something that I couldn't bear the thought of. They've been through enough. I'm sorry, and I hope one day you can find it within yourself to forgive me."

Flare continued to look forward at the wall opposite, as though she was trying to see through it.

She didn't acknowledge that he had said anything at all.

Jack, having realised that he wasn't going to get an answer, left the hospital wing.

Bullet watched him leave and turned back to Flare.

"Thank you."

"For what?"

"For putting our last option back in motion."

Bullet leaned down and pecked her forehead, and made a brisk exit from the ward to catch up with Jack.

Jack was in the conservatory putting on his jacket while Youth fiddled with the gel earpiece when Bullet caught up with him. Youth handed Jack the gel for him to put in his ear, and then made some adjustments to the camera on Jack's jacket and checked his tablet to make sure they had a clear visual. He pulled over a case and handed it to Jack.

"This is everything you'll need. Some clothes are in there too, and at the bottom, there's a compartment with some nifty little gadgets to help you out, should you need it," Youth opened the suitcase and went straight into the compartment to reveal its contents.

"This little laser pen is actually a bug detector. Shine it into nooks and crannies of a room, and if the laser turns green, it's bugged. This pen is a tranq dart. You push the top down as though you're going to use it and it shoots. Aim it at someone, and they'll fall unconscious in three seconds, but the unconsciousness only lasts for an hour so, you know, think before you click. This tablet is for email and video call only, on a different frequency, so that it can't be traced or detected, so if you get anything you can send it straight to us securely. There's a knife with a lock pick on it, a spare gel earpiece, x-ray vision glasses, and this pack of gum isn't actually gum, it's a flash drive. Sound good?"

"Uhh… yeah…" said Jack.

"Cool! Catch ya," Youth bid him farewell and walked away whistling to himself.

Jack crouched down by the case, curious about the gear he was provided. He lightly brushed his fingers over everything, and then shut the case.

"Rocket's outside with the car ready to take you there," Bullet informed him.

Jack nodded in response.

"Are you ready, boy?" asked The Spectrum, approaching them with his hands, as always, clasped behind his back.

"Yeah… look, about earlier… " Jack began but was cut off with The Spectrum raising his two palms to Jack's face.

"No need. Absolutely no need."

Jack gave him a slight grin, feeling grateful and respectful of the person that this man portrayed.

He turned to Bullet.

"What do I do if they find out what I'm doing?" he asked nervously.

"If you think someone is on to you, all you have to do is say: 'I don't think the Black Bullet is dead'. As soon as we hear that, we'll be right there to get you out."

"How will you get there that fast?" Jack continued, panicked.

"Boy… trust her. Trust them all," The Spectrum instructed.

A car horn from outside broke the silence that ensued, and Jack made his way down the glass staircase towards the door.

"Good luck, Jack!" Bullet shouted.

Jack turned and gave a half-hearted wave, and walked outside.

Bullet sighed with pent up tension she had been holding in all day.

"Sleep."

"I beg your pardon?"

"We should have let him sleep. He must be exhausted; he's been here for two days, and he was with Flare for three. He hasn't slept in that entire time," Bullet rambled.

"I think the boy will do just fine, my dear. He can sleep on the road there. But, I'm sure all will be okay."

The Spectrum made his way back to his office, leaving her on the balcony alone, watching Jack and Rocket get into the car and take off like a bat out of hell. The moment had come.

Although, it felt like it never would.

Neon had a mole.

One that he'd never see coming.

Chapter Five

Colour Coded sat in the Yellow Youth's room, crowded around four different monitors. One was the footage from Jack's jacket that Youth fitted before he left.

Another was floor plans of Neon's headquarters.

The bottom left was footage from Sparrow's drone showing the perimeter of the building.

The fourth, however, was completely different. It showed an electronic mind map, Neon being the centre point, with lots of branches off of him full of information; the date on which they created Prismatic, the date on which the ones who worked under him left Neon for The Spectrum, every mission and objective they worked on under Neon's authority, everything Neon had done since they left them – that they were aware of – and the skills and weaknesses of Neon from the time that they knew him.

Youth and Bullet were sitting in seats right in front of the monitors, while Tide, Lab and Gecko stood at the back of them with Sparrow, who was controlling his drone around the boundary of Neon's base.

"Does Flare know what's happening?" asked Lab.

"Yup," answered Bullet.

"How did she take it?" Tide cut in.

"Pretty much as you'd expect," Bullet replied, not for one second taking her eyes off of Jack's camera screen.

The Lavender Lab, a small plump woman in her mid-forties, checked her watch.

"Speaking of Flare, am I needed for anything? She'll need her next dose of morphine very soon, and I need to refresh her bandages."

"Flare is your first priority, Lab. Go do what you have to do to get her back on her feet. We've got this," Bullet instructed.

"Right you are, then," Lab squeezed Bullet's shoulder lovingly before she left, Bullet holding her hand in response.

Everyone loved Lab, she was like the gang's mother figure.

"Lab, can I have some morphine?" Gecko giggled.

"If you ask me that one more time, son, I'm going to start getting really worried."

"What do you mean 'start'?" He scoffed.

Lab chuckled as she walked away.

A few minutes later, Rocket walked in.

"That was fast," Tide claimed.

"Remember who you're talking to, Tide," Rocket said proudly.

"Did Jack sleep in the car?" Bullet asked, concerned.

"No. I think he tried to. But, his head is kind of all over the place. He was quite quiet all the way there," Rocket explained.

"Probably fearing for his life," Tide jeered.

"Once he's in there he'll be fine," said Gecko.

"I was talking about Rocket's driving," she confirmed, giving Rocket a look of disappointment, but was met with a look of sheer pride on his part.

"I'm going down to the garage to service everyone's cars. If we get the distress code from Jack, we need to be ready, and I don't want to take any chances," Rocket said, but only received mere grunts from everyone too concerned with the monitors in front of them than with his sense of initiative.

"You know, it's great working with you all. I feel so appreciated!" Rocket mocked, as he walked away.

Nobody said anything, but they were all smiling amongst themselves for keeping up their pretence.

As his footsteps got quieter, Tide had a very visible epiphany.

"Rocket! Can you fill up the water tank in my car in case it's needed?"

"Comes as part of the service!" Rocket's voice echoed back down the hall.

Satisfied, Tide turned her attention back to the monitors in front of everyone.

Gecko leaned closer to Jack's monitor over Youth's shoulder.

"Are they wearing uniforms?"

"I think so," said Youth, "I'll get a screen grab."

He hit some keys as though he was a pianist, and a picture loaded up on a fifth monitor to the left of the clustered four. He had screenshot a man walking past Jack, and zoomed in on his chest.

A dark grey one-piece suit fitted the man, and a white triangle with a grey 'P' was on his chest to the left-hand side.

Bullet pressed into her ear to activate the gel earpiece.

"Jack, how many men does Neon have working for him?" she asked, her eyes boring through his camera screen.

He didn't respond.

"Jack, can you hear me?" she asked, worried.

Jack did a 360-degree turn as he walked, showing two men on either side of him.

"He's being escorted," Youth confirmed.

"They're taking him straight to Neon," Bullet thought out loud.

"Youth, send that screen grab and a couple more to my account, maybe even a short clip too. I'm going to start working on mimicking that outfit," Gecko stated before disappearing out of Youth's room.

Youth battered the keyboard, taking shots from Jack's camera and emailing them to Gecko.

"Wait," Bullet exclaimed, "isn't it going to be noticeable whenever Jack has to press his ear to talk to us?"

"He doesn't," Youth replied, "he has the prototype, which was the one that had a continuous outgoing frequency. I just connected it with ours."

"So, he can hear everything we're saying without us having to press it?" Tide quizzed.

"No, because we still have to activate ours," he sighed, "that's the only difference. Our gel pieces have a pressure point that, when pressed, allows us to be heard. Jack will be heard any time he says anything."

Bullet nodded in understanding.

"I'm going to go for a swim in the lake," Tide announced suddenly, leaving Bullet, Youth and Sparrow by the monitors.

Youth turned and watched her leave, smiling.

"It's cute that they think we don't know they're sleeping together."

"Youth, Gecko's gay," Sparrow mocked.

"It's a good thing I'm not talking about Gecko then, isn't it?" Youth retorted, turning to look at him.

The penny finally dropped.

"What? Tide and Rocket?"

"Are you seriously saying you didn't know?" Bullet laughed.

Sparrow looked as though he was trying to calculate a very large sum in his head and failing miserably.

Ignoring their stares, he looked back to his tablet.

"It looks like there's approximately sixty to eighty people outside. Men to women ratio about... three to one."

"They all seem to be wearing that uniform," said Bullet, squinting at the perimeter screen.

"Ladies and gentlemen, we have lift off," Youth announced, as Jack's camera approached a large dark grey door in the converted warehouse building. His camera turned to see the two men walking back down the corridor.

"I don't recognise this hall…" Bullet whispered anxiously.

"Neither do I," Youth agreed, as he zoomed in on the floor plan, "and it doesn't seem to be anywhere on this either."

"Has he moved premises?" Bullet asked.

"He can't have. Rocket dropped him off here, and I have footage of them entering," Sparrow said.

"Then where the hell are they?" Youth enquired.

Bullet took a moment to examine the situation.

The building was the same size as before, but Jack's camera image revealed vents on the walls up by the ceiling.

It was clear to her now.

"They're underground,"

The revelation took a minute to sink in for Youth and Sparrow.

Neon was expanding.

He had a plan.

Jack stood nervously at Neon's door as the distant footsteps of his escorts quickly faded away into silence. Hesitantly, he chapped the door, made of thick steel.

There was no answer.

He just stood there, unsure of what to do, until suddenly the doors opened, slow, mechanically.

The room was dark.

A small light illuminated a desk with papers and a computer on it. Jack eased his way into the room, as the thick doors shut behind him just as slowly as they opened, scraping along the stone floor as they did so.

"You have a lot of explaining to do, Jack," said a voice.

Jack jumped.

"I do?"

He shook his head, annoyed with himself.

"I mean, yes, I do. I know I do."

"Well, that's a start," said the voice.

Movement at the desk had Jack freeze like a statue, filled with nothing but fear and discomfort.

Neon leaned forward into the light. His baggy eyes were much more baggy than when Jack last saw him. His face was pale, his grey hair usually combed neat and tidy was a frantic mess atop his head.

"Where've you been, Jack?"

Jack tried frenziedly to remember what his cover story was.

All he could remember was the Black Bullet and The Spectrum staring at him.

"Sit down," ordered Neon.

Jack made his way over and sat in the seat in front of Neon's desk. As he sat down, he recalled how comfortable the seat in The Spectrum's office was in comparison to this one.

"Where. Have. You. Been," Neon growled.

Jack swallowed nervously.

"They found us. I had to stay low to make sure I wasn't found before I could come back."

"How did they find you? You were in a safe house," Neon grilled him.

"I don't know how they found me. They just showed up."

"How?"

"Sorry?"

"How did they show up? In a car? On a boat?"

"Three cars and a helicopter, sir."

Neon stood up and slowly made his way around the table before leaning on it and facing Jack. He glared at him menacingly.

Calculating.

Was he on to him already?

"It's been almost a week, Jack. All you had to do was grab her and question her about Bullet."

"I did what you taught me."

Neon jumped up and kicked his table.

"If you did what I taught you, you wouldn't have been caught!"

The table screeched back across the concrete, paper slid on to the floor, tubs fell over. Jack felt the sweat drip down his forehead and stream down to the tip of his nose.

"The girl, Flare, is she still alive?"

Jack nodded, anticipating Neon would be angry about this as well.

Bullet, Youth and Sparrow watched with bated breath as they witnessed Neon leaning over Jack, his camera viewing the top of his wrinkled suit.

"Good."

Jack perked up, surprised at his reaction.

He remembered Bullet telling him about repeating Neon's words.

"You're happy that the Fuschia Flare is still alive?"

"It's an upside, I suppose. They'll feel taunted now. Killing her would fuel their need to take me out. As much as it would be a mess because of their emotions, it would be within a quicker time frame. But, having her back will keep them busy for a while. Allow me to finish my plan."

"What plan?" Jack asked curiously. "Can I help?"

"Oh, yes. You will be of much help."

"What do you want me to do?"

"I want you to go back. I want you to turn yourself into them."

"What?" quizzed Jack.

"Jack, repeat his words!" Bullet's agitated voice nipped his ear.

"When you go back, they'll interrogate you. They'll ask you why you did what you did. What kind of things am I planning. You're going to tell them."

"But, why?"

"Jack, come on, man!" Youth cut in. "Repeat his words!"

"Because even if you tell them the truth, they'll be no further ahead than they already are. They'll then emotionally blackmail you to be a mole. You will accept the mission. You will report to me, and tell me the objectives of your mission they set you."

"So, you want me to go back to them… tell them why I was told to capture the Fuschia Flare, and if and when they ask me to spy on you for them, accept the challenge?" Jack repeated.

"No 'if' is necessary, because they will ask you to do just that. But, yes. Precisely," Neon nodded.

Bullet and Youth sat in horror, as they let Jack's words register.

"Bullet… he knew that's exactly what we'd do if we got our hands on Jack."

"Yeah, but he doesn't know that we've already done it."

"Doesn't he?" Sparrow thought aloud. "How do we know this isn't a ruse? How do we know that he doesn't know Jack was with us for two days, and that he's in there to get information for us?"

Bullet couldn't find a response to settle his anxiety.

She silently agreed with them.

They didn't know Neon's intentions.

It made her very uneasy.

"What did you find out?" Neon asked obsessively, leaning towards him, his eyes drilling through Jack's face. "Where is she? Is she alive?"

"Yeah, I just told…"

"Not Flare! Bullet! Is the Black Bullet alive?" Neon yelled, his patience breaking.

Jack considered the cover story that he received from Colour Coded.

He decided to go against their wishes.

"I don't know, Neon."

"Don't know what, Jack?" Bullet asked through his earpiece. "We can't hear Neon, only you."

54

"You don't know?" Neon repeated furiously. "Why the hell not?"

Jack relished in the silence to get his wits about him for the grilling he knew would come from both Neon and Colour Coded for going with his gut.

"The Fuschia Flare doesn't know where the Black Bullet is. She claimed none of them does. I believe her."

"What are you saying, Jack?" Neon questioned further.

"Jack, what the hell are you doing!" Bullet pierced Jack's ear again.

Jack braced himself.

It was too late now.

He had already spoken out loud and it was nothing like the cover story Gecko gave him before he left Colour Coded headquarters.

He inhaled deeply, and slowly let it escape.

There was nothing else for it now.

"She's missing. The Black Bullet is missing."

Chapter Six

Youth sat with his head in his hands in front of the monitors, while Bullet paced the room behind him, agitated. Sparrow kept his face to his tablet screen, his head subconsciously shaking in scepticism.

"Why the hell would he do that?" she moaned.

"I don't know, but he must've had a reason," Youth replied.

"Well, whatever it is, he's not telling us. He's not saying anything," Bullet growled, still pacing. "Jack? JACK? Please talk to us, tell us what the hell is going on, why did you go off brief?"

Gecko came fleeing into the room hearing the commotion through his earpiece.

"Bullet, I swear that's not the back story I gave him!"

"I know, I know; I was read in. I don't know what he's doing, and he's not talking."

"Has he used the distress code and we missed it?" Sparrow asked.

"No, he definitely hasn't," Youth confirmed, "I've set an alarm to go off whenever each distress code is spoken and there's been nothing."

"So, he's just being a dick?" Gecko snarled, shaking his head in disbelief.

"Look, guys, until he talks to us, we can't make assumptions. He maybe didn't have a choice," Bullet suggested, trying to be reasonable.

Sparrow shrugged his shoulders suggesting a hint of possibility, while Youth and Gecko looked at her unconvinced.

Jack knew exactly what he was doing in their opinion.

They just didn't know why he was doing it.

Bullet stopped in her tracks, deep in thought, racking her brain for a possible reason as to why Jack would say she was missing rather than dead. She tried to put herself in his shoes.

Or in Neon's.

Why would the Black Bullet being missing be better than her being dead?

What did Jack think could come from that positively?

Was he really on their side, or did he take the opportunity to get back to Neon? She felt really unsettled, and that's a feeling she was never accustomed to.

"Gecko, how's that uniform coming along?" she turned to him.

"Well, I tried to doctor the images a little to get the specific shade of grey they use, but I'm still not sure if it's the right one. But, just the logo to get printed on and that'll be it."

"How long?"

"Ten minutes tops. You want me in there?"

"It might be our last choice," Bullet confirmed.

"I'll get on it," Gecko replied, and left for his quarters.

Bullet looked at Sparrow, who was unusually quiet and studying his tablet intently.

She watched him suspiciously, before turning her attention to the monitor with Sparrow's live drone footage, looking to see what he was examining so closely.

She noticed two vans had arrived, and something was being offloaded to Prismatic, but they couldn't see properly.

"Can you move the drone, Sparrow?" Bullet requested.

"I've tried every angle, it's either blocked by the building or by the van doors. I can't see properly without attracting attention."

"There's a crap heap of people taking part in the delivery," Youth acknowledged.

"Or the pick-up," Sparrow offered, catching their attention, "I wasn't exaggerating, I can't see what it is they're handling, nor if they're loading or unloading the vans."

"Bullet, Jack's heading outside with Neon!" Youth expressed in a frenzy.

Bullet's head snapped towards Jack's camera footage, showing him behind Neon climbing stairs and heading outside.

Sparrow came over to join them in watching.

"Jack, I know things haven't gone to plan, but please try and get a look into those vans and see what's going on," Bullet reached out to Jack.

Jack quite clearly wandered away from Neon towards the busy people at the vans. His camera turned suddenly, showing Neon waving him away from the commotion, agitation written all over his face.

"Oh, sorry, I assumed this is what we were coming out to deal with," they heard Jack shout to Neon as he turned away from the vans to continue following him.

As Jack turned, Sparrow clocked something.

"Youth! Screengrab!"

57

It seemed as though Youth just smacked the keyboard, and a picture loaded on the fifth monitor.

"Zoom in there,"

Youth followed his lead and closed in.

They stared in horror and confusion at what they saw.

"Is that… blocks of cocaine?" Youth asked.

"That's what it looks like to me," Sparrow agreed.

"Well, I hope that's what it is," Bullet added.

Sparrow and Youth looked at each other perplexedly before turning to Bullet for elaboration.

She met their lost gaze.

"Either that, or it's C4,"

They all looked back to the screen grab.

"That would be a worrying amount of C4…" Youth whispered in horror, his eyes wide like an owl.

"Uhh… Bullet," Sparrow said, breaking the silence, "you might wanna look at Jack's camera."

Bullet turned her attention to Jack's footage, which was lying sideways against the gravel land with black shoes facing it. The feet turn and walk away, leaving the view of a cigarette butt and some bushes.

"Jack?"

Bullet closed her eyes, praying for an answer.

"JACK?"

"Did you guys hear anything? I didn't hear him go down," Sparrow asked.

"JACK!"

"No, I didn't hear a thing," Youth replied.

"Goddammit, Jack! Answer me!" Bullet screamed.

The silence was unbearable.

Soul destroying.

Endless.

"How the hell did we miss this?" she roared.

"We were looking at the vans, Bullet!" Youth defended.

"There's three of us! Did it really take three of us to watch one monitor?"

"Bullet?"

"For God's sake, Jack's hurt!"

"Bullet."

"WHAT?" she yelled, spinning round putting her face in Sparrow's, who merely looked terrified.

"Umm… that wasn't me, love," he quivered.

"Bullet! Are you there?"

"Jack? Jack, are you okay?"

"Yeah, I'm fine. This is the first chance I got alone."

"Dude, why did you take your jacket off?" Youth asked. "We have no way of keeping tabs on you."

"More importantly… why the fuck did you say the Black Bullet was missing?" Sparrow growled through the radio.

"Something occurred to me when I was in there," Jack explained, "I'm sorry, I know it wasn't the plan, and I can't go into a lot of detail right now; he'll be back any minute."

"What's happening right now?" Bullet probed.

"He asked me to fix his electrical system. He's been working on an underground bunker for months, and it's ready now. But, they're struggling with the electrical supply. I didn't even think, I took my jacket off, sorry."

Bullet sighed with relief.

"A bunker?" Youth turned to Bullet.

"Sounding a lot more like C4 now, isn't it?" she replied. "Jack, was that C4 they were loading on to that van?"

"Opposite," Jack replied, "it was C4 he was having delivered. I don't know why yet."

"Shit. Keep us in the loop, man," said Sparrow, "and put your jacket back on!"

Jack's camera started to move and thrash around while he put his jacket on. As Gecko came back into the room in his newly made Prismatic uniform.

"So, he's okay, then?"

"Yeah, he's fine," said Youth.

"Still want me in there?"

"Yeah, definitely," Bullet replied.

"Sure thing. I'll go grab Rocket to take me there," he said, as he left once more, for a time frame unknown to everyone.

The whole time, Jack has been audibly grunting and moaning, using colourful vocabulary trying to work out the wiring.

"Having fun there, Jack?" Sparrow mocked.

"Yeahhh… this sure is an old building. I don't think this power box has been touched for years," he replied. "How old is this warehouse?"

Youth started tapping on the keyboard and within seconds loaded up articles with information.

"The warehouse was built in 1919 for agricultural purposes; the company sold farming goods and so on. They were shut down during the Second World War due to rations, and the warehouse was then used for manufacturing bullets and other ammunition. It then moved on to be a warehouse for retailers in 1946, before it was condemned and shut down in 1968. So, yeah… old building," Youth explained.

"Wow… it was a rhetorical question. But, thanks," Jack chuckled.

"Jack, Gecko is on his way to back you up, he's going to blend in wearing the uniform they all have," Bullet informed him.

"Thank God. I don't think I can do this on my own. I gotta quit talking, he's coming back."

Jack turned around to see Neon approaching him.

"Well, can you do it?" Neon asked him.

"Yeah, getting an electricity supply to the bunker shouldn't be a problem. It's just going to take me a while."

"How long?"

"A month. At least. The wiring for the warehouse itself is old, it needs renewed before I can do anything with the bunker."

Neon started to pace, looking anxious.

"Is there a problem?" Jack asked.

"Yeah, I need it done in a couple weeks. Can you not just cable up the bunker and leave rewiring the warehouse?"

"Well, I suppose, yeah, but if I do that, the wiring of the warehouse won't last long."

"That's fine, doesn't matter. Just make sure I have a supply in the bunker," Neon walked away from him towards the delivery-taking place.

"So, you're not bothered about the warehouse anymore, then? The bunker should be my main priority?" Jack shouted after him.

"Spot on, Jacky boy!" he replied without turning around.

Jack began re-jigging all the cables and putting the panel back on the electricity unit.

"Well, sounds to me like he's planning on blowing up that warehouse and keeping himself safe," Jack uttered, continuing to fiddle with the electric panel.

"Yeah, me too, but… why build a bunker? Why not just go somewhere else entirely?" Bullet pondered.

"I don't know, hopefully I'll know more soon. I'm gonna head back to my room soon so we can talk better then."

Jack started heading back towards the warehouse but went through the delivery entrance instead.

He walked in amongst stacks of C4.

"Are you guys seeing this?" Jack muttered, as one of the van doors slammed shut, causing him to turn and look. The other van was being loaded, also with C4. "What the hell?"

"He's unloading from one van and loading into another?" Youth questioned.

"I have no idea," Bullet admitted.

Jack quickly turned and navigated his way through the corridors, hallways and doors, until he reached his room.

The room was small, a dark shade of green, navy blue carpet, a metal-framed single bed still made, his case at the bottom sat in the corner. On the wall at the bottom of the bed, hung a mirror. Jack stood in front of the mirror, knowing everyone would then be able to see him.

"Jack, before you speak, take out the laser pen and check for bugs," Youth instructed.

Scoffing at the fact that he forgot, Jack rummaged in his bag and took out the laser pen, shining it around the room.

"Remember, things like the clock, the bed, corners of the room," Youth instructed again.

Jack pointed the laser everywhere Youth told him to and everywhere else he could think of, but it didn't turn green.

He threw it into his bag and flopped down on to the bed, exhausted.

"They're doing something with that C4 and then shipping it off. I just can't think what he'd be doing," Jack said openly.

"Jack… explain the cover story. Why'd you change it without telling us?" Bullet asked.

"I'm sorry. I didn't have time to tell you, because it only occurred to me about two seconds before I said it," he explained, "but, my thoughts were: if I say you were missing, rather than you're dead, it gives me a chance to lead him on a wild goose chase, rather than start gunning for the rest of you."

Bullet sat back, surprised.

That was a rather good plan.

"And it's just as well, because now it gives us an open opportunity to get Colour Coded in here without him lurking around."

"Jack, I'm impressed," Bullet admitted, "not because you went against your objectives that we gave you, but your reasoning makes a lot of sense. I'll read in The Spectrum later tonight. Jack… take a load off. Try and get some sleep, okay?"

"I'll do my best, Bullet. Can I take my earpiece out?"

"Sure," Youth answered, "but keep it on you just in case. We can't hear you until it's in your ear anyway."

Jack took the earpiece out and dropped it on to the small bedside table before taking off his jacket and folding it on to the floor, making sure to aim the camera towards the door. He shuffled into the small bathroom in the corner of his room and ran the tap, splashing his face with cold water. Something occurred to him.

He leaned back into the doorway and looked at the time.

Five past six in the evening.

It was Friday.

Neon would be away playing poker with his friends.

Then again, with everything going on, he might have given up that luxury.

Although, it was his only vice. Something Neon did to switch off and relax. Jack had no earpiece, no camera, no one to tell him not to go to Neon's office.

He dried his face and re-shuffled his jacket to aim the camera elsewhere before leaving the room.

He tried to remember where the entrance to the bunker was and began taking turns and doors until he jogged his memory.

And then it hit him: at the back of the loading bay.

Jack made his way out of the warehouse and walked around the back, knowing there would be less people there, but still kept an eye out for anyone watching him. He opened a side door into the main hall and took a sharp right to the door he was thinking of.

Jack went down the stairs, making his way along the flame-lit stone corridor until he reached the door at the end.

Slowly, he wrapped his sweaty palm around the doorknob and twisted but to no avail. It was a good thing he put the knife/ lock-pick in his pocket before he went to see Neon before. He pulled it out of the leg pocket of his canvas trousers, looking behind him cautiously, before beginning to pick the lock.

"Come on, Jack," he whispered to himself, "you've never done this before, but it doesn't mean you can't, there's a first time for everything so just give it a little wiggle around in there and hope… " he stopped dead when the door unlocked.

"YES!"

In a frenzy, he scrambled to his feet and opened the door, forcing it back over the stone floor that it rumbled across earlier.

The room was pitch black; he couldn't see a thing.

Jack went back out to lift a torch from the wall and went back into the office, leaving the door ajar behind him. Hurriedly, he went straight to Neon's desk and began to rummage. He found papers on the C4 shipments; a man named John Smith.

Typical.

Jack took a picture on his phone and put the paper back where he found it. He went through the drawers of his desk.

The top drawer was stationary stuff, but the second drawer made him freeze.

A handgun lay in there, alone, with only a clear plastic box of bullets for the company. The bullets were black.

"The Black Bullet," Jack breathed to himself.

He took another picture on his phone and went to the third and last drawer.

It was a filing cabinet.

He flicked through the folders looking at the labels and found nothing titled Colour Coded, but he clocked something very odd.

A folder with the header: "Old Prismatic".

He pulled it out, bubbling with curiosity and nerves at the thought of being caught. He opened it.

And there it was.

A poly pocket labelled The Black Bullet.

One for The Red Rocket.

One for The Fuschia Flare.

One was missing; there were only three, and there should have been four.

There was nothing on The Lavender Lab, The Green Gecko, The Silver Sparrow, The Teal Tide or The Yellow Youth.

Maybe Neon kept them somewhere else?

Or perhaps he didn't know anything about them?

But, who was the fourth member of the original Prismatic? One was definitely missing.

Without even attempting to read them as a means of boosting his speed, Jack started pulling out all the papers and took pictures of as many as he could.

Something caused Jack to freeze.

Noise. The bunker door opened.

Someone was coming.

Frantically, Jack stuffed everything back into the poly pockets and threw it into the drawer. He waved the torch around like a maniac trying to put it out, but nothing was working.

As he darted for the door, he noticed a hook on the wall next to the doorway. He stuffed the torch into it and held himself to the wall behind the door, being as stiff and still as possible. The person about to join him stopped at the entrance, their shadow stretching into the room before them.

Jack hunched up, trying not to touch the door and give himself away.

Someone took the same torch Jack had used and walked into the room, shining it around.

They had on the Prismatic one-piece suit, short black spiky hair, glasses, and a tattoo of the yin yang symbol in a ball of flames on their neck.

Jack shut his eyes tight and held his head up, the sweat devilishly tickling the side of his face as it trickled from his sideburns and down his neck. The man walked around the room, holding the torch out far in front of him.

Jack was now suspicious.

He didn't seem to be used to this place. He didn't seem like he had even been in the bunker before.

Jack decided to sneak out of his hiding place, slip out quickly and lock him in. Just as he was making his way around the door, a voice had him jump out of his skin.

"Jack?"

He slowly turned around to face a very amused Gecko standing in front of him.

"Aw man, I nearly shat myself."

"Didn't you know I was coming?"

"Well, yeah, I knew you were coming, but I didn't think I'd bump into you in Neon's bunker!" Jack defended.

"Find anything useful?"

"No, nothing. I think Neon knows better than to keep his prized possessions in the one place everyone knows he is regularly," Jack fibbed.

"Fair enough. Let's get out of here before someone sees us."

Jack didn't want to lie to him. But, he wanted to find out a little more about the people he was working for before he continued on this endeavour.

He tried to ask them, but no one said anything.

Unfortunately, deception was the only way.

Chapter Seven

Bullet was sitting in the hospital wing with Flare, Tide and Lab. They were chatting and laughing. It was nice for Bullet to see Flare smile like old times. She had been through a lot.

Then again, so had Bullet.

But, Flare was the one she was most concerned with.

"I think you should just tell us, Lab. Come on, you know you want to," Tide teased.

"Oh, blimey… the last boyfriend I had was short and stout, just like yours truly, and he worked for a newsagent."

"A newsagent? What a catch! Did he own it?" Tide pried.

"Nope. He was the paperboy. Used to go out on his bike at five a.m. every morning and deliver the free paper to the village."

"Seriously?" Tide scoffed.

"Yup."

"What age was he?" Flare probed further.

"Well, he was two years older than me at the time so he'll be… forty-eight, forty-nine now?" Lab admitted, her cheeks going a bright shade of red with embarrassment.

"Oh, my God!" Tide exclaimed, entering an endless fit of the giggles.

"Wonder why that ended," Flare joked.

"Actually, it ended because of me. I wasn't ready to settle down with anyone. I didn't want to string him along," Lab reflected. "But, you know what, at the end of the day, he did that one thing that made him happy. Like I do now with my beautiful little family."

Bullet looked on as Lab put her arm around Flare and gave her a loving squeeze, while she stretched her other hand across the bed and held Tide's as Flare leaned her head on Lab's shoulder.

Bullet watched the three of them laugh and giggle.

After everything she had been through in her life, Bullet couldn't help but feel grateful, and consider how lucky she was to have people like this around her every day.

She stood up and leaned over Tide to hug Flare.

"I have to go."

"Aw, no, why?" Flare pestered, as she took hold of Bullet's wrist with her good arm and pulled her down next to her on the bed. "Just stay, we were having such a good time."

"And you all still can, but Jack and Gecko are checking in at eight p.m., and it's ten to. I also have to wake Youth up," Bullet explained, as she wriggled out of Flare's grip.

"Youth tired?" Lab asked.

"Yeah, he's been non-stop since Flare was taken, and he's been kept going all day sorting those earpieces for us and getting Jack geared up for going back to Neon, and then keeping tabs on him and... yadda yadda yadda," said Bullet, walking to the bottom of the bed. "Jack was exhausted too, so when he went for a nap, I told Youth to do the same."

"And Gecko's okay?" Tide asked.

"Yeah, he's there in his disguise. Rocket just got back actually... just thought I'd let you know," Bullet said, winking at the other two before walking away.

"Oh, right... umm... thanks," Tide stuttered nervously.

Bullet passed the spiral staircase and made her way along the corridor to the Yellow Youth's room. He was fast asleep upon her arrival, starfished across his bed, on top of the covers, fully clothed. Peaceful.

"I thought it'd be best not to wake him," The Spectrum's soft voice broke the silence from behind her as she spun around to face him.

"Sir, I didn't even see you sitting there."

"So I gathered," he replied, checking his snazzy gold watch strapped around his wrist. "Nearly check-in time."

Bullet joined him and sat down in the seat that Youth occupied earlier that day. "Okay... I think it's... this one?" Bullet muttered to herself, as she pushed a button to video call Jack on his tablet. It rang for quite a while before a face appeared on the screen.

"Good morning," Gecko greeted them through a yawn.

"It's not morning, hon. What're you up to, Gecko? Where's Jack?"

"Well, we came back to Jack's room, and I sat on the floor trying to do a new floor plan to include the bunker. Must've dozed off because... you calling is the next thing I remember, and," he leaned over the top of the tablet and brought back a piece of paper, "I only have five lines drawn on this," Gecko held the paper up to the camera.

"Uh-huh, where's Jack?" Bullet coaxed further.

"He's right over there," Gecko announced, turning the tablet to face Jack curled up on his bed, sound asleep. "He didn't even stir when this thing started vibrating like a… "

"Don't even say it," Bullet cut him off, knowing exactly where he was going with that sentence. "So, what do we know?"

"Well, Neon is definitely up to something. That bunker he's built is fit for him and about two other people, three at a push."

"I was informed about the C4 that Neon was bringing in and then shipping out, do you have anything on that?" The Spectrum asked.

"Nothing yet, sir. But, it's the first thing on our to-do list for…" he started, another yawn interrupting him, "for tomorrow. That is, if that's okay with you, sir?"

"Certainly, get some well-deserved rest," The Spectrum ordered. "Also, try and position Jack's other jackets with the cameras attached around the room before you go to bed. It means everyone can be your security while you both sleep."

"Will do. Good night, sir. Bullet," Gecko bid them farewell, and the screen went black.

Bullet slouched back in the seat, spinning it slightly from side to side.

"Well… you hoped he'd get some rest," The Spectrum reminded her.

"I know. But, I really thought we'd have a lot more to go on by now."

"Jack has only been there for a few hours, Bullet, you can't have it both ways. However, I agree with your feelings you displayed earlier. The boy was extremely tired. He needed to rest. And now he is. So, for now, let him sleep. Maybe you should do the same."

"Nah," Bullet replied in disagreement, "at least not until Youth wakes up."

"As you wish," The Spectrum said as he got up to leave, "but, if you become tired, make sure to wake up the Yellow Youth. We cannot, under any circumstances, leave them hanging in the balance with no one monitoring them, am I understood?"

"Crystal clear, sir."

"Good night, Bullet."

"Good night, sir," The Spectrum left her alone.

Bullet turned her attention back to the screens in front of her and watched. An hour crawled by.

And another.

And another, even slower than the previous one.

Bullet made herself a cup of coffee with the machine in Youth's room and went back to her seat in front of the monitors.

Something happened.

She put the cup down and leaned into the monitor showing one of Jack's coats that Gecko placed in the room. She dotted quickly between all four.

Something moved.

Nothing was happening now.

But, something definitely moved.

And then again.

The door handle.

Someone was trying to get in.

The handle rocked up and down and then stopped. Bullet's finger hovered over the button ready to call the boys back. She stared so hard she thought her eyeballs might dry up and fall out. Nothing seemed to happen again.

Bullet let out a sigh.

"IT WASN'T ME! I DIDN'T!"

Bullet jumped out of her skin when Youth woke up with a fright. He looked around confused and rested his eyes on Bullet.

"Did I fall asleep?"

"Yeah, and then nearly had me shit myself when you woke up. Get over here."

Youth rolled out of his bed and shuffled over next to Bullet, slumping into the seat next to her.

"I need coffee," Youth moaned.

Without saying a word, Bullet handed him her freshly made cup.

"Anything exciting happen?"

"Someone tried to get into Jack's room."

"Seriously?" Youth perked up and focused on the monitors.

"Yeah, they're gone now, I think. It happened just before you woke up."

"Neon?"

"Well, I can't see through doors unless they're open, Youth," Bullet snapped.

Youth cowered away from her.

"Sorry, I'm just tired."

"You know, you've been so focused on everyone else sleeping, but you're the one that's been awake the longest. Go to bed, Bullet. I got this."

"You're sure?"

"I've had my hour long power nap. That plus, I've been napping here and there whenever I can, whereas you haven't slept at all. I'm all good. Go, seriously."

Bullet ruffled his wavy blond hair and headed for the door.

"I'll keep my earpiece in, shout me if you need anything."

Bullet walked back along the hall and climbed the spiral staircase, passing by two floors as she made her way right to the top.

She opened the door to her room, and quietly closed it shut behind her.

Getting ready for bed, she changed into her black tank top and black shorts, and walked barefoot across the black marble floor and crawled into bed. Bullet fumbled underneath her pillow and pulled out an old crooked photograph.

Two happy young girls were playing together in the park. She looked at the photograph longingly.

As she welled up, a tear escaped down her cheek. Bullet began to cry and turned to look out the window. The stars all winked at her as they sat like a beautifully clustered orchestra around their conductor.

"If you're out there Jenna. I miss you. And I'm sorry," she whispered, looking back to her photo.

She tucked it safely back under her pillow and turned on to her side.

It wasn't long before her subconscious grabbed her.

The courtroom was small and cramped, no seat was empty as Bullet sat in the witness stand, an older man in a suit standing in front of her menacingly.

"What did you see?" the man growled.

"I didn't see anything."

The walls were closing in.

"So, not only did you not see my client rape your friend, you didn't see anyone rape her at all. Yet, you claim it happened?"

"It happened!"

"How do you know?"

"She told me!"

Bullet could feel the air being stolen from her as the walls, the chairs, the people, the lawyer, all edged closer to her.

"She told you? And that means it's fact, does it?"

"She wouldn't lie! She committed suicide because of him!"

"No. She took her own life because she couldn't face the lies she had told."

"Jenna…"

"She's a liar, and well you know it, isn't that right?"

"Please…"

"Admit that you know nothing. Can you admit that Jenna Harvey was wrong about who attacked her?"

"Leave me alone."

"Answer the question."

"She was my best friend!"

"That wasn't the question, Miss Wells."

Everywhere Bullet looked, a person sat glaring at her, waiting, wondering.

Jenna's memory was hanging in the balance, her reputation being put in the firing line, and the only way to save it was all down to Bullet.

The world was running out of oxygen, for Bullet was using it all. Her white shirt stuck to her with sweat, her bun was now hanging at the top of her neck instead of the top of her head.

The world started to swim.

Bullet was drowsy.

She toppled off the side of her seat slowly and began to fall. She kept falling. Jenna was falling with her.

Her surroundings were black, like she was falling into nothing.

She reached out her hand trying to grab Jenna who was fading away the closer Bullet got.

She disappeared, but Bullet continued to fall.

"NO!"

She sat upright on the concrete floor.

The room was dark, empty and cold.

Bullet stood up, spinning around hoping someone would find her. She was wearing blue jeans and a white T-shirt; the same outfit she wore when she met him.

"Hello, Georgina."

Bullet spun around.

A man with grey hair combed back stood in front of her in a pair of bright red trousers, a white shirt and an orange blazer. He smiled at her ceaselessly.

"My name is Neon. I'm going to help you find the man that attacked your friend."

"I know who attacked her."

"Yes, and he walked. He's a free man."

"He shouldn't be."

"I know. That's why I'm going to help you find him."

"It doesn't matter if we find him or not, he was found not guilty. Everyone thinks he's innocent."

70

Neon walked towards her and placed his hands gently on her shoulders.

When he looked into her eyes it was as though he could see into her mind.

Into her soul.

As though he knew everything about her.

"Who said we were going to enforce the law?" he asked with a sinister smile. "We're going to find him, and enforce justice for Jenna Harvey. Yes?"

Bullet stared at the bright white ceiling of her room, the moonlight giving it an almost unbearable glare.

Her bed was not neat like it was when she crawled into it three hours before; a pillow was on the floor, her duvet was damp and strewing all over the mattress, its cover was pulled off of two corners.

Bullet got up and went over to open the window.

The cold night's breeze was much welcomed and wrapped around her like a cool blanket. Her wavy hair hung like rats' tails as the damp sweat dried in the gentle wind that swirled around her as she looked at the view. The moon's reflection in Loch Lee doubled the source of light.

The grounds were beautiful. The castle style building used for Colour Coded had much land surrounding it, decorated with beautiful flowers, and a fountain trickling in the courtyard at the front.

Bullet found it very calming.

She left the window open and walked back over to her bed, the wind howling softly around her room. She picked up her tablet from the bedside table and activated it. The screen showed Jack's jacket camera still facing the door. At eleven p.m., it was no surprise that they were still asleep.

She swiped left and saw another view of the door. She swiped again to see a view of the boys sleeping, Jack still curled up on the bed, Gecko sprawled out on the floor using Jack's case as a pillow. She watched for a while, remembering more about Neon.

How he found her.

How he understood her.
Sympathised with her.
Listened to her.
How he helped her find Jenna's attacker.
And how he helped her kill him.

Chapter Eight

Jack and Gecko made their way through the crowds of people to the main room of the warehouse.

Neon stood at the front signing something for a man wearing a blue cap and a denim shirt, no fresh skin could be seen for the tattoos that covered his arms and neck, and Jack assumed the same could be said for the rest of his body that was covered by clothes.

Gecko saw men taping boxes shut and went over to join them, blending in effortlessly while Jack continued on.

He watched the men intently.

Some were unwrapping packages, while others were repackaging. Some boxes said 'BB', some said 'FF' and some said 'SS'. He pretended it didn't faze him as he clocked Neon watching him.

The tattooed man walked towards him with the clipboard. Jack noticed the strange signature that Neon provided him with.

It's not the one he was used to seeing Neon sign with.

"Who's he?"

"No one. Ready for your mission?" Neon asked.

"As ready as I'll ever be."

"Good. Follow me."

Jack followed Neon out of the main hall and entered the bunker.

"You will go to Colour Coded and hand yourself in. This is another phone number I have; you will memorise it, and then throw this away. You will find out everything you possibly can about their plans. You will call me every evening at nine p.m. with an update. You will spend a week there, maximum, and should they not provide you with the mission I believe they will, you will find a way out. That is the objective of your mission. Understood?"

"Yep, call you every night at nine p.m. on this number that will only be in my head, find out everything I can, and leave after a week, if not before. Simple enough."

"Quite," said Neon, eyeing him suspiciously. "Close the door on your way out."

Jack walked out briskly and made his way back to the main hall. He scanned the room seeking out Gecko, whom he found in the corner looking at a notice board.

Jack walked up behind him and brushed against him.

"Oh, sorry, pal," he said, ushering his head to the corridor and walked out. A few minutes later, Gecko joined him.

"So, we're going back?" Gecko said.

"Yeah."

Gecko pressed his finger in his ear ready to get in touch with Colour Coded, but Jack grabbed his arm.

"Not here."

Being as nonchalant as possible, they walked through the living quarters and went into Jack's room, closing the door behind them and locking it.

"Bullet, you there?" Gecko asked.

"Yeah, we're here, Gecko. Rocket's already getting the car primed, he'll meet you and Jack over the other side of the hill eastbound to the warehouse in three hours," Bullet responded.

"Right, about that… just take Jack. I think I should stay here."

"Why?" Youth probed.

"I was taping up boxes this morning, and I found something weird. Neon isn't doing a thing with C4. Go on, ask me what he's actually doing."

"Okay… I was going to ask that anyway. So, what is he doing?" Bullet humoured him with agitation.

"He's getting cocaine shipped in *disguised* as C4. His team remove it, replace it with ground salt, dress it back up as C4 again, and ship it out."

"Do you know why?" Bullet asked.

"That's the question I was going to tell you *not* to ask me… I have no idea."

"I don't know if this is important, but my gut is telling me to inform you that his signature's changed… I don't know if that's helpful or not, but it was really weird to me. It looks nothing like his name," Jack added. "Also, the boxes that are being packaged have initials on them."

"Initials?" Bullet asked, "What did they say?"

"Some said 'SS', some said 'FF' and some said 'BB'. That's all I saw although, I think there was another one but I couldn't make it out without being obvious. Sorry guys."

"No, that's good, Jack. I can hopefully work with that," Youth reassured him. "Hang tight, you'll be back soon."

"Gecko, I don't feel good about leaving you there. I want to run it by The Spectrum," Bullet said.

"Okay. If he wants me back with Jack, then that'll be the plan. I just think someone should stay on the inside."

"I'm with Bullet, man. I don't think you should stay. He doesn't know you," Jack chimed in.

"All the more reason for me to stay."

"Yeah, but, if he doesn't know you, you'll never find anything out. That, plus, he's ruthless. He gets more ruthless with every passing day. You only just got here so you don't know much about how he runs things… if you put one toe out of line, he will kill you," Jack pleaded, "so, just come back. I'll be coming back here anyway; someone will be on the inside."

Gecko paced the length of Jack's room, running his hands through his jet black hair and scratching at his stubble.

"Fine."

All of a sudden, an alarm went off, swarming the room with red flashes, and a voice came over a tannoy system.

"This is a personnel alert. All staff must report to the main hall, repeat, all staff must report to the main hall."

"What the hell is that?" Youth burst out.

"We've been summoned," Jack explained. "Stick with us, guys; I might be able to whisper some information."

Jack and Gecko made their way back to the main hall, joining in with the other workers who were jogging steadily to meet their boss' demands.

Jack couldn't help but think that they stood in blocks like an army when they arrived in the main hall. Echoes of footsteps broke the silence as Gecko and Jack followed the man in front and took their place facing Neon on the steps at the front.

"Ladies and gentlemen. I have some disturbing news to share," Neon began, standing brazen and still like a statue, towering over his employees. "As you know, there is now a bunker that I had built for myself to have somewhere quiet to work. Someone in this room didn't think that was vital, and they entered my private lair for reasons completely unknown to me."

Gecko and Jack looked at one another with a clear expression of fear and anticipation.

"I would like the intruder to step forward. Step forward knowing that you will be treated not nearly as harshly as you would if you don't step forward and I find out that it was you," Neon threatened, eyeing each and every member of his organisation individually.

His eyes fell on Jack, and lingered for a moment, before moving on to Gecko.

Jack felt the vein in his neck pulsate profusely, and he heard Gecko swallow rather loudly with tension. Nobody in the room moved a muscle.

They looked amongst each other seeking out the culprit, hoping that they would come forward knowing Neon's remorseless nature.

"No one?"

Again, nobody did or said anything, especially Jack and Gecko.

"Very well, then. I now have no choice but to have security pace the perimeter of the grounds every night for the foreseeable future. After nine p.m. every night, leaving your living quarters will be strictly forbidden until the perpetrator is caught. I don't need to tell you that if you are found anywhere on the premises other than the living quarters, serious consequences will follow your capture."

Neon strategically paused to let his words sink in with the crowd.

"Good. You may return to your duties."

Everyone spontaneously scattered like ants.

Jack and Gecko turned to go back to Jack's room.

"JACK BURNS!" Neon's voice rang out over the room.

Jack turned to face Neon, who was still at the opposite side of the room.

"WITH ME," Jack headed towards Neon, and keeping his head down, he began to whisper.

"Neon has placed security around the building because someone broke into his bunker. I've been sent back which is fine for me leaving, but I don't know how we'll get Gecko out. We're going to need a plan."

"We hear you, Jack. We'll work something out," Youth replied.

"Just do what you have to do to stay safe, guys," said Bullet.

Jack walked towards Neon and left with him into his bunker, knowing he was getting ready to leave.

Bullet turned to Youth and Sparrow, leaning forward and running her fingers through her hair. She pulled the zip down a little on her black leather biker jacket. The pressure of this endeavour was getting higher and higher by the second.

"What're we gonna do?" Sparrow asked.

Without even thinking, Bullet pressed into her earpiece.

"Everyone, this is the Black Bullet. You're all needed in the Yellow Youth's quarters. A situation needs Colour Coded."

Bullet slouched back in the chair while Youth continued monitoring Jack and Gecko's cameras, and Sparrow was manoeuvring the drone to the other side of the warehouse.

A couple of minutes later, footsteps were heard, and Tide and Rocket entered. In behind them, The Spectrum entered, looking forever fresh as a daisy.

Breaking the silence was Lab.

"Someone wanted to join in the fun," she announced, helping a limping Flare into the room.

Sparrow immediately grabbed a seat and spun it towards her as she crashed on to it.

"Hon, this is maybe a little soon," Bullet suggested, concerned.

"If I spend another night in that hospital wing, I'm going to kill myself," Flare exclaimed.

Bullet flinched at her words.

"I just want read in, I'm not jumping in with two feet."

Bullet looked at The Spectrum, who nodded gently with his approval.

"Okay," Bullet walked round by Youth and referred to the monitors, "as everyone knows, Jack was hooked up with cameras before he went back to Neon, as was Gecko, and we've been monitoring them both since they got there."

"Along with me keeping an eye on the perimeter with the drone," Sparrow cut in.

"We also know that Neon has built a bunker underneath the warehouse and I've been trying to update the floor plan with its location," Youth added.

"I don't know if you heard earlier on, but Jack informed us that Neon is planning to send him back here as he somehow knew that we would ask him to spy for us. But, he's sent Jack back to retrieve information and pass it along to him."

"Much like he's doing for us," The Spectrum clarified.

"Exactly. Now, there's a problem; Jack will get out easily because he'll have clearance from Neon. For Gecko, on the other hand, it's going to be tricky. Neon has authorised security to man the outdoors and nobody is allowed out of their living quarters after nine," Bullet continued.

"So, why doesn't Gecko just leave now? It's six thirty," Flare asked.

"Because Jack is leaving just now to come back to us. If they both slip out at the same time, it'll be too noticeable," Youth replied.

"Well, what's the plan?" Rocket asked. "The car's out the front, ready to go."

"Are all the vehicles serviced?" Sparrow asked.

"Yup, every single one is up to spec and ready whenever they're needed to be. Why?"

"Because I was thinking it might be best to take multiple vehicles. One takes Gecko, one takes Jack, the other would be a decoy?"

"Yeah, let's do that," Bullet stated, "so, Tide can go with Sparrow, Rocket can take his car, and I'll take the bike. When we get there, I'll take Jack, and Gecko will go with Rocket."

"Are you planning on taking different routes home?" The Spectrum intervened.

"Yeah, we will. Sparrow, you take the A85," Bullet instructed.

"A… eighty… five…" Sparrow muttered to himself as he tapped roughly on his tablet.

He looked up to everyone staring at him.

"I'm a pilot, not a driver. I don't know roads!"

"Uh-huh," Bullet mumbled, smiling, "Rocket, you take the A9."

"Sure thing, love," Rocket confirmed before leaving the room.

"I'll come back the long way around the A90. Lab, you might want to get some fresh bandages and antiseptic at the ready. We don't know how ugly this is going to get."

"On my way!" she replied, heading out to the hospital ward.

"Everyone good?" Bullet concluded.

They all nodded in confirmation and got up to leave.

Bullet noticed Flare looking rather unhappy.

"Youth could use some help with those monitors, Flare," she whispered.

Flare beamed and pushed on a table with her good arm, her chair rolling smoothly over to Youth who greeted her with a smile.

"Hey, stranger. Been a while!" She rested her chin on his shoulder as he began typing.

Bullet flashed a satisfied smile as she left.

The night air nipped them as a red Volkswagen, a silver Ford and a black motorcycle left Colour Coded HQ. The Spectrum watched from his office window, Lab and Flare at his back as they rolled off of the property and disappeared behind the trees.

"Do you think this one will get ugly?" Lab asked The Spectrum.

"I can neither confirm nor deny my concerns at this moment. Many of us have certain fears and reservations about many things, but everyone is always apprehensive about the unknown. I am no different," he replied, not taking a break from watching the headlights travel away from them on the tight, winding roads that would lead them to Jack and Gecko.

And Neon.

Jack walked out of the warehouse, keeping his head high and his walk a brisk one. The guards didn't bat an eyelid considering it was a minute past nine.

Brazenly, Jack gave them a wave as he walked off the premises and headed for the hill to the east of the warehouse as Bullet had told him.

"Jack, it's Tide, can you hear me?"

"Yeah, I can hear you. Where's Bullet?"

"She's on her motorcycle; we're all on our way, but listen, don't climb the hill. We're coming in from the south. Hide away somewhere to the side of the road. We'll find you."

"Right, okay. How long you guys gonna be?" he enquired, looking around for somewhere to stay low.

"Won't be too long, bud. About twenty minutes. Gecko, be ready to make a run for it by then," Rocket cut in.

"I'm ready right now, gang. Just give me the all clear," Gecko answered.

Jack walked for around ten minutes, looking back to see how far out of site he was from the warehouse. He came across a ditch just off the main road and crouched down into it, leaning back against a big rock and using his case as a seat looking both ways down the road for headlights or any other sign that Colour Coded were close.

In the distance, Jack saw the lights from two cars and a singular light at the back which was clearly Bullet's motorbike come down a road and then disappear behind a field.

Gradually, engine noises got louder and louder.

Jack started to panic.

"Guys, I can hear you, you're close. Cut out the engines and turn off your headlights."

He could no longer hear anything. He got up and walked down the road to meet them.

"Put your case in my car, Jack," Rocket offered, "I've popped the boot."

"Thanks," said Jack, walking around to the back of Rocket's red car and flinging his case in.

"Hey! Be careful with that, I can still see you remember!" Youth screamed in his ear.

Jack merely chuckled.

"Sorry."

"Gecko, we're ten minutes away on foot. Wait for our signal," said Tide.

"I'm ready. What side am I going for?"

"We'll go for the…"

"North side," Jack cut Tide off.

She looked at him very taken aback, forcing him to suddenly feel anxious.

"It's only got one door, there won't be as many guards at that side."

"He's right," said Sparrow, who had pulled out his tablet, "there's only two guards there. There's six on the south side and four on both the east and west sides."

Bullet walked over to them as she pulled off her black helmet, letting her brown hair drop down on to her jacket, a swing in her hips as she paced over in their direction.

For Jack, the world stopped.

He couldn't decide if he was more frightened or in awe as he eyed every inch of her. This was someone who, if she was scared, never let it show.

The Black Bullet was ready.

"What're we waiting for?"

"We were doing a guard count, I'm just checking the rest of the grounds. Don't want any surprises," Sparrow replied.

"Where's your drone positioned?" Bullet enquired, as she went into the boot of Sparrow's car.

"Bird's eye."

"Okay, you guys go. And stay low. I'm going to set up shop here," she ordered.

"Fine, but you're not doing it across my car!" Rocket warned her.

Bullet rolled her eyes as she set up the stand on for the sniper, and they all started running into the field in stealth mode. Jack couldn't help but remember the last time Bullet pulled out one of her guns in his presence.

The closer to the warehouse they got, the more they began to spread out. Tide went towards the back of the warehouse with Sparrow, while Rocket and Jack ran to the front. Rocket stopped at the south-east corner just before the entrance to the compound, while Jack ran past him to the north-east corner.

He could see Tide at the north-west corner.

"Guys… the guards rotate. There's six on this side right now," Tide whispered.

"That means they've done a full 180 since we got here. How long has it been since we checked the drone?" Bullet's voice cut in.

"Six minutes," Sparrow replied.

"They rotate every three minutes... Neon is taking no chances," Jack muttered. "What's the plan?"

"We need a distraction," Rocket said.

"Gecko, are you by the north side door?" Sparrow asked.

"I'm right on the other side of it. Hurry up! There are guards in here too!" he whispered frantically.

"I have an idea," Jack said.

"Well, get ready to execute it in ten seconds. We're about to go down from six guards to four," Bullet intervened.

They all sat as still as possible, and after a moment, the six guards moved to the east side of the warehouse by the entrance, while four guards came around from the west side.

Jack moved down to the compound area where the vans once were and scooped up four decently sized rocks, and as hard as he could, lobbed two of them over the wire fence as far as he could make them go. As soon as he threw them, he ducked back into the bushes and ran up towards Tide, and threw the other two to the west side of the building. The four guards divided into two and split up to investigate the noise.

"Now, Gecko," Jack forced as quietly as he could.

Gecko flung the side door open and ran straight for Jack who was now opposite the door on the other side of the fence. Tide followed him down there, while Rocket threw another rock into the property before running around the way he came and darted straight back down the field to the car.

Jack, Gecko and Tide ran as quietly as possible to meet Sparrow.

They had barely gotten to the north-east corner of the premises before the alarms were going off in the warehouse, and guards were in a frenzy.

"Guys, do not let the alarms panic you. Stay. Low," Bullet ordered.

They did as instructed.

They kept low.

But, a guard had run to the entrance of the compound area, and Gecko literally bashed right into him. They scrambled around on the ground; Gecko was whimpering and clearly scared.

"Tide, Sparrow, run now!" Jack shrieked, as he dived on top of the guard in an attempt to free Gecko.

Tide and Sparrow ran past them, although Sparrow seemed hesitant.

"GO."

Reluctantly, Sparrow continued to the road as five more guards arrived just as Jack took power of the situation. He was rugby tackled to the ground, and Gecko was grabbed again.

He couldn't see.

There were so many men sprawled everywhere, all Jack could do was flail around with his arms and legs hoping he caught somebody other than Gecko.

"Jack, try and stay low. I'm going to fire," Bullet said.

"No, Bullet, don't!" Tide's exasperated voice came back. "You're missing, remember? Don't give yourself away. We're almost there."

The sound of a revving car had everyone distracted as Rocket's red Volkswagen came billowing up the road with no intention of stopping, and he was heading straight for them.

At the last second, Rocket slammed on the breaks and yanked the steering wheel, the side of the car now skidding towards every one of them.

All but one guard leapt out of the way.

The last one standing merely fell back a little, and all four doors to the car popped open.

"GET IN!" Rocket yelled.

Jack and Gecko scrambled to their feet, and Jack as good as toppled himself into the back seat. The last guard grabbed on to the back of Gecko's shirt and floored him.

He went down hard on to the concrete.

"No, you don't!" Jack muttered.

Rocket's voice almost deafened everyone's ear.

"Bullet, SHOOT!"

A gunshot reverbed through the night air alongside the wailing of the warehouse alarm. Sparrow's silver Ford came hurtling up behind them with Tide in the passenger seat as Rocket was dragging both Gecko and Jack to the car and hurled them in.

"Rocket, bring Jack to me!" Bullet cried.

Rocket left half of the rubber from his tires on the road, the smoke billowing out the back of them from the wheel spin as he whirled the car around and went back down the way he came. He screeched to a halt by Bullet who was back on her bike.

Dizzy and in shock, Jack tumbled out of the car and went straight to her, climbing almost drunkenly on to the back of the bike. Rocket continued down the road, and Bullet took off back up the way, passing the warehouse at top speed. She rode for a few minutes, checking her mirrors constantly, but thankfully, no one seemed to be following. Bullet couldn't understand why Jack's grip got more loose as she went on.

She tried to slap his arms awkwardly as she rode.

Was he falling asleep?

Panic-stricken, she pulled the bike over, and Jack merely fell off into the mud at the roadside.

"Jack?" Bullet yelped, yanking her helmet off and dropping it to the ground.

"Oh, my God… Jack… I thought it was clear, I'm so sorry!"

She clawed at the bullet hole in his shoulder, watching his eyes roll into the back of his head.

"Jack, stay awake," she pleaded, "Sparrow, come back. I shot Jack. I fucking shot Jack! I can't take him on the bike!"

"Jesus! I'm turning around now!"

"God, Jack, please hang on," she wept, "please, please hang on, I'm so sorry."

Sparrow's car skidded to a halt on the other side of the road, and both he and Tide got out to help Bullet get Jack to the car. Tide opened the door, and they flopped Jack's unconscious body into the back seat just as loud revs could be heard in the distance. The view from the top of the hill showed guards leaving the compound on quad bikes.

Four quad bikes; eight guards.

Tide climbed in the back beside Jack, and Bullet slammed the door shut behind her.

"Whatever you do, do not take the long way!" she snapped at Sparrow, before picking up her helmet and mounting her bike. Both car and bike sped off up the hill frantically.

Bullet knew they had a good head start on the quads.

Losing them wouldn't be difficult.

But, keeping Jack alive… that part was unclear.

83

Chapter Nine

They flew on to the premises of Colour Coded at top speed, and before they had even stopped, Lab and Rocket came running out through the main door.

Bullet hopped off her bike and let it crash on to the gravel that formed the driveway. She ran over to Sparrow's car and yanked the back door open.

The blood was everywhere.

Rocket and Sparrow hauled Jack out of the car, wrapping each of his arms around the back of their necks and dragging him inside. Lab led them in, all the while trying to shout to Jack through his unconsciousness.

Bullet flung her helmet off, about to follow them in when she noticed Tide still in the back seat of the car, staring wide-eyed at the back of the driver seat. She had already shot one person, it didn't feel wrong for her to assume she had unknowingly hurt Tide too. Bullet backtracked and went round to the other side of the car and opened the door.

"Are you okay?" Bullet asked as she searched over Tide's body looking for injuries.

"Come on, honey, we have to get in there."

Tide said nothing. Did nothing.

Didn't even flinch.

"Tide…"

Slowly, almost dead-like, Tide turned her head to face Bullet who was crouched down next to her holding her arm trying to coax her out.

"There was so much blood. It wouldn't stop."

Bullet noticed her hands.

Her light blue fleece.

Her dark blue jeans.

All stained in Jack's blood.

"I tried… I tried to keep him awake. Sparrow drove as fast as he could. I tried to keep him awake. The blood… it went everywhere. I tried to stop the bleeding. I tried."

"Tide, this wasn't you. This was all my fault; I didn't think he was going to get out of the car. I didn't even know I'd hit him until I got him on the bike," Bullet tried to explain, although, it felt more like she was trying to defend herself.

She was.

"Come on, honey. Please. Come inside, we'll get you cleaned up," she offered.

Tide said nothing.

Tears openly flowed down her cheek like a stream would flow down a mountain. Bullet rubbed her eyes in frustration, trying her best not to break down, trying her best to keep it together.

She pressed into her ear.

"Rocket, Tide needs you."

He needed no coaxing. Seconds later, Rocket ran outside and met Bullet at the car with Tide.

"Hey you," he smiled at her, "you did good."

As soon as he started talking to her, Bullet picked herself up and forced the legs that were made out of jelly to move as fast as she could make them. She ran across the foyer and up the glass staircase to the conservatory and down the corridor.

She followed the blood trail.

It felt as though the hospital wing was miles away as her rasping grew more harsh with every step she took, forcing herself not to stop, or even slow down. She made it.

Everyone else was there other than Jack and Lab.

"Where is he?" she panted, looking around aimlessly for him.

"Lab's working on him," said Youth.

She went to go through to the back room where Lab does her private consultations. Sparrow stepped in front of her, blocking her way, and Youth held her arms from behind.

"Bullet... Lab's working on him. Let her do her thing," Sparrow interjected.

Bullet glared at him.

Sparrow merely stared back at her waiting for her to settle.

"She's good at what she does, Bullet. You know that," Youth reassured her. "Come on. Sit down."

Youth guided her over to a vacant bed next to Flare's and sat her down gently before sitting down next to her.

She looked at him, feeling lost.

Feeling scared.

Useless.

But, more importantly, feeling guilty as sin.

Youth put his arm around her and rubbed her shoulder. Gecko struggled off of one of the other beds and limped over to them, shuffled up behind her on the mattress and wrapped his arms around the two of them.

A very silent moment passed before Rocket walked in carrying Tide in his arms who, at this point, was openly crying into his neck.

Bullet, Gecko and Youth got up, and Rocket placed Tide down on the bed.

Looking at her inconsolable friend, Bullet climbed in next to her, letting Tide snuggle in while Rocket pulled a chair over, sitting it next to the bed and lowering himself into it, not for a second letting go of Tide's hand.

Gecko climbed in next to Flare, while Youth sat by Bullet and Tide's legs.

Sparrow merely paced the room nervously.

No one said a word.

They didn't have to; they were all thinking the same thing.

Jack might die.

Neon might be on to them now.

Jack might die.

Apart from Bullet; that's not what she was thinking as she stroked Tide's damp hair. In the silence of the hospital wing, only one thought passed through the Black Bullet's mind.

Jack might die… because of her.

Lab appeared from the consultation room, bloody and tired.

Bullet, Youth and Gecko stood up instantaneously as Lab came over to the two beds that they had all gathered by. Her face was straight, giving nothing away, until a little smile broke out.

"He's going to be absolutely fine," she announced as sighs of relief were released across the medical wing. "The bullet was a through and through to his shoulder. It caught his clavicle, a little of which is broken. He lost a fair bit of blood, but he's now stable."

She walked over to Tide who was still laying stiff on the bed.

"He didn't pass out from blood loss, sweetheart. It was shock. You did good."

Lab flashed an immensely proud smile to an emotional Tide who began to sob again, but this time with relief. Rocket squeezed her hand in moral support.

"Is he awake?" Bullet whispered.

"He's sleeping. I decided to give him a generous dose of morphine so I could re-align his collarbone. You'll be able to talk to him in the morning. Gecko is out and home, safe and sound because of what you did. Nobody is blaming you, Bullet."

As much as Bullet heard Lab's words loud and clear, she didn't believe them.

Yes, Jack would be okay.

But, she was fully to blame for his life being in danger.

"Bullet," The Spectrum's deep voice penetrated the ward.

Bullet turned to face him.

"My office, now," The Spectrum walked away.

Bullet looked at everyone who merely looked as concerned for her as she was for Jack.

Without a word, she followed him out and to his office.

"Take a seat," he said, ushering her to the gold couches that faced one another across a red fluffy rug and an oak coffee table with a glass top.

She dropped down on to it.

Clinking and clanging broke through the crackling of the fire as The Spectrum poured two glasses of whiskey and brought them over. He handed her a glass and sat down on the other couch in front of her.

"Thought you could use a drink."

"In actual fact, I could really use a do-over."

"If that were possible, you know I would make sure you got it."

In silence, they took a sip of their drinks. It nipped the back of Bullet's throat delightfully as she swallowed, letting it wash through her like a cold wave on hot, dry sand.

"Tell me what you're thinking," The Spectrum demanded.

She pulled her gaze away from him and looked out the window at the night sky. In light of the frenzy that Colour Coded had just been through, the world seemed very calm.

Somewhere out there, however, Neon was infuriated and who knows how ruthless he was now being with his staff, and especially his security, who failed to do their job on the first night of it being implemented.

"Bullet. Tell me what's in that head of yours."

"Nothing."

"Don't lie to me," The Spectrum jagged her.

"I'm not," she explained, "I don't know what to think about first. I'm thinking about everything and anything all at the same time. To the point where it feels like there's nothing there," Bullet dropped her head into her hands and ran her fingers through her long brown hair.

Without even realising it, she had started to cry by the time she lifted her head up to look at The Spectrum. "I don't know how I messed this up."

"You didn't."

"I shot Jack."

"Yes, you did. But, you didn't mess anything up."

Bullet stood up and went over to pour herself another drink. She gulped it down with extreme ease.

"If you're going to say I didn't mess anything up because we went there to get Gecko out and we did, I'm going to get really mad. I don't care if you're my boss."

The Spectrum merely observed her as she downed the rest of the remaining fluid and poured yet another glass.

"Why did you fire your weapon?" The Spectrum probed.

"Because Rocket told me to," she said, before downing her third glass and pouring another.

"And where was Jack when Rocket told you to fire?"

Bullet paused for a moment. She knew what he was doing and turned to face him, taking another gulp of whiskey.

"Come on, humour me. Where was Jack when the Red Rocket asked you to shoot?"

"He was in the back seat of the car."

"And where was the Green Gecko?"

"He was on the ground. The guard had pinned him down, he was kneeling on Gecko's back," she recalled.

"So, neither Gecko nor Jack were in your line of fire when Rocket gave the order," he stated as he stood up and walked over to her, "Hmm?"

"No."

"No," he confirmed.

"But, that doesn't change anything," she snapped angrily.

"You're right, it doesn't," he agreed, surprising her, "Jack is still in the hospital wing with a bullet hole in his shoulder that caused a broken clavicle. All of which you created."

Her tears continued to flow, now more profusely than before.

The Spectrum stepped closer to her. He was so close to her that she could smell the whiskey on his breath mixed with the scent of his aftershave.

"What is the difference between someone who is to blame and someone who feels responsible?"

Bullet shook her head and shrugged her shoulders, unable to talk through her tears.

"Someone who is to blame is an individual who did something wrong and knowingly so. Someone who feels responsible is a person who believes that, somehow, one way or another, the onus is on them when an unfortunate series of events occurs," he said softly, putting his hand on her arm and taking the glass out of her hand before putting it down. "You may feel responsible. But, you are not to blame."

Bullet fell into him. The Spectrum caught her and hugged her tightly.

He knew what kind of woman he was dealing with.

The girl in her late twenties, as much as she was talented, a good shot, and extremely lethal when cornered, was also a fragile and good-hearted one. This was the girl that everyone knew of.

The legend.

In some places, the myth.

The one who, one minute she was there, and then she was gone. The one who had neutralised two terrorist plots without the Secret Service or the government even having a clue. But, as much as she was a hero, a saviour, and a warrior... she was still human.

A knock at the door interrupted them.

Lab walked in, a look of sympathy in her eyes at the state that Bullet was in.

"God, you didn't half get yourself in a tizzy, girl," she said, spreading out her arms, inviting Bullet to go and hug her. Bullet obliged, running to her mother figure, The Spectrum looking on.

Lab gave her a tight squeeze, rubbing her back comfortingly.

They let go, and Lab looked into Bullet's eyes.

"Are you ready for this?" she asked her, ominously.

"Ready for what?" Bullet replied, the feeling of dread filling her rapidly.

"Jack's awake."

Bullet was stunned. It had been a hell of a night.

Frantic.

Nerve-wracking.

Not to mention terrifying.

It took a moment for Lab's words to sink in as she smiled lovingly at Bullet.

"He wants to see you."

Chapter Ten

Red-eyed, tired and worried about what was to come, Bullet made her way back to the medical ward.

It was empty.

Flare and Gecko had both been released out of the Lavender Lab's observation and were now back in their own room.

Every sound, loud or quiet, carried through the hospital wing as though it was leading Bullet to Jack. She stood outside the consultation room door.

She didn't want to look at him. She didn't want to see the result of her actions.

But, for some reason, he wanted to see her.

Slowly, shaking, she placed her hand on the door handle and reluctantly pushed it open.

A very sore and drowsy Jack turned to look at her slowly. She held his gaze for as long as she could before cowering her head down to look at the floor.

"You shot me," he murmured, still looking at her.

Bullet looked at him. He had no expression. He was just staring at her.

"I'm sorry, Jack," Bullet said, "I'm so sorry. It was an accident. I didn't know you were going to get out of the car, and Rocket yelled for me to shoot just as you did, and… I know you hate me, but trust me when I say that you don't hate me nearly as much as I hate myself," she rambled, trying as best as she could to fight back the tears from returning again.

Jack's expression didn't change. He kept her gaze.

Bullet was beginning to feel frustrated.

Why wouldn't he say anything to her?

Did he hate her that much?

"Jack, please say something!" she pleaded. "It was an accident. I didn't set out to shoot you. I was aiming for the guard, and you got out of the car…"

"Are you saying this was my fault?" Jack croaked, still staring at her, still with no expression.

"No! Not at all! Jack, I'm saying it was mine. I'm to blame. I fired my gun, I didn't know you were going to get out of the car."

"Exactly. You had no idea."

Bullet was confused.

"I shouldn't have fired my gun at all," she said, thinking that was where Jack was going.

"No. If you didn't shoot, Gecko would have been taken, or worse... killed," Jack batted back.

Bullet looked at him. She had no idea what was going on.

Did he blame her or not?

"Jack."

"Bullet."

The frustration started to fill her. Bullet had no idea what kind of game Jack was trying to play.

"I don't know what you want me to say."

"I want you to say what you're thinking. I want you to tell me the truth."

Bullet took a moment.

She recalled the event from earlier that evening.

How she observed Gecko bumping into the guard and tumbling to the ground through the scope on her rifle. How Jack tried to help him. How Rocket pulled up. How Jack managed to get into the car, but Gecko got grabbed again. And how Rocket told her to fire, but Jack had gotten out of the car. How she packed the gun away, and everyone came down to meet her. How she hadn't even realised she caught him in her line of fire until he was on the back of her bike.

"Tell me the truth, Bullet."

Bullet hesitated. She stumbled over some attempts at forming words.

"It was an accident!"

She had no idea what happened. It just burst out of her, and it didn't stop there.

"It was an accident. I was aiming for the guard and you got out of the car just as I was pulling the trigger. I caught you as well as the guard. I didn't even know I'd hit you! I did everything I could to get you back here as quickly as possible. It wasn't my fault, and I'm really really sorry it happened." It poured out like fluid from a bottle, like a waterfall over a cliff edge. Like she had bottled everything up.

Suddenly, Jack smiled.

"Thank you," he chuckled, flinching at the pain in his shoulder, "I didn't care if you believed that I didn't think it was your fault, or everyone else didn't think it was your fault. I wanted *you* to know. I wanted you to believe in yourself that it wasn't your fault."

"Jack, I just feel so guilty."

"Bullet... what's the difference between someone who is to blame, and someone who feels responsible?"

Bullet froze.

That couldn't be a coincidence.

She was about to answer him when he beamed an enormous sheepish grin at her.

"I have to tell you something."

"What?"

"Your earpiece is broken," he admitted, "I don't know when or how it happened, but I can hear you all the time when you speak and everyone around you. I heard you talking to The Spectrum and it was killing me. I knew it wasn't your fault, and I kind of hated you for blaming yourself."

Bullet, for reasons best known to herself, let out a laugh. The tears openly started to flow again. She walked over to the bed and sat down beside him while she removed the broken device from her ear and placed it down next to Jack's.

Now, there would be no inevitable eavesdropping.

"And now I need to ask you a favour," he requested, "if you don't want to, I'll get it. It's been a long night for everyone."

"Anything, Jack. Ask me."

"Will you... umm... will you sleep here tonight?" he stuttered. "I don't want to wake up to no one. And if I got to choose, I'd pick you anyway. I feel safe when I know you're around. I can't explain it." Jack looked away, incredibly embarrassed, kicking himself for speaking too soon.

Bullet got up and walked around to the left-hand side of the bed. She climbed in next to him, leaning on his good shoulder and snuggled up to him. Bullet had never snuggled into anyone.

She had never met anyone she wanted to snuggle.

"For the record," she mumbled, leaning comfortably on his chest, "I feel safe when I know you're around too."

Both Jack and Bullet were smiling.

They were safe. They were content.

They fell asleep.

Jack woke up to a sound. As Lab was checking his monitor and levels, she caught his eye.

"I'm glad to see you two worked things out," she whispered, gesturing to Bullet who was still sound asleep on Jack's chest.

He smiled as he watched her lay there peacefully, grazing his fingers along her arm.

"There was nothing to work out. It was an accident."

"I know," Lab replied, continuing to check that everything was in working order, "did you tell her that her earpiece was broken?"

"Aye. She was mortified that everyone heard her cry," Jack scoffed.

Lab shook her head with a smile.

"She's one hell of a girl."

"Like no other," Jack agreed, "so, when can I get out of here?"

"Oh, you're not out of the woods yet, Jack. As much as the bullet missed all the important stuff, it broke your collarbone. We need to make sure it didn't hit nerves or tendons and that there's no torn muscle or tissue, and I can't check for any of that that until the wound has healed a little, which will only happen if you move your arm as little as possible," Lab explained, "that plus the fact that the guards got a good few blows into you. There's a lot of bruising on your back and down your legs, and I'm sorry to inform you, but you've got a beauty of a black eye forming."

"How long?"

"A couple of days, and that's just for me to check your movement and the sensation in your hand and up your arm. After that is dependent on how the former goes."

Jack was clearly displeased with her response.

"Let me put it this way: I know you care about her. I can see it. Better than everyone else. I knew it the first time I met you, and I knew it the first time I spoke to Bullet after she met you," Lab informed Jack, "I know you want out of here. I know you want to stop Neon; we all do, but unless you do what I tell you, you won't make a full recovery. Don't rush things and make it worse. Keep your arm in that sling. Take your time. For her. Not only will she want you fully recovered, she'll *need* you fully recovered. Agreed?"

Jack looked at Lab, impressed.

He was surprised at her empathetic demeanour.

But, more importantly, he was impressed at her tug on his heartstrings.

Her stab at his kryptonite, if you will.

"Don't look at me like that. One, I'm a doctor. And two, that girl is like a daughter to me. As is Tide and Flare. Gecko, Sparrow, Rocket and Youth are like my sons."

"And The Spectrum?" Jack probed lightheartedly.

"Don't even go there, buddy boy," she warned him, laughing.

93

Bullet curled up a little before she woke up to Lab and Jack laughing amongst themselves.

"Hey there, sleeping beauty," Lab smiled at Bullet.

"Ugh, I honestly don't feel like any kind of beauty," Bullet mumbled, positioning herself on her elbow and leaning her head on her palm.

"Oh, don't be silly. You're always my beautiful girl," Lab said, "now, mister. How do you feel? Do you need more morphine or are you good?"

"Nah, I think I'm good, thanks. You're my favourite doctor," Jack winked at Lab.

"Yeah, on second thought, I think you're okay for the morphine as well," she said, rolling her eyes at Bullet before leaving them alone.

Jack turned to look at Bullet, who held his gaze.

"Hey."

"Hi," Bullet smiled.

"How'd you sleep?"

"Like a baby. You?"

"Like a... junkie."

Bullet laughed.

It had been so long since she had felt as content as she did then. She was happy.

It was a welcome stranger to her life.

"That's actually the first time I've slept since... since I became the Black Bullet... and not had a nightmare."

"What do you have nightmares about?"

Bullet considered telling him.

He was high on morphine, there was a chance he'd maybe forget. Then again, there was a chance he would remember, and that was a lot to bombard someone with about a person's past.

Especially someone who had just been shot.

Especially someone who had just been shot by the person who was opening the can of worms.

"Just about my past, it's a long story."

"Well, the doc just said I'm going to be here for a while, so you know, I have time," Jack offered.

Bullet got up off the bed and turned round to look at him. Those deep hazel brown eyes looked back at her, patient, willing, ready to listen.

"Maybe, one day. But, not today."

Jack nodded with understanding.

She smiled and took his hand before leaning down and giving him a peck on his forehead.

Bullet left the hospital wing and walked along to the conservatory.

For the first time in a long time, she felt awake.

Not awake, muddling along until she got to go to bed again, awake.

Awake, awake.

Like she could run a marathon and then complete a military level obstacle course, awake.

It felt wonderful. That feeling too was a welcome stranger.

She sat herself down in her black chair in the upper foyer, looking out at the sun up high in the sky.

It sparked curiosity in her. Bullet pulled out her phone, which showed the time as 2:15 in the afternoon. She and Jack had slept for over thirteen hours.

"Afternoon, sleepy head," Sparrow greeted her.

He came over and joined her, sitting in his silver chair.

"Hey, Sparrow, how'd you sleep?"

"Great, to be honest. You?"

Bullet nodded, smiling uncontrollably.

"Yeah. Really great."

"Good! I take it you talked to Jack?"

"Yeah, I did. We worked everything out."

"Bullet, there was nothing to work out. We all heard you with The Spectrum last night. Tide, Lab, Flare and Gecko burst into tears just listening to you!" he informed her, and then a smile crossed his face. "Youth did too, but he begged us all to keep our trap shut."

Bullet laughed happily.

"Yeah, I took my earpiece out before I went to sleep last night," she said as she went back to looking out the window, and her smile began to fade.

"What's up?" Sparrow probed.

"He's still out there somewhere. He's still planning something. He's still looking for me. And he's still expecting to hear from Jack."

"Well, let's get planning then," he announced as he pushed his finger into his ear.

"This is the Silver Sparrow. We need everyone in the conservatory. There's a situation that needs Colour Coded."

It was weird for Bullet that she couldn't hear anything electronically, that she couldn't hear Sparrow in her ear as well as right next to her.

95

One by one, everyone arrived. The Spectrum walked in at the back of everybody.

"Good afternoon, all. I know everyone had a rough night last night, I trust we slept well?"

Everyone nodded in confirmation.

"Excellent," he exclaimed, "Sparrow, you called a meeting?"

"Yeah," he began, "I did. We all know Jack's in the hospital wing, and Lab doesn't think he's going to get out within a week, which was how long Neon had given him before he was to find a way back, so we need to come up with a story for him to feed Neon that keeps him here."

"Why don't we have him keeping Neon on his toes?" Gecko asked. "I mean, the guy is ruthless but, he's also obsessed with Colour Coded, especially Bullet. If we get him to say something like: 'I'm on to something, I think she's alive, but I need more time to confirm it', then it buys Jack time but, it'll also have Neon reeling. There'll be more of a chance he'll make a mistake then."

"Yeah, but the thing is, Neon never changes his plans unless something physically happens," Bullet replied, "so, if Jack tells him he may be on to something, it won't be enough for him to budge."

"He'd have to say he's found her," Youth clarified.

"But, then Neon would want to see him with me right away, so it still doesn't buy him time."

"How about he just ignores him?" Tide suggested. "I mean, for all Neon knows, we killed Jack when he came back to us, and maybe he doesn't know us as well as he thinks he does."

"Or he does know us, but he doesn't know Jack as well as he thinks he does because he's changed sides," Sparrow interjected, "which he has, really. I second that, I think we should just have Jack ignore him."

"He should call him tonight though, and then as of tomorrow, ignore him," Youth added.

"Third that," Rocket said.

"Fourth," said Gecko.

"Fifth," Lab joined in.

"Are we all in agreement?" Bullet asked.

The answer was unanimous. Jack was going to ignore Neon if and when he called after tonight.

"Okay," she said, "the next thing we have to worry about is where we go from here. We know Neon is bringing in cocaine dressed up as C4, taking out the cocaine and repackaging it with salt, while maintaining the C4 aesthetic. We know that the cases have weird initials on them, that his signature has changed, and that

96

he's built a bunker that fits him and potentially a couple of other people. We know he has a lot more staff now, and he also now has security. The only thing we don't know is… "

"Why?" Jack cut in, hobbling over to the crowd.

"What the hell do you think you're doing? Do you not remember our conversation earlier?" Lab snapped at him.

She looked him up and down. He looked terrible. Blood trickled down to his hands from the bottom of his upper arms.

"Did you just yank those tubes out!"

"I remember, and I still agree. I'm not planning on doing anything stupid, I just want to try and help," Jack explained as Lab let him have her seat, and she stood instead, "and no, I didn't yank them out, I was careful. Are you impressed?"

"No, I think you're an idiot, and if you ever do that again, forget Bullet, I'll shoot you," Lab pierced.

"Guys," Sparrow cut in, impatiently, "we've cleared up the fact that we know a couple of things about him here and there, but we don't know why. With all that in mind, what are we going to do?"

"I think this is one of those times that I'm het," Youth suggested.

"What do you mean, Youth?" asked The Spectrum.

"I think I should investigate the things that we know about him. Like the cocaine. That amount of cocaine must be gang related. He may be talking to dealers," Youth explained, "why, again, is unknown. But, that, to me, seems like a better place to start."

"Yeah, but we need to find out why so that we know what to do next," Flare defended.

"The 'why' part is something we don't know though," Youth debated, "but, the changes that he's made is something we do know. We need to work with what we've got. That alone could give us an answer to the 'why' question."

"I have to say, Flare, as much as your argument is one hundred per cent correct, I do agree with Youth," said The Spectrum, "and, furthermore, if we're working behind the scenes, keeping ourselves to ourselves, remaining quiet, it backs up the implication that Jack is, for whatever reason, indisposed to be able to call Neon at nine p.m. every night."

Flare backed down instantaneously, understanding his point.

Everyone seemed to be on the same page.

"So, that's the plan? Research what we have so far and see if we can connect the dots and learn something?" Bullet clarified.

"I would highly recommend that path above all other possible routes, yes," The Spectrum confirmed, as he walked by everyone to make his way back to his office, "and I'm sure you can all decide amongst yourselves who takes what task, because I can assure you that everything isn't getting left to the Yellow Youth. I also think it goes without saying that Jack, Flare and Gecko can participate in this, since it isn't strenuous work, yes?"

"It shouldn't be a problem. Although, if you're struggling at any point, you let someone know and stop, agreed?" Lab instructed, dotting her gaze between all three of them, but paying particular attention to Jack.

They nodded in agreement.

"I have the footage from all the cameras stored on my hard drive. I'll screen grab as much as I can for us to work from," Youth announced, and got up to leave.

In dribs and drabs, everyone followed him out.

The only ones left were Jack and Bullet.

He sat there smiling at her, but Bullet did not return the gesture.

"I can't believe, after everything, you got up and walked out of the hospital wing," she glared at him, "it isn't a real hospital, Jack, you can't just discharge yourself because you don't want to be there."

Bullet stood up and leaned on the railing to look outside.

"You need to recover sooner. And that'll only happen if you do what Lab tells you."

"Lab told me to take things steady, keep my arm in my sling, and not overdo it," Jack explained smugly, "I walked down a corridor. My arm is still in its sling. When I needed to stop, I stopped. I'm following the doctor's orders."

Bullet wasn't amused with his smug attitude and whipped around to face him.

"I need you well, Jack."

"And I just need you, Bullet."

Without giving her a second to argue, Jack kissed her.

It took her by surprise, and at first she didn't know what to do.

But, he didn't pull back.

Neither did she.

For a man so well-built, and with such a tough nature, his lips were incredibly soft. It was like the world was swept away from her.

Nobody else existed other than her and Jack.

The thought of pulling away crossed her mind, but in all honesty, she really didn't want to. She wanted more.

Her heart was racing. Sparks flew. The butterflies felt very real to her. Her legs felt like jelly, and she staggered back against the railing. Jack didn't waver; his body followed hers like a magnet.

Quickly, their kiss became very intense.

Bullet held the sides of his face and ran her fingers through his hair as she pressed herself into him. Jack's hand gripped on to her hip and slowly, he slid it around behind her. She could feel his bicep against her ribs as his hand made its way up her back.

After a while, Bullet tried to slow everything down, and they both pulled away. His brown eyes were mesmerising to her.

Both of them felt the struggle to get their breathing under control.

"Please tell me you left your earpiece out, too?" Bullet whispered.

Jack chuckled, still holding her close to him.

"I did, yeah."

"Good."

They hovered around each other delicately, their lips brushing again.

Every cell in Bullet's body was springing to life like fireworks.

Jack pulled his head away, beaming at her like he was the happiest man on the planet at that moment.

"Come on, then," he said suddenly, taking her hand and pulling her across the seating area, "we've got work to do."

Bullet did everything she could to get to grips with herself again as she let Jack lead her along the corridor to the spiral staircase. He was right.

They had a lot to figure out.

It was time to put all the emotions to one side and get one step ahead of Neon.

Chapter Eleven

It was extremely quiet in the Yellow Youth's lair as everyone was looking at photos, rewatching camera footage, updating the warehouse floor plan, or researching the C4 packaging scheme. Hours had gone by since Jack and Bullet had spent their moment alone in the upper foyer, and for a moment, it was like it had never happened.

The concentration had taken over.

Bullet watched him looking at photos; he was clenching his eyes shut and opening them wide, trying to focus. Bruises were starting to appear on his face from his fight with the guards at Neon's warehouse. He grabbed the back of his neck and rocked his head from side to side. He was stiff. Sore.

Exhausted.

"Jack," she said, inviting him to make eye contact, "go to bed."

"No, I'm fine," he claimed, looking back at the stack of photos Youth had printed off for him.

"You've been struggling for a while. I've been watching you."

"Oh, really?"

Bullet blushed and looked away.

"I'll keep going for another half hour, and then I'll stop. I promise," he stated.

Bullet nodded with approval and went back to looking at the screen grabs of Sparrow's perimeter footage.

"Okay, we think we've finished the floor plan," Tide announced, getting up from her seat and stretching.

"Let me have a look," Jack requested, taking the sheet of paper that Flare handed over to him.

He scanned it over.

"Yeah, that seems about right."

"Now that that's one thing done, I was hoping it would be okay for me to stop? I'm getting quite stiff and tired," Flare asked delicately.

"Of course, honey. Go," Bullet approved, "have a good sleep."

"Wake me if you need me for anything," Flare smiled at Bullet, walking out looking visibly exhausted.

Jack squinted at the floor plan, looking confused.

"Jack, I swear to God, go to bed," Bullet snapped.

"No, no, I'm fine but… this doesn't make sense."

"How?" Tide asked defensively. "We looked at the video from your camera and worked out the dimensions in respect to the bunker entrance and drew it on. It's as exact as it can be."

"No, I'm not disputing you and Flare's efforts, it's smashing how you did that so quick without going in with a measuring tape but… his bunker is right over electrical lines that connect to the warehouse."

"Yeah, so?" Sparrow asked.

"Well, then, why was he asking me to wire up his bunker with electricity? Why didn't he have it done at the time? They had direct access to a source."

"Maybe it was like you said: maybe it was all too old. I mean, you said it yourself that the generator panel looked as though it hadn't been touched in years," Rocket offered, "Youth gave you the warehouse history. It was abandoned for years before Neon got his hands on it."

"But, if it was me, or anyone else, they would have wired it while they had access to the source," Jack said, "so, why didn't he?"

"Because there was a reason he wanted you to do it?" Youth suggested.

"Or, because something was going on at the time that he couldn't?" Bullet offered.

Silence followed.

Fear started to live in a very dense nature for everyone when it came to Neon.

What was he up to?

"Okay, so I've been digging around as much as I can regarding the C4 packaging scandal that he seems to have gotten himself into," Youth began, typing frantically on the keyboard, "now, I haven't got much, but this is something that keeps popping up."

He hit a couple of keys with gusto and an article appeared on the plasma screen at the other side of the room. It contained a picture of a heavyset man in his late thirties with a bald head.

"His name is David Watt," Youth continued, "he's been associated with a gang called The Lion's Den in Glasgow. His street name is… Ditch. A little odd."

"Where can we find him?" Gecko asked.

"In a graveyard."

101

"So, he's dead?"

"Well, if he's not, he's going to wake up pretty angry," Youth joked.

"Gang warfare?" Jack asked.

"Well, no one really knows. His death was quite elaborate and the police are stumped," Youth explained as he loaded up another article.

It showed the Wallace Monument in Stirling with Watt's body impaled on the topmost spike of its structure.

"What the hell?" Jack breathed, looking at the article in horror.

"I see what they mean about it being elaborate," Tide scoffed, "what a way to go."

"What's this guy got to do with Neon?" asked Sparrow, who had suddenly gone stiff and defensive.

"The Lion's Den are suspected of a lot of criminal activity, but their main line of duty is drug trafficking. David 'Ditch' Watt was the only one from the entire gang that had ever been arrested," Youth said.

"So, he got caught during a deal?" asked Tide.

"No," said Youth, "he was accused of raping a young girl; Jenna Harvey, twenty-three, studying History at Stirling University. Orphaned at age twelve. She took her life during the trial. There are no pictures of her."

"Good," Bullet said suddenly.

So suddenly that it caused heads to turn with curiosity.

"I hate it when they show pictures of rape survivors. They've been through enough, they should be left alone," she defended.

"So, what's significant about The Lion's Den?" Sparrow asked, getting more impatient. More defensive.

"Well, it might be something… but, it might be nothing," Youth said, smacking hard on more keys and loading another report up on the plasma screen, "but, Prismatic, which contained Bullet, Flare, Rocket and yourself, Sparrow, was created in 2012. So was The Lion's Den."

Everyone looked at all the articles that Youth had loaded up on to the screen.

"You think this was his funding project? This was how he got his money to finance everything?" Tide asked.

"It's possible," Youth suggested, "but, that's all I've got so far."

Bullet looked at the article about Watt being accused of rape.

About him going through a trial and being found not guilty. She read about how there was plenty of evidence to convict him, but the jury cleared him. How the public and Jenna's foster family were up in arms about it, and rightfully so.

Her stomach churned chaotically, suddenly turning into a whirlpool.

She read and reread the article, but there was no mention of anything else important. Looking away from the screen, she noticed Jack eyeing her suspiciously.

She didn't know what to do.

If she should say something or not.

She was trying to muster something up, but thankfully, was interrupted.

"Guys, speaking of when Prismatic was founded, I've just thought of something," Gecko interjected, staring frantically from one photo to another, to another, and then back again, a look of horror flooding his face, "and it's not good."

"What have you got?" Bullet asked, pulling away from Youth's briefing and Jack's stare.

"The boxes... Jack noticed that some of them had initials on them, like 'FF', 'SS', and so on. We counted four that we got screen grabs of; the other two are 'BB' and 'RR'."

"And?" asked Sparrow impatiently, "we already knew that."

At this point, Jack, Tide and Youth were looking at Sparrow and Bullet with a very calculating manner. They were acting extremely weird.

Rocket, too, was a lot quieter than he had ever been before. Almost mute.

"Yeah, we did, but I think I might know what they stand for," Gecko said, turning to look at Bullet. "When you worked for Neon at Prismatic, who were the first people there?"

"It was Sparrow, Flare, Rocket and... me..." Bullet answered as she trailed off with the realisation hitting her hard in the gut.

"'BB'... the Black Bullet. 'FF'... the Fuschia Flare. 'SS'... the Silver Sparrow. And 'RR'... the Red Rocket," Gecko thought out loud as he wrote on the whiteboard, sticking up a photo of each box with the relevant initials on it.

"There isn't one box with two different letters on it?" Youth asked.

"Nope, not that I can see in the photos or the footage," Gecko confirmed.

Jack sat in silence, his brain going wild, trying to take everything in. Trying not to think about the look that Bullet had on her face when Youth found the article about David Watt. Like she recognised it.

Like she knew about it already; and all too well.

That was a thought for later.

He focused with all his might on everything Gecko just said.

And then it hit him.

"Youth, can you pull up the footage from my jacket cam when I approached Neon after Gecko arrived?"

Youth turned back to the computer, and after hitting a few keys, the footage played on one of the four monitors. Jack struggled to his feet and hobbled over to him, leaning over his shoulder.

"What're you looking for?" he asked Jack.

"Get ready to screen grab, I'll tell you when."

The deliveryman that was loaded with tattoos was taking back his clipboard after Neon signed it for something. He was walking towards the camera, getting closer and closer.

"NOW."

Youth slammed on the keyboard and a picture loaded on another one of the four monitors. At this point, everyone was crowded around the computers, keen to see where Jack's head had taken him.

"There, zoom in there," Jack instructed, pointing to the clipboard in the gangster's hand. Youth zoomed in, focusing on where Neon had signed the form.

"His signature. You said you thought it was different?" Sparrow clarified, looking between Jack and the monitor.

"Yeah, and it is. Can you flip this so that it's vertical?" Jack asked Youth.

"Can I fli... can I flip... yes, I can flip it," he chortled, as though amused by the insinuation that it would be a tough job.

A couple of clicks and Youth had flipped the photo ninety degrees to the right. Jack cocked his head a little to the side to get a more level view of Neon's handwriting.

Jack didn't like what he was about to say to everyone one little bit, but he was pretty sure he was seeing what he was seeing.

"Is it just me, or does that look like it says 'The Spectrum'?"

At his words, everyone joined in with the imitation of puppies being teased with a bone.

"Yeah," Tide agreed, "it really does."

Rocket threw his pen down on the table, annoyed at all the possibilities of what Neon could be up to, none of them being good.

"What the hell is he doing?" Gecko asked the room.

"It looks like he's setting everyone up," Bullet said, "the boxes with our initials on it, signing paperwork as The Spectrum, swapping out cocaine for salt, dealings with drug dealers... He might be trying to make us a target."

"To who?" Tide asked. "The Lion's Den?"

"Or another gang," Rocket offered for the first time in quite a while.

Everyone's head was spinning. They were wracking their brains for a solution or even a reason to Neon's weird activities. Youth started typing frantically on his keyboard.

"Youth, what're you doing?" Bullet asked him.

He didn't answer.

He didn't even acknowledge that she had spoken.

Bullet leaned towards him, carefully.

"Youth? Where's your head at?" she probed again, getting concerned.

She tried to look at his screen, but it was all coding and binary. That was his thing, that's what he did, what he was best at. Bullet could never understand it no matter how much she tried. The concentration on his face was immense. Strained.

He was typing in a frenzy, and now, Bullet wasn't the only one who was a little worried.

"Youth, buddy... what're you doing?" Rocket asked him, gently smacking his shoulder.

Suddenly, he smacked a key with extreme force, like it was his grand finale to a masterpiece he had played.

"Done," he announced.

"What's done?" Bullet demanded.

"I just hacked into Police Scotland's database; I have everything on The Lion's Den."

"Youth, The Spectrum specifically said you were never to hack into anything unless... "

"It was absolutely necessary," Youth said, cutting Tide off in her tracks, "I know. But, I have a hunch, and it's gnawing away at me."

He loaded up a zip folder and opened it.

He clicked through some more folders and found surveillance photos of men that nobody recognised. Youth flicked through them. No one said anything more about his severely illegal hacking adventure he just went on.

Youth stopped on a photo.

"Recognise him, Jack?"

Jack looked hard at the photo. His eyes nearly stretched double their size in shock.

"That's the delivery guy that Neon signed something for!" he announced, looking from the screen grab to the hacked surveillance photo.

"And according to these reports, that man's name is Andrew Watt," Youth stated.

"Watt... please tell me that that's a coincidence," Rocket pleaded.

"Nope," Youth said, staring at the monitor, filled with disbelief, "this is Andrew. David Watt's brother."

Bullet's heart sank.

Neon was coming after her.

After everything they did together, he really was seeking out revenge by putting the Black Bullet, along with the rest of Colour Coded, right into the line of fire of what was clearly one of the most dangerous gangs in Scotland.

Neon was boxing them in from all sides.

Chapter Twelve

Bullet stormed into her room and slammed the door shut. Her high heels almost cracked the black tiled floor as she paced her room, panicked, scared, and at a loss on how to tackle this problem that they had come across.

Neon was setting them up.

He was planning on having them killed, making sure he had nothing to do with it. Even if they all died, no one would miss them. They gave up their identities to do this job. To help people.

To keep people safe.

That was how Neon roped them in.

Well, her at least.

The one idea that everyone, to this day, agreed with: it would be too dangerous to have everyone's identity mixed with their Colour Coded lives.

It had to be one or the other.

She paced to the bed and drove her hands frantically under her pillow and pulled out her photo.

Jenna was so happy. She didn't deserve everything that happened to her.

Bullet remembered how proud of her friend she was when she decided to take Watt to trial five years ago.

Five years.

It felt like it was maybe a week ago.

But, if that was the case, she would just be meeting Neon right now.

It really was a while ago.

A knock at the door interjected her thoughts as Jack delicately creaked the door open.

"Hey."

"I just need to be alone."

"No, you don't," he replied, coming in and shutting the door, "I think you've been alone for long enough."

He walked over to the bed and sat down on it, watching her walk the length of the room and then back again.

"I don't want to talk."

"That's fine."

Bullet continued to pace. She was nervous when he was sitting there.

She was nervous whenever he was near her.

She was even scared to think in case he heard her thoughts. Bullet kicked herself mentally for even thinking something so stupid.

She turned back to walk yet another length.

Jack caught her eye.

Bullet quickly looked away and kept pacing, running her fingers through her hair, rubbing her eyes, trying to be calm again. Trying to be who everyone thought she was.

The Black Bullet.

The woman that was made of steel; that was always so grounded.

That didn't let emotions get the better of her.

She wasn't that woman. She was weak. Bullet turned once more to pace the room. Jack was still looking at her.

"What?"

"What?" Jack retorted, holding his innocent hand in the air, "I didn't say anything!"

"You didn't have to, your eyes said it all for you."

She started to pace again.

"Stop," Jack insisted.

"Stop what?"

"Stop pacing, you're driving me crazy!"

"Hey, you're the one who invited yourself in here. I didn't ask you to come."

"Don't do that," Jack nipped at her.

"Do what?"

"Don't push me away. I've already told you I'm not going anywhere."

Bullet flapped her arms against her sides like an agitated penguin. She turned away from him and leaned against the window, still gripping her photograph.

"What's going on with you? You've been acting really weird since Youth put that guy's mug shot up on the plasma."

Bullet didn't say anything. Jack was getting too close.

Too involved.

It scared her.

She didn't want him to judge her. She wanted it to be like it was in the upper foyer. He couldn't know about her.

Could he?

"Bullet... you've seen him before, haven't you?" he pushed, getting up off the bed and coming over to her.

He leaned on the other side of the window, trying to see her face.

"Just tell me the truth, there's nothing to be scared of."

Bullet scoffed at his comment.

He would be scared.

There were no two ways about it.

She had always wanted to confide in someone. Even The Spectrum didn't know about her past. That's how Colour Coded worked.

No pasts.

Just the present. What you see is what you get.

"It doesn't matter," she croaked.

"If it matters to you, then it does matter."

She couldn't take it anymore. It was becoming too much.

A tear escaped again. She stared at the luminous dream catcher hanging in the sky, complimented by stars of all sizes surrounding it.

It loomed over the earth like a person looms over a meal.

"Bullet," Jack stepped in closer to her, "I don't think you realise just how much seeing you like this is killing me. Please, just talk to me."

His being so nice was making it really hard to lie to him.

This would have been so much easier if he was just a dick, pure and simple. Someone she didn't like.

Someone she didn't want to share her life with.

"Jenna Harvey..." she started, her tear ducts turning into Niagara Falls.

Jack noticed the picture in Bullet's tight grasp. He reached out for it, and instantly she let go. Looking at the picture, he immediately recognised both the girls.

The one on the left was Bullet.

The one on the right was a clear resemblance to Jenna Harvey.

"She was your friend," he said sympathetically.

Bullet nodded a verification.

"She was my best friend."

Jack looked at the girl that stood in front of him. He couldn't help but think how magnificent she was. This girl buried everything to help people without attracting attention.

In his eyes, that was the definition of a hero: someone that just wanted to do good.

"Tell me what happened."

Bullet walked to the bed and collapsed on to it, Jack right at her back.

He crouched down in front of her, his hand on her knee. She closed her eyes, recalling everything that happened that night and thereafter.

"We went to a friend's house warming party. Someone we went to school with had just bought this enormous bungalow, and we hadn't seen him in forever. I remember Jenna was so excited; she used to have this massive crush on him. Watt was at that party," she said, looking Jack in the eye for the first time since she walked to the window.

"The night went on, both of us were pretty drunk, and I was in the hall waiting for someone to come out of the bathroom. There was this... hellish, horrible scream... that came from the bedroom. I ran in and..." Bullet's voice faded away as her sobs took over.

Jack got up and sat on the bed next to her, taking her hand.

"You saw them."

"No, I... I saw her. And someone fleeing out of the bedroom window. But, David Watt was the only one that was missing from that party even before we called the police."

"And I bet he claimed he left earlier."

"Yeah, he did," she confirmed.

Bullet squeezed Jack's hand. She couldn't believe she was saying this out loud, let alone to another person.

"After that night, Jenna wasn't the same," she continued, "she was jumpy, jittery, quiet and I mean *quiet*. I was with her for every interview, every appointment, court date, doctor's visits, you name it. She was scared; everyone constantly asking her 'are you sure you were raped?', 'are you sure you want to press charges?', 'are you sure you're ready for this?'. And these weren't just people, this was the police and lawyers asking all these questions."

Jack shook his head in disbelief at her words.

"Anyway," she began again through her sniffles, "it came to the trial, and he claimed the 'sex' was consensual. I was asked for my testimony as a corroborating witness. I didn't even think about it, I instantly said yes. I was up there and... I was ripped to shreds. They said I was a waste of the court's time because I didn't actually see anything, so I couldn't place Watt in the room, and so I couldn't prove that Jenna was raped. He walked."

"Aw, Bullet," Jack breathed, the hate of seeing her hurt was more than visible, "he didn't walk because of you. He walked

110

because there was some kind of doubt with the jury. A technicality. Not you."

"The doubt was my testimony. I didn't see anything, I couldn't prove it was him. I let her down," Bullet sobbed, "and it's like she knew it was all going to crumble, because she killed herself the day before."

"Look," Jack twisted himself on the bed to face her, "what you went through was terrible, and I can't believe you've kept this to yourself for so long. But, Jenna would be proud of you for what you've done since."

Bullet got a fright. She looked at him, wondering how he knew what she had done.

"What do you mean?" she asked forcefully.

"All the good. Helping people, not asking for anything in return, having everyone's back. Jenna would have forgiven you. Now, you need to forgive yourself."

Bullet got up and walked over to the chest of drawers, leaning back against it. She shoved her hair out of her face and pulled a tissue out of the tub that sat on top of the unit to dry her eyes.

"Neon found me right after that," she admitted.

"What?" asked Jack, baffled, "How?"

"I don't know how he found me, but he did. He knew my name, my history and everything that had happened with the case. He said we were destined to meet because he was going to help me."

"How was he going to help you?" Jack probed, filled with worry.

"He was going to help me find meaning in my life and find closure. Find myself."

"Did he?"

Bullet thought about Jack's question. It was one that she had asked herself a lot over the years, and to this day, had never come up with an answer.

"I used to think he did," she admitted.

"And what about now?"

"Why?"

"What?" Jack asked, perplexed.

"Why is it so important if I felt like he helped me or not?" Bullet clarified, "I knew him once. That's it."

Bullet stormed into the bathroom and started taking her makeup off.

"Seriously?" Jack snapped, following her through and standing in the doorway. "Why do you keep pulling away from me when

111

things get uncomfortable? What have I done to make you think you can't trust me?"

"You kidnapped Flare and beat the crap out of her, for one!" Bullet burst out.

The flood gates opened and regret filled her to the brim.

Without a word, Jack about turned and went straight for the bedroom door.

"Jack, wait, I'm sorry! I don't know why I said that!"

"Because you believe it."

"No, I don't!"

"Well, what DO you believe?" he yelled.

"That what you did to Flare is literally the only thing you've done wrong since I've known you, but I completely understand why you did it!" she screamed, begging him with her eyes to forgive her.

Jack shook his head and went to open the door, but Bullet came to the back of him and pushed it closed again.

"Please don't leave," she whispered.

They stayed still for a moment, their breathing accelerating drastically.

Bullet leaned on Jack, running her hand down his back.

"What do you believe?" Jack asked again, not moving away, nor turning his head.

Both of them stood exactly where they were.

"I believe you."

"That's not what I mean and you know it," Jack sniped.

He turned around so that his face was right in hers. He gazed into those deep, dark eyes that looked back at him.

"How did he help you?"

Bullet held Jack's gaze, manically trying to figure out what to say to him. Regret had turned into confusion, which turned into anxiety, and back to confusion.

She was drowning.

Bullet tried to turn away, but Jack grabbed her around her waist forcefully and held her close.

"How did he help you?" he snarled.

Bullet closed her eyes. She saw Jenna standing there, smiling at her.

That smile that Bullet never saw in the last year of Jenna's life.

She nodded her head.

Without opening her eyes, Bullet let it out.

"He helped me to find David Watt... and avenge my best friend."

Jack's eyes slowly closed in mental rejection.

"Neon convinced you to, and helped you to kill David Watt," Jack explicated.

Bullet nodded. Jack let her go.

They stood there staring at one another.

Bullet tried to keep his eye, hold his gaze, but she buckled, the tears still flowing, her anxiety levels through the roof. She was shaking. She folded her arms defensively and looked at the floor.

"He told me after that that it was the beginning of a new era," she continued, "that the Black Bullet was born."

"And Georgina Wells was dead," Jack stated.

Bullet went numb.

She looked at the man facing her. His gaze was different.

It was cold, judgemental, condescending.

"How did you… "

"Neon had a file on you in his office. I managed to take pictures of it on my phone and… I read it," Jack admitted, shuffling on the spot at her reaction.

"Bullet… I've known about your past the whole time."

Chapter Thirteen

Jack and Bullet were still in her room on the top floor of Colour Coded headquarters. Much time had passed since Jack revealed that he knew about Bullet's past.

Bullet was now pacing again; this time angry rather than anxious.

Jack stood still, his eyes following her back and forth like a riveting tennis match.

Occasionally, she would stop and look at him, about to say something, and then change her mind and continue pacing.

It was the most awkward and guilt-stricken that Jack had ever felt.

"Why? Why would you do that?" Bullet burst suddenly, exasperated.

"The file was there, I… I wanted to know who I was working for," Jack defended.

"You were working for Colour Coded. We told you how we run. No history. Just us."

"I know. Look, I'm sorry, okay?"

"How much did you read?" Bullet asked, ignoring his apology.

"What?"

"Is that all you know? What else did you find out?"

"I don't know anything else."

"Don't lie to me, Jack."

"I'm not lying, I swear, that's all I know! I mean, jeez, how much more could there possibly be after all that?"

Bullet stared at him, waiting for the penny to drop.

"There were two other files in there," Jack said.

"Mm-hmm, and who were the four people that worked for Neon?"

"You… Rocket, Sparrow and Flare."

"Okay, so, what do you think was in the other files?" Bullet interrogated him. "Or do you already know?"

"I'm telling you, I don't. I just looked at yours."

"Because we all have a past. We give them up because we're not proud of them; we want a fresh start, we've been involved in criminal activity, or, like me, all of the above," Bullet reiterated. "You're absolutely sure you didn't read anyone else's file?"

"No... but I was going to," he admitted, "I was planning to take pictures of everything, but all I got was yours and then I heard someone coming so I hid, and that's when I bumped into Gecko."

"Gecko said you didn't find anything," Bullet stabbed at him, her eyes piercing through him.

She knew, deep down, that if anyone should be bombarding someone with questions, it should be Jack asking her.

"Why, if you knew the whole time, why on earth would you put me through that and make me tell you? Why would you make me say it out loud?" she pleaded.

"Because you had to say it to someone," Jack explained, coming towards her slowly. "You can't keep things like that to yourself, it messes with you. It eats you from the inside out."

Bullet looked at him, calculatively.

She was trying to read him to see if he was lying or if he was sincere.

In all honesty, she didn't have a clue.

"But, the file... was just a file. It was plain. Black and white. Facts. 'This is what happened'. Dates, times, locations. There was nothing about you in there."

"What're you talking about? The file was *about* me."

"There was no emotion. There was nothing of you. The real you."

Bullet's heart sank.

The man that entered her room earlier; the one that seemed to care about her, and wanted to know everything about her, appeared to have returned.

"The girl that saves lives and asks for nothing. The girl that does so much good but doesn't want anyone to know it was her. The girl that blames herself and is ready to give up everything because she made a mistake," he said, gesturing to his shoulder. "The girl who's beautiful smile has always hidden a grave and horrible secret. That girl. You. There was nothing in there about her, and that's the bit I wanted to know about."

Bullet stared at him completely stunned.

This was NOT the reaction she was expecting. But, she couldn't deny that her heart was pounding with sheer joy that this was how he was taking it.

"You're not going to leave?"

115

Jack smiled at her encouragingly.

"No."

He made his way towards her again.

This time, Bullet didn't back away.

With no warning, she burst into tears, and Jack grabbed her, holding her as tight as he could with his one arm. The pressure she was putting on his shoulder was excruciating, but he didn't care.

He'd go through any amount of pain to be right where he was in that moment.

"Aren't you glad you got to tell me in your own words?" he whispered.

As the tears still streamed down her cheeks, Bullet couldn't help but smile.

Someone knew.

Someone knew, and they weren't mad at her.

They let go.

Jack looked at her with a smile, holding her hand, like he was proud of her.

Bullet felt like a huge weight had been lifted. It was as though she was floating, yet her feet were firmly on the ground.

"How can you be so okay with this?" Bullet said, the voices of disbelief in her head still gnawing at her. "I killed a man, in cold blood, and you're looking at me like all I've said is that I stole a car and took it for a joy ride."

Jack's smile faded.

He looked down at the floor, contemplating on how he was going to answer her.

"Because I've got a past, too," he admitted, "I've done things that I'm not proud of. I've got history, baggage… whatever you want to call it. It's also the thing that Neon holds against me."

"He holds what against you?" Bulled pried.

"Everything," Jack replied, turning away from her and walking aimlessly across her room. "Everything and anything. He used it as leverage against me all the time and he'll probably continue to do it. So, yeah. I get it."

Bullet walked up behind him and placed her hands gently on his back. She slid her hands down and around his waist, feeling him tense at her touch, and rested her head on his shoulder.

"I can't believe this is happening. I can't believe you know and you're still here."

"At first, when I read it, I thought: how could someone do something like that?" he explained, "but, when Youth put up those

116

articles about The Lion's Den and Watt, and then Jenna... I knew. Neon emotionally blackmailed you."

He turned around to face her again, maintaining her hold on him.

"Tell me how."

"Jack..."

"Tell me how it happened," he pleaded, "don't leave anything out."

"Jack, I can't," Bullet said, starting to pull away from him.

Jack wouldn't let her.

"Yes, you can. You just did it. You've told me the first half, and admitted how good it feels that someone knows. Now, all you have to do is keep going," he said encouragingly.

"No, I don't mean it like that," Bullet explained, "I literally can't tell you. Not without compromising other people."

"What other people? There's a good chance I don't know them."

"You do. They're here," she said, "they're members of Colour Coded."

Jack looked at her, confused, trying to figure out what she was trying to tell him.

Like an avalanche, it occurred to him.

"The other files?"

"Two out of the three original members of Prismatic are involved, yes. One in particular," she admitted. "That's why I'm panicking, Jack. It's not just my life that's in danger. It's other people's, and it's all because of something I did."

"Something he encouraged you to do. Something he made you feel like you had to do because there was no other way. He indoctrinated you, Bullet."

"Yeah, and I let him do it!"

"Not willingly. He was saying all the right things at the right time. You were vulnerable, there's nothing wrong with that. What is wrong is someone taking advantage of it. We're going to fix this."

"How? We've used up every route there was to take. We don't have any other options left, other than to wait."

Jack paced the room, deep in thought, figuring out a plan.

"There might be another way," he informed her.

Bullet watched him pace for a bit and then stop to meet her eye. He raised his eyebrows, flashing her a sheepish smile.

It was like a mental conversation was happening, a wavelength all of their own, as Bullet figured out what he was implying.

"No, Jack."

"Why not?" Jack exclaimed. "It's the perfect plan!"

"It's a stupid plan; he'll kill you."

"No, he won't," said Jack proudly, "he needs me, remember? I have to get power into his bunker."

"You've been shot in the arm. You didn't get in touch with him when you were supposed to. What in God's name would you tell him?"

"That you all held me here. Bound and gagged."

Suddenly, Jack took his mobile phone out of his pocket, threw it hard to the tiled floor and stomped on it, twisting his foot like a dance.

"You took my phone off of me so that I couldn't reach out for help. I managed to break free and as I was escaping, someone shot me."

"You were seen by his guards, there's a pretty good chance he's informed Neon that you were helping Gecko to escape."

"You really think those guards are still alive?" Jack asked, almost mockingly.

"You really think it's wise to assume they're not?" Bullet stabbed back.

"Yes."

"Are you insane?"

"Quite possibly."

A staring contest ensued.

Bullet was desperate to have Jack back down from his plan while he was trying to suppress the will to smile at her serious face.

Suddenly, Bullet stormed past him and out the door. Without any hesitation, Jack followed her curiously down the spiral staircase, passing by a couple of floors, and along a corridor.

He recognised it.

They were on their way to The Spectrum's office.

The doors to his room towered high; higher than Jack remembered.

Bullet knocked and awaited an answer.

"Come in," The Spectrum's low tones echoed, and Bullet threw open the doors.

The pair walked in, never stopping as they made their way to The Spectrum, who was posed with deep authority at his desk up the marble steps at the far end of the vast room.

Jack, following Bullet's lead, sat down facing him.

The Spectrum's expression was curious. Calculative. Speculating.

He raised his eyebrows, which asked a question with no need for verbal back up.

"Jack believes he has a plan, and he'd like to run it by you, sir," Bullet explained.

Something inside Jack fell over. It was heavy. He felt very much in the spotlight as both Bullet and The Spectrum looked to him, waiting for him to speak.

"Uhh… well, sir… umm… I believe it would be prudent for me to go back to Neon now," Jack stuttered.

The Spectrum sat back in his stylish, dark brown leather chair, clasping his hands over his chest. Thinking.

"Why?"

"It's the perfect time," Jack claimed, "I have a bullet hole in my shoulder which makes for a good cover story about trying to escape. I can say I never called him because I was being held with force by Colour Coded. He'll take me back, he needs me for his bunker setup."

"Won't the guards have told him about your presence at the entrance to the warehouse grounds when trying to detain Gecko?" The Spectrum enquired.

Jack saw Bullet giving him a very smug 'I told you so' look out of the corner of his eye.

He ignored it.

"Sir… I don't think those guards had much time to explain themselves when Neon got his hands on them."

"And you can back up that statement with evidence, yes?"

Jack shuffled in his chair uncomfortably.

"No, sir, but… "

"Then it's settled," The Spectrum announced, cutting Jack off, "you will remain here until you are fully recovered, and Colour Coded will come up with another plan of action."

He went back to doing his paperwork like nothing ever happened.

Bullet went to get up, gesturing with her head that he should leave too.

Jack wasn't happy with the outcome. And he made a decision.

"I'm going back," he declared.

"I beg your pardon, boy?"

"Jack, what're you doing?" Bullet questioned him, stunned as she returned to her seat beside him.

"My decision has been made, Jack. You briefed me with your potential plan, and I deemed it unsuitable considering the circumstances. The answer is no."

119

Jack stood up with gusto.

"With all due respect, sir... I don't actually work for you," he stated, finding confidence from somewhere he didn't know existed when it came to facing this man. "I'm going back, and you can either help me or cut off your nose to spite your face."

Jack about turned and headed for the door to his office.

"It's your choice," Jack announced, without even turning back or slowing down. He disappeared from view.

Bullet was stunned.

She never knew there was a side to Jack like that. But, then again, he did inform her that he too had a past.

This time, it was Bullet who found herself smiling out of pride. But, also in disbelief at his stubbornness.

Despite everything, Jack was going back to Neon.

Chapter Fourteen

Bullet made it to the hospital wing as Jack was gathering up his things. He was buttoning up his bloodstained jeans when she walked in.

"Looking forward to your trip?"

Jack looked around to face her as she leaned in the doorway, arms folded, her black leather trousers glistening against the light.

"If you've come here to try and make me change my mind, you're wasting your time."

He fiddled with the fly on his jeans, frustrated at failing to fasten it with one hand. Jack started messing around with the strap on his sling, as the rest of Colour Coded entered the wing, The Spectrum at their back.

"Is it true? You're going back to Neon?" Gecko asked.

"Yeah, I am," Jack confirmed, carefully sliding the strap of his sling over his wounded shoulder, grimacing with every millimetre.

The Lavender Lab rushed over, slapped his hand away, and holding the bottom of his elbow, slid the sling off for him.

He smiled at her with gratitude.

"Before you go anywhere, at least let me refresh your bandages."

"Take those ones off, but don't put new ones back on," Jack instructed.

Lab looked at him, perplexed at his demand.

"If my cover story is going to work, I can't be bandaged up. I also need you to make it bleed."

"Jack!" Bullet interjected.

"I'm going back to him assuming the role that I escaped Colour Coded with my life by the skin of my teeth. If it looks healed, he'll know I'm lying."

Lab had a look of sheer horror on her face.

"Mate…" Rocket began, walking in front of everyone towards him, "at least let me give you a lift to the other side of the hill."

There was a moment of still air as Jack nodded, accepting Rocket's offer.

The silence was unbearable.

There was nothing anyone could do to stop Jack from proceeding with his plan, and yet, nobody wanted him to go through with it.

"Jack," Gecko said, him too stepping towards him, "just give us a bit more time. Neon said you should return in a week. We have another five days yet until he's expecting your return. We can come up with something, you don't have to do this."

"Yes, I do," Jack replied.

Lab helped him get out of his grey polo top, his bare torso on show for everyone.

Jack was a very fit young man. However, the bruises on his ribs and back were now a horrific mix of blue, yellow, black and brown. He groaned as he gently lowered his arm.

Looking at Bullet, Jack remembered everything she told him, and he unwillingly recalled the state she got into when she did.

"There's too much at stake to hang around any longer," Jack continued on as Lab began to peel off one of the bandages, "and you all know it, you're just too scared to ask me. But, I'm prepared to go back. So, I am."

"I'm coming with you," Gecko announced, "you'll need back up."

"I'm afraid that is not possible, Gecko. Everyone saw you there. Your return will be extremely noticeable," The Spectrum replied. "As much as we don't want Jack to do what he is about to do, he is right. It is the one method that makes the most sense."

The Spectrum walked right up to Jack as Lab peeled off the second bandage. He towered over him sitting on the bed, his hands clasped behind his back.

"I admire your tenacity, Jack. Whatever you need, the resources of Colour Coded are at your disposal."

The Spectrum thrust out his hand, waiting for Jack to respond.

Stunned, Jack took it, and they gently shook hands.

"Good to know I finally got your respect, sir," Jack smiled, pulling his hand back.

"My respect for you didn't start just now, boy. It didn't start when you rightfully disobeyed my instructions in my office a while ago. It started when you marched into this very hospital wing and apologised to the Fuschia Flare before going back to Neon precisely one week ago. That, Jack, is the sign of a good man with values. As is this."

Jack felt rather embarrassed at The Spectrum's compliment. He looked at Flare who flashed him a slight smile.

Bullet remained very quiet. She was torn.

Torn between what Jack was planning to do and how everybody was treating him. She was incredibly happy that they were being supportive of him, showing him very clear gratitude by their gestures.

However, she did not, under any circumstances, want Jack to return to Neon's company. This man that seemed to adore her, wanted her safe, brought down the wall that she had worked so hard to build around herself with one simple glance. The man that she trusted.

Jack Burns.

The man that she was falling in love with.

Out of selfishness, she wanted him to stay here. To be safe. She wanted him to let his wounds – that she made – heal properly. Not make them worse to keep up a story for a vindictive and extremely dangerous man.

She made her decision.

"Gecko can't go with him, but I can."

"Okay, that has to be the worst idea on the planet, Bullet," Sparrow snapped, "he definitely knows what you look like."

"I didn't say he was going to see me, did I?" she retorted. "I'll stay off premises, keeping a look out through my sniper rifle."

"Bad idea," Sparrow murmured, walking away in a strop.

Bullet looked at The Spectrum who held her gaze reluctantly.

"Can I talk you out of this at all?" he asked, seeming unconvinced at his own question.

"No, you can't," Bullet replied, "Jack's not going in there alone. Gecko can't go and no one else has experience of blending in."

"Well, Sparrow spent a little time teaching me how to work one of his drones, so there can be two keeping an eye on the premises at all times," Youth added. "As well ask Jack's first-person cameras. You didn't take them off, did you, Jack?"

"I wouldn't even know where to start, pal."

"Well, then you're all good on that front."

Jack smiled at Youth for his support.

Lab helped him put on his bloodied white T-shirt that he was wearing on the night of the shooting.

"There's something else," Jack informed them.

Everyone's head jerked like a meerkat, giving him their undivided attention.

"I'm not wearing an earpiece this time."

"Jack, that area is non-negotiable," Bullet interjected, "we need to know where you are and what you're doing at all times."

"And you'll know that with my camera."

"I'll be there, I won't be watching your camera footage."

"Well, then you can keep in touch with Youth to hear where I am and what I'm doing at all times," Jack snapped, "I can't keep up the charade with everyone yapping in my ear 24/7, so the solution to that is not to have the source."

Bullet let out a loud sigh.

She got up and walked out of the infirmary, everyone watching her whizz by as she disappeared out the door. The clicking of her boots echoed down the corridor, fading away while getting faster.

Jack struggled to his feet to go after her, but Lab took hold of his arm. She shook her head at him sympathetically.

"I'll go, wait there until I come back, and I'll sort your wound so that it looks 'fresh'."

Lab, too, disappeared out of the infirmary, leaving a group of concerned faces in her wake.

Bullet went to her usual alone place.

The conservatory above the foyer began to get dull as the sun tried to hide behind the hills and the billowing clouds fell lower in the sky.

She was sitting down on her black armchair, this time not looking out at the view, but staring at her feet, holding her head in her hands.

"Honey?"

Lab's voice startled her. Her quiet footsteps had followed Bullet down the corridor almost like she was trying not to be heard.

"I think you need to just let him go."

Bullet looked at her horrified, unable to believe what just came out of her mouth.

"I know it's hard, but he's doing this for us. For you. You need to let him go. But, let him go and you stay here," she suggested.

"He's not going in alone. Someone has to be nearby in case things go wrong."

"You were there for what he said to The Spectrum, weren't you? He doesn't work for us. He doesn't have to adhere to our rules, Bullet. I know it's hard, but it's what he wants to do. I don't particularly like the idea either."

Bullet started to sob.

She had cried more in the last three days than she had in her entire life. Lab sat down in Gecko's green chair next to Bullet's and held her hand in both of hers.

"Where's your head going these days, sweetheart?" Lab pried gently, trying to make eye contact with her. "You've been very quiet and distant as of late."

Bullet thought carefully about how she should answer that question as she tried to suppress the will to continue crying.

Tell her the truth.

But, not specifically.

"Neon has information about my past. And a couple of other people in Colour Coded. He's using that information to either bring me out of the darkness or throw me under the bus. Either way, he's going to win."

"Your past is your past. When you come here, you drop everything about your history."

"I know, but, the thing is, the rest of Colour Coded are on to it. I have information in relation to Neon's drug scam that I can't tell them without arousing suspicion, and nobody can know about my past."

She rubbed her eyes that were low and baggy with exhaustion. Frustration ran through her like a derailed train crumbling across concrete.

"And you're worried that Jack will find out?"

"Jack already knows," Bullet admitted.

Lab leaned back a little in the chair.

That changed things slightly.

"How much?"

"Most of it. But, he found out because Neon has a file on me and he saw it. Jack's pretty sure has one on Flare, Rocket and Sparrow as well but, he didn't manage to get to them," Bullet explained, wiping her red cheek to rid herself of the stray tears that were managing to escape. "The worst bit is… I don't mind that he knows. I trust him."

"He is an interesting character," Lab chimed in, "but, I think he's got his mind so set on this plan of his, and he's so confident in it, that he'll actually be okay when he goes back."

"But, how can we guarantee that?"

"Oh, darling, how can we guarantee the outcome of anything we do?" Lab looked at a very upset and rundown Black Bullet.

Forgetting that they were work colleagues and nothing more, Lab pulled her over and sat her on her knee. She wrapped her arms around Bullet, who burrowed into her, hugging her back.

"When Flare runs into blazing fires to put them out, how do we know she won't perish? When Rocket gets in a car chase with a criminal, how do we know he won't crash? When you get into a shooting match with a terrorist, how do we know that you won't get shot?" Lab whispered in her ear. "It's faith, honey. Trust. We trust in each other's skills within Colour Coded, and we have faith that they'll come home. It's the only way we can keep going and not lose it."

"But, I'm in love with him, Lab," Bullet stammered through more tears.

"I know you are, honey, I can see it and I can't imagine what kind of scenarios your brain is racing to right now. But, you know he's right. He has to go back."

Bullet openly cried into the second person's arms in two days.

What was happening to her? This isn't who she was. She was strong. Reliable. Dependable. Daring.

Resilient.

She did her job and then forgot all about it, ready for the next one.

The Black Bullet never pondered, never worried, never doubted.

She just did what she had to.

The Lavender Lab rocked her back and forth, like a mother with a child, holding her tight. Bullet looked outside at the sun setting behind the hills of the highlands, realising the time, and loosened her grip on Lab.

"I need to go and help prep him," she said, leaning on Lab's offered hand to get up from her lap, "thank you, Lab."

"I'm always here for you, sweetheart. You know that."

Feeling slightly better from the impact of Lab's loving and supportive smile, Bullet ran back down to the hospital wing.

She entered into an empty room.

He hadn't left without saying goodbye, surely? Where else would he need to go before he left?

The Yellow Youth.

Bullet ran to the spiral staircase and went up a floor, and ran along the corridor to Youth's lair. She went in to Youth playing a video game.

He spun around with fright when she barged in.

"Bullet, what's going on?" he asked, concerned by her frantic persona and her red cheeks.

"Where's Jack?"

"He's on his way down to Rocket's garage… why… "

Without letting him finish, Bullet ran back to the spiral staircase and went back down to the floor below. She ran out to the conservatory and down the glass staircase to the foyer, but instead of running to the exit, she took a 180 and ran back down the hall of the ground floor, the white tiles blinding her as they reflected the setting sun. Bullet took a right and sprang down a small flight of stone steps and into the garage.

The space was definitely an enormous one as it ran the whole length and breadth of the building, the walls painted red which could only mean one thing: the Red Rocket's lair.

The garage was Colour Coded's basement area which must have housed around thirty vehicles, in a variety of colours specific to the individuals of the organisation.

The engine of the Red Rocket's Subaru was already running, and panic-stricken, Bullet ran in between all the cars and past her motorbike hanging in bits from Rocket working on it to reach the car.

Rocket was in the driver's seat, revving the engine to check the car.

"Rocket!" she yelled over the noise of the engine growling.

He saw her pass around the front of the car and turned the engine off.

"Bullet, you okay?"

"Where's Jack?"

"He went inside to find you after he put his stuff in the boot," he told her, "he was worried about you. He said he had something to tell you before he left."

"Where did he say he was going?"

"He didn't, he just said he was going back in to find you and asked me to wait."

Bullet ran back to the stairs at the other side of the garage and went up to the corridor.

She ran along to the foyer again and went to go back up the stairs, until she clocked him outside the front door in his bloody clothes, looking out to the hills. She sighed. Slowing down her breathing, she walked outside to meet him.

The noise of the door opening caused him to turn around and notice her.

Bullet tried to be calm and contained, much to her body's reluctance, and she walked over beside him, staring out at the hills too.

"I heard you were looking for me," she said calmly.

"Yeah, but I noticed the sunset and I got distracted. Kind of reminded me of you."

"Me? How?"

"Bright, warm… trying to hide from the world."

Bullet shuffled on the stoned path awkwardly.

The evenings were getting colder as they entered into October and the wind brought with it an icy chill.

It didn't seem to bother Jack at all.

"So, why were you looking for me?" Bullet asked.

"Why were you looking for me?" he replied. "I spoke to Lab at the infirmary, she said you went to find me, and she hadn't seen you since."

"I wanted to help prep you," she said, "and say I'm sorry."

"For what?" Jack asked, this time genuinely perplexed.

"For being so hard on you. I just care, and I still think this is a really bad idea. I don't want you to get hurt."

"The reason I'm doing this is because I don't want *you* to get hurt."

"Which brings us to a stalemate," she finished.

Silence wrapped around them like the cold breeze the evening brought.

"You have the number to Youth's hotline?"

"Yeah, it's on speed dial."

"Don't leave it there. Memorise it, and then delete it, just in case Neon gets a hold of your phone. If ever you dial it, delete it from your call logs."

"I will."

"If you need to get out, call and tell us you're 'homesick'. We'll come for you."

"I got it."

"And don't jump into mission mode right away, give it a little time so that it doesn't raise suspicion… "

"Bullet, I got it," he cut her off, turning to face her.

Not giving her a choice, he pulled her into a hug.

Not that she needed a choice. She wanted to hug him.

She didn't want to stop hugging him.

"I have to go," he whispered in her ear.

"I know."

Bullet felt herself holding him tighter, Jack returning the gesture.

"Is that why you're not letting me go?"

"You can bet your ass that's why."

Jack chuckled softly, placing his chin on top of Bullet's head that was resting against his chest.

She pulled away and looked up at him. Even with her high-heeled boots on, Jack was still a good foot taller than her.

Rocket's car pulling round to the front of Colour Coded HQ ruined the ever-intense moment that they were having together. As Jack was letting her go to walk to the Subaru, Bullet pulled his arm back towards her, losing herself in his hazel brown eyes again.

"I love you."

Jack smiled a mad smile.

"I love you too."

Reluctantly, she let his hand go and watched as he got into Rocket's car, and they sped down the driveway, the small stones pinging backwards frenziedly in the wake of his wheel spin.

The car reached the main road and took a left out of view.

Jack was on his way back to Neon, with no earpiece, no direct method of contact other than a replacement phone when he was in the clear, and a camera that didn't record sound.

But, nevertheless, he was on his way back.

Hopefully, for the last time.

Chapter Fifteen

The hot water hitting her skin was refreshing and welcomed as Bullet tried to wash away the stress of her day. She could feel the water massage her head as it beat down on her scalp and made its way through her hair. She closed her eyes and tilted her head up towards the shower head, letting the water pour across her face and down the front of her body. She caressed the shampoo into her hair, making sure she didn't miss a strand, and began to rinse it out. She did the same with her conditioner and began washing her skin with the bar of soap on a small shelf in the corner of the shower cubicle.

Bullet stepped on to the tiled floor, feeling fresh but tired at the same time. She was trying her best not to think about Jack, although admittedly she was struggling.

If he had listened, he would have been there with her.

Instead, his stubbornness allowed everyone to cave to his plans, and he went in there, despite the danger that he was putting himself in.

Bullet lay in her bed staring at the ceiling, in her pyjamas, wondering about him.

Rocket wasn't back yet.

She wondered if he was already there. If he was okay. If he had spoken to Neon.

If he was safe.

Her brain was racing. She was restless.

She adjusted her pillow and turned on to her side.

Closed her eyes. Took a breath.

Nope.

She couldn't shut off.

Maybe she was hungry.

Bullet got up and put on her black silk dressing gown, and barefoot, made her way down the spiral staircase. As she passed the first floor, planning to make her way right down to the bottom, she heard murmuring coming from Youth's room. There were a few muffled voices that she could hear.

She made her way along and stood outside the door.

Youth, Sparrow and Tide were taking the first night shift keeping an eye on Jack.

"What the hell is he doing?" Tide asked.

"I don't know… is he lost?" Sparrow replied.

"I highly doubt it, he was working for Neon for two years in that warehouse before the whole thing with Flare happened. When he went back the last time he definitely knew his way around," Youth added.

"Then why the hell is he walking around in circles?" Sparrow enquired.

"Maybe he's not, maybe it just looks the same to us but it's actually different passageways," Youth suggested.

"No, it's the same. Even the cracks in the walls are exactly the same," Tide informed them.

Bullet walked in. She had heard enough.

"What's wrong?"

Everyone stood upon her entry.

"Nothing, what makes you think anything's wrong?" Youth lied, forcing a very fake smile at her.

"Because you talk loud, and Jack's walking around in circles," Bullet retorted. "Next time, if you're going to lie, make it even slightly believable."

Bullet walked to the monitors, watching as she witnessed what they were saying about Jack. His camera was walking around the same areas, down the same corridors, along the same passageways.

"Has he been in touch?"

"No, absolutely nothing," Youth replied.

"Who met him at the entrance?" she enquired, turning to Sparrow.

"Neon did, along with two guards," Sparrow answered, "but, it seemed pretty amicable."

Sparrow loaded the footage he recorded of Jack's arrival to the warehouse on to one of the monitors.

Bullet observed as Neon ran out to Jack who was pretending to be a lot worse for wear than he actually was. She recognised the warmth that Neon displayed when he put his arm around Jack's waist and helped him inside.

"If Jack was pretending to be in really bad health, why is he just cruising around the corridors?" Tide asked, baffled.

"Where did they go when he managed to get inside?" Bullet asked.

"He was taken to his room, he sat down on the bed, his jacket came off for a second, I think so that they could look at his wound, and then the jacket went back on and this started," Youth explained.

"How long has he been wandering for?"

"The best part of an hour," Sparrow replied.

"An hour?" Bullet spun around, stunned. "And none of you thought this needed Colour Coded?"

"We thought it might just be us thinking it was a problem and he was actually travelling around the place," Tide defended.

"Seriously? Look at the floor, look at the walls, the doors, the…" Bullet went quiet.

She noticed something.

Something she was surprised that Youth didn't notice first.

"What's wrong?" Youth pressed.

"I saw something, shush," Bullet instructed.

Her gaze was pulled to the screen like a magnetic force. She was trying not to blink in case she missed it.

What she'd miss, she didn't know yet.

"THERE!" she yelled, thrusting her finger out towards the screen.

"What?" Sparrow asked.

"It's exactly the same as before," Tide added.

"No, I saw it," Youth chimed in.

"It flashed," Bullet announced, "it flashed or… jumped, like it was on a loop or something."

Youth was typing frantically on the keyboard, trying to limit the video feed to the section where they saw it. Footage loaded up on the third monitor, secluding the section of footage.

This time, everyone saw it.

"Youth, what can you do?" Sparrow probed.

"I can trace the feed and check if it's still live or not," he replied as he was, yet again, slamming the keys hard and in a frenzy.

"It's not live."

"Shit. Call everyone. This needs Colour Coded. I'm going to get The Spectrum," Bullet ordered.

Sparrow went on to the earpiece to wake everyone up, but Youth lifted a clear panel on the wall covering a bright yellow button and thumped it, sounding a wailing alarm.

Bullet ran along the corridor, her bare feet sliding on the tiles as she made her way along to The Spectrum's room.

As she was reaching the door, he appeared in his tartan dressing gown and slippers, shoving his glasses on.

"Jack?"

"He's in trouble."

"How?"

"Someone wore his jacket and walked around for a while, ending in a circle. They looped the footage and sent it back to us, playing it on repeat," Bullet explained as they ran back along the corridor to Youth's room.

"How long?"

"It's been just over an hour now, sir."

They entered the Yellow Youth's lair at the same time as the Lavender Lab ran in, where everyone was gathered in their nightwear, and Youth switched off the alarm.

"Do we have any way to get in touch with him?" Flare asked.

"We can call him but it'll put him in even more danger than he's already potentially in," Sparrow replied.

"Rocket, get Bullet's motorbike, your Subaru and Sparrow's Ford out the front and ready to go," The Spectrum demanded.

"Yes, sir," he replied, running from the room.

The Spectrum made his way to the monitors next to Youth.

"Bullet tells me this has been going on for an hour?"

"Yes, sir," Youth replied.

"Why wasn't this noticed sooner?"

"They fooled us, sir. We thought everything just looked ridiculously similar, and Jack was heading somewhere. It was just before the Black Bullet came in that we considered possibilities as to why Jack would be walking around in circles, I'm sorry."

"Don't apologise to me, son. You can apologise to Jack if we get him out in one piece."

"We *will* get him out in one piece," Bullet growled at her boss, who turned to face her in shock at the tone she threw in his direction.

"We need a plan," Tide interjected, "arguing amongst ourselves isn't helping Jack."

"Whatever we're doing, I'm in on it this time," Flare announced.

"Lab?" The Spectrum turned to her.

"I medically cleared her this morning. Other than her arm which needs to remain in the cast for another week, she's good to go," Lab responded.

"So, what do we do?" Flare asked, trying to contain her excitement at being involved again and maintain a serious tone.

"Sparrow, what's the security situation?" The Spectrum enquired.

Sparrow lifted his tablet, and Youth lifted another to activate the drones and assess the boundaries of Neon's warehouse.

133

"There's a lot more guards than there was before," he said, his nose almost touching the screen.

"There's six down each side of the building, four at the entrance, and one in each corner of the grounds. Getting in is going to be no easy feat," Youth added.

"Unless…" Sparrow drifted off.

"Unless what, Sparrow?" Flare pried.

"Unless we don't take the car. Do an air drop-off."

"Would that be possible?" Flare demanded.

"You'd need to fly pretty high so that it doesn't cause suspicion, which rules out an abseil entry," Bullet said.

"And also, sky diving is a real hit or a miss, and the parachutes would be more than noticeable," Gecko added.

"So, then how?" The Spectrum snapped, getting frustrated and impatient.

The room went quiet, as everyone racked their brain to quickly come up with the most effective solution.

Tide moved suddenly.

"Youth, can you load up the new blueprint that Flare and I drew up?" she asked.

Youth dunted on the keys rapidly and loaded the requested picture.

Tide studied it carefully.

"The sewage line."

"Pardon?" Flare jumped in.

"We can get entry through the sewage line. Underground. We'll never be seen, and I doubt Neon would expect it," Tide offered.

"Anyone have any objections?" The Spectrum looked around the room at all the faces looking at him.

"I'm not going through a sewage pipe!" Flare stated adamantly.

"That's fine, you were always going to be waiting in the car," Bullet said.

"What? Why?" she demanded.

"Your arm's in a cast, Flare."

"Yeah, but…"

"GIRLS," Lab cut in. "Take it easy."

Flare slumped into a seat behind her and crossed her arms sourly.

"Everyone, get dressed, collect your gear and get going. Quick, march!" The Spectrum ordered, and instantly everyone got up and swarmed down the hall to the spiral staircase, Flare, Lab and Gecko going down, while Bullet, Sparrow and Tide went up.

Bullet's was the only room right at the top, as the spiral staircase led straight to the door of her room. She burst in and grabbed a pair of trousers out of her chest of drawers and jumped into them. She chucked her nightgown on to her bed and pulled on a T-shirt while her feet fumbled around to get into her boots.

In all black, as usual, she went over to a mirror on the far side of the room and held her palm against it. It bounced outward slightly, and she swung it open, entering a hidden room.

The Black Bullet's arsenal.

She lifted a handgun off a hook already in a holster and strapped it to her thigh. She grabbed a silencer and slid it into her pocket as she walked down and reached for a long black bag. After opening it, she checked that all the parts for her sniper rifle were there and ready to go, and zipped it shut, flinging it on to her back.

She headed out, grabbing four boxes of ammunition, two in each hand and stuffed them into the pockets of her leather jacket.

On the wall by the door, hung a variety of knives, all different shapes and sizes, all in a sheath. She snatched a dagger off its holder and ran out of the armoury, whirling the door shut behind her.

At the front of the building, everyone but Gecko had gathered by the vehicles, including The Spectrum, ready to go. But, there was only two.

The Spectrum had asked for three.

"Why's there only two?" Bullet enquired.

"There's been a change of plan, Bullet," Rocket told her, "we're taking my modified transit van and your bike. We'll explain it more in a minute."

Rocket had Bullet's black Kawasaki motorbike positioned close to his red van, her helmet sitting precariously on the seat with her gloves inside.

"Who're we waiting on?"

"The Green Gecko," Tide replied.

"Now, remember everyone, this is the first mission in a while that has included all of us. Follow protocol. Your name to their name and then your message. Understood?" The Spectrum ordered.

Bullet nodded as she shoved her radio into her ear and pressed on it.

"Bullet to Gecko, you almost ready?" she asked.

"Gecko to Bullet, I'm on my way down the spiral staircase," he responded.

"Okay, I'm going to park on the other side of the hill to the west of the warehouse," Rocket stated.

"But, the hill to the east isn't as high, it'll be faster to get over," Flare informed him.

"I know, so they'll see that coming," Rocket replied, "Tide knows the pipeline locations, so she'll go on the bike with Bullet who will get as close to the warehouse as possible without being seen or heard. They'll start working on gaining access to the sewage line while you guys hike your way over to meet them."

"Flare, Rocket and I will stay in the car and then steadily make our way around the hills to get closer to the warehouse. If we do forty miles per hour, it's three miles from where we're doing the drop off to the warehouse going over the hill; that buys you just over an hour and a half to get in and find your way around," Youth added. "I'll be scanning the network to see if there's any live security cameras on the inside and hack into their feed, while Flare's looking over the blueprints to note the fire exits and work out where extinguishers would be... you never know."

"Lab," The Spectrum walked over to her, "hold the fort. Keep your earpiece in. Be ready for our return."

"I will. Be safe everyone," Lab pleaded, as she backed away to the door of HQ.

"I can't believe he didn't even make it a day," Tide expressed as she climbed on to the back of the bike while Bullet put on her gloves.

"I know. Neon's definitely up to something. He knows more than he's letting on to Jack," Bullet replied.

She swung her leg over the bike, and it sprung to life at the push of the button, as did the van on their left while everyone climbed into the back.

The Spectrum sat in the front with the Red Rocket.

Bullet looked up at him. Rocket gave her a nod, and Bullet returned the gesture.

She kicked up the stand, Tide wrapping her arms around her waist, ready to get going.

Tide was right.

It was ridiculous that he didn't even make it through a day.

What the hell happened?

How did they get on to him so quickly?

It must have been from the night when they launched Gecko's escape plan. They must have remembered him being there.

Well, Jack might not have lasted one day being safe.

But, he also won't last one night being in danger.

The situation was about to be Colour Coded.

136

Chapter Sixteen

Bullet twisted the accelerator on her bike like her life depended on it.

Hers didn't. But, Jack's did.

The winding country roads seemed a lot more tortuous at high speed, but Bullet didn't slow down.

She was in control.

More than she had ever been.

Tide clung on as tight as she could as she looked over Bullet's shoulder, watching the tight turns arrive at top speed, shutting her eyes tightly while Bullet tilted the bike almost horizontally to take the bend.

Coming in from the north meant that Neon's warehouse was downhill.

Bullet yanked in the clutch and stamped on the gear lever until she got to neutral and switched off the engine, gently gliding down the narrow road. She carefully alternated between the front and back break, trying not to slam it too hard and skid, creating noise.

She had the bike crawling along silently, bringing it to a complete stop, and let Tide hop off before she put the stand down.

Elegantly, she swung her leg over the bike and ducked down low, taking off her helmet and placing it down on the ground next to Tide's blue one.

As she moved over closer to her, Tide was looking through a pair of binoculars by the bushes.

"Anything?" Bullet whispered.

"Six guards on each side still, one at every corner, and four at the entrance to the compound. This is going to be insanely tricky," Tide replied.

"What way to the pipe?"

"It runs down towards the warehouse up in the north-west corner."

"Okay, let's go. Try not to rustle the bushes too much," Bullet instructed as they began to carefully crouch-walk through the shrubs and bushes that outlined the warehouse grounds.

"Bullet to Rocket, we're just about to reach the sewage pipe, what's your twenty?"

"Rocket to Bullet, we're just pulling up to the drop off point. Your hour and thirty minutes start in two."

"Bullet to Rocket, copy that."

Ducking as low as they could, they continued along, Bullet keeping one hand around the back of her bag to make sure it didn't catch on anything and bring any unwanted attention to them.

After a few minutes of stealth walking through the straw-like tall grass, they disrupted a bird cowering out of the cold in a bush nearby. It took off with a powerful thrust from its broad wings, breaking twigs and branches on its journey, and a torchlight swung rapidly in their direction.

Without thinking, Bullet and Tide rolled on to their side and played dead. The light from the torch broke through the bushes, grazing the top of Bullet's leather jacket. She held her breath like it would make a difference, holding as still as possible, trying not to think about the fact that she could feel herself sinking into the mud.

They heard the men shouting, and two guards ran towards the property entrance.

"Army crawl," Bullet hissed at Tide lying in front of her.

Frantically, they shuffled along through the muck, twigs and branches sticking into them from all angles, Tide's feet flapping like a fish out of water in Bullet's face.

The water pipe wasn't far away.

Neither were the guards.

The shouting got louder and louder as the cast iron pipe sticking out of the ground got closer.

Tide reached out and slapped her hand on to it, dragging herself over to the other side as Bullet wrapped her fingers around Tide's ankle and went over with her.

Keeping out of view, they stayed completely still.

The voices got louder. Torches were flashing around their general direction. Branches were crumpling under the feet of the guards.

"C'mon man, there's nothing there!"

"I'm telling you I saw something."

"Can you see anything now?"

"Well, no, but…"

"Because it was a bird. Just a teeny tiny wee bird, deciding to do a flittin' at two in the morning, so stop being a nugget wrapper, we need to get back to our posts. You know what Neon'll do if he comes out and we're not there."

"Yeah, I know. Sammy didn't deserve that."

"Aye, neither did John, and neither do we, so c'mon!"

The guard that was closest let out an agitated groan, and about turned, the footsteps finally getting quieter as they ploughed their way back through the bushes and out to the main road.

Bullet and Tide let out a breath.

"That… was far too close for comfort," Tide breathed, lying flat on her back trying to keep herself under control.

"You're preaching to the choir with that one. Okay, so this is it?"

"Yeah."

"How the hell are we supposed to get in there?" Bullet stressed through her clenched teeth.

"Worry not, my friend," Tide whispered with a cocky smile, "the pre-seventies sewage systems had entrance holes, sort of like vault doors. All we have to do is find one and pry it open."

"Great… Where? And how? Unless you've got a tiny little toolkit hiding on that skinny little body of yours, we're done."

"Since when are you the one full of doubt? That's Sparrow's role in the gang. We're gonna bring Jack home, Bullet," she reassured her, keeping her tones low.

Tide looked down towards the warehouse. There was a wheel on top of the large pipe just before it disappeared into the ground.

"Well, that one will be too close to them to open it without them hearing us," she informed, "let's go this way."

Keeping low, yet again, they made their way further afar from the warehouse, the floodlights lighting up the grounds like that of a football pitch, making it glow in the midst of the hills around them. They followed the pipe back for a good while until they came across another panel with an old rusty wheel on the top.

"Okay, this should be far enough," Tide announced, speaking in normal tones.

"I hope so, I don't want to have to crawl another mile to the next one," Bullet joked.

Tide flashed her a smile and pulled a crowbar from up the back of her blue hoodie.

Bullet looked on in disbelief.

"Are you kidding me?" she asked, laughing.

"Well, it's not a tiny little toolkit, but considering these types of contraptions are pre-seventies, I kind of thought I'd most likely need one," she replied with a smile, placing the crowbar into the edge of the panel.

"If your ribs are cracked, I won't be surprised. Was that not killing you when we were crouched down? Or hiding?"

"I'll admit it was a little uncomfortable," Tide said sarcastically, leaning as hard as she could on the tool.

The panel wasn't budging.

"Nothing?"

"Not even a creak," Tide confirmed, panting from the strain, "but, it was never going to be a simple job. Can you hold this here?"

Tide held the crowbar in place for Bullet to take it. As soon as she took hold of it, Tide scrambled on top of the pipe, not having to worry about her balance as the pipe was so big, and leaned her foot on top of the crowbar.

"Right, let go," she instructed, and Bullet took her hand off of the crowbar.

Tide was about to put her full body weight on the crowbar, but Bullet interrupted her.

"Here," she said, dumping her rifle bag down and walking overreaching her hands out, "lean on me."

Tide grabbed Bullet by her wrists and steadily placed both feet on the crowbar.

She started giving light bounces on top of it, the crowbar starting to grow flimsy under her weight.

"I don't think it's going to go," Bullet said, keeping her head down looking at the panel.

"I'll try it from the other side," Tide offered.

They struggled over the other side of the pipe and laid out the same setup, Bullet taking Tide's hands and Tide bouncing on the crowbar. The panel made a small creaking sound.

It was loosening.

"And now from the front," Tide said, quickly getting worn out from the difficulty of the job.

This time both girls were on top of the pipe, but swapping roles. Bullet held on to Tide this time as she forced her weight hard on top of the crowbar with her feet.

It creaked again.

"Right, now we just need to slacken the turning wheel, and we'll be good to go," Tide said cheerfully.

"What tool are you going to whip out for that?"

For show, Tide stretched her hands further out of her sleeves, looking at Bullet.

"The tools which I was born with."

She slammed her hands on to the iron wheel, her feet grinding through the dirt and grass, pushing with all her might.

140

Bullet jumped over to the other side of the pipe and joined in on the effort to unlock the now loosened panel into the old sewage pipe.

"Nah, it's not happening, the ground is too slippery," Tide expressed.

Bullet checked her watch, stunned at the time.

"Holy sh… we've been at this for over an hour," she informed Tide, who remained deep in thought.

Tide went into her little dark blue hip pouch that she was wearing and pulled out a neatly coiled rope.

"Been dying to see what this can do," Tide said excitedly as she tied it to one of the spokes on the wheel.

"It's rope, Tide."

"It's got little bits of plastic in it, makes it really hard to break but means it can be as narrow as it is to fit into tight spots," she explained, looking up at Bullet's still very baffled expression.

"Let me put it this way, if you were stuck down a hole, this could pull you out with your entire arsenal attached to you and not snap."

Bullet was mightily impressed, as she watched Tide line herself up with the angle that she had to pull the wheel to as a means of opening it. She jammed her feet up against the pipe, now unable to slip. Bullet stood beside her, also taking a hold of the rope in between her black leather gloves and placed her muddy boot on the side of the pipe.

"Ready… GO!"

Bullet could feel her hamstrings bulging in the back of her thigh as she pushed herself away from the pipe as hard as she could. Tide's toes were crumpling against the pipe at the ground as she continued to lean backwards, almost lying herself flat on the ground.

They were groaning and moaning, their joints in agony, trying to breathe through the pain.

"Sparrow to Bullet, we've reached the top of the hill, what's your status?"

Bullet ignored him.

The rope was surprisingly holding like Tide said it would. She could feel it breaking through the leather on her gloves, rubbing against her calluses.

If this is how it was for Bullet wearing gloves, she couldn't imagine how Tide was managing to cope.

The wheel moved slightly, letting out a sound of its age as rust scraped against rust.

"Keep going," Bullet groaned, as they continued to strain themselves by the old pipeline.

"Sparrow to Bullet, are you okay? We're around twenty minutes out," he repeated.

But, the wheel was moving.

Suddenly, they let go of the rope, bouncing into bushes as the rope bounced back, landing across the top of the pipe.

They lay in the grassy field panting.

"You okay?" Bullet asked.

"Yeah... that panel is putting up a helluva fight," she panted back, "but, we should be good to go now."

"Your hands, Tide," Bullet said as she leaned over to grab her wrist.

Tide's palm was rubbed raw, the skin broken, blood threatening to start trickling down her hand.

"I'll be fine."

"Sparrow to Bullet, can you hear me? What's going on?" Sparrow nipped in their ears as they scrambled to their feet.

"Bullet to Sparrow... we're fine. Got into a fight with the pipe entrance. We're almost ready."

"Sparrow to Bullet, we're midway through our descent down the hill to the west of the warehouse."

"Bullet to Sparrow, copy that. What's your twenty?"

"Sparrow to Bullet, we're at the south-west corner of the warehouse, are we anywhere near you?"

"Bullet to Sparrow, head north about a mile and a half and you will be."

"Sparrow to Bullet, E.T.A is approximately ten to fifteen minutes, hang tight."

"Tide to Sparrow, the guards are on full alert, Bullet and I were almost compromised. Take it easy. If you need to take the long way to us then do it."

"Sparrow to Tide, I hear you. We'll do what we have to."

Bullet strolled over to Tide who was wrapping a cloth around her stinging hands.

She was worn out. Tired. Aching.

As was Bullet.

"Right, now to open it," Tide said, getting ready to go at it again.

"I'll do it," Bullet said, gently pushing Tide away from the wheel, "I have gloves on."

She braced herself before she began forcing her body weight away from her arms with as much force as she could muster up.

After a few attempts, the wheel came loose, throwing Bullet off her feet as she slid down the side of the pipe.

Her muscles were burning with pain, her hands numb with the pressure she put into turning the wheel, her feet throbbing with the force she was throwing on to them. Tide hobbled over and sat down next to her.

"Let's just pretend that was the easiest job in the world whenever they decide to get here," she joked.

Bullet smiled.

She couldn't even force a laugh out she was that tired.

Her breath was visible in the cold night air as she panted heavily, leaning her head back against the pipe.

Suddenly, she sat bolt upright.

"Is that how it's going to be when we're getting into the warehouse?"

"It should be easier to open from the inside. It won't have been exposed to the natural elements, the notch is on the inside, and there'll be more of us," Tide explained, "it's a plus all around."

Bullet nodded and slouched back against the pipe again, closing her eyes, praying that they would make it in on time to save Jack. There was a noise.

A scuffle.

A branch snapping.

Bullet's head darted ninety degrees like someone snapped her neck. She pulled her handgun from the side of her thigh, holding it out in front of her, cocking it. Sparrow and Gecko appeared from behind a bush with their hands in the air.

"What you going to do with that?" Gecko asked sarcastically.

Bullet sighed with relief, lowering her arms to the ground.

"You scared the shit out of me!" she growled.

"Sorry," Sparrow said, "we didn't know how much noise would carry back to the warehouse so we chose to be as quiet as possible until we found you. Are you ready?"

"Yeah, we got it open," Tide announced, gesturing to the panel.

Sparrow walked over to it and turned the wheel effortlessly, like it had been that way the whole time. Gecko helped him to lift the heavy iron panel up.

The smell that burst out was horrendous. The four of them looked into the darkness. Gecko pulled out his torch and shined it in. It looked worse on the inside than it did on the outside, and the exterior was pretty ugly.

"Are we sure this is the only way?" Gecko asked, a disheartened frown inhabiting his forehead with disbelief.

The stares he received from Bullet, Sparrow and Flare were enough of an answer for him. There was no other way.

Bullet pressed her finger to her ear.

"Bullet to The Spectrum, the four of us have reunited, and the old sewage line door is opened. We're going in."

Chapter Seventeen

One by one, they dropped into the sewage pipe, Bullet leading the way. Her leather boots crashed into the old, thick sludge that used to be trickling water, grimacing at the sound.

She pulled out her handgun, activating the torch on it that joined the other streams of lights coming from Tide, Sparrow and Gecko's torches behind her.

"A gun? Really?" Sparrow scoffed before Tide smacked his arm.

"Do you really want to take any chances when it comes to Neon?" Bullet retorted over her shoulder.

They began down the tunnel. Their footsteps echoed both forward and backwards, down the cast iron tube. They took it slow at first, but that turned into a brisk walk, which soon turned into a steady jog, and then finally into a slow run.

"Here's a panel," Sparrow announced, aiming his torch up to the top of the tunnel.

"That's the first one we've come across, which means it's the one at the edge of the grounds. We probably want the next one," Tide said.

They kept running, trying to maintain their speed.

"Rocket to Bullet, we are in position," he tickled everyone's ear.

"Bullet to Rocket, we're almost at the underside of the warehouse. Keep you posted," she replied.

The further down they ran, the worse the smell got. Almost unbearable. Almost.

In the distance, there was an odd shadow on the roof of the tunnel.

The next panel.

Their access to the warehouse to Jack. To Neon.

"Thank God we made it, I think I'm going to throw up with the smell in here," Gecko panted.

They stood directly under the door to the tunnel, shining all four torches on it, studying it.

"What do you think?" Bullet asked Tide.

"I think we'll never know how stiff it is if we don't try and open it," she replied.

"Me-ow!" Gecko purred.

"Sparrow, give me a boost?" she asked, although it seemed more like an order rather than a request.

Sparrow clasped his hands together and bent over slightly as Tide lodged her foot on to his palms and launched herself up towards the door, Sparrow rising with her.

Tide fiddled and fumbled with the latches on the underside of the panel, but to no avail.

"Nothing?" Bullet enquired, tucking her gun away.

"Nope, hee haw," Tide replied, dropping down from Sparrow's grip.

"Right, well, use this then," Gecko instructed, rummaging in his jacket pocket. He pulled out a small container.

"What's that?" Sparrow probed.

"Lab gave me a few of these, it's hydrochloric acid, she said it would definitely be a good help in getting in here."

Tide and Bullet looked at each other, despising the fact that there was such a thing called hindsight in the world. She took the bottle from Gecko as he ushered her to be careful with it, and this time, Sparrow gave her a boost instead of Tide.

"Go for the hinges, Bullet. When it dissolves, we'll just push the panel," Tide instructed.

"Okay," she said, getting ready to splash the acid.

"And try not to get any on you, or you'll be severely burned," Gecko reminded her.

"Yeah, I got it," she sighed.

"And remember I'm right underneath you," Sparrow groaned under her weight.

"Aye, okay, I get it!" she snapped, her voice carrying up the tunnel.

Everyone went quiet. Anxious. Anticipating the next stage of the mission.

"Sparrow, move backwards a little bit. I'll splash it forward," she instructed.

Sparrow shuffled as far back as he could, his feet slanting up the curve of the tunnel edge. Bullet carefully took the lid off of the bottle, and slowly pulled back her arm.

She splashed the acid.

The hinge to the right and some of the outside rim began to bubble and sizzle like something from a sci-fi movie. Being cautious as to not step underneath the panel, Gecko handed her another bottle.

As steadily as she did before, Bullet removed the lid and reclined her arm behind her, and splashed. It was a little squint. She got more of the panel itself than the hinge, and none of the rims was touched at all.

"I might need to do that one again," Bullet considered, studying the acid searing through the iron pipe.

"It should be good," Tide confirmed. "Gecko can you lift Sparrow?"

"Why?" he squinted at her.

"Because he's the stronger one out of the two of you to lift the panel. I'll give Bullet a buddy up since she's got the gun,"

Gecko rolled his eyes that were filled with reluctance.

"Guess I don't have a choice then, do I?" he sighed. "But, we'll need to wait five minutes for the acid to settle."

"Why five minutes?" Sparrow probed.

"Because that's what Lab said, and this is her thing," Gecko retorted.

"Okay, so let's plan," Bullet suggested. "We lift the panel and do a preliminary 360 check. Have you got your mini-drone with you, Sparrow?"

"Sparrow Junior is tucked away safely in my backpack," he replied proudly.

"Okay, so you release the drone into the warehouse and stay down here to scope the place out. Keep it high to the ceiling, we don't want to fly it around a corner and bump into a guard. Now, if you're Neon, where would you hold a prisoner?" Bullet asked.

"In the bunker," Gecko said, "it's restricted access, it's underground, there's no electricity: it's the perfect place."

"So, Sparrow flies the drone, I'll read the blueprint and give him directions to the bunker, Bullet sits up there in the warehouse keeping a lookout, and Gecko… does what?" Tide asked.

"I'll just stay here with Sparrow, that way there's an extra person to go to the panel we got in through to keep a lookout up there when it's needed," he offered, "unless there's something else?"

"Did you bring that uniform with you?" Bullet requested.

"Yeah… you want me to go back in there?" he gasped.

"No. I want you to leave it here," she replied, "I'll wear it."

As Gecko jumbled around in his bag, Sparrow, Tide and Bullet continued to discuss their next objective.

147

"Sparrow, when you find Jack, wherever he is, keep the drone there so that Bullet has a way back that's clear of guards. Or a way that has the least amount of guards," Tide suggested.

"Yeah, that's a good idea," Bullet confirmed.

Gecko threw the uniform to Bullet who caught it and threw his bag over his shoulder, giving her a nod.

They were ready.

Bullet put her finger to her ear.

"Bullet to The Spectrum, the door is open and we have a plan in place. We're about to make entry."

"The Spectrum to the Black Bullet, run your plan by us all please."

"Bullet to The Spectrum, we're doing a preliminary 360 check when we lift the panel, Sparrow's mini-drone will be released into the warehouse to seek out Jack while Tide gives him directions from the blueprint. Once we have a location and know what we're up against, I'll enter."

"Youth to Sparrow, isn't the mini-drone the device with the short life span?"

Bullet's heart sank.

She turned to look at Sparrow, annoyed and frustrated.

"Sparrow to Youth… I was just about to tell them about that."

He stood in front of them looking nowhere in the vicinity of their eyeline, the whole six feet of him felt very small as he felt their gaze bearing into him.

"How long will it last, Sparrow?" Tide pried.

He shuffled awkwardly, still trying hard to not catch anyone's eye.

"After some previous tests on this particular drone, its battery life is approximately fourteen minutes."

"Fourteen?" Gecko exploded.

"It's a really small machine! There's only so much it can do!" Sparrow defended.

"Well, that's fine, but you could've mentioned that before!" Tide snapped.

"You never asked!"

"Oh, is that the only time we get information now?"

"GUYS!" Bullet butt in, standing between them. "All this is doing is wasting time that Jack really doesn't have a bucket load of. All we can do now is change the plan. Sparrow, locate Jack and get the drone back here once you do. I've dealt with terrorists, I can deal with this."

Bullet turned to face Tide and put her hands on her shoulders, ready for her boost up to the panel.

"Gecko to The Spectrum, we've amended our plan slightly, however it remains pretty much the same."

"Youth to Colour Coded, I've deactivated the pressure point in the earpieces, we can all hear everyone all the time so… watch who you bitch about," Youth smiled.

"The Spectrum to Colour Coded, the distress code word is 'battle stations' if you need back up. Stay safe everyone."

Gecko and Tide had Bullet and Sparrow at the ready for hiking them up to the pipe door. In silence, they nodded their counts to three, and thrust. Bullet and Sparrow slammed their hands flat against the base of the panel and pushed hard, Gecko and Tide tried to remain as stiff and still as possible as they were pushed down on.

After some force, the panel lifted and wobbled on their hands, as Bullet and Sparrow navigated it over to the side.

"Careful," Bullet whispered.

They placed it down, slowly, steadily, straining to keep their balance as well as to keep the noise level down.

They looked around. The room was run down, dank and musty. Abandoned and silent.

Bullet swung her arms over and pulled herself up through the floor.

She stayed in crouch, shining her torch around. It was as though they were outside, but they weren't really. This was a part of the warehouse that was forgotten about right at the back of the building. She looked at Sparrow and nodded, and he took the drone that Tide handed him and sat it on the warehouse floor.

Gecko lowered him back into the sewage line so that he could activate the control pad, while Tide set a timer for fourteen minutes. She held up three fingers and began to count down.

Three. Two. One.

NOW.

The drone sprung to life.

Thankfully, it was a lot quieter than Bullet had anticipated as it slowly lifted from the ground and glided through the air away from her. She could barely hear a thing. Her heart was racing like a driver of an F1 tournament.

They might get away with this.

Bullet looked down through the trap door, watching Sparrow do a virtual tour of the warehouse on his tablet.

"Anything?" she hissed.

"Nothing so far," Gecko replied.

More silence, as Sparrow concentrated on keeping the drone higher up out of sight but not too close to the ceiling that he might hit it and lose control, or more frighteningly, break the drone.

The sweat was dripping from him as he felt the pressure heighten more and more with every second that passed. After some twists and turns down corridors, he made his way into the main hall.

"Tide, I'm in the main hall facing east," Sparrow informed her in hushed tones.

"Okay, that means you're facing the entrance to the warehouse," she explained, "Neon's bunker is to the north, Jack said it's through the door in the north-west corner."

He navigated his way over to view said door.

"It's shut," he growled.

"There's a gap up there you might be able to get through," Gecko pointed to his screen, "must've been where the extension began a couple years back."

Sparrow aimed for the gap that was pointed out to him and carefully guided the drone through. He rotated the cameras, looking around. It was a tiny hallway type of room, with only one door facing west.

"That's the entrance to the stairs down to Neon's bunker," Gecko announced.

"And it too is closed," Sparrow groaned.

"Bullet what do we do?" Tide looked up at her.

In all honesty, she had no idea.

It was too much to risk waiting for someone to walk through the door, especially in the small hours of the morning. Bullet pulled out of sight of them, sitting herself down on her backside, looking around, taking a breath.

Thinking.

There was only one thing they could do.

She went back to the trap door.

"Pull the drone out," she ordered.

"But, we haven't found Jack," Tide expressed anxiously.

"Pull it out of there, and keep a look out for as long as it'll last until you need to bring it back here. I'm going in."

She pulled out her handgun to check it was fully loaded and emptied a box of bullets into her jacket pocket.

"What if Jack isn't down there, Bullet?" Gecko asked.

"Then I'll come back out of the bunker and go with places Tide suggests that he could be. You know where his room is?"

"Yeah, I circled it on the map," Tide confirmed. "Bullet, I really don't like this."

"Neither do I, but we've got to keep going. The drone is running out of time and so is Jack. Sparrow, you remember how to set up the sniper?"

"Yeah, but I'm a little busy at the minute, Bullet," he countered.

"I can see that, darling," she came back sarcastically, "I want you to walk Gecko through it. When it's set up and you've brought the drone back, I want you on the ground two yards back in the direction we came from, aiming up at the entrance; you'll know it's not me because I'll tell you I'm approaching. If anyone comes, shoot them. Gecko, I want you at the panel we came in through, and Tide I want you to never walk in front of Sparrow whatsoever. Understood?"

They all nodded, for the first time in a long time openly showing an expression loaded with fear and severe anxiety.

It was a waiting game for them now.

Bullet held her gun out in front of her and tried to remember where the drone went. The corridor walls were a bland, cream colour and the floor was plain cement. She tried to recall the drone's route to the main hall.

Two immediate lefts, a second right, a second left and then a first right.

Glancing around every corner before she moved, she proceeded through the warehouse. It felt like forever, and then, all of a sudden, it was as though the main hall swallowed her up.

She made it.

Bullet went straight for the door in the north-west corner like Tide had said, constantly checking behind her.

Quietly, she opened the door and went through into the small hallway.

"Bullet, we have you in our sights," Tide informed her.

"Just open the door and I'll fly Junior down first," Sparrow instructed.

"How much time do we have?" Bullet breathed.

"Six minutes and thirty-two seconds," Tide announced.

Split second decision.

"Fine," said Bullet, who carefully and steadily twisted the doorknob to the bunker. It opened.

"Okay, I'm going in," Sparrow confirmed.

"WAIT," Bullet hissed.

The door was ajar. She stood behind it, straining her head to the hinges.

She could hear something.

Talking. Maybe shouting.

151

Maybe Jack?

"Take the drone back, he's down there. I'm going to get him."

Without giving anyone a chance to argue with her, Bullet entered the torch-lit passageway gun first and began to make her way along. The noises got louder.

Her breathing got faster, her heart racing more and more.

It was screaming.

And shouting.

It was Jack and Neon.

Chapter Eighteen

"Did you really think you'd get away with this?" Neon yelled at Jack, dragging the sharp blade up his arm. "Did you really think I wouldn't find out?"

"I don't know what you're talking about!" Jack screamed.

The sweat poured from him relentlessly as he struggled in his restraints, never taking his eyes away from Neon's knife.

The side of his face was throbbing, a neat bruise starting to show through. His bare torso was covered in blood after Neon had messed with his bullet wound that he had attained a few days before.

The room was dark, lit only from a candle that Neon had set down nearby.

Other than them and two men standing completely still a couple of yards behind Neon, it was totally empty.

A sharp, excruciating pain burst across Jack's thigh as Neon scuffed him with the knife. Blood began to trickle from the exit, slowly and tauntingly, like lava in a volcano.

"Please…" Jack begged, "I did everything you said."

"You didn't call at nine p.m.," Neon hissed. "WHY?"

"I couldn't! I was bound and gagged," Jack lied.

"And the camera in your jacket?" Jack's mind raced. He didn't know how to explain that one away.

He didn't know how he knew about it in the first place.

"They must've planted it on me…"

"How could they have if you weren't ever caught by them?" Neon pried arrogantly.

"When I went back, when they had me restrained, they must've attached a camera on to… "

"The camera was *stitched* on, Jack! And it was BEFORE I sent you back to them. Do you really think I'm that stupid?" Neon snapped. "I took you in. You were a lost cause, but I took you in. I gave you a bed, I gave you food. I trained you, taught you everything I know, and this is how you repay me?"

Neon was barely even an inch away from Jack's face holding the tip of the knife just centimetres away from his eye. Jack leaned away as much as he could with his hands bound behind the metal chair on which he sat. His wrists began to nip from the strain of him leaning as the tightly bound cable ties rubbed through layers of skin.

"I don't know how they got there then."

Jack didn't think it was possible, but Neon's face grew even more infuriated by his persistence to lie to him. Without looking away from Jack's eyeline, Neon placed the tip of his knife into Jack's wound on his shoulder, and slowly twisted it, torturing him.

Jack writhed and squirmed, panting through gritted teeth, his eyes shut as tight as they could go, trying to endure the harrowing pain Neon was causing him. The nerve shocks flooded down his arm and across his chest like a tsunami hitting a tiny village.

"I just want to know why," Neon hissed, removing the knife and watching Jack slump with relief that he had done so.

Jack remained quiet, trying to get his bearings back.

"Why, Jack?"

Jack stayed silent. His brain wouldn't allow him to perform such a simple task as speaking, words would not come to him, his jaw would not unclench.

The truth could not be spoken.

"WHY, JACK!" roared Neon.

"Because I had to make them believe I was on their side!" Jack bellowed.

The dizziness was beginning to get intolerable as he continued to hyperventilate, his lungs feeling as though they were the size of an avocado. As though there wasn't enough air in the world to keep him alive.

"Still going with this story, are we?" Neon growled.

"That's the truth," Jack breathed. "I swear."

Jack looked away from him, forcing himself to take deep breaths and try and steady his heart rate.

Try and ignore the pain pulsing through him.

He glanced around the room. The bare floorboards creaked with every move that was made by any party, and the stone walls seemed cold and ancient. Jack had no idea where he was. That fact filled him with nothing but dread and anxiety.

If he had no clue where he was, then there was a good chance that Colour Coded didn't know either.

This was the end for him.

He wasn't going to be rescued.

His mind drifted off with him, as he recalled the feeling that soared through him when he kissed Bullet. When she held him.

When she smiled at him. When she clung on to him like there was nothing else in the world that she wanted to cling on to.

A tear escaped from the corner of his eye and travelled down the side of his swollen cheek. He wanted to see her.

Just one last time.

His gaze rested on one of the men at the back of the room.

The deliveryman.

Jack could recognise those tattoos and beady eyes anywhere after that day. The man just stared at him, still as a statue.

Dead in the face.

Expressionless.

Dead.

The blood around his mouth sat dry, the cord around his neck unwavering, the hook on the wall slanting downward under the man's weight, the tip of his toes dangling just above the floor and no more.

Horror hit Jack like a sucker punch to the gut. He threw himself around frantically, his chair screeching across the floor.

His head shaking uncontrollably from side to side was a scene from a mental institution. Abruptly, he sat forward and let out a scream like he had never screamed before.

With a look of confusion, Neon looked around behind him at the two dead bodies hanging from the wall and then back at Jack.

"I forgot about them," he claimed, turning his back and walking over to them, eyeing them up and down as though admiring the Mona Lisa. "People hang up paintings or their kid's drawings, but… this masterpiece couldn't be hidden away now, could it?"

"How… how did…" Jack started, but as much as he tried he couldn't finish. Neon picked up the candleholder so as to move the light closer to them, and held it up to their faces.

"I snapped their necks. See?" he said, gesturing to their neck area. "See that wee bit sticking out the side there? Do you know how to do that?"

Neon turned to Jack menacingly.

"I'll show you!"

He put the candle back down on the floor and went around behind Jack. He placed the palm of his hand firmly on the side of Jack's head.

"I put this hand here… he'd be lying face down on the floor obviously… but I put this hand here on the side of his face, aligning the underside of my middle knuckle with his temple," he explained, demonstrating to an enchained Jack while he talked, "you hold it firm, and then with your other hand, you just *punch* right into the

155

side of his neck, but when you do, apply force to the side of his head."

For a minute, Jack thought he was actually going to do it to him. He thought Neon was going to end it all there.

For a minute, Jack actually wanted him to.

But, he didn't.

"There's a certain satisfaction from doing it that way," Neon explained further, "it's either that incredulous noise that it makes… SNAP! Or it's just the idea that you've literally detached their head from the rest of their body without breaking the skin. Or it's both."

Neon picked up the candle again, this time walking back over to Jack.

"Let me get a look at you."

He leaned in, assessing Jack's red puffy cheek, his bullet wound, the nicks and cuts across his body inflicted by Neon's knife.

"There isn't as much as I thought there would be," he thought out loud, looking down at his legs. "Just a few grazes here and there."

Without looking up, he smiled.

An awful, demented, sinister smile.

"I know, I thought so, too," he glanced up at Jack's curious expression. "You could use a little more."

Before he had time to consider what Neon was talking about, a searing pain hit Jack's chest and slithered down to his stomach. He couldn't even decipher what it was as he clenched his eyes shut and let out a cry.

The hot wax singed its way through Jack's skin, every pore melting into nothing, the smell of cooling wax and burnt flesh filling the air.

"Oops, sorry!" Neon chuckled sarcastically.

He held the candle up in front of his face, staring at the flame like he was seeing one for the first time.

"I've always found the fire to be extremely interesting, haven't you?" he asked Jack.

Neon bent down to Jack's feet, which were securely attached on to the legs of the chair, and yanked off his shoes. He threw them behind him, one of which smacked against the legs of one of Neon's masterpieces, although he never looked around to notice.

Jack tried to lean in any direction he could as a means of observing Neon, but no matter what he did, he couldn't get a decent view.

"I just love how fire keeps us warm when we're cold… we can't be too warm though, or we'll die. But, we can't be too cold either, or we'll die. Life is so funny, don't you think?"

Jack said nothing. The time had come.

Neon had officially lost his mind.

"I'll show you what I mean," he insisted.

Jack retracted his last thought about Neon. He hadn't lost his mind.

He knew exactly what he was doing when he held the candle against Jack's toes, slowly running along each one, and then moving over to his right foot. He could feel the soft skin turn to liquid in seconds, his socks smouldering and singing, nipping its way up his foot.

Jack was losing the energy to express pain anymore. The thing he felt most was merely just reluctance now.

Reluctance at being with Neon, with having to listen to him, with having to endure his torture methods, with not being with Bullet.

Reluctance at being alive right now.

"Come on, Jack," Neon teased, "you know that as soon as you start talking, as soon as you start telling me the truth, I'll start to go easy on you. I have all the time in the world, and I have very few hobbies; I don't mind filling my time with inflicting pain on you. I'm really rather enjoying myself actually."

Jack breathed deeply.

The room was spinning.

Earth's movement in the solar system had sped up immensely, and Jack couldn't keep up. Neon was breaking away into three different figures and then back into one, and Jack couldn't work out which one was the real thing.

"Why did you really come back? Why did you lie?" Neon probed.

Jack tried to talk, but words still wouldn't form. His throat was extremely dry, unlike the rest of him. He tried to lick his lips, but nothing worked. He was completely parched, and his mouth had a horrible taste.

Watching him, Neon had an epiphany.

"Hang on… I think I had this fine gentleman bring me a bottle of water a while ago," he said, looking at the unidentified man hanging from the wall.

"Yeah, I did, because when he went to get it, that's when I killed my friend over here," he continued, referring to the tattooed deliveryman.

He walked up to the dead man that Jack didn't know and reached around behind him. Pulling his hand out, he presented a bottle of water to Jack, who only by looking at it, realised just how thirsty he was.

Sauntering over to him, Neon unscrewed the bottle cap and leaned Jack's head back. Carefully, he dribbled a little water into his mouth. Loving the sensation of the fluid washing over his very dry mouth, Jack slurped at the water for not even a second.

As quick as it had begun, it stopped, and Neon downed the rest of the bottle. He crunched the empty plastic container in his hand and threw it to the side.

"Fair's fair," he informed Jack, "I've been doing all of the work, all you've done is just sit there."

He walked around to face Jack, and leaning his hands on Jack's thighs and pressing into his newly placed cuts, Jack grimaced with pain.

Neon smiled.

"So… why did you betray me?"

Jack was tired. Exhausted.

The will to keep trying, or even to live, was gone.

"Bec… because I fell in love," he croaked.

"Awwwwww! Isn't that just adorable?" Neon almost seemed convincing, but in a flash, he was back to his menacing self. "Fell in love, what kind of pussy excuse is that? Okay, lover boy, fell in love with who? The Fuschia Flare? She got Stockholm Syndrome now?"

Jack was like a half shut knife. His eye felt heavy and his muscles felt weak.

He didn't know how long he had been here for, but it felt like days. He didn't know how much longer he could cope with this, but he really wanted it to end now, in any way possible.

"The Black Bullet… she's alive," Jack murmured, "and she's going to kill you."

Chapter Nineteen

Bullet quickly marched down the passageway, her gun extended in front of her, ready for any guards that might be keeping a lookout. Even the door at the end of the infinite passageway was fearsome. Like an old Victorian gate, its dark brown door was held in place by black metal hinges that protracted across part of the door front.

Like the house of a Lord.

Bullet stood outside the door, her heart a pounding timpani, her breathing rapid, her pores open to the environment around her and sweat free falling from them. Her leather jacket squeaked as it stuck to her damp skin, loose strands of hair matted to her forehead.

A noise behind her had her duck down and do a 180, pointing her gun to the door. As quick as it started, it stopped.

An odd, echoey clunking sound. Once again, she was surrounded by nothing but the sound of the flames licking the air around them. She listened intently as Jack gave her up.

As he admitted he was in love with her.

As he said she was going to kill Neon.

That was her cue.

She kicked the door in, surprised at how little it moved under her tenacious move, and flung her hands out in front of her, ready to fire her gun.

"STOP!" she yelled, pointing her gun aimlessly around the dark room.

Nothing.

She flicked the switch on her torch and shone it around cautiously.

There was no one there. No Jack. No Neon.

No nothing.

Nothing but a speaker sitting on the floor.

Bullet walked over to it, confused and horror-struck as Neon and Jack's voices continued to project from it.

"She's alive?" he grilled Jack.

"Yeah… and she's pissed at you…" Jack croaked.

"And you knew the whole time?"

Silence.

Jack's screams penetrated the air, almost bursting the speakers, and Bullet ran from the room.

"Youth, we were played! There's a speaker in Neon's bunker, it seems like it might be getting recorded live, can you track the feed?"

"I'm on it. Get out of there!"

Bullet made her way to the end of the passageway and climbed the stairs to the bunker door.

It was locked. Confused and panic-stricken, she fumbled with the handle, but the door didn't budge.

The noise.

Someone locked her in.

"Gecko, Sparrow, Tide, get out! Now!" she cried, continuing to claw frantically at the door.

"What about you?" Sparrow shrieked.

"I'll meet you all at HQ! GO!"

Bullet took a step back and began forcefully thrusting her foot at the door. It began to loosen, but not enough. She could hear people shouting on the other side.

They were heading for the old sewage pipe.

"Sparrow, take position behind the sniper. You're going to have company. Tide and Gecko, run back to the open panel and make your way to the van," she instructed.

"Copy that," Sparrow replied.

"Stay safe, Bullet," Tide pleaded.

"We're on our way to the van, but we're not leaving without you," Gecko informed her in between breaths, as he ran with Tide back up the sewage line.

Bullet fired a couple of shots at the hinges before twisting to fire at the lock, and gave the door one final blow with her entire body weight. In the small hallway, there was an outcry from multiple voices in the main hall.

"She broke the door, she's out. Take aim!" a man cried.

Guns cocked and clicked, and silence settled in the warehouse.

A gunfire had Bullet jump out of her skin.

Her sniper.

"One down," Sparrow reported.

Sparrow... his drone.

Bullet looked up at the gap between the wooden wall and the ceiling. Bits of the wood were crooked, so she positioned her foot on a piece that was sticking out of the otherwise flush wall near the bottom and, fumbling slightly, thrust herself up to the gap, reaching it with her ripped gloves and taking a firm hold.

She positioned her dangling leg on another piece of uneven wood, trying to get a half decent stance, and pulled herself up to the gap. Her head just fit through and no more, as she cocked it to the side and navigated herself through.

A quick head count showed that twelve men and one woman stood outside, guns aimed at the only exit to where Bullet was. She swung her arms through and hung over the gap. Nobody could see her.

"What's she doing?" a man whispered.

"She's surrounded. Outnumbered. She's probably cowering in the corner like a baby."

"Neon said she's lethal, so don't bank on that, Brian," the woman snarled.

With no hesitation, Bullet began to fire.

She made her way along each man, all of them falling like dominos, no one having a chance to fire back as they tried to work out where the shots were coming from.

The woman stood watching in horror and dropped her weapon.

"DON'T SHOOT! DON'T SHOOT!" she cried helplessly. "Wherever you are, I've lowered my weapon. Please don't shoot."

"Kick it away," Bullet instructed.

The woman burled around and looked behind her, trying to find the source of Bullet's voice.

"Kick it away," Bullet forced again.

The woman kicked the gun across the room and Bullet lowered herself down the wall. She flung open the door, gun clearly exposed and marched straight over to the woman who was backing away from her.

Bullet slammed her against the wall, sticking her face into the whimpering woman's.

"You work for Neon?"

"Unfortunately," said the woman.

"What's your name?"

"Anna… Anna Hamilton. Please don't kill me."

"I'm not going to kill you, Anna. Where is Neon?"

"I-I-I don't know. I swear, he went into that bunker yesterday and I haven't seen him since," Anna claimed. "He said you were dead, and he had to deal with a traitor."

"Jack?" Bullet probed.

"Yeah, yeah the Burns guy. Jack Burns. He went down there with him, I swear I never saw them leave."

"Why are you here, Anna?" pried Bullet as Anna began to cry. "Just tell me why."

"My husband went missing… Neon promised to…"

"Help you find him?"

"Yeah… how did you…"

"It doesn't matter," said Bullet, "did you find him?"

"Yeah, he was dead. A stab wound to the neck. But, Neon wouldn't let me leave, he said I owed him and he could really use my skills."

"Skills?"

"I'm a prison officer."

Bullet slowly released her grip on Anna.

"Go. Get out of here. But, whatever you do, don't go back to wherever you're from. That's the first place he'll go looking for you," Bullet said, as she walked towards the door that would lead her to the old sewage line.

Anna went to leave and turned back.

"Hey… umm… only one man went to the sewage line. Everyone else turned back when they heard you shoot the door. It's all clear," she informed Bullet. "But, the other guards will be on their way."

As she stood at the door to leave, Bullet nodded to Anna with gratitude and ran as fast as she could down the corridors, making her way to the condemned section of the warehouse.

"Sparrow, don't shoot, I'm coming in."

She approached the trap door and dropped down into the sewage pipe, the smell there to greet her once again. Sparrow was gone.

Not taking any time to linger, Bullet ran up the pipe.

Noise followed her.

Looking over her shoulder, she saw three figures drop in and chase after her. Guns started to fire. Bullet started to zig-zag. She thrust her arm backwards and fired, hoping that the bullet hit someone.

The footsteps maintained. She heard no one fall.

She fired again, and again. And again.

From the sound of the struggle, only one out of the three was chasing her now.

The light shining in from the night sky was visible at the location where they entered the pipe a while ago. It travelled towards her until she stopped underneath it and leapt up, grabbing the edge.

Bullet started pulling herself up, in a frenzy, gasping and panting, shaking with adrenaline.

Something pulled her back down.

Bullet landed flat on her back, splashing into the sludge, the stench covering her. The man bowled over her feet and fell down face first. He barely even made it to his hands and knees when Bullet fired, catching him lethally in the back of the head.

The man slumped back on to his front. Dead.

"Bullet?" Rocket yelled in her ear. "Bullet, are you there? Can you hear me?"

"Yeah, I'm here," she whispered, relieved that she could hear nothing but silence, "is everyone okay?"

"Sparrow just got here, Tide and Gecko made it back a while ago. I'll meet you at the drop off point, you know where it is?" Rocket asked.

"I know what road it's on, I'll find you, just get out of here."

"The outside looks clear, you should be good to go," Youth claimed, as he held on to Sparrow's tablet.

"Copy that," Bullet replied, as she stood up and took one last leap at the edge of the open panel, and pulled herself out.

Exhausted, she rolled off the side of the pipe and on to the cold, frosty grass field. She scrambled to her feet and ran along the edge of the field, the grass crunching under her boots, branches and twigs whipping her face ferociously.

Her small cuts nipped in the chilly air as she ran over the uneven earth, the roadside coming closer and closer. Out of nowhere, machine guns fired from the warehouse perimeter. She ducked low, still running, still frenzied, still panicked.

Her bike sat as though everything in the world was just dandy. Bullet threw herself on to it, leaving her and Tide's helmets at the side of the road, and after her bike roared to life, she took off down the hill, leaving the essence of rubber from her wheels on the tarmac.

"I'm on the bike, E.T.A ten minutes. Meeting you from the south," she yelled over the noisy wind hitting her face, her long brown hair blowing around dementedly behind her.

"We're watching out for you," she heard Rocket niggle her ear.

She took the bends like moto racer pro, sticking out her knee to brush the concrete if needed. Bullet knew that she should take her time, what with the temperature being so low, the type of road she was on, and the fact that she wasn't wearing a helmet, but there wasn't enough time.

Where the hell was Jack? How did Neon plan that so brilliantly? How did he know anything?

Had they rushed into their plans too soon?

Bullet felt nothing but guilt. She knew she should have done more to stop Jack from leaving.

Now, she had no idea where he was, and Neon had managed to play them all.

He was one up, again.

Colour Coded were back to square one.

Chapter Twenty

Her hair sat as though it was trying to grow up the way rather than down the sides of her head as Bullet got off of the bike, windswept and exhausted.

The back doors to Rocket's red van were open, Tide and Gecko were gulping on bottled water as though it was their first time drinking it, while Sparrow and Youth had their noses pressed up against their tablets and laptops.

Flare jumped out to meet Bullet as she approached them on foot and bounced into her arms like a puppy greets its' owner after a long period of time. Bullet clung to her, appreciating the human contact after what was an incredibly shitty mission.

She failed.

Bullet couldn't believe Neon had managed to play her so easily.

So many questions swarmed in her mind that she couldn't process anything at all.

How did he know? How long had he known for? Where the hell were they? Was he ever planning to keep Jack, or was he merely a pawn in this chess game they seemed to be playing?

Was Jack okay?

"Are you okay?" Flare asked, releasing Bullet from her grasp.

"As good as I can be," Bullet informed her, giving her an attempt at an encouraging smile, and walking to the van with her.

"Youth... anything?"

"He's good. I wasn't aware he had these skills. He's bouncing the signal all over the place, but I'm chasing him," he replied, never looking away from his laptop as he battered his keyboard furiously with concentration.

Rocket got out from the front seat and walked around to greet her.

"Bullet," he called out, throwing a bottle of water to her, "I saved one for you. You alright?"

"I just want to know where they are," she snarled, still angry at herself and everything in the world. "I want to find Jack and bring him home."

"We'll find him, it'll be okay," he reassured her, giving her a bear hug and thumping her back like she was one of the guys. "Come on, sit down, take it easy for a bit while we figure this out."

Bullet perched herself on the step into the van and took a drink of her water. It was only when it splashed around her mouth and down her throat that she realised just how thankful she was that Rocket kept a bottle back for her.

She was incredibly thirsty.

Bullet looked into the night as the countryside presented itself in a calm and reserved form.

There was nothing wrong out there. The trees leaned in the wind, the sound of small branches crashing off of one another and the leaves brushing against each other in the distance was a soothing sound for her. She could hear the crickets whistling to each other, and birds singing in preparation for the morning sun making an appearance.

Everything was as it should be out there.

But, it was a whole different story for them.

Bullet looked into the van; Youth and Sparrow were still busy with their electronics to pay attention to anyone, Rocket sat with Tide who was in between him and Flare, as each of them tried to keep her warm, while Gecko had one of his shoes off to give himself a foot rub after all his running.

She leaned upward a little to peak through the small window into the front, but there was no one there.

"Rocket, where's The Spectrum?" she probed.

"He went for a walk up the hill when you gave us your E.T.A," he explained, "said he had some thinking to do."

"Are the earpieces still active?" Bullet asked.

"Nope!" Youth interjected, his eyes remaining glued to the screen of his laptop.

Bullet took a gulp of water and placed it down on the floor of the van.

She took her gloves off and dropped them down next to her bottle and stuffed her sore hands into her pockets.

"I'm going to go look for him," she said and began strolling up the road in the direction Rocket informed her of.

The Spectrum always liked his walks.

He had done for as long as the Black Bullet had known him. He used to walk regularly through the forest trails in the Cairngorms since the Colour Coded headquarters were up there.

He enjoyed nature; the fresh air, the sounds and, above all, the sights.

166

"Nothing could ever beat it," he always told her in his wonderfully masculine voice that could melt chocolate, "it's a good reminder of how beautiful life actually is, no matter how ugly it may look to us sometimes."

Bullet strolled along at her own pace, recalling The Spectrum's words as she looked out into the darkness that the early hours of an October morning brought.

The birds' lament echoed through the air as she head up the main road that stretched from Tay Forest Park to the Cairngorms.

About a mile up the road, she saw him in the distance, standing looking out across the valley to the hills that stood proudly in the distance, hands clasped behind his back.

She approached him, unsure of what his reaction would be in regards to them failing their mission. Standing beside him to admire the scenery, the pair stood in silence.

It had been an incredulously long day, and The Spectrum had done nothing but listen in as everyone interacted over the radios, and waited in anticipation as he witnessed the sounds of Bullet, Tide, Sparrow and Gecko struggle and pant while they carried out their objectives.

Bullet looked at him.

Every time she observed him looking at the views up in the highlands of Scotland, he always had a look on his face as though he was seeing it for the first time.

She loved that about him.

Actually, she loved everything about this father figure she had.

"Are you okay?" he asked, breaking the silence that Bullet couldn't decide was awkward or pleasant.

"No," she stated.

"Are you hurt?"

"No."

"Then what's wrong?"

"We failed," she replied, surprised at the question.

"You failed, did you?"

"Yeah…" she said, although it sounded more like a question.

"How so?"

"Because we came away empty-handed, and almost died in the process."

"Ah, yes," he said placidly, "the joys of a mission."

"Exactly," Bullet agreed, "so, we failed."

"No."

"No?"

"No," he confirmed, eyeing her carefully over the top of his spectacles as she turned away from the view to face him.

"One cannot fail a mission when the mission is not yet completed."

"But, I don't understand," Bullet countered, "we went in there for Jack, and we didn't get him."

"Exactly."

Bullet tried to reach his wavelength, but the powers that be wouldn't let it happen. She knew he was talking in riddles; it's what he always did. He would drop small hints so that they could come to a realisation on their own.

But, it wasn't happening tonight.

"I still don't get it," she claimed.

"The mission to find Jack is not yet complete," The Spectrum explained, he too turning away from the view to pay attention to her. "Jack has still not been found, therefore, the mission to find him is not complete. Henceforth, you cannot have failed your mission, as you have not met its end thus far."

Whether it was fatigue, worrying about Jack, the proceedings of the night, or all of the above, Bullet was completely unable to wrap her brain around what The Spectrum was trying to tell her.

"But, we searched the warehouse…"

"Yes, you did, and very professionally I might add. However, like every mission, there are objectives, and their quantity varies with every mission, yes?"

"Yeah…" Bullet humoured him.

"Precisely. So, the mission is to find Jack. Searching Neon's warehouse was merely an objective; an objective which now *is* complete," he explained further, watching the penny drop in Bullet's mind. "So, this needn't be considered a failure, but an objective that has been carried out, but alas, to no avail. All this has done is extended our mission further."

He turned back to the view, satisfied with his explanation, and also with his reassuring her.

It definitely worked; Bullet unquestionably felt ten times lighter.

"But, we're still running out of time."

"No, no, no, no…" he whispered confidently.

"Neon was torturing Jack. We don't know how long it'll take before he gets bored," Bullet argued, beginning to panic again as the sounds of Jack's screams started to echo in her mind.

"If he gets bored, he will not kill him. He needs him."

"I think at this point the wiring of his bunker is the last thing he's concerned about, sir."

"I fully agree, which is why I wasn't referring to that," he batted back at her. "I'm talking about you."

Bullet's heart stopped.

Did he know?

She looked at him trying to suss out if he was aware or not. Although there was no point, she could never read him anyway.

"Quit firing questions around in your head, girl. I know how you two feel about one another. I pray that you don't feel any resentment toward any party when I inform you of this, but the Lavender Lab told me after Jack left for the second time," he admitted. "Nevertheless, Neon needs him. The one thing he wants is you. He knows that Colour Coded were using Jack to penetrate his organisation from the inside, so he knows we'll go looking for him. But, he's trying to lure you out."

"Well, it's working," she acknowledged.

"Well, don't let it," The Spectrum ordered her.

"I can't help it. I need to make sure he comes home."

"And you do not trust your colleagues to perform that task?"

"Yes, of course, I do, but …"

"So, then you will let them," he declared. "It's not up for discussion, Bullet. Neon thinks you're missing. We need to keep it that way for you to be safe."

This one, he didn't know.

Nobody heard Jack telling Neon that Bullet was alive. Their earpieces only transmit their voice, not third parties.

After the number of times she had to remind Jack of that, she kicked herself for forgetting so easily.

"Sir…" she began tentatively, "there's something I should maybe run by you…"

Already, The Spectrum looked unamused as he awaited the bad news that was clearly coming.

"Go on."

"Hypothetically… if Jack told Neon that I was alive, and that he was in love with me, and that I was pissed off to the point I was going to kill him… how bad do you think that would be?"

"Hmm… it would certainly stunt our advantage slightly. Why?"

"Well, consider our advantage stunted."

"I see. Well, that's a bit of a game changer, isn't it?" he said, seeming unfazed by the news.

The Yellow Youth nipping in their ear was what interrupted their conversation.

"Guys, I'm sorry to interrupt, but I think I have something."

"Can you take the earpieces off trigger release, please?" The Spectrum requested.

Thrilled that she didn't have to take her hands out of her pockets, Bullet burrowed them in further, praying that her fingers would thaw soon.

"Youth, did you find them?" she asked, dodging past any greetings or small talk.

"Yeah, but it might be wrong. It's saying they're at the warehouse."

"Well, that can't be right, we were just there," Bullet thought out loud.

"Is there anywhere you didn't check?" The Spectrum asked her.

"Sparrow manoeuvred around the whole warehouse with the drone once he located the bunker," Bullet informed him.

"Yeah, I did, and I admit I didn't find anything... but Bullet, I think they're still there as well," Sparrow interjected.

"Why?" The Spectrum cut in.

"Well, I've been eyeing the view from my main bird that's observing the perimeter, and the exterior guards are still in position, in ranks, on duty. Why would you have someone guarding something that you didn't care about?"

"Well, he has been one step ahead of us," Gecko offered. "Maybe he's doing it as a mirage to keep us busy and away from finding out wherever he actually is."

"Or he wants us to think that," Bullet suggested. "I mean, it's perfect. Make us think that's what he's doing to throw us off the one place we know he usually is. It'd be like hiding in plain sight, and it's totally a Neon thing to do."

"I agree," Youth chimed in, "especially when I've just hacked the server, which is also at the warehouse."

"There are no servers anywhere in that warehouse," Sparrow threw out there. "We watched Jack's cam for hours, and I flew around with the drone, there was nothing."

Something occurred to Bullet.

The reason why the wiring wasn't done, the reason they think being that something else was happening that prevented them from being able to do it.

"Guys... what if the bunker we know of isn't the only one he had fitted?"

"What makes you think that, Bullet?" Flare jumped in.

"Everything does," she began, "everything is pointing to them being there, even the whole reverse psychology that Neon is trying to play. But, remember the wiring? It wasn't done, and Neon wouldn't explain why to Jack, he just said he couldn't do it at the time."

"That would be a bloody good reason why," Rocket offered.

"It could also just be that Neon's bunker is a lot bigger than we knew about. There might be a door disguised in the room as something else, that leads to another room," Gecko added.

There was silence at both ends of the radio as everyone pondered over what they were discussing.

"Well, Tom Cruise would be super proud of us, eh?" Sparrow randomly put out there.

"What do you mean?" Tide probed.

"Because this mission literally just turned into Mission: Impossible," he replied.

"We're on our way back to the van everyone," The Spectrum informed them, as he and Bullet began speed walking back down the road, "start brainstorming."

"E.T.A?" Gecko asked.

"Fifteen minutes," Bullet answered, "we'll brainstorm too, and we can collaborate when we get back. I want a mission go in thirty."

"But, all options are basically centred around the prospect of having to go back to Neon's warehouse?" Flare clarified.

"Yeah, they are," Bullet replied.

"Swell. Just swell," she said sarcastically.

"Folks, this is anything but ideal, however, regrettably, it is the cards of which we have been dealt. All we can do now is take them and play them as best we can," The Spectrum nodded to Bullet, who took heed and requested Youth reinstate the trigger release.

"We can't go back in the way we came," Bullet informed him.

"I know," The Spectrum admitted.

"How the hell are we going to get back in?" she probed, praying for him to have a backup plan for a situation like this.

But, never mind the response he gave her being at the bottom of the list of possibilities, it wasn't even on the list at all.

"You will enter with guns ablaze. If it's the Black Bullet he wants, then the Black Bullet he shall get."

171

Chapter Twenty-One

Everyone at the van was buzzing, getting organised, preparing to go back to Prismatic, yet again, and face Neon. Bullet and The Spectrum made it to the van with five minutes to spare from the given estimated time of arrival.

"Plan?" The Spectrum jumped straight to it as they approached everyone.

"Well, I had an idea," Sparrow began. "I brought this with me and didn't even realise."

Sparrow held up a small black device, indecipherable to anyone who wasn't as tech savvy as Sparrow and Youth were.

"What is it?" Bullet asked.

"It's an infrared thermal imager," Youth explained. "When he realised he had it in his bag, he thought we could clip it to the drone that's there now and scan the ground looking for thermal activity."

"I like the sound of that," Bullet confirmed, "where's the drone now?"

"It's tucked down in the bushes on its pad, charging," Sparrow said.

"How long will charging it up take?" The Spectrum enquired.

"The best part of thirty minutes, sir. I'll need to be somewhere pretty close to be able to fly it back to me."

"How close?" Rocket asked.

"Like… the main road, pretty much," Sparrow said sheepishly.

"What the hell, Sparrow?" Flare outburst.

"Look, it was made for hovering in one place, which it *can* do for a long period of time, but as soon as you start flying it around, the battery drains quicker than a shallow bath. I'm sorry."

"Mate, don't apologise, we didn't know we'd need it for this," Youth comforted a very pity filled Sparrow. "So, when the drone is fuelled up and the scanner's attached, how long do we have roughly to find the hidden bunker?"

"Probably about twenty minutes, maybe less," Sparrow explained, hating himself more as he continued to answer questions about the drone that was his pride and joy.

"The best way to find him quickly would be for me to shoot the drone high up over the warehouse giving a bird's eye view, and then lowering it to the section that looks the most convincing for where Jack might be."

"Okay… so, we do that. Say we locate him… then what?" Tide questioned. "We can't exactly just walk in the front door and we can't use the sewage pipe again; they'll be all over it."

"And it's too late to get back to HQ and get the chopper to go in from the sky; that plus, we already ruled that out," Gecko reminded them.

"Maybe not," Youth offered, running his fingers through his blonde wavy hair as he racked his brain. "Neon has servers… which means he has an internet service… which means he has phone ports."

"So?" Flare probed. "That's great, he's joined the twenty-first century. How does that help us?"

"The utility lines," Youth explained, "they need to connect to the building that they're giving signal to. That's how phones work, and you need a phone line to have internet. If we can find the nearest utility pole, you could get in by climbing up it, shuffling along the wire, and gain access to the warehouse through the roof."

"Well, they definitely wouldn't see that coming," Gecko joked, "but, can't you get electrocuted if you do that?"

"You can if a ladder bumps against a power cable while it's on the ground. But, if someone can get up there, travel along one line and avoid all the conductors at each end, then they'll be as safe as a bird – which regularly sits on power lines and doesn't get electrocuted, so… you know."

"Okay, so Bullet goes in through the roof. What are the rest of us doing?" Flare enquired to the group.

"Well, if Sparrow locates the bunker and Bullet gets inside the warehouse, then I have a plan," Gecko announced. "It's bold. But, I really think it'll work."

"Please enlighten us, Gecko," The Spectrum requested.

"Well… once we get confirmation that Bullet's inside. I walk up to the front gate with you, sir," he explained.

"That's not happening," Bullet immediately shot down.

"Now, now…" The Spectrum stopped her, holding his hand up with authority, gesturing for her silence, "I'm keen to hear where he's going with this. Go on, Gecko."

"You walk up with me dressed in the uniform of Prismatic and ask to do a trade. Me for Jack. You let the guards take me and then

Bullet shoots them with the silencer. After that, we get Jack with the element of surprise."

"That won't work," Sparrow interrupted, "he doesn't want you, he wants Bullet, so she would need to be the trade."

"I'm alright with that, so long as I get in there," Bullet volunteered.

"Yeah... but, no," he continued ominously, "I don't think we need to do the trade. It's a good idea, but unnecessary. If you go back as the Green Gecko dressed in Prismatic uniform, then Neon will know for certain Jack was working with all of us and not just Bullet, and it'll put him in even more danger. But... if you turn yourself in, without The Spectrum, they'll take you straight to Neon to determine your punishment."

"And then Bullet can shoot the guards with the silencer, and they'll both have the element of surprise," Tide finished.

"Exactly," Sparrow finished, folding his arms as he awaited a reaction to his idea.

"We could also set fire to the warehouse when you get to Jack. Burn any coke that's still in there. And Neon too, if he doesn't get out on time," Flare advised.

"That actually might be a great way to get them out of the building, if it's been set alight," Rocket chimed in.

"I've heard enough," The Spectrum's voice shut them all up.

He eyeballed everyone, his hands clasped behind his back.

"This is the plan: Upon any confirmed location by Sparrow's drone, Bullet enters the warehouse via the utility pole. Gecko hands himself in as a means of being taken straight to Neon when Bullet confirms she is in the bunker passageway. As soon as the guards walk in with Gecko, Flare will set up the exterior of the warehouse to be set ablaze. It will be in the bunker passageway that the guards will be eliminated since nobody else will be down there. Bullet and Gecko will then make their way to Jack, wherever he is... and Neon *will* be shot on sight."

Bullet looked at The Spectrum, stunned at his orders.

Shot on sight.

He really wasn't messing around this time.

"Shoot to kill, or maim?" Bullet clarified.

The Spectrum merely raised an eyebrow before walking to the front of the van, hands still clasped behind his back.

"Rocket, I'm going to need to borrow some fuel," Flare said to him as he wheeled Bullet's bike into the back of the van.

"Aye... that should be fine... I'll give you some out of the bike," he grunted at her, struggling with the bike as Sparrow took the other side and they eased it up the ramp. Everyone in the van pulled their legs in to make way for the bike as he latched the wheels down in the middle of the van floor.

"Right, let's go. Buckle up, everyone," Rocket said, jumping out of the van and slamming the doors shut behind everyone while they took their seats at the side. The van rumbled to a start, and Rocket pulled away from the edge of the road with a jerk.

"I've never been a fan of his driving," Tide said, rolling her eyes.

"Well, he gets you from A to B before you've even plugged in your seat belt. Can't moan about that," Youth replied.

"Oh, I can absolutely moan about that. He drives like a maniac. I'm happier on the back of Bullet's motorbike than I am in a car with him."

Bullet took a break from staring at her boots to force a smile at her, before resuming again.

She was annoyed.

Jack was exactly where they thought he'd be, just in another section that they didn't know about; at least that's what their educated guess was. She would be fuming if they went back there again, and confirmed that they really were just grasping at straws and talking a load of crap and Jack really wasn't there at all.

She would lose him.

She would lose the first concept of happiness that she had ever had since Jenna was alive.

She would lose the first glimmer of hope that she had received in almost five years.

That wasn't good enough.

Bullet could hear everyone murmuring between themselves about the plan, the next objective in their mission. They were whispering echoes as she lost herself in her own head.

She was exhausted, but alert.

Hungry, but not in the mood to eat.

Her eyes felt heavy, but she didn't feel sleepy.

She was very confused, extremely irritated and beginning to get rather angry at everything.

Shooting Neon shouldn't be a problem.

He blackmailed Jack to kidnap Flare, had her beaten to a pulp – for which Jack had to get drunk to do – and he was trying to set them up in relation to an extremely dangerous gang, all the while knowing Jack was working for them, and then took him and tortured him to draw their attention.

Yeah.

Shooting Neon shouldn't be a problem.

"Hey," Gecko said loudly, waking her out of her daydream, "you're awful quiet."

"Just… going over everything in my head," she replied, leaning back against the side of the van as it tumbled along the country roads.

"We'll be in there together. We'll be in constant communication. It'll all be fine," Gecko reassured her, reaching over and rubbing her knee encouragingly, flashing her a smile.

"I'm just worried that he's not in there," Bullet admitted.

"If Sparrow doesn't see anything on his infrared thingy-ma-jig, then we'll go back to HQ and amend the mission. We're not giving up on him, hon," he assured her. "But, I really do think he's in there."

"You do?" she asked.

"Yeah, I really do. It makes absolutely no sense for him to be in there… which crazily makes it make sense because, well, it's Neon."

Bullet sighed, praying that he was right; that they were all right.

She really wanted Jack to be there. She wanted him home, safe, and with her.

She'd give anything to make that happen.

As though someone hit the mute button, everyone fell completely silent as they felt the jolt of Rocket pulling in and slowing the van to a stop. He chapped on the window that was between the back and the front.

Bullet opened the door and hopped down on to the roadside, everyone else following her as they swung their bags over their shoulder. Youth jumped down and stood next to Bullet, while Rocket walked around to join them.

Nobody was talking, even though they were a decent distance away from the warehouse. They were all ducked low; Tide looking through her binoculars, while Gecko stepped into his uniform, and Sparrow was once again nose to screen to check up on his drone.

"I saw a utility pole over there," Rocket said, pointing over into the field near the Prismatic headquarters, "I don't know if it's the closest one, but it definitely looks like it connects to the warehouse."

"It'll probably be the only one since we're kind of out in the middle of nowhere. Thanks, Rocket," Youth confirmed, thumping his back before he went into the van to get fuel out of Bullet's bike at Flare's behest.

"Come on, we need to inspect that utility pole until Sparrow gives us the signal," Youth said, taking her arm and walking with

176

her into the bushes. "Guys, I've activated the pressure points on the radios. We're going to the utility pole, so if you need us just stick yer finger in yer lug."

They climbed over the wire fence and ran over to the utility pole, keeping low and out of sight of the guards in the grounds of the warehouse.

Bullet crouched down next to Youth who was looking up at the pole. It had metal spokes sticking out the side of the wooden post, giving her a method of climbing.

"Right, see that bit there? It looks like a fuse box," Youth asked, pointing up to the top of the pole.

"Yeah, I see it," Bullet confirmed, craning her neck and squinting under the night sky.

"Good. Whatever you do, DO NOT touch that," Youth warned her. "When you get to the top, you'll need to make a leap to the line. Do not, under any circumstances, swap to another line when you're making your way along, as that's where the currents are. When you stretch from one to the other that makes you the conductor… you get me?"

"Unfortunately, yeah," Bullet said, "I don't think I'll need to switch, but it's good to know."

"Great stuff. Right, let's go back," Youth said, turning around to run back to the fence.

"Guys, do not move. One of the guards is having a nosy. Get down," Tide's concerned voice came on the radio.

Bullet leaned over to Youth and rolled on top of his back as a means of preventing any reflections from his bright yellow waterproof anorak. The light of a torch skimmed over the top of them, as they lay as still as a fallen tree. The light came back along the way. Youth started to squirm and struggle underneath her.

"Stop! What's wrong?" she hissed in his ear.

"Spider! There's a fucking spider on my arm!" he breathed so high-pitched that a dog could hear him.

Nobody could ever forget how Youth had a really severe phobia of spiders.

Bullet recalled a time when they were sitting by the lake watching Tide do lengths and the tiniest little spider crawled over his foot…

He fainted.

Without making too much movement, Bullet tried to lean over and swipe it off.

"Okay, guys. All clear," Tide's voice brushed over their inner ear.

"Right, come on, we can go now," Bullet said, nudging him. "Youth?"

She rolled him over and watched in horror as he cried like a baby, struggling to breathe.

"It's okay, I got it, it's gone," she assured him, stroking his arm in an attempt to console him. Youth couldn't move. Bullet flipped him on to her back and crawled towards the fence. Rocket's face was a picture as he noticed their method of return from the utility pole.

"What the…"

He jogged towards them while Bullet grabbed Youth's arms over her shoulders and stood them both up.

"Spider," Bullet said simply, rolling her eyes.

Rocket's look of understanding was followed by one of immense amusement.

"Come on, buddy. There's no spiders in my van," Rocket comforted him as he scooped him over the fence and carried him over to the back of the van, sitting him down on the edge.

Bullet walked over to Sparrow.

"Where we at?" she asked him.

"The drone's finished charging, I'm just about to fly it over. Although I'm still trying to work out where it is so I can get closer and use less battery power," he replied, squinting at the screen as he tried to load up the live footage.

A picture popped on to his tablet screen; it was dark, creating immense difficulty in making anything out. It began to rise, coming up over a wall, near the entrance to the warehouse grounds. Sparrow held it in a hover.

"Got it," he announced and began to jog up the road.

Bullet went with him, jogging at his back, keeping her eyes peeled for guards as well as the drone.

"Stay low, Sparrow," she instructed, catching a glimpse of a man facing the entrance, holding a machine gun.

Both he and Bullet kept low, almost running while bent over at a right angle, like frightened chickens running from foxes.

Sparrow stopped at the side of the road not too far away from the junction into the warehouse and rotated the camera on the drone. Bullet looked over his shoulder to the screen and saw herself and Sparrow crouched down on the road.

The camera began to move towards them and Sparrow cocked his head up, taking hold of the drone.

In the same fashion, they ran back to the van. Sparrow went straight for his bag and pulled out the odd-looking device that he had shown everyone earlier.

"Okay, Sparrow's attaching the scanner to his drone. Gecko and I need to be in position for the possibility of it showing something. Flare, I want you up there with Sparrow," she said to Flare who was sitting in the van next to Youth with her arm around him. "Be ready with the petrol to go in and soak wherever it is you need to soak to get a slow starting but containable fire."

"Sure thing," Flare nodded at her.

"Rocket, lights off, no engine running until the last person is heading back to the van, agreed?" she asked.

"Yeah," he shrugged, "if I need to start the engine for any other reason, I'll let you know."

"Youth, honey, you okay?" she asked almost maternally.

He merely nodded in confirmation, but he looked like hell.

His eyes were almost glazed over.

All because of a spider.

"Anything you want to add?" she offered him.

"Other than the radios being on constant, we're now all in the know. Time to get started," he croaked, downing the rest of his water and crawling into the van to help Sparrow.

Everyone started to pace, did their little tricks that they would do before a mission to prepare themselves and remain calm.

Bullet cracked all of her fingers, then her neck and gave her legs a shake. She took out her handgun, topped up the bullets, fitted the silencer on and slot it back into her holster.

Sparrow jumped out of the van with his drone, Youth at his back looking a little more pink in the face.

"We're good to go," he said, turning to Flare, "ready?"

Flare picked up a metal can that Rocket used to hold the fuel he extracted from Bullet's motorbike and joined Sparrow as they ran up the road.

Everyone watched from the distance as Sparrow and Flare ducked down low, leaning close to one another as they kept themselves close to the screen of Sparrow's tablet. They could just make out the outline of the drone as it took off towards the warehouse and then flew up high. Bullet and the rest of Colour Coded listened in on Flare and Sparrow whispering their thoughts out loud.

"Okay, so the bunker is at that side there," Flare said, pointing to the screen.

179

"Well, that stretch of orange there will be the passageway, the one that's lit up by fire torches," Sparrow replied.

"Well, if there's fire, why isn't it red instead of orange?" Flare probed.

"It's deep underground, so the scanner can't read the levels as much..." he said, drifting off as he tried to concentrate.

"There's an orangey-yellow blob thing moving around there," Flare said, pointing to the screen again.

Sparrow lowered the drone down towards the warehouse so quick it looked as though it was merely falling. The drone was hovering over the north-west corner of the grounds near Neon's bunker.

As it got closer, the scanner revealed that the orange blob that Flare spotted was moving around a static one, which was a very pale yellow in colour. Sometimes, it was right against it, and other times it was distanced and erratically moving back and forward or circling the lighter coloured one.

"What is that?" Flare asked, squinting at the screen.

"That's a person," Sparrow said, stunned at what he was witnessing, "that's... that's people."

"Jack and Neon?"

"My thoughts are yes, it's Jack and Neon."

"They must have a severely low body temp. How can they be walking around in the bunker if they're yellow?"

Sparrow scrunched up his face like a sponge, scanning through every possible reason why the colours were as they were. He checked the battery in the scanner, as well as the tablet and the drone itself.

All was good.

So, what was happening?

"Unless they're not in the bunker," Sparrow suggested, rotating the camera, lowering the drone, rising it up again, trying to be sure. "Sparrow to everyone, the mission is a go. There's another room *underneath* the bunker," he whispered, watching Flare study the tablet.

"And there's definitely movement in there."

Chapter Twenty-Two

"Go for it, Bullet," Sparrow said, as he centred his drone over the top of the warehouse getting a full and clear view of the entirety of the property.

Bullet checked her gun again before emptying her pockets to get a rough count of her ammunition one last time and clambered over the wire fence once again. She waited for the signal from Tide who was looking through her binoculars again.

"All clear."

Bullet ducked down and ran through the field, retracing the steps that she and Youth took earlier. The metal spokes on the side of the pole were a little higher up than she realised.

Bullet swung her arms back and jumped, grabbing the spokes on either side tightly and securely. With nothing to plant her feet on, she wrapped her legs around the post and, very awkwardly and uncomfortably, shuffled upward, placing her feet firmly on the bottom spokes that she originally clung on to and began to climb.

Bullet considered how it never seems to look high from the ground, but as soon as she reached the top, the queasiness hit rather quickly.

Yet now, she had to jump.

And she had to be careful not to hit any other cables than the one she was aiming for. Or touch the 'fuse box' which, at that moment, was right next to her.

Bullet leaned out from the post, keeping her outstretched arm straight and her legs bent and began to swing from side to side while hanging on with one hand to the uppermost spoke of the pole

One. Two. Three.

She was mid-air for only a split second, but at that height, it felt like an hour. The wire fit snugly in the folds between her fingers and her palm.

"You okay, Bullet?" Youth asked, concerned.

"I'm all good," she answered, looking at the ground far below her as she dangled from the phone line, "sort of."

Bullet looked along the line that she was clinging to.

The warehouse seemed like it was miles away.

"It's going to take me a while doing this monkey bars style, I take it I can put my feet up too?" she asked, trying hard not to look down at the field beneath her.

"Yeah, just don't touch anything else," Youth reiterated.

"Don't touch anything? Gee, you haven't mentioned that up until now."

Like an acrobat, she effortlessly tucked her knees up to her stomach and latched her feet around the phone line. Locking one foot over the other, she pulled her body along like you would pull a rope downward and dragged herself across the field, over the perimeter fence, above the side of the warehouse, until she hit the topmost point of the roof.

Carefully and quietly, she dropped down on to the metal slates and made her way across the roof, looking for a way in.

"Sparrow," she whispered, "how many exterior guards and what's their twenty?"

"Uhhh…" Sparrow deactivated the thermal scanner in front of the camera on his drone and rotated it above the warehouse as he did a quick head count, "there's been some re-shuffling since we arrived. There's four in the front by the entrance which is the east side of the building, two to the north and south… Bullet there's only one on the west side at the back of the warehouse."

"Take him out," The Spectrum chimed in.

Bullet couldn't help but notice how his tone had changed since they all learned that Jack was there even though they didn't find him the first time. Fair enough; it was because Neon let nothing slip.

Not even to Jack, whom he apparently trusted.

Bullet glanced quickly over the roof of the building and spotted the male guard a little to her left. She stretched out her leg to the side and leaned the rest of her body weight on top of it. The man was now directly below her.

Whistling.

She closed her eyes defiantly. This part she hated.

Bullet knew this man was most likely innocent; being bribed or blackmailed by Neon like most of the others who worked for him.

I wonder what he had on Jack, she thought.

Focus.

She positioned herself at the edge of the roof, quietly pulling her knife out of the holder on the inside of her jacket. Twirling the knife in her fingers making sure she had a good grip, she dropped from the roof. Bullet landed on the man's shoulders, forcing him to drop firmly to the ground without any chance to let out a yelp, let alone a cry.

Immediately, she plunged the knife into the side of his neck, seeing the tip appear through the other side, and yanked it back out at another angle. The man let out a light gurgle on his own blood before going completely still. Silent.

Lifeless.

Bullet rubbed the man's shoulder, bowing her head down and closing her eyes.

"I'm sorry," she whispered.

"What for?" Youth nipped in her ear, knocking her sideways with fright.

"Nothing, I was just… I hate killing people that I know nothing about. He didn't do anything to me or anyone I know."

"He stands between you and Jack. He did something. Now, keep going," The Spectrum demanded.

"Yes, sir," Bullet gave the obligatory response before heading to the only door on that side and carefully tugged on the door handle.

It clicked open and she slipped inside, closing it shut quietly behind her. The room she entered was one she had never seen before on any of Jack's footage or Sparrow's drone footage.

It was small; white walls and a plain concrete floor enveloped the room that only had a table and two chairs, one on either side, over to the right-hand side of the room.

Maybe Neon's old office?

Another door, wooden with a frosted glass window, sat on the opposite wall to the left-hand side of the room.

"Okay, I'm in the warehouse. Tide, where am I in comparison to the main hall?" Bullet asked.

"You go through that door and you'll be in the main hall," Tide said.

"Sparrow, any heat movement in there?" she enquired, standing behind the door trying to see any movement through the frosted glass.

"Nope, you're all clear," he confirmed.

Bullet walked through the door into the empty hall.

Three rows of tables were laid out just like the last time she passed through.

As much as there were no bodies, twelve patches of blood were spread out by the door to Neon's bunker from when Bullet shot them before. She also clocked the door off its hinges leaning against the wall with bullet holes in it. No need for a locksmith anyway.

Bullet entered through the door to the top of the stairs that led down to the passageway, the heat from the fire torches lined down either side hitting her in the face.

Taking her gun out and extending it in front of her, she made her way down the stairs and along the concrete corridor. The door at the end wasn't as she had left it. It was hard for her to see in the flickering light, but something was hanging on the front of it. She continued down the hallway, the shape slowly turning into something distinctive. A person.

A dead person.

It was a woman.

As Bullet approached the door, horror filled her from the bottom up like flood gates had been opened, her hands feeling numb and her arms began to shake.

"Oh, my God. No," she breathed, unable to believe what she was seeing.

"Bullet, you okay? What's going on?" Flare probed, worry shining through in the tone of her voice.

"It's Anna," she whispered as she felt herself welling up, "Anna… Anna Hamilton. I grilled her earlier and then spared her. I told her to run…"

"What's wrong with her?" Rocket asked, although believing he already knew the answer.

"She's dead. A nail has been hammered into Neon's door and she's hanging from it by a cord," Bullet described, studying the woman she really genuinely hoped would run away and make a normal life for herself. "Her neck has definitely been snapped."

"So, you're in the passageway?" The Spectrum confirmed, as though he hadn't heard anything she had just said; or worse, he didn't care.

"Yeah…" Bullet replied, wiping the tears from her cheeks, "yeah, I am."

"Good. Gecko, get in position," The Spectrum ordered coldly.

"I'm just about to head in," Gecko replied.

The Green Gecko walked up the road and turned into the warehouse grounds from the entrance.

Immediately, he held his hands in the air, offering surrender.

Every guard at the front aimed their machine gun at him, one shouting out into the night, and the others came around from the sides, also lifting their weapons and taking aim.

"Woah, woah, woah! Don't shoot, please! Don't shoot! I come in peace, I need to speak to Neon," Gecko said, beginning his charade.

"You betrayed him," said the guard closest to him, "we were told nobody comes in and nobody gets out. That order applies to everyone." He leaned his head closer to the gun, taking aim, his finger hovering dangerously over the trigger.

"I know, I know. I made a mistake. I listened to that fucking idiot, Jack Burns. He told me to go with him, said he'd change my life. All he did was steal what little stuff I had and then fucked off and left me in the middle of the night," Gecko lied convincingly.

"Oh, yeah? Where did he go?" asked another guard.

"I have absolutely no clue, hopefully in front of a train," Gecko said, hating himself immediately and trying not to show it. "Can you take me to see Neon?"

The guards looked between each other.

"Pat him down," the guard at the front gestured to another, and he came down to Gecko, swinging his gun behind his back via the strap and patted Gecko down.

"He's clear," he announced as he walked back to his colleagues.

"Come with us," the man closest announced, turning his back to Gecko and walking to the warehouse. Two of the guards took Gecko by each arm and as good as dragged him into the warehouse behind who seemed to be the head of security.

"Do you not all need to go? Only three of you?" Gecko said, subtly dropping a hint to everyone; namely Bullet.

"There needs to be at least four on watch," the guard to his left informed him.

They walked through the loading bay and into the main hall.

"Wow, this room is way bigger than I remember!" Gecko exclaimed, his squeaky voice bouncing off all the walls. The guards ignored him as they headed for the door down to Neon's bunker, passing the patches of blood along the way.

"Holy crap, what happened in here?" asked Gecko, knowing full well what happened there.

"We executed workers for conspiring to run. We hung their leader on the front of Neon's door. Wait 'til you see," the head guard lied, opening the door.

"Jeez, it's warm in here. Could've used a heating system like this in the living quarters," he said, trying to seem cool and inconspicuous.

As they walked down the corridor, Gecko could make out the shape of the body that Bullet saw earlier, and sure enough, their feet didn't seem to be touching the floor. This was one hell of a long passage.

Where the hell was Bullet?

185

She was supposed to be here.

An extremely calm Green Gecko began to panic immensely, seeing that his saviour wasn't here.

"There she is. Little Anna. It's a shame really, she was a good-looking girl. But, we decided to make a spectacle of her… "

A weird pinging sound was heard and the guard in front dropped to the floor.

It happened again, grounding the man on Gecko's right. The remaining guard, confused beyond belief, did a 180 thinking someone was behind them until he was floored at the pinging sound too. Gecko found himself spinning round to the entrance, just as the guard had done.

"Gecko, help me down from this, will you?" Bullet said dryly.

He about turned again, suddenly noticing it was Bullet hanging from the door.

"What the hell?" he said, running to her and hiking her up and lowering her down, "I thought you said that girl was hung from the door; even the guards said… "

"As soon as I heard you asking the guards not to shoot, I lifted her down and unbound the cord from around her neck and I carried her into Neon's room," Bullet explained, cutting him off. "Come on, you ready?"

"Ready as I'll ever be," he replied, straightening his glasses on his face.

"Here, take this," Bullet instructed, handing him her bloody knife.

Reluctantly, Gecko took the knife.

"I really don't want to know who your knife is wearing," Gecko said.

"It's a good thing I wasn't going to tell you then, isn't it?" Bullet said as she took a hold of the door handle and twisted it.

"Wait," Gecko said and lifted a torch from one of the metal holders on the wall, "we'll need this, remember?"

Bullet pushed the door open and flung her gun up in front of her, aiming it about the room, checking behind the door as Gecko never left her side. He immediately clocked the woman lying on the floor just in from the doorway, quite clearly placed gently down. If it weren't for the fact that she quite clearly had a broken neck, Gecko would have considered that she was merely sleeping.

"Clear," she announced, "Sparrow, we're in the bunker. You're sure there's another room underneath?"

"Positive, Bullet. There's definitely a room underneath you and there's definitely someone in it," he replied.

Bullet walked by the speaker, which was now silent, and across the room looking for an anomaly to suggest a trap door or pressure panel. Gecko went over to the desk and had a rummage around.

"I don't see anything that could lead us downward," Bullet informed everyone.

"Well, don't look for anything fancy, Bullet. There's no electricity down there, remember?" Youth reminded them.

"So, it's most likely something that's concealed or... dressed up to look like something else," Gecko walked around the edges of the room running his hand across the walls but flapped his hand by his side from no result.

"Nothing."

"There has to be something," Sparrow snapped, "keep looking."

"It's a room. A square room. There's only so many places you can look," Bullet retorted.

"Well, there's obviously something you're missing. Think like Neon, Bullet. What would he do?" Youth said calmly, trying to diffuse the tension.

"If he was down here all the time and had a secret room that no one was allowed access to, he'd put the entry somewhere nobody could go," she thought out loud.

Bullet looked at the desk sitting in the middle of the room. The stone slabs that sat underneath it were very misplaced in here. It didn't go with the rest of them.

They were bigger.

So, maybe it wasn't meant for decoration.

Chapter Twenty-Three

Gecko and Bullet lifted the table to the side, and hastily kicked the chair away to expose the larger slabs. The empty space revealed that one of the large slabs, unlike all the other ones that formed this section of the floor, had an iron hoop to one side.

A trap door.

"We've found it," Bullet informed.

"Great!" Youth shrieked with glee. "Well done! What's the plan now, sir?"

"Bullet, get down there. Gecko, pull out," The Spectrum ordered.

"Pull out?" he asked, confused. "What was the point of me coming in here?"

"To take out more guards. Come back out so we can take out the rest."

"Do we really need to take them all out? Some of them are most likely innocent," Gecko pleaded, looking to Bullet for her to step in.

She didn't know what to say.

Bullet had never heard The Spectrum talk like this.

It was as though something had really ticked him off or even tipped him over the edge. She tried to think back to everything that had happened to figure out what it could have been.

Nothing stuck out.

Bullet began to get annoyed, angry even. She couldn't understand why he was being like this, and now she was wasting time thinking about it when Jack needed her.

"Look, sir, I don't know what's wrong with you but, Gecko's staying here. We're not killing anyone else other than Neon, that's not what we're about. We can hand them over to the police when we're done and frame them for the fire or whatever. Now, we're going down. Flare, get ready to strike."

Giving her boss orders wasn't exactly how Bullet saw this mission going, but Jack was her main priority, and The Spectrum was being extremely counterintuitive when it came to the details of this mission.

With no further thought, Bullet lifted the trap door.

It revealed stone stairs that led into nothing but darkness.

Trying not to let it bother her she began to descend the stairs, clicking the button on her torch and lighting up the tight, narrow stairway. It went on straight for a while and then curled to the left, making it difficult to navigate around. After they turned the bend, a door stood in front of them. The screams on the other side were imminent, loud and particularly identifiable.

Jack was still alive.

Before Bullet could kick the door in, Gecko shuffled down in front of her awkwardly, trying to stay as quiet as possible.

"Go back up the stairs a little, I have an idea," he whispered to her perplexed expression, "just follow my lead."

"Gecko, what're you..."

"Just go!" he hissed at her.

Stunned at his attitude, and a little black affronted for giving in to him so quickly, Bullet backed up as she was instructed and crouched on a step just before the bend, clicking her torch off. Gecko tried the door quietly, Jack's scream making him jump with fright.

The door was open.

Taking a breath, Gecko stormed in.

He sprawled out flat on the floor, moaning and groaning, stumbling to his feet.

"What is the meaning of this?" Neon bellowed, stomping towards him crazily, eyes wide, his back hunched and blood part of the way up both his sleeves. "How did you get in here!"

"Your shitty guards opened the floor and threw me down. Go shout at them!" Gecko growled.

"Who the hell do you think you are?"

"The one who escaped," Gecko admitted, "but, I came back because I got the information I thought you'd want to hear."

"I don't care! I've got more pressing matters to deal with, and my friend here has been doing a wonderful job of helping me with that," Neon said, stroking the side of Jack's face, and then punching it.

"More pressing matters?"

"YES!" Neon roared.

"Like the Black Bullet?" Gecko said, knowing he'd grab his attention.

Neon stopped dead and turned around slowly to face him again.

The smile on his face was that of the devil.

"You have information?"

The look he gave was as though Gecko was offering him a cigarette and Neon hadn't had one in decades but really wanted one.

"I do," Gecko admitted, a smile shown through slightly due to his smugness that his plan was working.

"Tell me," he uttered through his teeth, the psychotic smile never fading.

"And then what?"

"What?"

"If I tell you, what will you do for me?"

"I'll let you live," Neon threatened, raising the knife he had by his side up in front of him.

Gecko looked at it, terrified.

"Deal!" he announced, watching Neon lower the knife, watching that God awful smile creep even wider to the sides of his face.

"She's outside."

"Outside?"

"Yep."

"She's here?"

"Yep. She's hiding, of course. Lurking somewhere in the shadows but yes, she's outside."

"And you know this, how?"

"Because I brought her here. She was asking questions about Jack and I told her I knew him; but as soon as I walked on to the grounds, the guards recognised me and practically dragged down to the bunker and then sent me head first through a trap door and… here we are."

"She's… she's going to kill you…" Jack breathed from behind him.

Gecko couldn't see much of him, but he knew he looked terrible.

"SHUT UP!" Neon boomed at him.

"…she's lurk… lurking in the shadows… waiting for you to… go outside… and then she'll shoot…"

"WHAT DID I JUST SAY!"

Neon smacked him over the head with his knife, splitting Jack's head open.

Jack didn't scream; he didn't even whimper or groan. His head merely dropped forward and hung there.

Gunfire exploded through the bunker loudly, ricocheting off of every surface. Neon dropped to the floor, flopping on his back and lying completely still, eyes closed.

Bullet ran through the door and straight past Gecko. There was so much he could have said, but knowing the situation, he too went straight to Jack.

"JACK!" Bullet shouted, taking his head in her hands and lifting it up to see his face. "Jack, wake up!"

Gecko leaned down behind him and checked for a pulse in his wrist.

"He's still with us, but barely," he said frantically.

"Untie him," Bullet commanded. "Flare, do it! Do it, now!"

"I'm on it!" she bellowed back.

"Jack," Bullet whispered, patting the sides of his face, but Jack was not waking up or even stirring, "Jack, come on, honey. Wake up. We're here. We're going to take you home, but you need to open your eyes."

"Got it. Who's carrying him? Me or you?" Gecko asked.

"Do you want to take my gun and potentially have to shoot people?"

Gecko bashed her out of the way and leaned Jack over his shoulder, that was his answer to her question. He stood upright and manoeuvred around the chair to head for the door, Bullet right at his back.

A sharp pain in the back of her thigh took her straight to the ground at the bottom of the stairs. Twisting awkwardly to find the cause, she was faced with Neon crawling menacingly towards her, clearly filled with anger; although a sense of glee was present as well.

Grimacing and groaning, Bullet pulled his knife out of her leg.

"Bullet!" Gecko's voice shouted from behind her.

"Get Jack out of here, Gecko! RUN!"

Gecko knew better than to argue with her and disappeared up the winding staircase with a limp Jack over his shoulder, his green T-shirt now stained a deadly shade of red.

"You don't get to do this to me. YOU left ME!"

"For a reason!" Bullet screamed. "One you know all too well!"

Neon started to cackle disturbingly, making his way slowly across the floor towards her.

"Does David Watt still haunt your dreams, Georgina?"

"That's not my name anymore."

"That'll always be who you are, Georgina Wells."

"Stop."

"Does Jenna still smile at you in the park when you shut your eyes?"

"Shut the fuck up!"

"Do you remember me teaching you how to break someone's neck?" he taunted, gesturing to the two men hanging from the wall behind him that Bullet tried to ignore.

"Do you remember doing it to David Watt?"

"YES!" she cried. "I remember. I remember everything, now please just shut up!"

"Bullet, shoot him! NOW!" The Spectrum cried into her ear. "Stop wasting time. Talking to him is no use, you know that!"

"Flare's doused the warehouse exterior with petrol and managed to dodge the guards, Bullet. If Gecko comes outta there with Jack she's going to light it," Youth warned her anxiously. "Just do what you have to do, and get out of there!"

"We need to stick to the plan, Bullet," Sparrow added.

"Come on, honey. Trap him down there and let him bake to death, just get out!" Tide encouraged her.

Bullet maintained eye contact with Neon as she listened to her colleagues. Her friends.

Her family... She knew they were all right. She knew she had to get out. Neon's beady eyes looked right through her as he continued to prowl towards her frighteningly, like a panther cornering its prey.

"What're they saying to you?" he said.

Not that Bullet was paying particular attention to this, but she couldn't remember the last time Neon blinked since they began their staring competition.

"Are they telling you to run and trap me down here? Are they telling you to maim me and take me back with you as a prisoner? Are they convincing you to kill me?" he taunted. "If you do any of those things... you'll be in a lot more danger then than you will be if I'm alive."

"What makes you say that?"

She had latched on to the hook that Neon had dangled in front of her. His eyes beamed with pride as he knew he had her.

Instantly, she kicked herself for taking the bait, but even she knew now that she was hooked. She wanted to know.

"Because I've been working hard these last few months. If I die, people have been instructed to act against you in the event of my death. People you don't want to mess with, and people you'd never see coming. Also, a lot of people, to the point that even your little team with all of your skills combined would be outnumbered," he explained, beginning to crawl towards her again.

Bullet found herself shuffling back towards the stairs this time, the knife he had plunged into the back of her leg still in her hand.

"However, if you keep me alive, not only do these people then have no instruction to attack you, but I then still hold all the cards. I can keep you all safe. I can keep your identity hidden. You just have to trust me."

"TRUST YOU?" Bullet yelled. "You blackmailed me! I killed a man, in cold blood, because you somehow convinced me, brainwashed me into thinking that it was okay because I was 'special'. Because it was special circumstances! But then I had to give up everything I've ever known and go into hiding. Become that missing person that would never be found."

"It didn't take much to convince you, darling. You were hurting. And you… HATED… that man. Despised him. And rightfully so, I mean, he did defile your friend without her permission," Neon said, almost sympathetically.

"I just wanted you to feel whole again. I wanted you to feel accomplished."

"And now all I feel is hatred. Towards myself. But, towards you even more," Bullet threw the knife with much force at Neon, who flung himself backwards and dodged it. Dragging her injured leg behind her, she pulled herself up the dark, tight staircase as fast as she could, making it to the underside of Neon's office.

Fumbling frantically, she lifted the slab up ready to shut him in the lower bunker. His pale, angry face appeared out of the darkness, lunging for her furiously.

In a frenzy, Bullet slammed the slab into its slot in the floor, jamming Neon's entire arm.

She listened to him scream.

It wasn't so much an outcry in pain but more like a roar of fury.

Exhausted, she rolled over, placing her entire body weight on to the slab and watched Neon's arm squirm and shake uncontrollably in pain. She could almost hear the bones crushing under her and the slab's weight over the noise of his bellowing cries.

Adrenaline flushed through her like an avalanche down a mountain as she tried to steady her hands to latch on to the hoop on the slab and lifted it slightly. Like rubbish into a bin, Neon's arm dropped into the stairwell, and Bullet repositioned herself back on top of the slab. Neon banged on the door causing Bullet to bounce with the impact of his angry attempts to free himself.

It was only then she noticed the smoke cuddling the ceiling above her.

Placidly, it glided over, swirling around in the air, and it wasn't long before it haunted the entire room since Flare lit the blaze.

With her good leg, Bullet tried to pull the solid oak table towards her, looping her foot around its leg. It moved slightly, but it was tough to drag over the concrete stonework beneath her. She was never going to move it in time before her body gave out from the effects of the fire. The smoke invaded her lungs maliciously, her coughing was out of control, and the drowsiness was very real.

Jack's smiling face looked at her. He held out his hand encouragingly, gesturing for her to take it. She remembered the feeling of his touch, his kiss, the silkiness of his short brown hair.

How her entire body sprung to life when he merely looked at her.

If this was the last thing she'd ever remember, then Bullet was ready to go. Jenna would be waiting for her, anyway.

She'd be in good hands.

Bullet always wondered how it would end; she always had it in her head that she would get shot. That was the situation she was in more often than not, so, to her, it made the most sense. Perishing in a fire had never crossed her mind.

But, there she was.

In the depths of the burning inferno of the warehouse, Bullet could feel herself drifting away.

"Bullet to Colour Coded… Go. Neon's trapped, but… so am I…"

On the floor of the bunker, nothing but blackness enveloped her.

It was neither hot nor cold there.

Nor was it scary yet, it wasn't a comfortable feeling either.

It was just a whole load of nothing.

Chapter Twenty-Four

The Red Rocket sat at Jack's bedside jiggling his foot nervously as he prayed that his new-found friend would wake up. A frenzy of tubes and wires extended from Jack's body, monitoring everything in his anatomy.

He was a mess.

A one-on-one with Neon turned out to be a lot more lethal for Jack than fighting off a group of guards.

The scoring around his wrists looked nippy and sore from having them bound together with wire behind his back. The entirety of his left leg was in a cast, leaving only his toes visible. He recalled the events of the night vividly in his mind, as the beeping of Jack's monitors echoed between his ears.

Gecko's frantic whining as he hauled Jack to the van from the warehouse, the building bursting into flames behind him, causing the guards to scatter and run while Flare sprinted back to them behind Gecko and Jack. His lifeless body slumped over Gecko's shoulder put the fear into everyone that they were too late, that they had failed their mission.

He kicked himself at not being more like the Black Bullet.

For following orders he didn't agree with; The Spectrum had demanded that he leave Flare and Tide at the warehouse to maintain and then put out the blaze, while he drove everyone back to headquarters, and let Sparrow travel back alone to join the girls in putting the fire to rest.

And hopefully locating Bullet.

But, the worst memory of the night for Rocket?

Bullet on the radio.

Weak. Fading away.

Giving her life to take Neon's.

Having changed their clothes, Gecko and Youth joined him in the infirmary.

"Any change?" Gecko enquired.

"His heart rate has sped up a couple of times. Lab reckons he's dreaming," Rocket replied, not pulling his line of sight away from Jack's body.

"I honestly couldn't feel him breathing when I was carrying him back to the van," Gecko explained, "I thought he was dead."

"So, did I," Rocket admitted.

"Well, you heard what Lab said," Youth told Gecko, "you saved his life. If you hadn't performed CPR, he would've died."

Gecko rubbed his eyes, exhausted and full of disbelief.

"Do we know anything about Bullet?" Youth probed.

"The Spectrum hasn't left his office since we got back. He's monitoring every word spoken by Sparrow, Flare and Tide. He said as soon as he knew, we would," Rocket explained.

"This is crazy," Youth said, "she risked her life to save Jack, who risked his life to keep us safe, and then she risked it all again to make sure Neon didn't escape. I can't believe he was ready and willing to have us all leave her in there."

"I think considering the situation, The Spectrum's doing everything he can," Gecko counter-argued.

"But, it's Bullet. The Black Bullet. Colour Coded wouldn't be a thing without her. None of this would be real. She's the glue that holds us together, if she dies… "

"She won't die. It's Bullet. She's gone through too much to let this be her end. She's built for more than this," Rocket thought aloud.

"I wonder what Neon was saying to her," Youth considered, "I mean, whatever it was, it was working. He was getting under her skin."

"He was using her past against her," Rocket said.

"Yeah, apparently she murdered someone?" Gecko chimed in again. "That can't be right. She wouldn't murder someone in cold blood."

"I don't know much about it," Rocket said.

Youth and Gecko looked at each other suspiciously.

"But, you do know something?" Gecko probed.

"I know that Bullet was in Prismatic before me. When I came, it was just her, Sparrow and Neon. Something had just gone down. She was all over the place."

"A mission?" Youth pried.

"I don't know. All I know is that when I came, they decided that personal pasts were forbidden from then on. Everyone had to drop everything for the organisation to work, and no one was allowed to ask people about their history."

"So, Bullet and Sparrow knew each other before that was implemented... do you think Sparrow knows about what Neon was saying?" Youth offered.

"Maybe... maybe not. I don't know. And I don't want to know. I like the system the way it is. It works. We know the people we know because of who they are now. Pasts make things complicated," Rocket snapped.

Lab entered from the back room. Her clothes were bloody and her hair was damp. Silently, she came to Jack's bedside and checked his drip, his pulse. She checked the incubator that was assisting with Jack's breathing and observed his heart rate monitor.

"What're you doing? Is something wrong?" Gecko asked, distressed.

"He's struggling to breathe on his own. He took a good couple of blows to the chest, his lung muscles are in shock," Lab explained. "Basically, it's like he's been winded, but it's more long-term; it's taking a while to wear off. But, since his body is so weak, I'm trying to help him breathe."

"Is there anything else life-threatening?" Youth probed hard.

"He's had severe head trauma. Gecko told me that Neon actually smacked the back of his head with the blade of the knife and that's when Jack became unresponsive. The blow fractured his skull ever so slightly, but a knife wouldn't be able to do that, so he had obviously been taking a lot of crap from Neon for quite some time, particularly to his head. His eye socket is cracked and his nose is broken, all of which could have been the cause of the blood coming out of his ears."

"His brain bled?" Gecko cried, horrified at the extent of his injuries.

"Slightly, yes," Lab confirmed.

"Will he be okay though?" Youth implored. "Please, Lab, tell me he'll pull through this."

Lab gave him nothing but a look of sympathy after she placed covers back over Jack's beaten and burned body.

"I can't promise you that, pet. He's not out of the woods yet. Right now, it's up to him to wake up and then we can assess how far he has to go before potentially making a full recovery."

She hated herself for making the three young men in front of her look nothing but disheartened and full of remorse at her words.

"Bullet?" she asked Rocket gently.

"Still waiting," he muttered.

Lab nodded, trying to remain hopeful.

"Right… okay. Well, I'm going to see The Spectrum. I have my earpiece in, I believe they've been put back on to pressure control?" Lab aimed at Youth, who nodded in confirmation.

"Right. Well, if anything changes, call me and I'll be right back," she instructed them, placing a comforting hand on Gecko's shoulder as she walked away from them and left the infirmary.

The silence that followed was one that none of them could bear.

They wanted to talk but didn't know what to say. They wanted to do something to help but didn't know where to start.

They were clueless.

Rocket stood up suddenly, kicking his chair away with anger, and paced back and forth at the bottom of Jack's bed.

"Are you guys going to stay here?" he enquired.

"Well, I'm not planning on going anywhere. Youth?"

"No, right now there's nothing I can do other than try and be here when he wakes up."

"Good. I'm going back, then," Rocket affirmed.

"What? To the warehouse?" Gecko probed.

"I can't leave Tide there by herself. Sparrow's only there to use his drone to help find Bullet. They'll need an extra pair of hands," he explained, and ran out of the room, energy bursting through him from nowhere.

Rocket fired down the corridor and near enough tumbled down the glass staircase after he had hurdled over the chairs in the conservatory.

He sprinted across the bottom floor and down the stairs to the garage, trying to process which vehicle would be better to take before he got there.

He needed one with more than two seats, so the sports car was out of the question, albeit it would have gotten him there faster. The van was low on fuel and he didn't have time to fill it up.

He went straight for the Subaru.

Every one of the vehicles down there had fingerprint controlled locks and the keys in the ignition for racy starts like this one.

The car sprang to life, and he navigated his way to the garage door, which opened upon his approach. Rocket stamped on the accelerator and flew around the side of the building, heading for the stone riddled route out of the property.

The Spectrum's authoritative figure by the fountain was anything but a greeting as the car squealed around the bend towards the driveway to the grounds.

The Red Rocket's feet stamped on the break, violently causing the car to skid uncontrollably over the stones as he held his breath, praying to every possible God under the sun that he didn't hit him. The Spectrum didn't move.

He didn't even flinch.

Rocket turned the wheel, flinging the car around sideways and clenched his eyes shut. The car came to a halt just inches in front of The Spectrum who was still dressed in his pinstripe suit. His expression was rather empty, like this was an everyday event that he was used to. Rocket let out a breath of relief, resting his forehead on the steering wheel.

A knock at the window caused him to stir with fright as he turned to The Spectrum looking down at him, his expression very much the same as it had been since he was first able to lay eyes on him after taking the bend at top speed. Rocket hit the button on his right, letting the window lower, feeling the cold air hit the side of his face.

"Where, might I ask, are you going?"

Lab, from hearing the commotion, ran out the front doors filled with worry.

"I'm going back," Rocket said, trying to be strong-willed.

"Oh, are you?"

"Yes."

"And who authorised that?"

No matter what he tried, Rocket couldn't swallow the lump that had suddenly appeared in his throat.

"I did," he croaked.

"Oh, did you, now?" The Spectrum asked, patronisingly.

Rocket's entire persona changed.

He was no longer nervous or worried about what The Spectrum might do.

Now, he was angry, as the worry for his friends and his girlfriend burst through him rapidly.

"They'll need an extra pair of hands, I can't just leave them there!" he cried. "If Bullet's in trouble, they'll need to get her out of there as soon as, and nobody… NOBODY… can drive like I can!"

The Spectrum merely stared at him.

He was hunched over to level with him by the car window, his hands clasped behind his back, his demeanour unusually calm.

"I was thinking exactly the same thing, Rocket," he admitted. "But, with one difference."

Rocket said nothing, waiting on his answer. The look of confusion was plastered very clearly across his face as The Spectrum held his gaze.

"What difference?" Rocket probed, irritated.

199

"That I will be in the passenger seat with you," he confirmed, still remaining annoyingly calm. "Are you too upset with me for me to join you and complete the mission?"

There was something about the way he spoke that had Rocket cower, feeling guilty for snapping at his boss. He looked away from him, shaking his head, allowing The Spectrum to travel to the other side of the car.

"Keep an eye on the boy," he said to Lab, "we'll be back soon."

"Do you think she's still alive?" Lab asked, her eyes wide with fear.

"I hope so. But, either way, we're bringing her home."

The Spectrum got into the car, and Rocket took off before he had even shut the door.

"I'm sorry, sir," Rocket murmured.

"Do not ever apologise to me, Rocket," The Spectrum replied modestly, "we each deal with worry and stress in different ways. This is your way."

"What do we do if she's dead?"

The Spectrum took time to think about this, as though he hadn't considered the possibility before now.

"We pray that Neon is dead as well."

"So that we're not in danger?"

"No. So, that the Black Bullet didn't die in vain."

Chapter Twenty-Five

Sparrow was holding back as Flare and Tide put out the last of the fire when Rocket and The Spectrum pulled up next to Sparrow's car. He walked over to meet them, a look of surprise on his face at their arrival.

"We didn't know you were coming," he announced.

"Neither did we," The Spectrum replied, slamming the door shut and walking around the car to stand beside him. The smoke from the defused fire billowed up into the night sky, the pungent smell intruding into their sinuses. Some of the wood was still smouldering as they approached the fallen warehouse, the metal slates from the roof half-melted and scorched.

"How bad was it?" Rocket asked.

"It went up like a bonfire," Flare shouted, "but, I made sure it was contained to only the warehouse. The bunker wouldn't have been touched."

"So, how do we do this?" Sparrow enquired.

"You'll need to charge up your drone again, we're going to need it. Clearing the debris from the entrance of the bunker is our best bet, and then we fly the drone in to make sure it's clear," Flare suggested.

"Do that. I'm going to stay in the car and listen to the radio; we need to be out of the area before emergency services arrive," The Spectrum instructed, walking back to Rocket's car.

"This may be out in the middle of nowhere, but we don't know how many passers-by there were, or if property holders nearby smelt the fumes projected from the flames. Get to it, folks."

"Yes, sir," Rocket said.

Sparrow went to an area at the side that was clear of debris, setting his drone down and preparing to charge it.

"Tide, you have the blueprints?" Flare asked.

"Right here," she said, pulling a folded bit of paper from the pocket of her blue jacket. She unfolded it while Rocket and Flare looked over her shoulder and observed the detailed floor plan of Neon's now destroyed headquarters.

"So, we're standing roughly here…" said Tide, pointing to an area on the blueprint. "And the bunker entrance was there."

"How long was the warehouse front to back?" Rocket asked.

"About one hundred and eighty yards, give or take. The main hall, or working area, was at the back near enough, the door to get to the bunker was there… so about halfway down," Tide said, looking up at the wreckage. "Is it safe to start rummaging yet?"

"I'll get the safety gloves and masks from the car, but maybe give it another five or ten minutes," she said, leaving them and heading to Sparrow's car.

"Okay, so where in this shit heap do we start looking?" Rocket asked Tide.

"Well, looking in from the front, the bunker entrance was over on the right-hand side. There's a bit of wall there that's still standing, so I'd suggest walking about eighty feet past that and then start sifting through the rubble," she replied.

Flare returned with four pairs of thick gloves and masks.

"I need to wear a welder's helmet?" Tide asked reluctantly.

"It's actually a visor that firefighters wear. There might still be smouldering materials buried underneath, and if metal rubs against metal, sparks will fly. It can blind you."

"And now I'm convinced," Tide said, taking a mask and forcing the strap over her forehead.

Flare and Rocket joined in and, after putting their gloves on, approached the burnt out mess of Neon's lair. A spare mask and gloves were left in case Sparrow found time to join them in the search.

Carefully, they clambered through the scorched heap and made their way to the chosen area. Cautiously pulling back wood, metal, wires and the like, they began sifting through the debris looking for the edge of the stairs down to the bunker.

Sparks burst once or twice, causing everyone to jump and be on alert.

"Ladies and gentlemen!" The Spectrum shouted from the edge of the building perimeter. "You have approximately forty-five minutes! Emergency services were called!"

"Shit!" Flare exclaimed, losing all cautiousness she had and started flinging everything back behind her. They all became careless.

Bullet was the main priority.

As well as their anonymity.

"I've got something!" Tide cried out, her head ducked deep within the rubble. "It's definitely the start of a large hole, but it's filled with debris!"

"I brought my toolbox, can we just smash through it?" Rocket asked Flare.

"And if Bullet's right on the other side of it, do you really want to take that chance?" Flare stabbed. "We need to do it by hand."

"That could take hours!" Tide exclaimed.

"You saw the footage, there were about eight steps down to the passageway and it was an extensively long tunnel; the whole corridor won't be filled. I'll dig through, but I think we'll need rope," Flare offered.

"I'll check the boot of my car. I'll bring my toolbox as well," Rocket said, frantically wading his way through the debris and pelting down to the car.

"Drone's charged!" Sparrow announced.

"Just on time!" Flare yelled back. "Bring it over!"

Sparrow and Rocket met in the middle and ran into the wreckage together.

Flare took the rope from Rocket as he plonked his toolbox down to one side while Sparrow set up his drone.

"How long is it?" she asked.

"No idea," he admitted, "does it matter?"

"I guess we don't have a choice now. Come here," she gestured.

Rocket went over beside her and Flare tied the rope around his waist before tying the other end around her own. She began pulling out poles, joists, and other damaged components of the warehouse, carefully making her way down one step at a time.

"You okay?" Rocket asked, staying firmly on the spot at the top of the stairs.

"Yeah… I count six steps so far. Start the drone," she replied.

Sparrow's drone sprung to life and he lifted it from the ground, leaving it to hover above the small route through the rubble that Flare had made.

"Ready when you are!" Sparrow shouted.

"Okay, bring it down!" she yelled, her voice echoing out of the tunnel. Sparrow lowered the drone down the stairwell carefully, keeping out of the way of any debris still down there. Flare's face came into view, and she ducked down to let it pass over her.

"Do you not have lights on this thing?" Tide asked, looking over Sparrow's shoulder at his tablet screen.

"Yeah, yeah, I do," he said, loading a menu and hitting a symbol.

Light projected from the tunnel as soon as he hit the button.

Having made his way past the debris, the tunnel was free and clear, all the torches burnt out, and Sparrow flew the drone along as fast as he could make it go.

Within seconds, he made it to the door into Neon's office, which was thankfully ajar. The reflection from the light bouncing off of Bullet's leather jacket was the first thing to catch his attention, and he navigated over to it.

Bullet lay unconscious and extremely still.

"Anything???" Flare screeched from the tunnel, worry beginning to get the better of her.

Normally, no news was good news; but this situation was different, and Flare hated every second of it.

"Yeah, we found her, but..." Sparrow trailed off.

"But, what??" she cried. "Does she have burn injuries? Where is she?"

"She doesn't seem to..." Sparrow said.

"Zoom in on her chest," Rocket suggested.

Sparrow was visibly shaking with nerves at the concept of them being too late as well as them running out of time.

Missions were always tough, but being against the clock messed with him.

"Flare! Flare, she's still breathing, but barely! Go! Go! Go!" Rocket yelled as he made his way down behind her.

She was merely a few feet in front of him as they both sprinted down the dark tunnel, only the lights from their masks illuminating the path a couple of feet in front of them while the rope that bound them was tumbling along at their backs. They burst through the door to Bullet's body lying on the trap door, a pool of blood on the floor around her right thigh.

"Bullet!" Flare cried. "Honey, can you hear me? It's Flare," she shouted, slapping the side of her face. "Bullet? Come on, babe... please!"

Flare gave herself a shake to focus and began doing a secondary examination of Bullet's body.

"No head trauma... arms are good... neck and spine are intact... no internal damage. Rocket, get her out of here."

He need not reply to Flare and the tears rolling down both cheeks as he lifted his friend over his shoulder and quickly walked out with her, Flare right at his back.

They travelled back along the passageway, following the lights from Sparrow's drone as he brought out his device.

Tide was halfway down the stairs, ready to help them squeeze Bullet out of the narrow entry Flare dug to gain access.

"Grab her feet and twist her around," Rocket said to Tide, who immediately crossed her hands over and took Bullet by the ankles. Rocket carefully slid her over his shoulder and held her under her arms at the bend of his elbows.

Carefully, they shuffled out with her and began making their way through the debris for the last time, with Sparrow guiding them as Tide walked backwards.

"You guys go, I'll catch up!" Flare said.

"What're you doing? We have to go!" Tide yelled.

Flare took something out of her pocket and watched them make their way back to the car, waiting for them to be well clear of the property before taking the pin out of the grenade and throwing it into the tunnel. She could have competed in an Olympic hurdling event the way she removed herself from the remnants of Prismatic headquarters. The explosion rumbled through the ground, bursting out of the bunker entrance, throwing rubble and dirt everywhere. Flare ducked her head down and kept running.

She knew she didn't have to do that, but in case Neon was alive, she wanted to make sure that he definitely didn't have an escape route.

When she reached them, The Spectrum was out of the car.

"There's nothing left behind that could be traced back to us?"

"No, nothing," Flare replied, panting.

"We need to get Bullet back to Lab for treatment. Flare, you're with Sparrow and me, Bullet's already in Rocket's car with him and Tide, let's move!" he ordered.

They all poured into their designated vehicles and sped off down the street. There was no way in hell Sparrow was going to manage to catch up with Rocket as he took off way ahead in front of them, especially when it came to the winding roads through the Cairngorms on the approach to Colour Coded HQ.

In Rocket's car, Tide sat in the back with Bullet who was sprawled out across the seats with her head on Tide's lap.

"Bullet? Come on, please. Wake up!" she said, patting the sides of her face with a gentle force.

Both Tide and Bullet's faces were covered with soot from the fire; although for completely different reasons. As much as Tide's skin was blackened from putting out the fire, Bullet's face was much more black from being stuck in there for so long.

She should've got that fire out quicker.

"Here," Rocket said as he squirmed around behind the steering wheel, "take my belt. Strap it around her leg; try and stop the blood."

Tide slid the belt through Rocket's fingers and wrapped it around Bullet's thigh just above her wound, yanking it as tight as she could make it go.

"You're going to be fine, do you hear me? Absolutely fine. No other option is good enough, Bullet," Tide yammered quietly as she fiddled with the belt buckle.

"Try giving her some water," Rocket suggested.

There was a couple of bottles of spare water tucked into the pouch on the back of the passenger seat. Tide leaned over Bullet and flicked it out, fumbling around in a frenzy to unscrew the cap while being jostled around from Rocket's frantic driving.

Carefully, she tipped it into Bullet's mouth, forcing her head forward so that she didn't choke. A lot of it dribbled out the sides of her mouth and on to the seats.

"It's not working," she sobbed.

"Is she still breathing? Hold the back of your hand to her nose," Rocket said, trying to watch her in the mirror as much as he could while keeping an eye on the road.

"I think so... Yeah, she is. But, barely. I can hardly even see her chest rising," Tide said, panicking frantically.

"Rocket to Lab, are you there?"

"Yes, I'm here, pet, what's going on?"

"We found her, we're on our way back, but she's unconscious from smoke inhalation, or blood loss, or both. How can we help her until we get to you?"

"If you don't have an oxygen mask, then do what you can to replicate it. Open windows, everything. Try giving her water."

"Lab, it's Tide, I've tried giving her water, but it doesn't work, it just spills everywhere."

"You need to peg her nose, tip some water in and clamp her mouth shut with two fingers at the little indent just under her chin."

"Like CPR?" Tide confirmed.

"Exactly, darling! Just like CPR, except instead of blowing into her airways you're tipping a tiny little bit of water into them."

"Won't she drown?"

"No, sweetheart, she won't drown. But, it will irritate her, which is what we want. We need her to cough up all that gunk in her lungs."

Tide broke down and started to cry.

"Come on, Tide. You can do this, babe!" Rocket encouraged her. "Come on. She needs you."

"Just a little bit of water, now. Like a cap full. Don't overdo it," Lab instructed.

Tide pegged Bullet's nose as instructed and tipped a little bit of water into her mouth. She put her fingers at the bottom of her chin and held her mouth shut.

"If she doesn't cough it up right away, then gently blow into her mouth and coax it down," Lab's gentle but firm voice tickled their ears again.

Tide leaned down and spread her mouth over Bullet's, and blew.

Instantly, Bullet writhed and juddered, coughing and spluttering everywhere. Black phlegm bounced out of her mouth as though from a slingshot, splatting against the window and the back of the front seat. Her wheezing was ridiculous, as barely any air was able to make its way down to her bunged up lungs.

"Good girl!" Rocket bellowed with delight.

"It's okay! Bullet? Bullet, it's Tide. You're okay! We're taking you home, Lab's going to help you, you're okay!" Tide said, thumping Bullet's back while attempting to hold her steady. She started to slouch backwards.

"Lie on your side, Bullet. Don't lie on your back," Rocket said to her.

Bullet's head had barely hit Tide's thigh when she was back up again, fumbling and squirming around.

"You're okay, Bullet," Rocket said comfortingly.

"No… no, she's not. Rocket, she's choking."

"What?"

"She's choking, she can't breathe!" Tide thumped her back frantically, with no clue what to do.

"Bullet, hang on, we're almost there!" Rocket cried out.

Once more, Bullet began to feel weak and drowsy. Her lungs were a shrivelling leaf on a twig of autumn. She felt herself slump into the back seat as the little oxygen she had in her system turned into CO_2, and her brain began to shut down.

Painfully and incredibly slowly, Bullet recognised that familiar feeling as she drifted into the unconscious once again.

Chapter Twenty-Six

"Lab, we need a gurney at the top of the stairs!" Rocket shouted as he turned on to the private driveway and floored it until he was at the front of the building, yanking the wheel down to the left as the car scraped violently across the stones.

"Get her in, I'm on my way," Lab replied.

Leaving the engine running and the doors open was the last thing concerning Rocket as he dragged Bullet's lifeless body out of his car and ran with her to the door, Tide right next to him while she opened the door for him to pass through.

Lab had just reached the top of the stairs when they made it inside. Bullet's limbs bounced all over the place as Rocket ran up the glass stairs two at a time with her, flinging her down on the bed.

"How long has she been unconscious for?" Lab asked.

"She stopped moving just under five minutes before we got back," Rocket said, running along with Lab beside the bed, "she's not breathing... I drove as fast as I could."

"I know, darling, I know. Let me get her into the consultation room."

"We're not leaving her!" Tide stated.

"Sweetheart, you've done your bit. Let me do mine," Lab said as they ran into the infirmary.

Reluctantly, Rocket let go of the bed and slowed to a standstill, grabbing Tide's arm as she tried to pass him and go with Lab and Bullet.

Frustrated, she flung her arms around and began to pace, openly crying and not caring who saw her.

"She died," Tide said.

"Lab'll get her back," Rocket replied.

"She died, Rocket. Dead. Her entire body shut down. She's gone."

"Lab'll get her back."

"There's nothing to get back, she's gone, it's... "

"LAB'LL GET HER BACK!!" Rocket yelled at her, his face in hers, tears welling up in his eyes. "She'll get her back."

"But, what if she can't?" Tide panicked, gripping Rocket's arms as a means of holding herself up.

Willingly, Rocket reached out and held her.

"She will. She has to. There's no Colour Coded without the Black Bullet," he whispered.

They held each other's gaze for a while, Rocket using every ounce of himself to fight back the tears.

"You don't have to be a tough guy all the time," Tide informed him through her tears.

"Yes, I do."

"No... you really don't," she forced, stepping closer to him. "Show me the man you really are. Show me the one who really cares about his friends, who doesn't want to lose them... show me the man that, deep down, is really fucking scared, just like I am."

He tried.

With everything he had he tried.

It was no use.

Rocket crumpled to the floor and broke down, leaning his head on Tide's legs and wrapping his hands around the back of her calves. She crouched down beside him, running her fingers through his gel-filled, spiky brown hair, resting her forehead on his, and cried with him.

"I've... I've never driven so fast... and it wasn't enough..." he sobbed.

"Aw, honey... don't do that. This wasn't your fault. You did everything right," she assured him. "I didn't put out the fire quick enough."

Tide rested herself down and held his head against her chest, rocking side to side with him as they both sobbed into each other.

Neither of them knew what the most prominent thought was; losing Bullet, Colour Coded falling through, Neon's plan coming into effect... Losing Bullet.

Bullet was the heart and soul of Colour Coded.

Even The Spectrum said so.

She was there when it all began. She always had everyone's back. She had the most useful skill when it came to dangerous missions. She never faltered when someone needed her, always giving them her full and undivided attention. And all of that could be ripped away from them, like a rug being swept away from under their feet.

Footsteps pattered down the hall sporadically. Flare, Sparrow and The Spectrum rushed into the hospital wing, a look of panic on their faces.

Not long after, Youth and Gecko showed up, their faces confusion stricken at all the commotion over the earpieces earlier.

"What happened?" Gecko asked. "Where's Bullet?"

He and Youth looked around at everyone, but they were all focused on Tide and Rocket sprawled on the floor in each other's arms. Focused on Rocket's state of mind.

Or lack thereof.

He was beside himself.

They thought the worst.

"Why are you sitting out here?" Sparrow snapped.

"Lab wouldn't let us go through with her," Tide cried.

Without a word, The Spectrum marched away from them heading to the consultation room where he knew Lab would have taken Bullet.

He barged into a sight that almost had him stagger back out the door.

Machines flatlining, a constant high-pitched sound filling the air, while Lab used the defibrillator on Bullet's chest.

An incubator had been situated into her mouth, just like Jack.

"Lab?"

"I'm working on it, get out," she said, not turning her sight away from Bullet's lifeless body lying in front of her.

"What's happening?" The Spectrum probed again, the shock filling him like a tank of water.

"I said I'm working on it, now, get out!" she yelled at him.

The Spectrum watched the Lavender Lab frantically shock Bullet's body. He watched Bullet jerk as soon as the shockwave was released. He watched the heart rate monitor continue to portray a solid line.

Everything was happening in slow motion.

If ever there was a moment that enforced just how fleeting life could be, then this was definitely one of them.

The Spectrum looked at the face of the girl he came across five years ago. One that he knew just by her attitude and how she composed herself that she had been through a lot in her few years of living.

The Black Bullet had a burden to bear. A big one.

The Spectrum didn't know what it was, but for her to be able to kill so easily, he knew it must have been something huge. He had, on many occasions, considered that she was a veteran; that maybe she had done a couple of tours and they had messed with her mentally. It would explain the weaponry expertise and the second-hand nature of which she seemed to possess when taking a life.

No histories.

That was the rule.

For this precise reason.

A thump from the defibrillator snapped him out of his daze.

He stumbled back to the door and hurled himself around the other side of it, pushing it shut with his back as he leaned on the door, eyes wide, body numb.

"Sir?" Sparrow asked as he hovered anxiously by the consult room door.

The Spectrum looked up at him and jolted as though he had just noticed him.

"She's working on it," he said blandly, "it's a waiting game now."

Gravity was sucking him to the floor when he made his way to the main section of the hospital wing. He tripped a couple of times over his own feet as he struggled to find his balance, the whole situation knocking him in every direction. The fear in each member of Colour Coded rose when they saw The Spectrum walk back to them in a daze, in shock, and in emotional turmoil.

"How is she?" Flare probed frantically.

"She's in the right place. For now, we wait for Lab's update," The Spectrum said, propping himself down on the bed next to the one that Jack's unconscious body continued to inhabit.

The hours dragged past tauntingly, and there was still no sign of Lab.

The morning sun had risen above the mountains, greeting them with a blinding glare.

Tide and Rocket had curled up together on a bed by the door and were now sound asleep. Gecko and Youth sat next to each other in silence on the bed opposite The Spectrum; Youth played a game on his phone while Gecko simply stared at the floor in his own little world. Flare sat with her feet up on the bed, her head dangling between her knees as she willed Lab to walk out of that room and tell everyone that her best friend was going to be okay. Sparrow was pacing. At first, it was fast, deliberate.

Now, it was just repetition, obligation, clueless on another way to deal with everything.

Everyone looked around at the same time; Tide and Rocket woke up, Gecko snapped out of it, Youth put his phone away, Flare lifted her head up and Sparrow stopped still.

The sound of Lab checking Jack's machines caught their attention.

"Lab, is she okay? Can we see her?" Flare hopped off the bed swiftly.

"Soon. Not right now," Lab replied.

"Tell us," Sparrow demanded, "and don't sugarcoat."

One by one, Lab made eye contact with each of them in the hospital wing.

"You have to understand… she lay engulfed in smoke for a really long time. She had a severe wound to her leg which she lost a lot of blood from. She was unconscious but clinging on by the skin of her teeth, thankfully. I did lose her in there last night," Tide burst into tears again, recalling how Bullet writhed in pain one minute and then slumped into lifelessness the next.

"How is she now, though?" Youth demanded.

"Alive. But, barely," Lab replied. "I lost her for a good fifteen minutes."

"What took you so long to come out then?"

"Sparrow!" Rocket snapped at him, stunned. "Bullet's alive, isn't that enough?"

"I had to do tests and monitor everything about her for the first few hours. They were crucial. She could easily have slipped away again, and I wanted to be sure. I didn't want to give you false hope."

"Her injuries, Lab?" The Spectrum's voice rung out across the room.

"Aside from the smoke inhalation which has clogged her lungs, she lost a lot of blood from the stab wound to the back of her leg. The blade scuffed the edge of her femur and damaged muscle tissue, tore through a tendon, and just nicked an artery and no more. She also has a cracked elbow which I can only assume was from falling. That is the full report."

"And now?" The Spectrum probed.

"She's critical but stable. I have her on oxygen, much like your boy here, I've cleaned out as much of the soot as I can, her leg is strapped up and she's had a blood transfusion to replace what she lost." Lab rubbed her eyes, exhausted from the job she had with Bullet. "Tide, I need to sort your hands, darling. They'll get infected if I don't."

Lab held up an antibacterial agent and some bandages, motioning for Tide to come over to her. Sheepishly, she left Rocket by the bed and went over, holding her hands out.

Amidst the silence of the room, Lab rubbed the gel gently into Tide's hands, who stood numb despite the raging sting that sprung to life in her palms, and after she placed a cotton pad across each

212

one, wrapped them up with the bandages she brought out with her from the back room.

"This is all my fault," Flare's whisper echoed through the noiseless room.

"What?" Gecko prodded.

"I set that fire."

"Darling, don't do that," Lab instructed. "You didn't know…"

"That she was in there? Yeah. I did. But, I did it anyway."

"You thought she was going to run out, Flare. We all did," Rocket assured her. "That was the plan. This isn't on you."

"I set that fire. I deliberately didn't attempt to contain it so that it would spread faster. I did it even though I knew I didn't know what kind of components were inside, what kind of gases could be released, if there were catalysts of any kind… but I took my flame thrower, and I blasted the fuel that I splashed everywhere."

"Bullet told me to run. Flare, she knew as soon as I was seen outside that that was your cue to strike, but she told me to run anyway," Gecko acknowledged, "she knew it was going to happen."

"We went into that room together. Remember?" Rocket said, walking over to her. "Where she was lying on the floor. Other than an injured leg, there was nothing that could've possibly stopped her from leaving, was there? She could've made it out on time, but she hung back to make sure Neon stayed buried in there."

"We should probably get proof of death," Sparrow said coldly, changing the subject altogether.

"There's time for that," Rocket snapped at him.

"Not if he's still alive there isn't."

"Mate, what is your fucking problem?"

"That we don't know Neon's whereabouts! That bothers me!"

"Does it? And Bullet lying in there fighting for her life while Flare blames herself for it doesn't bother you?"

"Of course it bothers me, but someone has to remain rational!"

"And you think you're the best candidate for that!"

"Guys, come on…" Tide sighed.

"Well, no one else seems to be stepping forward!" Sparrow ignored her interruption.

"Maybe that's because now is not the time!"

"Then when is? If we leave it too long he could have upped and left by then, starting yet another scheme to kill us, maybe this time succeeding!"

"GUYS!" Youth exploded. "Shut the fuck up, will you? Maybe now isn't the time for mollycoddling, maybe it's not the time to deviate from thinking ahead, but I can assure you it's definitely not the time for acting like a couple of fucking kids fighting over who's got the best race car!"

Stunned, everyone eyeballed Youth.

He was always the calm one, laid back, ready for anything.

To see him lose control the way he did was a shock to the system.

"I couldn't have said it better myself," The Spectrum added, mirthless at their behaviour.

"This... is a breakdown in team effort. It is a breakdown in communication. It is a breakdown in supporting one another. It is also letting Neon *win,* which is something that, under no circumstances whatsoever, I will allow. Get. Your act. Together. NOW," The Spectrum stormed past everyone in the infirmary like a man on a mission, heading for the door.

"Flare," he said as he passed, "my office. Now."

Full of self-hatred, Flare shuffled awkwardly around the bed and followed her boss out of the infirmary.

It wasn't long before she was facing the entrance to his grand office that was always so warm and always so tidy. She entered the room, noticing the back of his head as he sat on the couch pouring himself a glass of whiskey. Another glass sat across from him, already poured.

"Sit, please," he asked quietly.

Flare did as she was told.

Lifting his glass and watching the golden fluid swish around in its fancy container, The Spectrum gathered his thoughts for what he would say to Flare. There was only one way he could think to go that Flare would resonate with.

"It wasn't that long ago that I had the Black Bullet in here. Sitting where you yourself are sitting. Drinking this very brand of whiskey, out of this very bottle actually," he said before taking a sip out of his glass.

He closed his eyes as the alcohol nipped his throat, giving him the kick that he had been hoping for.

"She too was suffering from the same turmoil that you are right now. Do you remember what that was regarding?"

"She shot Jack by accident."

"By accident? So, you don't think that she was responsible?"

"No, of course I don't!" Flare defended. "Are you insinuating that I do?"

"I'm not saying one way or the other, Flare. But, by reacting to Bullet's condition the way you did, I can only assume you believe Jack's gunshot wound was Bullet's fault."

214

"That's completely different!"

"Is it? Please elaborate for this silly old man. Explain to me how it is different," The Spectrum nudged her gently.

"We could have had a successful mission without me setting that fire."

"Bullet could have had a successful mission without having to fire her weapon."

"On purpose, I sat in wait, looking for my cue."

"Bullet took aim, waiting to see if her skills were needed, also on purpose."

"I deliberately set the warehouse on fire."

"Bullet deliberately pulled the trigger."

The Spectrum pointed to her glass, ushering her to take a drink. She needed one.

It had been one of the longest and toughest nights that they had endured in a very long time. If not *the* toughest.

"You see now how both events, although different methods were used, had the same kind of outcome?"

Flare nodded, her eyes welling up as she took a large gulp from her whiskey glass.

"So, I'm going to say this one last thing, and then that'll be the end of this train journey your mind has gotten itself on," The Spectrum announced. "I said this to Bullet as well, so take heed like she did, alright? Feeling responsible for something and being to blame for something are two completely different things. If you're responsible, you played an important role in the said situation, but you didn't purposely attempt to cause harm. However, if you are to blame, you did do it on purpose, with malicious intent, and premeditated actions. You may be responsible, Flare. But, you are not to blame."

Flare's reaction was very much like Bullet's; she burst into tears like she was needing someone to confirm that it wasn't her fault that her best friend was at death's door.

"Go. Try and sleep."

"I want to be near her."

"Then sleep in the infirmary tonight. But, either way, sleep. That's an order. Rest yourself while knowing that this was not, in any way, your fault," She forced out a smile at him, as unconvincing as it was, and left him alone in his office with only his whiskey for company.

He heard her footsteps die down as she travelled along the corridor, while he poured himself another glass.

"It was mine."

Chapter Twenty-Seven

Everyone was sound asleep in the infirmary. Nobody was prepared to retire to their own quarters in case there was news of Bullet's recovery. The only one who couldn't close her eyes, who couldn't let her body rest no matter what she tried, was the Fuschia Flare.

The Spectrum's words echoed in her mind. She could see his point; that even though the situation was different between Bullet's mishap and hers, a lot of the factors were very much the same.

The main one being that both of them were not deliberate. Unintentional. An accident.

But, Flare still couldn't get out of her head that Bullet fired her gun just as Jack moved to help Gecko, whereas she set the fire knowing full well that Bullet was still inside.

She didn't set the fire with the assumption that Bullet wasn't in there.

Flare knew she was. Yet, she lit the fuel and watched it ignite like a furnace.

Bullet was meant to run out. Flare knew she had the know-how to navigate her way through the beginnings of a fire; she taught her everything she needed to know.

But, instead, she stayed inside. Knowing that there was a fire engulfing the entire building, she didn't come away from the door so as to make sure Neon didn't get out either.

Sparrow was right though; they really do need to get proof of death before they start making assumptions about anything. He was dead though, there were no two ways about it.

Nobody was getting out of there alive without help.

Did he have help?

No! Of course, he didn't. He was down there alone with Jack, Gecko got him out, and Bullet trapped Neon in. The remaining guards scattered as soon as the fire broke out.

He's toast.

But, Flare couldn't help but worry that something was wrong. Neon was always prepared and one step ahead; everyone knew that. Everyone worried about that.

And they all hated it about him the most.

It would be the most frustrating and soul destroying thing in the world if he was alive after everything Bullet did to make sure he wasn't an issue anymore.

Flare looked at the sun burning high in the sky as the afternoon arrived to greet the sleepy organisation. Lab appeared out of the back room and checked on Jack. She noticed Flare in a daze, staring outside with her mind racing about everything.

"Honey, have you slept?" she whispered to her, making sure she didn't wake anyone else.

Flare jolted with fright at her voice, shaking her head as an answer to her question.

Lab finished fiddling with Jack's monitors and walked over to her bed, propping herself down on the bottom of it.

"Staying awake for days on end isn't going to make Bullet better any faster. She's got a lot going on, it's going to take time, sweetheart."

"I wish I could sleep, Lab, but, I just can't. Every time I close my eyes all I can see is her lying there, bleeding out, being swallowed up by the smoke from the fire that *I* set."

"Didn't The Spectrum put your mind to rest about this? Flare, this isn't your fault. Nobody blames you for this, darling. Nobody, apart from you."

"Have her test results shown you anything?" Flare probed, ignoring Lab's attempts at consoling her.

"Do you want me to sugarcoat it or should I just say it like it is?" Lab checked.

"Just rip off the band-aid," Flare instructed, positioning herself on the bed and taking a breath, getting her wits about her to hear the news.

"She has mild carbon monoxide poisoning from the fumes. Her lungs are weak but saveable; the thermal damage wasn't as bad as I thought since she was away from the flames, it was mainly the smoke that caused the most damage. What didn't help was the blood loss from the knife wound to the back of her thigh; it was quite extensive, but I used the blood I have in stock to replace what was lost. She's got a fight ahead of her, but... she's a tough one. I'm really hopeful."

"That's... she's lucky to be alive, Lab."

"Exactly," Lab agreed. "Flare, she's alive because *you* fought to get her out. She's alive because Tide managed to put out the fire. She's alive because Rocket got her back here in jig time. You saved her life. You all did. Rocket was torturing himself too; he was blaming himself because he should've driven faster. As was Tide; she was blaming herself for not putting the fire out quick enough. You all rescued her."

"So, I should forgive myself for almost killing her because I helped to save her?"

"If you can do that then, yes," Lab said. "But, I know full well it's not that simple."

"No, it's not," Flare confirmed. "All I keep thinking is I should've waited until I saw Bullet before I lit the place up."

"Yeah, and Neon might have been right at her back and he could have gotten away as well," Lab retorted. "Look, none of us are oracles. We don't have a crystal ball, and hindsight is most definitely a bitch at the best of times. There is no way you can go back and change what happened. But, you can rest assured that when you first thought you had done the wrong thing, you did everything you could to make it right and to redeem yourself."

"I know… I get what you mean. I just don't want her to die."

"I'm going to do everything in my power to make sure that doesn't happen, darling. But, nobody can forgive you for this."

Flare looked up, doleful at Lab's words.

"You can't forgive someone when there's nothing to forgive," Lab assured her. "Nobody blames you for this, just like nobody blamed Bullet for Jack getting shot."

"Yeah, that's what The Spectrum said."

"Well, listen to him. Because he's right," Lab said, nudging her playfully in an attempt to cheer her up.

Lab cautiously looked around. The gang were still fast asleep, emotionally and mentally exhausted from the series of events of the last couple of days. Those last couple of days that no one had slept through, minus one or two catching a couple of hours randomly.

"Do you want to come through and see her?" Lab asked.

"Is that allowed?" Flare asked, shuffling around on the bed preparing to get up.

"You'll have to wear a face mask and an apron to prevent the spread of germs in both directions, and use disinfectant mousse on your hands before you go in. But, yes. It's allowed."

Lab's hand brushed gently on the back of Flare's shoulder as she guided her round to the back room. She put on her rubber gloves before bursting an apron out of a packet, while Flare covered her hands in disinfectant before putting on the apron that Lab was holding out for her. She adjusted the facemask over her mouth and nose, positioning the straps behind her ears as Lab opened the door.

Flare couldn't even begin to count the number of wires and tubes that were attached to Bullet's completely still body.

If you took all of it away, she would look like she was simply sleeping, just like everyone else was as they waited for more news about her physical state.

A strange box covered her head with a single tube extending from it and attaching on to a machine by Bullet's bedside. Numbers fluctuated back and forth on the device's screen. Flare had no idea what it was but it couldn't be good.

"What is that?"

"It's an oxygen box. Inside it the air pressure is a little higher than normal so that the carbon monoxide is removed quicker from her bloodstream and replaced with oxygen. That's the one I'm trying to fight off first, because, as much as it's mild, if I ignore it for too long it could easily deteriorate and kill her."

"Oh, my God…" Flare breathed as she tiptoed over to the bed.

Bullet's hair was puffy and frizzy as it spread out around her head in the confinements of the clear box that had been carefully placed around her from the neck up.

Her skin was still stained black with soot from the smoke.

One leg was on top of the covers, showing a mass amount of bandaging around Bullet's rather muscular thigh, while the other remained under the covers. Flare noticed a bag in the corner which contained Bullet's clothes that had been cut off, Lab following her line of sight.

"I can only imagine the grilling I'm going to get when she learns that I cut through her leather."

Flare smiled at her comment.

Slowly and gently, Flare wriggled her fingers under Bullet's, giving them a loving squeeze while a tear managed to escape down her cheek.

"I'm so sorry," Flare whispered softly. "Please wake up. Fight whatever demons you have to, but just wake up."

Lab's expression was filled with nothing but sympathy and love as she watched Flare have her moment with Bullet. Her two girls, with the friendship they had that was much like a sisterhood, was her pride and joy, one that she felt blessed to witness every day. For her to watch this was a lot harder than she was prepared to let on.

"Will she make it?" Flare asked Lab blatantly.

"I honestly can't answer that, darling. I'm doing everything I can for her. Much like I'm doing everything I can for Jack. The pair of them need to just keep hanging on to have the best chance. That part is down to them entirely," she said, adjusting the bandage lining on Bullet's leg before walking around to Flare.

"I'll give you a minute, sweetheart. Just don't touch anything, okay?"

"No, I won't. Thank you, Lab," Flare said, flinging her arms around Lab's neck and holding her tightly.

Lab didn't hesitate. She wrapped her arms around Flare in return, kissing the side of her head comfortingly.

"Don't thank me yet," Lab said, letting her go and rubbing her eyes.

"Have you slept?" Flare enquired.

Lab merely chuckled.

"No… I haven't had time. But, I will. When she's clear of carbon monoxide, then I'll sleep."

Lab left, shutting the door quietly behind her.

The room was rather spacious, but when everything was piled into it – the bed, the machines, the utensils – it made it seem rather cramped. A chair hid behind the door, and Flare pulled it forward towards the bed.

She thumped down into it, taking Bullet's hand again.

It really did look like she was just sleeping.

If only that was the truth.

Bullet had always put herself in harm's way to protect everyone, but she had done it numerous times for Flare alone.

"Bullet… I don't know if you can hear me. Even if you can, I feel like an idiot for even trying this. Please wake up. Please live. I'm so sorry I let you stay in there when I ignited the fire. I was following orders, I was sticking to the plan, I was… I was hoping you'd come running out and we could leave together. I was wrong, and I'm sorry. Now, I get how you felt when Jack got shot. You pulled the trigger, so it was your fault. I used the flame thrower, so this is mine," Flare rambled in low tones, fiddling with Bullet's still fingers between her own.

Her hand was cold in Flare's warm grasp. She wondered if the rest of her was just as cold.

She wondered what it was like… Was it like a dream? Was it nothing but darkness?

Flare recalled her little rant she just had and considered the possibility… could Bullet even hear anything? Where was she? What was it like? Was she in pain?

The list went on and on.

Flare would have given anything to swap places with Bullet.

To save her.

That plus, Bullet was very forward thinking. If she was okay, and Flare was back in hospital, shit would get done. There would be a proof of death on Neon.

The drug scam would be getting investigated.

There it was.

Flare knew what she had to do.

She had to stop moping around. Keep busy. Be productive.

Put everything to rest, once and for all.

That way, if the day came that Bullet woke up.

Or *when* the day came for Bullet to wake up, there would be no stress.

Everything would be dealt with.

If that wasn't making amends… if that wasn't a true gesture of apology, Flare didn't know what was.

Chapter Twenty-Eight

Bullet walked through the corridors of Colour Coded HQ.

The place was quieter than it had ever been. Nobody seemed to be around. There was no furniture, no curtains, no tables in the hallways, or beds in the infirmary.

Nothing.

Her heels echoed as they always did, except this time, they echoed further. Louder.

"Hello?" she called out, listening to her voice carry in every direction around her.

She climbed the spiral staircase and went into what she knew as her room.

The black tiles were there, the walls were still black with the white skirting creating that familiar border between them and the floor.

But, like everywhere else, that's all there was.

No bed. No units. Not even her mirror on the wall.

Nothing.

Bullet headed back down the spiral staircase and went straight down to the first floor.

She pondered over what The Spectrum's office looked like as she made her way there. Even if nobody else was here, and nothing else was here, there was no way that he would leave the building.

When she entered the room, dread filled her when she witnessed that it was exactly the same as the rest of HQ.

There were no logs in the fireplace. No fish in the aquarium. No sofas, not even the rug.

The curtains were all gone, along with The Spectrum's desk and chair on the small, marble podium at the back where he would always be upon most arrivals.

The Spectrum, too, was nowhere to be seen.

This wasn't right.

She couldn't figure out what the hell was going on.

Bullet couldn't remember anything as much as she tried to. She blacked out in Neon's bunker after the fire started and then woke up lying on the floor of the infirmary.

Anything in between those two moments was a complete blank.

She sauntered back along the corridor, beginning to panic a little.

Was Colour Coded still active? Had everyone left? If they had, why did they just leave her lying on the purple tiled floor of the hospital wing? Did they perish in the fire and she somehow made it back?

What the hell was going on?

She wandered back along towards the spiral staircase and went out to the balcony, the place she always went when she needed to think.

Jack's back faced her as he leaned on the railing, looking out through the glass front of the building at the view.

"Jack?"

He spun around, surprised at the sound of anyone's voice, let alone hers.

"Bullet? What the hell are you doing here?"

"Where is here?"

"Well, it's Colour Coded headquarters... but, I think we're on another plane or something."

"Another plane? Like the Astral plane?"

"More like the Akashic plane," Jack said firmly.

"The what plane?"

"Akashic plan. It connects all the different planes in existence. The Astral plane is where we go after our lifetime is finished... apparently."

"How do you know all this?" Bullet pried, rather amused at his extent of knowledge on a subject she would never associate him with.

Jack turned away from her, contemplating his answer.

She had been honest with him. It was only fair.

"I had a sister. She was a pretty spiritual person; she used to talk about all this stuff. Life after death, where we go, karma, yin and yang, the whole shooting match. That was her faith."

"You *had* a sister?" Bullet probed further. "What happened?"

"It's a long story."

"Well, it seems to me that we have plenty of time, don't you think?" Bullet coaxed him.

Jack shuffled uncomfortably on his feet.

Turning away from her again, he went back to leaning on the railing of the conservatory, looking out of the window. His mind's eye was recalling that moment in his life when everything turned upside down.

"Abby went missing. Just over two years ago. I have no idea what happened and neither do the police. She went to work and just never came back. My niece was put into care because I and the rest of my family were deemed unfit to take care of her," Jack explained.

"Was she your little sister?"

"No, she was two years older than me. She worked for an optician at the reception desk. She loved her job. She loved her life."

"Was her husband questioned?"

"She wasn't married. She had a deadbeat boyfriend who knocked her up and then fucked off. Abby was a single mum. The best one on the planet, if I do say so myself," Jack told her, not once giving her even a second of eye contact. "Abby's body was never found. The police tried to say she'd run away, that she didn't want to be a mother anymore and couldn't face telling everyone, so she just disappeared. But, that's not who she was. Abby loved her daughter more than anything. She loved her family just as much as we loved her. She wouldn't have given that away for anything on the planet."

"So, she's never been found?"

Jack shook his head, mournful at the thought of where his sister could be. What she went through. Not knowing if she was alive and in pain, or dead.

"And let me guess, Neon offered to help you find her, but first you had to help him?"

Jack looked at her for the first time. His eyes told her everything she needed to know.

She nailed it.

"Where did you meet him?"

"I got a lead that a guy who hung out in a bar 24/7 on the east side of Edinburgh might know something. One of those finger in many illegal pies type of guy. Neon overheard me questioning him in the bar and stopped me outside. He told me that he also had his finger in many pies, and could round up some information to help me find her if I came and worked for him."

"What did he have you doing?"

"At first, I was his delivery boy. He was in the world of drug lords, and he had me shipping packages from A to B. Picking up payment, if they had it, and bringing it back to him, as well as relaying any other orders that his 'clients' asked for."

"What kind of drugs?"

"Some hard, some harmless. Weed mostly. Some ecstasy. Heroin, cocaine, speed," Jack listed for her. "I did that for about a month and then he had me answering his phone to take the orders. I did that for less than a month, and then he had me act as his debt collector."

"So, if there were people who owed him money...?"

"I'd go and scare the bejesus out of them. 'Do whatever I had to do to get him his money'," he quoted.

A moment passed by as Bullet processed everything Jack told her.

Neon always had an M.O. that occasionally changed, but lately, from the intel that Bullet had been gathering, this seemed to be the one that he preferred. It was easy, straightforward, and quick to execute.

Right up his street.

"Why the hell are you here?" Jack burst out suddenly. "I mean, I know I'm here because Neon tortured me. What happened to you?"

"I'm here after I went back to get you," she explained, "and we did. You're probably in the hospital wing now. Well... not that I can see you..."

"If you got me out then that's where I am. Just not on this plane."

"Are we dreaming?"

"I don't know... I don't think so. It feels pretty real to me, don't you think?"

"Yeah... it's a bit echoey though. Too quiet."

"Bullet, tell me what happened," Jack changed the subject. "You got hurt trying to save me?"

"We set the warehouse on fire. But, I stayed back to trap Neon in the lower bunker. After that, I don't remember."

"Who got me outside?"

"Uhhh... Gecko did. Him getting out of the building was Flare's cue to set the place on fire."

"And she did it even though you were still in there?"

"The plan was for me to follow Gecko out. I didn't. But, even at that, she was just following orders."

The pair of them fell into silence looking out at the view, which normally was magnificent no matter whether it was sunny or rainy outside, but right now, it was bland.

Boring, even. Lifeless.

"Are we dead?" Bullet questioned.

"I really don't think so. I think this is like 'limbo' or something," Jack suggested.

"Why?"

"Because, a while before you showed up, I saw a man walk past outside and then fade away. The Akashic plane is where everyone passes through to get to the plane their supposed to be on. The Astral plane is where souls go when their bodies have died and they're moving on. I don't think we're there. There would be people outside. I went out for a walk; there is literally nothing."

"So, what? We just sit here until something happens?"

"I think we're supposed to go one way or the other."

"How?"

"Haven't figured that part out yet. I haven't seen a big bright light telling me to go into the afterlife," Jack said.

"Are you expecting to?" Bullet pried.

"I don't know. Sometimes I hope I do. Other times… I think my life was just starting to get good," he said as he turned to face her, "and that was because of you. I don't want to leave you."

"I don't want to leave you either," Bullet admitted. "Jack, you have no idea how thrilled I was when we went in there and found you alive."

He put his arm around her with a smile and continued to look out at the very plain and un-giving view.

Bullet just looked at him.

Every cut and every bruise was gone.

His arm didn't need a sling from her shooting him.

His usual stubble was gone, just like the bags under his eyes and the scar that she had once noticed on the back of his neck. His eyes were bright and healthy.

Right there, he was everything that she had ever wanted for him.

Safe.

In no pain.

Just like she was.

And, better yet, they got to be in that state together.

"I wonder what everyone's doing…" Bullet thought out loud.

"Probably panicking about you being at death's door."

"And you."

"Mainly you," he smiled at her, "and rightfully, so."

Bullet looked away, embarrassed.

To this day, it was hard for her to take any kind of compliment. Jack showered her with them constantly, so, one way or another, she was going to have to get used to it.

But, she could tell by his attitude and his forced smile that he felt like they all loved her, and no one was bothered about him.

"They love you, Jack," Bullet assured him. "When we got you home after I pulled the trigger... Tide was beside herself. She thought you had died in the back seat with her. Rocket and Gecko never left the infirmary until you woke up. And I was... well... you know the state I got myself into."

"They really all felt like that?"

"Yeah, they really did. And I know that, right now, they're all in the infirmary routing for both of us. Not just me."

"We're not done, yet. We have to go back."

"I know. I don't know what happened with Neon, and then there's the whole drug scam he's set us up for. He said that, in the event of his death, people had been ordered to come after us. We need to be there to make sure no one else gets hurt," Bullet informed him.

"Yeah, that's all valid. That does need sorted. But, that's not what I meant."

"You've been talking to The Spectrum too much. Quit talking in riddles, Jack," she nudged him.

"We have to go back. *We're* not done yet. You and me. Us. We've got so much further to go than this. We're not meant to die yet,"

Bullet felt herself welling up at the sentiment he put into his words.

He wasn't joking around.

His eyes, that always talked louder than he did, were saying that he genuinely meant every word.

"This..." he said, gesturing to Bullet and himself, "this was meant to happen. I'm not prepared to give up on that."

"Neither am I," Bullet admitted.

"So, let's go back. Let's find the way. Together."

Chapter Twenty-Nine

Flare had Youth in a headlock, her thumb and forefinger nipping his ear as she dragged him into his room. He whimpered and squirmed in her grip, but he couldn't break free.

"Stop struggling!" Flare yelled.

"I'll stop struggling if you just let me go!"

"Oh, so you can go back to the infirmary!"

Flare shoved him across the room, ignoring that he almost bowled over a table behind him.

"That's where we need to be! If Bullet wakes up then… "

"Then Lab will call us!" she snapped, cutting him off as Gecko followed them into the room, curious about the commotion.

"What's going on?"

"We have work to do," she growled, "are you prepared to help?"

"Well, yeah, of course I am. But, you know, if Bullet wakes up we should maybe be there."

"We'll be there when she wakes up because Lab will let us know when she does. In the meantime, we need to keep busy and get to the bottom of all of this. There's still a lot of work to do!"

"She's right," Sparrow announced from the doorway, "there's lots to get done. Don't you think it'd be nice to have Bullet wake up and not have to worry about anything? It can be our 'Get Well Soon' present for her. Something meaningful."

"Not like you to be so sentimental, Sparrow," Gecko mocked.

"Thanks," he said sarcastically, "she's my frie… my family, too. I want her better as much as everyone else. We all deal with shit differently."

"This is getting us nowhere, stop insulting each other," Flare snipped at them.

"How can we help?" asked Rocket, walking in with Tide at his back.

"We need to do a think-tank. What do we know?"

"We know that Bullet's fighting for her life and we're not with her," Youth scoffed.

"Will you give it a rest, Youth!" Sparrow pierced him.

"I'm sorry, I just don't feel comfortable with this," he admitted.

"Well, let me put it this way," Flare interjected, "the sooner we get to the bottom of this, the sooner we can go back to Bullet and Jack."

Youth slumped into a seat beside him, his mood mimicking that of a five-year-old.

"So, again, what do we know?"

"We know that Neon was signing off on stuff as The Spectrum, and packets of cocaine dressed up as C4 were being delivered to him only to be replaced with salt before getting sent back out, with initials on it that we believe belong to Rocket, Sparrow you and Bullet," Gecko rhymed off.

"We know that Neon had a bunker built under the radar within the last year. But, he had a backup bunker underneath for whatever reason," Sparrow added.

"It was his torture chamber," Gecko announced. "Seriously, you guys didn't see it down there. There were two bodies hanging from a hook on the back wall by wire around their necks, which were clearly snapped in half by the way."

"And that's where Bullet trapped him during the fire?" Flare said.

"She was lying on top of a door when we found her. I'd imagine that's where he is," Rocket chimed in.

"Okay… what else?" Flare asked.

"Well, we know this guy is important," Youth said, loading David Watt's picture up on the plasma again. "The Lion's Den gang member that was accused of rape and then walked, but turned up dead on top of the Wallace Monument in Stirling."

"Didn't you also say he was the first person from the Lion's Den to ever be arrested?" Tide asked.

"I did, yeah," Youth said. "Jack also identified his brother as the delivery guy who dropped off all the cocaine dressed as C4."

"And I can identify him as one of the dead men hanging in Neon's torture chamber… torture bunker… thing…" Gecko announced.

"WHAT? Are you serious?" Flare probed.

"I'm no expert, and there was a lot going on when Bullet and I were down there, but I'm pretty certain. Those tattoos are rather in your face," Gecko replied.

"Well, that's a bit of a game changer," Rocket confirmed.

"How important was he in this gang?" Sparrow asked Youth.

"As far as I can tell, he was pretty high up. If he wasn't the drug lord, he was definitely second-hand man," Youth said. "I have a feeling that Neon was running it though, it's too coincidental that Prismatic and this Lion's Den started running at the same time."

"I'm telling you, it was his financial plan!" Tide said.

"Or his backup plan... if Prismatic failed then he had something to fall back on," Rocket offered.

"No, the financial plan makes more sense," Youth said, "we don't earn money from what we do, but it still needs funding. Bills need paid, things need bought, people need fed, yadda yadda yadda..."

"Well, that's pretty much everything," Sparrow said. "So, what's first?"

"Proof of death," The Spectrum announced, standing with his hands clasped behind his back. "That is most definitely top of the list. Rocket, get the cars ready."

"How many, sir?"

"Two; Yours and Sparrow's."

"Yes, sir," Rocket shuffled past him in the doorway and headed down to the garage.

"Thank you. Proof of death will be Sparrow, Flare and Tide's mission, since they've been down that way before and know where to look. Youth and Gecko, I want you to track down any known associates from the Lion's Den. Get a location on them, and then Gecko will go with Rocket to track them down. I want earpieces set to pressure activation, and formal code used when communicating. Understood?"

"Yes, sir," they murmured, almost harmoniously.

"Good. I'll have my earpiece in also, as will the Lavender Lab. If you need any of us, just call out."

"And if there's any change?" Youth asked, his passion and anxieties forcing him up out of his seat. "If anything happens with Bullet or Jack?"

"You'll all be the first to know. Now, hop to it."

The Spectrum left them in Youth's room, walking away with his hands still clasped behind his back.

"We'll tell Rocket that he's to come back up here to wait in case a gang member is found," Flare said, heading for the door. "Right, guys... grab your gear. Meet you all out the front in ten."

"Sure thing," Tide confirmed.

Flare, Tide and Sparrow left Youth's quarters with haste.

"Where do we start?" Gecko asked Youth.

"We start where everyone always is... social media," Youth smiled.

"Facebook?" Gecko scoffed. "I'd never have thought of that."

"You'd be amazed at the number of nosy parkers there are on there. The joys of a 'search' bar," he giggled.

Youth clicked on the search bar and simply typed: The Lion's Den.

Search.

Many people came up in the search, some of them with the surname Lion, or Lyon, and some of them with the letters 'Den' in their first names.

Youth scrolled down and saw a page for the TV show with the same title, skipping past it immediately, going straight for the posts from people with 'The Lion's Den' somewhere in their status updates.

"These are just about the TV show," Gecko said, leaning over Youth's shoulder to look at the monitor.

"What about this one?" Youth asked, clicking on a link. "Aw, that's someone that works on the set for the TV show... typical."

They continued scrolling, looking through everything that they could.

"Wait, go back," Gecko's voice boomed in his ear.

Youth moved the page back up.

"What did you see?"

"I saw something that said... there, that one. 'It's obvious they're doing it, how can the police not catch them'. That sounds ominous enough to be something."

"It does indeed," Youth agreed, clicking on the post.

After they both scanned over it quickly, Gecko read aloud.

"Everybody's heard of the Lion's Den gang in Glasgow, probably people trying to piggyback on the Lyons who constantly feud with the Daniels. It's obvious they're doing it, how can the police not catch them? I'm pretty sure one of them stays next to me in Bearsden because he's constantly got people chapping his door late at night, and they leave a few minutes later with a packet that they never came with. The police have searched his house twice but they've never found anything incriminating? Surely, there's something that will give them away... people get hurt with this kind of stuff! You heard about all the shootings between the Lyons and Daniels. It's only a matter of time. This HAS to stop.'"

"Well, this guy is angry," Youth stated.

"Aye, you're not kidding," Gecko agreed as he read over the post again. "Bearsden?"

"That could explain how they're getting away with it. Bearsden is really well-known for being quite a wealthy area; if they're dealing from a well-off neighbourhood, dress good and have a nice

231

car and stuff, the cops probably won't look far before apologising for taking up their time," Youth suggested.

"And if they're successful drug traffickers, then they could probably afford Bearsden," Gecko said, trailing off as he went deep into thought. "Do me a favour, will you? Do a search and see how much houses in Bearsden go for."

"Why?" Youth pried.

"Just… work with me here."

Youth began typing on the keyboard. He loaded up a search engine for house hunters and scrolled down.

"Okay… a smaller house there going for one eighty-five…"

"Use the filters, they'd be using something that had a lot of rooms; one, maybe two for their drug storage, and then the others to house gang members. There'd probably be a garage, or a shed. Driveway."

Youth zig-zagged his mouse across the mat viciously, clicking and typing as he took in Gecko's instructions.

"Cheapest one is three forty-five now."

"What area are those ones in?"

"Hang on, I'll do a frequency search with the postcodes," Youth said, typing frantically again, catching on to what Gecko was trying to do.

"Seems to be the south-east side of Bearsden."

"Is there anything in the middle of it all? Like a famous bar, or a hotel or something?"

"No… but, there is a golf club. It's called Douglas Park Golf Club."

"I bet you anything that's where they meet their clients, get orders, discuss business…"

"Let's see what the club's firewall is like," Youth suggested, beginning to type away on the keyboard while Gecko started pacing, rubbing the back of his tense neck.

Even if the golf club proved a dead-end, Gecko was pretty certain he had a place to start sniffing around for someone who was a member of the Lion's Den, or at least an associate.

"Okay, got their client list," Youth announced.

"Already?" asked Gecko, flabbergasted.

"I'm born for this, my friend," he sniggered playfully. "Okay… do any of these names look familiar?"

"Jeez, there's a lot of them," Gecko observed, "are they in order of the date they signed up?"

"No, alphabetical, but I can look at the date that they joined. Why, what you thinking?"

"I'm thinking that it would take the gang a bit of time to get things up and running, get a steady flow of income… maybe a year."

"Okay dokey, loading up everyone who joined in 2013 onwards," Youth declared, smacking a couple of keys, still beaming from Gecko's comment about how fast he worked.

Youth loved to impress everyone.

"No. Way," Gecko said.

"What? What?" Youth snapped out of his daze.

"There," Gecko replied, pointing to the monitor. "Kevin Watt joined the club in August 2013. Can we see his activity?"

"I should be able to dig that out," Youth informed him, trying to be humble about his skills.

"Joined in 2013, opted for the premium membership, visits once a week… never plays a game of golf, always sits in the clubhouse ordering food and drink," Youth read out.

"And that's a lot of food and drink for one person to eat all on his lonesome," Gecko noticed. "Six whiskeys, two steak lunches, one chicken en croute, and a bottle of house red for the table."

"That's what most of his order history looks like."

"He's wining and dining people."

"And it seems he's related to Andrew and David Watt."

"Well, that would be a massive coincidence if he wasn't."

Gecko and Youth continued to stare at the screen with no intention of looking for anything else, satisfied with their speedy and efficient work.

"Good job, man," Youth said, holding up his hand.

"Right back at ya, buddy," Gecko replied, giving him an epic high five with glee that they got another lead.

"Yellow Youth to The Spectrum, we have something. Will we come to you or will you come to us?"

"The Spectrum to Youth, I'm on my way. This better be good."

"Youth to The Spectrum… it is, sir. Believe me. You're going to be pleased."

Youth started to do research on Kevin Watt as Gecko slumped into a spare seat, relieved and proud of his efforts.

If they could take down an entire gang as well as Neon… that would be a pretty wonderful day.

Bullet would have nothing to worry about, and she could concentrate solely on her recovery.

At the end of the day, that was all everyone wanted.

Chapter Thirty

The Spectrum walked in without announcing himself and sat down by Youth and Gecko.

"Talk to me."

"This is Kevin Watt. He's a cousin of David and Andrew, both of whom are now dead," Youth began.

"He lives on Boclair Road in Bearsden, and has an account with Douglas Park Golf Club, but he's never played a game in his life," Gecko continued.

"That's a shame. A man with integrity is a man who plays golf," The Spectrum stated. "Keep going."

"Being a cousin, we believe him to be part of the gang, but also because he's listed as receiving unemployment benefits, yet he can afford to live in a house in one of the wealthiest streets in Scotland," Youth said. "We believe that the two brothers were running the whole shindig, but now that they're dead, Kevin is the man in charge. I checked his phone records; once a week he called a mobile number that isn't listed to any name in particular. I cross referenced that with Jack's numbers, and it's a match to the one that Neon supplied him with."

"So, Neon is in constant contact with this gentleman?"

"Yes, sir," Gecko confirmed.

"However," Youth jumped in, "considering David Watt was murdered and no one knows who did it or how on earth he ended up on top of a monument, and Gecko is certain that Andrew Watt's body was in the lower bunker when he went with Bullet to rescue Jack, the common denominator is Neon. We can't state solidly if he's arranged for him to contact him to exchange business discussions or because he's fallen victim to his threats."

"That doesn't matter. You found a link. That's exactly what we're looking for. You said you have his address?"

"Yes, sir," Youth affirmed.

"Gecko, you're up, son. Rocket will take you. Visit Mr Watt in your Prismatic uniform, tell him you work for Neon and that he sent you. I want to see his reaction to Neon's name, find out if he's scared of him or admires him."

"What will I say when we find out which way he swings?" Gecko checked.

"May I?" Youth offered.

"By all means, m'boy," The Spectrum welcomed Youth's input.

"If he admires him, tell him that the Lion's Den's biggest rival went after him and set fire to the warehouse; that way, we can find out if they have any competition in the drug trafficking world. If he says they don't have one, then just say that's what Neon told you to say, and that he'd understand the message. Put him on the spot both ways," Youth offered.

"Good man," The Spectrum approved, "and if he flinches at Neon's name?"

"At this point, sir, I'm out. Sorry," Youth recoiled in embarrassment.

"No need for apologies. Gecko?"

"He could say that he overheard Neon talking about him and how he had him under his control," Rocket chimed in, leaning in the doorway, "and he considered the possibility that he'd like to join some of Neon's workers in the planned revolt against him. Offer him a way out. If he accepts, then we bring him back here."

"Yes, I do like the sound of that," The Spectrum considered, "but, if he doesn't accept?"

"Then I tell him to swear he won't say anything, and if he agrees, then there won't be an anonymous phone call to the police and we'll leave him alone," Gecko offered.

"Good. Well done, gentlemen. Efficient work, done quickly, and thoroughly checked out. Now, go. Rocket, I take it Sparrow and the girls have left already?"

"Yes, sir. Around twenty minutes ago," Rocket replied.

"Good. Well, we haven't heard anything on the earpieces so no news is good news. Off you go."

"Righty-ho!" Gecko said, getting up and heading for the spiral staircase to go to his room and get his things. Rocket was right at his back, planning to head downstairs.

"The car is already round the front, meet you outside in ten?" Rocket offered.

"Yeah," Gecko accepted, "but, do me a favour? Wear that ridiculous red cap you sometimes put on. And your leather jacket. I need you to look like a henchman."

"What? Am I not waiting in the car?"

"A big, strong man like you? Of course not! If things go pear-shaped, I want you in there with me. You fight better than I do."

"Yeah, I can't deny that," Rocket laughed.

"Aye, very good," Gecko batted back as they went their separate ways on the spiral staircase.

Just as Rocket swung the driver door open to get in, Gecko was walking out of the building with his bag. He flung it in the back before climbing in the passenger seat, Rocket taking off before his door had even closed.

"You could at least wait until I put my seatbelt on," Gecko scoffed at him.

"Or I could go now and get a head start."

"Oh, that whole thirty seconds, if that, makes all the difference, eh?"

"Sometimes it does, actually. Take Bullet for instance."

Gecko instantly went quiet.

"If I had driven any slower, she probably would've died."

Gecko picked at his nails feeling very guilty and not knowing how to deal with it. He looked up at Rocket who was paying attention to the road.

"You did good, Rocket."

"Not good enough," he claimed.

"She's going to be okay."

"You really think so?"

"I don't really know what to think, to be honest. I'm just choosing to believe that she's going to be okay. No other outcome sits well with me," Gecko admitted.

He revealed a side of himself that Rocket had never seen before.

One that was prepared to fight to the death for Bullet.

He knew that his comment about 'Bullet not making it wouldn't sit well with him' was kind of a threat to anyone who worked with Neon.

Rocket reckoned Gecko was probably one of those silent but deadly types. Seemed like the loveliest guy on the planet that wouldn't harm a fly, but if you crossed him, it would turn into a whole other story.

"How long until we get there?" Gecko interrupted his train of thought.

"Umm… probably about three hours. Get comfy," Rocket replied.

"What music do you have in here?" Gecko asked, turning on his CD player.

A rock band blasted out of the speakers.

"You call this music!" he shouted over the noise.

"It's the Foo Fighters! They're class!" Rocket defended.

"What else do you have?"

Gecko took the CD holder from the slot in the door and started to thumb through it.

"Oh, now, this'll do."

He pushed a disc into the player and put the ejected one in the now available slot in the case.

"What're you putting… Oh, come on! Really?"

"You can't argue with Blondie, my friend. Why are you moaning? It's in your collection!"

"Yeah, Tide put it there," Rocket admitted.

"Oh, she did, did she?" Gecko teased. "How's all that going?"

"How's all what going?"

Rocket put up a wall.

"Aw, come on," Gecko pushed, "you're always with her. Sparks fly constantly. Whenever something goes wrong she runs to you. The first time you ever cried was in her arms. Rocket, no one's judging you, we're all happy for you both."

Rocket remained silent, navigating his way down the winding, twisting roads through the Cairngorms.

"We all know you've been seeing each other since, like, the week after The Spectrum brought her into Colour Coded. And you've changed since."

"What?" Rocket finally piped up. "How?"

"You're not all, you know, 'check me out with my big, bulging biceps' kinda guy anymore."

"Aw, piss off!" Rocket dismissed him.

"Look, you're a good-looking guy. I'm the first one to admit it, believe me. I get why she's with you. You is a fine piece'a ass!" he laughed, putting on an accent and lightening the mood.

It worked.

Rocket burst out laughing.

"But, you have to admit… you know you are. Any reflective surface and you were admiring yourself in it. You loved yourself more than anything. And then you met Tide; it was like you found something that you love even more."

Rocket's expression was one that clearly agreed with him.

"I do love everyone more than myself though."

"Yeah, *now* you do," Gecko ridiculed him devilishly.

"No, no, come on. I always have."

"Well… you had a funny way of showing it, darling," he teased him.

"Hey, I'll crash this car and make sure your side gets it," Rocket warned him jokingly.

"Well, aren't you just a big ray of sunshine."

The pair laughed as they continued down the road, Blondie playing in the background.

Hours passed by, and Rocket turned the car on to Boclair Road in Bearsden.

The evening traffic had not long fizzled out into nothing. At the back of eight p.m., everyone was settling down to all their TV shows or soap operas, ready to see the night in before bed.

"Where about is it?" Rocket asked.

"Should be somewhere on the left," Gecko replied, looking out at all the houses, checking their numbers. "I think it's this one here."

"What, that one?"

"Yeah, yeah, yeah, just stop here,"

Rocket pulled in to the side of the road just down from the house.

"Right, buddy boy. Get changed in the back," Rocket told him.

"Yeah, I'm going," Gecko scoffed, climbing through into the back and flinging himself on to the seat. "No peeking, now. I'll tell Tide."

"Aw, damn, you figured out my ulterior motive," Rocket announced sarcastically as Gecko slipped into the one piece suit he made for Prismatic.

He lifted out his bright green binoculars and leaned on the edge of the passenger seat to steady his visual as he held his eyes up to the scopes and peered at Watt's house.

"See anything?"

"Lights flickering through that window at the front. He's watching TV," Gecko said, "you ready, henchman?"

Rocket slipped on his cap.

"Ready."

Gecko and Rocket got out of the car and walked along the pavement until they reached the gate that would lead them up to Watt's house.

The white wall had a black metal fence positioned on top of it. The mono-blocked driveway was large with an Audi TT residing at the end of it.

In comparison to the rest of the houses down this stretch of road, this little white one with black framed windows was rather small. However, in the great scheme of things, it was still a big house, which really just spoke volumes for Watt's neighbours.

By the built-in double garage, the front garden was elegant and tidy, with a different array of flowers planted and beginning to wither in the autumn weather. When they got to the door, Gecko took a breath before battering on it.

The wait seemed like forever.

Rocket looked at the window where the TV was shining through, and suddenly, the blind flicked shut.

Someone was eyeing them.

Several minutes later, the door opened to reveal a man in his late thirties, a receding hairline atop his head and a scar down his face, standing in the hall.

"Yeh?"

"Kevin Watt?" Gecko asked.

"Aye, whit ye wantin'?" Watt asked, his Glaswegian accent extremely prominent.

"Neon sent us," Gecko lied, pulling back his jacket to show the logo on the uniform he made.

Watt leaned out of the door, looking up and down the street as far as he could see before stepping back to let them through.

He didn't look pleased. But, he didn't look scared either.

He did, however, look incredibly angry.

The living room was large and rather pleasantly decorated.

A feature wall that had gold leaves on a stone grey background covered one side, while the rest of the walls were a light shade of cream. The white fluffy rug in the middle of the room complimented the black leather couches against the dark hardwood floor. It was clean and very well maintained; not what you'd expect from the gangster that just opened the door.

Rocket stood with his hands stuffed deep into his pockets, aiming his head down but keeping his eyes on Watt.

Even Gecko considered the fact that he looked rather formidable.

"Whit's he wantin'?" Watt growled.

"He told me to tell you that your biggest rival against the Lion's Den just attacked him. They set the warehouse on fire."

Watt's eyes widened in horror.

"The drugs? Where eh they?"

"Gone. All of it."

"Shite."

Watt's eyes darted about the place frantically, his mind racing as he wondered what to do.

"Is… is he angry?"

"What do you think?" Gecko threatened him.

239

Watt started pacing, looking as though he was going to burst into tears.

"Has he heard fae Andy yit? 'Cause ah've no. An' he wis meant tae be hame b'noo."

"Are you… are you kidding?" Gecko pried.

Watt looked at him, confusion filling his face slowly as he shook his head slightly, not having a clue what Gecko was asking about.

"Watt… Andy's dead. I saw his body. Neon broke his neck."

"Whit the…" Watt stumbled over his words. "Naw… naw, yer fuckin' lyin', ya prick!"

"No, I'm not, I swear. I went in when he was interrogating Burns. You know who Burns is?"

"Aye, Jack Burns, ah know 'um," Watt screeched impatiently.

"Neon was doing a number on him, and I was sent in to deliver a message. Your cousin was hanging from the wall. As an example, according to Neon."

Gecko and Rocket looked on as rage slowly built up in Watt.

This man was now a volcano ready to erupt.

"Am gony fuckin' kill that bastur'!" Watt let rip. "He 'hinks he kin dae this 'cause he knows a couple'y 'hings? He can get 'imsel tae fuck!"

"Woah, woah, woah… wait," Gecko pleaded with him after he pulled a gun out of a drawer in the side unit, "wait a second, okay? We can help you."

"Aw, kin ye?" Watt mocked him. "How?"

"There's a few of us at Prismatic that hate him just as much as you do. Making false and empty promises, emotionally or physically blackmailing us to keep us in line, executing people in front of us to put the fear in us. We're done with it. We're planning a way out. But… we need a leader," Gecko enticed him like a pro. "You'd be a perfect fit."

"Ye want me tae help ye'z aw get oot fae under 'uhm?" Watt repeated, making sure he was hearing him right. "Eh ye mad? Neon'll go pure ape shit, man!"

"Yeah, and who's he going to have to do his bidding after the biggest bulk of his 'workers' turn against him?" Gecko persuaded him.

Watt was clearly taken by his offer.

His arm that was irresponsibly waving the loaded gun around had went rather still, hanging safely down by his side.

"How m'ny folk eh weh talkin' aboot?"

"I don't have an exact head count, but I'd say about... seven eighths of Prismatic. If not more," he offered. "How does that work for you?"

Watt tossed the gun back down on the unit, nodding his head, ready to join forces.

"Aye. That wurks fur me, man."

"Good stuff. Come with us. We'll take you to your new followers. They've been anticipating your arrival since I suggested we talk to you."

"They really 'hink am the way tae go, aye?" asked Watt, a look of pride taking over him.

"Oh, aye. It's the best idea they've heard in a long time."

"Right, nae bo'er, son. Am wae ye, aw the way, man, a hunner pur cent."

Gecko winked at Rocket as he followed Watt to the door and went outside. They waited on the step as he locked his front door, and walked down the driveway to the pavement, Rocket hanging back slightly.

"Where eh ye parked?" he asked, looking up and down the street. "Dae ye's drive, aye?"

"Aye. That's our car just over there."

Gecko guided him down to Rocket's car, who was still hanging back from them slightly. Pulling one hand out of his pocket, he pressed his finger into his ear.

"Red Rocket to The Spectrum, we have the package. Estimated time of delivery is three hours."

"The Spectrum to Rocket, good job boys. This is the beginning of the next step. Get home safe."

Rocket let a glimmer of a smile escape as he unlocked the car with his fingerprint at the door handle. The Spectrum nipped their ear once more, making their souls soar with pride.

"You've done Bullet proud."

Chapter Thirty-One

It was just after eleven at night when they arrived back at Colour Coded headquarters with Kevin Watt in the back seat of Rocket's car.

Gecko and Rocket were rather happy that Watt had done nothing but moan and groan about Neon all the way back, telling them all about the goings on that he knew of regarding the man they were all after.

"Whit the fuck is this?" Watt pestered them as they pulled on to the driveway of the grand structure that was their home. "This isn'y Neon's pad!"

"Just trust us, Kev. You're in the right place," Gecko said.

"Is this ee's new place or suh'n?"

"Sort of," Gecko replied cryptically.

They slowed to a halt at the front of the building before Gecko got out of the car with Watt following his lead and doing the same.

The Spectrum stood at the entrance in his usual stance; hands tucked behind his back, peering at them over his small spectacles.

"Mr Watt," he greeted him, "thank you for joining us. Please come in. We have a room ready for you."

"Who're you?" Watt probed.

"Someone who has a proposition for you," The Spectrum replied, giving nothing away.

He nodded to Rocket, giving him the go-ahead to park the car in the garage. Rocket drove off, causing Watt to spin around, his face questioning everything.

"Where the fuck am ah?"

"You're safe, Mr Watt."

"Mah name's Kev, mate."

"That's lovely, Mr Watt. Please, come inside out of the cold," The Spectrum offered, holding the door open for him.

Watt walked past him cautiously with Gecko who led him up the glass stairs at the right-hand side of the foyer and through the conservatory. Gecko said nothing as he reached the spiral staircase and climbed up to the next floor where he, Tide and Flare resided and walked along past all of their rooms to the end of the corridor.

The interrogation room.

That small, bland room that Jack had once sat in not too long ago.

"Take a seat, Kev. We'll be with you shortly," Gecko said, holding the door open as Watt passed through.

"You're no' a fuckin' Prismatic worker!" Watt cried. "Who eh ye? Dae ye wurk fur the government're suh'n?"

"You're right and you're wrong, Kev," Gecko informed him, "I don't work for Prismatic, but I'm not a government worker either. You could call me a freelancer with an interest in Neon. Sit tight."

Gecko slammed the heavy door closed and locked it as he witnessed an angry man clawing the other side of it, screaming at the top of his lungs. Rocket, Youth and The Spectrum appeared at his back as he pulled the key out of the door.

"Is there only cuffs in there? We might need a straitjacket, he's a wee bit angry."

"Where's Bullet when you need her?" Youth said dolefully.

"Now, now, Youth. We can do this. Rocket, do you recall the self-defence manoeuvres that Bullet taught you last year?" The Spectrum asked calmly.

"I think I remember, sir."

"Well, let's hope you do. By the sounds of things, you're going to need them," The Spectrum said, referring to Watt's continuous anger outburst that he was taking out on the door.

They walked into the room and looked through the window, observing Watt as he banged frantically on the door, occasionally kicking at it.

"It's a good job Bullet suggested reinforcing that door. It used to be a flimsy wooden number," Rocket determined. "So, I restrain him, we get him to the table and Gecko cuffs him up. What're we doing after that?"

"We play a special quiz game. It's special because only he answers questions, and we get to choose which questions we ask him," The Spectrum said.

"We interrogate him," Youth translated.

"We do indeed," The Spectrum clarified, "did you find anything out about him on your journey home?"

"Well, it kind of came across as though he's the hierarchy of the Lion's Den, but he didn't want to be," Gecko explained. "Basically, his cousins died, and Neon just sort of told him it was now his duty to run the business."

"So, he's been forced to do something that he doesn't want to… do we know how he's being wrangled into doing it? Blackmail?"

"We think so," Rocket continued, "he didn't say it outright, but he said Neon told him about his cousins and sort of implied that he'd go down the same route if he didn't step up."

"Hang on…" Gecko interjected, "Rocket, he implied at the house that he didn't know Andrew was dead. He freaked out when we told him."

"So, he lied? About which one; Neon threatening him about it or the fact that he didn't already know?" Rocket probed, angrily.

"Well, that's definitely something to bring up with him in there," The Spectrum suggested. "Did he say anything about Neon's drug scam? The cocaine getting swapped for salt?"

"We tried to tip-toe around it and get him to mention something but he never did," Gecko said, "I don't think he knows about it, sir."

"Good. Run with that, and then merge into the lie he told you. But, be careful in there. Whether he lied or not, this man has been through an emotional hurricane because of Neon and we're about to add an earthquake."

Rocket and Gecko left the observation room and stood between the only barricade that separated them from Watt. Slowly and quietly, Gecko turned the key in the door, the click drowned out by Watt's cries of anger.

"Ready?" Rocket checked.

"Not really."

"One… Two… THREE."

They burst into the room taking Watt by surprise. But, that didn't affect him much.

He threw a punch towards Gecko, and Rocket grabbed his arm, pulling it back so his hand was stretched into the air above him. Watt leaned backwards with the pressure that Rocket was putting on him before he was grabbed by the scruff of his top and thrown on to the table.

Gecko lunged over and trapped his arms against the desk while Rocket put the cuffs on him.

One hand was secure in the handcuffs before Watt swung his entire body around and caught Rocket in the face with his elbow, hurling him to the floor. Gecko was clawing at Watt's T-shirt when Youth ran in like lightning and forced the deranged man's head down on the table while Gecko fumbled with the cuffs around his other wrist.

"You okay, man?" Youth shouted over to Rocket who was still on the floor.

"Yeah…" he groaned.

Rocket got up off the floor and rammed the seat into the back of Watt's legs.

"Sit down!" he growled as Watt fell back into the chair.

"You fuckin' tricked me, ya wee prick!"

"Actually, everything we told you was the truth. We want Neon. And we believe you can help us," Gecko said, sitting down in one of the seats opposite him. "But, we need some information."

"Well, if ye dinny know any'hin', whit makes ye 'hink ah know?" Watt's voice boomed in Gecko's face.

"Because you work for Neon. We don't," Youth chimed in.

"You said ye'z did… so ye did lie tae meh!"

"Yeah, one little white lie, but you're used to worse than that from Neon, aren't you?" Gecko pried.

Watt leaned forward to his enchained hands and ran his fingers through what hair he had left on his head.

"Fine. Whit dae ye'z wan'y know?"

"How long have the Lion's Den been in collaboration with Neon?" Youth asked.

"Ehhh… aboot four, five years ah 'hink. Mah maw hud jus' been taken tae hospital an' that wiz in 2012… so aye, five years."

"And how long have they dressed up their cocaine as C4?" Youth pried further.

"That wiz jus' recent. His Pristmatic 'hing had a front; apparently experts in dealing wae explosives fur eh government or suh'n," Watt hung his head down and closed his eyes. "Ah dinny know how it aw worked though."

He hated that he was ratting out the one man who had him wrapped around his little finger.

He also couldn't figure out why it was so easy for him to do it.

"So, how long has he been committing the drug scam in their name?"

"Whit drug scam?" Watt asked perplexedly.

"Are you going to tell us that you didn't know that Neon was replacing the cocaine with salt, redressing it to look like C4 again and then shipping it back out?" Gecko interjected.

"Naw! Whit's he dain tha' fur?!"

"Because he's trying to make you a target," Gecko said.

"While making us a target," Youth added.

"And saving his own arse," Rocket jumped on the bandwagon.

"Eh?! Tell meh how?"

Youth took a pile of photos that were folded up in his inside pocket and flattened them out in front of them.

"These boxes; they have initials on them, see? 'BB', 'FF', 'RR' and 'SS'," he said, laying them out side by side to face Watt. "Have you ever seen them before?"

"Well, aye, ah huv'. That's how they git delivered tae us at the hoose," Watt said, eyeing each photo carefully. "But, only the wans th't we haun oot personally. The rest go straight tae whoever ordered thum."

"And this signature?" Youth put down a fifth photo. "Is that the usual signature or has it changed recently?"

"Neon telt Andy thit he'd bro't someb'dy else oan tae the business deal, and he hud ee'z trust tae sign off oan shit wae his signature."

"Well, we can confirm that he was lying. He was forging that signature without anyone's consent."

"So, does this bastur' even exist or did that wanker j'st make up a name?"

"No, he exists," Gecko confirmed. "The gentleman you saw outside when we got here? That's who he's setting up."

"An' who's he?" Watt probed back at them.

"Our boss," Rocket said without hesitation, "Neon's setting all of us up. The initials 'RR' are mine." Rocket slammed the table and stuck his face in Watt's. "He's setting you up as well as us, Kev. Help us fix it."

"Ah don't even know where 'e is!" he yelled back at him.

"We've got people looking for him, you don't need to worry about that. What you need to do is tell the rest of your buddies in the Lion's Den what he's been doing and to cut all ties with him."

"So… yur no gawny haun me o'er tae eh polis?" Watt clarified.

"No," Gecko replied simply, "you do what you want, when you want, however you want. You don't bother us, we won't bother you."

"But, your gang need to know that we had nothing to do with this. You fix it at your end and we'll fix it at ours," Rocket hissed in his ear as he continued to tower over him in a very sinister fashion.

"Aye, fine, whatever!" Watt agreed, leaning away from him.

"You'll help us?" Gecko checked.

"If ye promise no eh grass me up, then aye, ye've goat a deal."

"Good," Rocket said, standing up and pacing slowly behind him. "Now, there's just one more thing to clear up."

"Aw, whit noo, man?" Watt breathed, exasperated.

"You lied to us," Gecko said outright.

"Eh? Aboot whit?"

"Your cousins."

"Ah didn't lie aboot thum! Yer aff yer heid, man. How did ah lie?"

"Let us make this very simple for you," Rocket paced his way around and behind Gecko to face him, folding his arms, glaring at him for a few seconds. "Did you, or did you not, know that your cousins were both dead?"

"Whit?"

"You messed up, Kevin," Gecko informed him, "you made out as though you were shocked at the news that Andrew was dead, but in the car, you told us that Neon had threatened you with 'what happened to your cousins'. So, which one is it?"

"Both! Or... neither... ye dinny get it!" Watt growled, frustrated.

"Then explain it to us," Youth piped up.

"Neon wis blackmailin' ev'rybody!" Watt exploded. "Obviously, ah knew aboot Davie 'coz he died five years ago after eh trial wis aw done an' that. Andy, ah genuinely didn'y huv a clue, man, honestly!"

"How was he blackmailing them?"

Watt started lulling his head from side to side, arguing with himself in his own head. He leaned backwards and stared at the ceiling while he let out a very audible sigh.

"Come on, man," Youth persuaded. "They're gone, mate. They're not being blackmailed anymore, so just tell us."

Eyes closed, Watt slung his head forward, his chin resting on his chest.

He remained there, making sure to avoid eye contact at all cost.

"Davie raped that lassie."

"Jenna Harvey?" Youth asked.

"If that wis 'er name then, aye."

"What about Andrew? And you?" Gecko pried.

"We helped 'um tae cover it up," Watt muttered. "That's how 'e goat away wae it."

"You gave him an alibi," Youth whispered, although more to himself than to the room.

Shockingly, a look of shame filled Watt's face, and he nodded to confirm Youth's murmuring.

Rocket resumed his position; he leaned on the table and allowed his face to prowl menacingly closer to Watt's.

"Why?" he snarled.

"Family, man. That's whit ye dae fur family."

"And what about innocent girls that would never ask for something as heinous as that to happen to them?"

Watt remained silent.

"As much as I respect you for being honest," Gecko continued playing good cop, "that still doesn't explain if you knew Andy was dead before we told you. So, what's the answer?"

"Well, considerin' aw the threats gettin' chucked at meh, and the fact ah hudn'y heard fae 'um in days, ah hud genuinely convinced masel' that 'e wis deid. Tae the point ah believed it," Watt opened up, looking them in the eye for the first time, "aw you's did wis c'nfirm it fur meh."

A knock on the window had them all bounce back a little.

Gecko, Youth and Rocket pulled away from Watt and left him alone in the interview room, letting the silence settle around him like mist on a cold winter morning.

In the small room with The Spectrum was Lab, looking serious as the pair of them whispered.

"Lab?" Gecko called out.

"What's going on?" Youth asked.

Lab turned to face them, eyeing each one of them individually before going back along with them again.

"Jack's awake. He's doing well. Understandably, he aches a fair amount, and he's rather stiff, but that's to be expected considering the extent of his injuries."

"That's good, that's… that's really good," Rocket said, drifting off.

They loved Jack.

They were really glad that he was okay.

But, none of them could hide the fact that they were hoping there would be news about Bullet.

Lab shuffled past them to head back along to the infirmary. They turned to look at The Spectrum who was merely beaming at them.

"You hoped it was Bullet she had news about," he stated like he read minds.

Although, their faces said more than their mouths did.

"Yeah," Youth admitted, Gecko and Rocket nodding in agreement.

"Oh, yeah! I forgot to tell you!" Lab cried out from behind them, watching them all spin on their heels to face her.

She flashed them a warm and happy smile.

"Bullet's asking for you."

Chapter Thirty-Two

Lab led the boys down to the infirmary. All three of them were dying to break into a run, but for some reason didn't want to seem too needy.

"Shouldn't we radio Sparrow and the girls to let them know?" Gecko offered.

"No," The Spectrum replied bluntly, "they have a very important job to do. This will only distract them, if not bring them back before they've finished."

"They're gonna be pissed at us for not telling them," Youth pointed out.

"So, be it."

They entered the infirmary to see Jack sitting up in bed.

"Hey sleepy head, nice of you to join us!" Rocket said, walking to his bedside.

"Yeah… thanks…" Jack croaked. "Where's Bullet? Is she okay?"

"She's in the back room, Jack. She's awake, but very in-and-out just now. She's got a long way to go yet, much longer than you do," Lab explained to him.

"You guys go see Bullet, I'll stay here with Jack for a while," Rocket suggested.

Gecko and Youth said nothing as they near enough sprinted for the door of the consultation room.

Bullet lay limp on the bed, seemingly in the same state as before, but the box around her head was open.

"What was that for?" Youth asked Lab, pointing to it.

"She had mild carbon monoxide poisoning. That was to clear it out of her system. Having the air pressure slightly higher when providing oxygen replaces it quicker."

Gecko approached her bedside.

"Bullet," he whispered, "it's Gecko. You awake, honey?"

The boys watched as Bullet's eyelids fluttered, her iris rolling forward from the back of her head.

"Hey… hey you. God, you scared us," Youth whispered as he stroked her hair gently.

Bullet's lips moved slightly but no sound came out.

"Don't try and talk, honey," Gecko pleaded, "you got trapped in the fire, you were flirting with death for quite a while."

Lab stood at the bottom of the bed watching her.

Bullet's lips continued to move.

"What's she doing?" Youth panicked. "Is she okay?"

"She's fine, she's just… she's trying to talk," Lab said, eyeing her carefully.

After a few moments of trying to mimic what she was doing with her mouth, Lab rolled her eyes and smiled at Bullet.

"Jack's okay, sweetheart. He's outside, he's awake."

Bullet's eyes drifted shut again, relief flowing through her. She felt as though she was being pinned to the bed.

She couldn't move.

Bullet couldn't recall ever feeling this weak before. The room was spinning slightly and the lights were a little too bright for her eyes to handle.

Jack.

Where was Jack?

"Screw this," Lab outburst.

She leaned behind Gecko at Bullet's left-hand side and clipped the machines to the frame of the bed before going around to Youth's side to do the same.

"Open the door for me, Gecko," she instructed.

Gecko hopped to it, instantly.

"What're you doing?" Youth jabbed at her anxiously.

"I'm a sucker for romance," Lab replied.

She rotated Bullet's bed in the room and then carefully rolled it towards the door, eyeing each side of the bed to make sure it didn't batter off of the door frame on the way out.

Cautiously, Lab wheeled the bed around to the main area of the infirmary and pushed it up beside Jack's bed.

"Hey, pal," Rocket said as he jumped up at her sudden arrival.

"Bullet… Bullet, it's Jack, can you hear me?" he grunted, trying to turn on his side.

"Woah, woah, woah, no moving around yet, mister. I sat you up; I said that's all you were getting for now," Lab called out, running around to his side and pulling him back down on the bed.

"I just… I just want to look at her," he uttered.

"In time, darling. In time," Lab promised him as she guided him back around on to his back, adjusting the pillows behind him.

Bullet's head turned slowly to her left, looking at Jack sitting beside her. A smile gradually crept on to her face as he looked at her, longingly.

Like they hadn't seen each other in years.

"Is she going to be okay?" Jack breathed, not taking his eyes off of her.

"I'm going to do everything in my power to make sure she is," Lab assured him.

The Spectrum, Lab and the guys watched on as Bullet and Jack continued to hold each other's eyeline.

"Let's give them a minute…" Gecko suggested.

They all departed the infirmary, leaving Jack alone with Bullet.

"Hey," he whispered, tears rolling down his cheeks, "I don't remember much… I remember Gecko's voice talking to Neon. I remember hearing the gunshot. But, then everything went black. I know that gunshot was you. I know I'm alive because of you, and you nearly died to make that happen. I'm so sorry. I thought the plan would work, I'm so so sorry."

Bullet used every ounce of energy, every fibre of her being, to force a slight nod at him. Her eyes were desperate to close.

She wanted to just drift off.

But, she wanted to keep looking at Jack.

She didn't want to ever stop looking at Jack.

Jack strained himself and reached over to take her hand, groaning and grimacing as he did so.

Lab and the guys came back into the sight of Bullet and Jack sound asleep; their fingers intertwined in the space between their beds.

"I was planning on putting her back in the consult room, but… I guess I'll just leave her out here with him," Lab said, welling up at the sight of them. Bullet and Jack got into the mess that they each were in for the other.

After everything, they were still clinging on to each other.

The pair were holding on to one another as they recovered.

Love story of a lifetime.

"Guys… you should go back to what you were doing," Lab insisted, "right now, the sleep to conscious ratio for these guys is in favour of sleep. Whether you're here or not isn't going to make much difference, I'm afraid."

"But, we want to stay with her," Youth pleaded.

"I know you do, darling, but she's not awake to see you all being there for her and routing for her. She doesn't need to see it, but I'm pretty sure she knows it nonetheless. Come back along tomorrow. You guys need your sleep too, remember? Please?" Lab implored.

Youth hung his head like a kid who had just been told he can't get another toy, and they all shuffled out of the infirmary.

"Sir," Rocket turned back to The Spectrum from the doorway, "what do we do with Watt?"

"Un-cuff him. Give him the guest room by my office, and make sure all the windows are locked as well as locking the door behind him."

Rocket left with his orders.

"Thank you, Lab," The Spectrum said.

"For what?"

He averted his eyes to Bullet and Jack and reverted back to looking at her over his glasses with his hands overlapped behind his back.

"Oh… that's my job, sir. And that's my girl. I'd never let anything happen to her. Or him."

"You went above and beyond with her. I've never seen you deal with anything that was as complicated as this was. You did it efficiently, and you didn't get anyone's hopes up. You have my sincerest gratitude for that."

"We all have pasts, remember?" she teased him slightly. "I've done this before. Go back to your team; I'll look after her."

"I know you will," he smiled at her, before taking a brisk walk out of the infirmary and down the corridor.

"Silver Sparrow to The Spectrum, we've completed our investigation. We're on our way back to headquarters."

"The Spectrum to Sparrow, drive carefully. It's late. Temperatures have dropped drastically and they've to continue dropping as the night goes on."

"Sparrow to The Spectrum, copy that. Our E.T.A is one hour."

The Spectrum reached Gecko and Youth who were in deep discussion outside of the guest room just before his office.

"Where's Watt?" he interrupted their conversation.

"He's in there with Rocket. We brought him some food. Rocket's just turning the water on for the room so that he can shower and stuff," Youth explained.

"Good. And I take it you heard the radio?"

"Yeah… why didn't you tell them about Bullet, sir?" Gecko asked.

"The roads are icy. I don't want him to speed. Especially, with Flare in the car, she'd be hounding him to step on it as a means of getting back quicker. Wouldn't you agree?"

"Yes, sir, I would," Gecko said with a smile.

Rocket walked out of the guest room and locked the door behind him.

"Windows are sealed?"

"Yes, sir," Rocket confirmed.

"Gentlemen, retire to your quarters. You've had an abrasive few days, and they've been anything but pleasant. You heard Lab; sleep is a must."

"Goodnight, sir," they all uttered, relieved at his order as they walked past him down the hall.

The Spectrum made his way to the conservatory.

He leaned against the railing, squinting through his own reflection in the window that stared back at him due to the bright lights on the ceiling meeting the dark sky outside. He could just make out the entrance on to the property.

This is where he would stand until Sparrow's arrival with the girls.

Anticipation was eating him alive. He should radio them to find out the situation.

Did we have proof of death?

Was Neon still a threat to them?

He could understand Gecko and Youth's questions about him not informing them of Bullet's recovery. But, he meant what he said.

He didn't want to distract them from maintaining their own safety.

How ironic it would be that they should kill themselves trying to witness their friend's recovery from a brush with death.

No.

They would remain in the unknown until they got back.

Strangely, the hour seemed to fly by as The Spectrum saw headlights turn into the premises of Colour Coded. He made his way down the glass stairs, observing the girls getting out of the car while Sparrow turned off the engine.

Their red cheeks were glowing as they entered out of the cold from searching the burnt out warehouse all night.

"We have news, sir," Flare outburst as soon as she saw him.

"It can wait. No matter what the answer is, it can wait."

Tide and Flare looked at him confused as Sparrow walked in behind him, shuddering from the nippy air outside. As soon as he joined him, he knew he had just walked into the middle of something.

"What now?" he moaned.

"Is she okay?" Tide punctured Sparrow's words.

"Yes," The Spectrum confirmed, turning his back to head up the stairs again. "She woke up earlier, as did Jack."

"How is she?" Flare pried. "Can I go see her?"

"No, she's sleeping now. She's nowhere near the clearing from the woods just yet. But, she'll get there, with rest and the correct treatment from Lab."

"What do you want us to do then, sir?" Tide asked.

"Sleep," he said simply, "it's been a horrific few days, uncomfortable for everyone here. Rocket, Gecko and Youth are already in their quarters. I, myself, am about to head to mine. I'd like for you three to do the same. After you," he said as he extended his arm ushering them to go to their rooms.

He watched them go.

The suspense was killing him; he knew he would never sleep.

But, he knew that they were all needing to.

The tension from trying to rescue Jack and almost losing Bullet had built up to bursting point in everyone, and yet they had to continue to work as though everything was just fine. He asked for a lot from them throughout everything, and they never wavered.

They never did falter with any task he set him.

He was very aware that his rescuing Flare, Rocket, Sparrow and Bullet from Neon was the best decision he had ever made. Taking on the rest into the team was just as good. He was very aware that he had the best team under his wing.

Never would he knowingly jeopardise that.

The Spectrum walked back to the infirmary and sat in the chair by Bullet and Jack's beds. The Lavender Lab was sound asleep across from them so that she was close, should something happen. He eyed Bullet's still and weak body.

His blatant stubbornness almost got her killed.

She fought his orders, but he forced them to be followed.

Her death would have been entirely on his hands.

Through the night, he observed her.

Jack, too.

But, mainly her.

His girl.

The Black Bullet.

The glue that held this entire unit together.

The Spectrum recalled the first day he met her.

She had gone out for a walk, and they crossed paths. As soon as he saw her, he knew something was troubling this girl. She was pale and exhausted and told him that she and her friends had nowhere to live. And so a relationship formed.

A beautiful father-daughter relationship.

He had always wanted a daughter. He had always wanted kids.

Alas, the opportunity never presented itself to him.

It wasn't long before the sunrise greeted him during his pleasant journey on the train of thought he had embarked upon. He could feel the heat hit the back of his neck like a UV ray in a tanning salon. Time flew by as he watched Bullet slowly and painfully get slightly better, and before he knew it, it was the late hours of the morning.

"YOU'RE OKAY!" Lab sprung to life behind him as her dream came to an abrupt halt.

He didn't even stir.

"Sir... what're you doing here?" she asked, swinging her legs off the bed and joining him.

"I'm just watching over her."

"I slept right opposite her all night."

"I know. I've been here all night."

"You ordered everyone to sleep, but you stayed awake?" she quizzed him.

"I wasn't in the least bit tired. I knew everyone else was. They're young, they've been working hard, they deserve their rest."

"You knew she was okay. You knew I was here... why couldn't you sleep?" Lab pried, pulling a chair over next to him and propping herself down on it, facing him.

Her eyes bore through him.

The Spectrum spoke to her. Easily.

Being in her mid-forties, she understood more. The Spectrum also had a suspicion that she had some form of training in counselling.

"I know the news that Sparrow, Flare and Tide have come back with is not good."

"How? They haven't even said anything yet."

"Precisely."

"I don't follow."

"They haven't said anything. If Neon was dead, if they found his body, they would not have hesitated in telling us."

"Well... you didn't tell them about Bullet until they got back."

"That was my choice; I wanted to make sure they got home safe in the low temperatures last night."

Lab caved.

She knew he was right, she just wanted to deny it until she was blue in the face. Without a word, she got up and checked Bullet's monitors before moving over to Jack's.

Sparrow shuffled into the hospital wing in his shiny silver dressing gown, his usual gel-filled, spiky hair, now fluffy and dishevelled.

He shook his head, and without a moment's hesitation, The Spectrum placed his finger into his ear.

"This is The Spectrum. All members please come to the hospital wing. A situation needs Colour Coded."

After a few minutes, the team walked into the infirmary in robes and slippers, yawning the morning away as they ran their fingers through their hair and rubbed their sleepy eyes.

"I was hoping to let you all sleep until whatever time your bodies woke you up at. I'm sorry for not fulfilling my original agenda."

"No worries," Rocket replied, "so, what did you guys find last night?"

"We don't have proof of death," Tide said, choosing not to beat around the bush.

Flare walked over to Bullet's bedside and perched on the side of the bed, taking her hand and kissing her forehead while sighs of annoyance fluttered through the hospital wing.

"Oh, come on!" Rocket yelled, kicking a nearby chair and turning his back as it flipped noisily on to its' side.

"Take it easy, son," The Spectrum said softly. "Do we know how he got out?"

"We think he was escaping even before Gecko made it out with Jack," Sparrow answered.

"There was another exit?" Gecko probed.

"Yeah… a tunnel. The door was disguised as a panel in the wall of the lower bunker. Which, by the way, I can assure you that Jack is the luckiest guy on earth to still be alive… the amount of blood down there was horrific," Flare interjected.

"Did you find its exit?" Youth asked, ignoring Flare's comment about Jack and pulled out one of his many tablets.

"Yeah, that's why the investigation took so long to complete," Sparrow continued, "he had a passageway dug all the way through the hill that sat to the west of the warehouse. You lift a boulder at the other side and you're halfway up the hill and free to go wherever you want from there."

"Bullet shot him," Gecko chimed in again, "was there a blood trail?"

"Yeah, and it was quite extensive. He'll be seeking out medical attention as soon as he can," Tide confirmed.

Silence ensued, wrapping itself uncomfortably around everyone as the news sunk in. Everyone other than Youth who was swiping frantically at his tablet.

Neon was alive.

And nobody knew where he was.

"So… what do we do now?" Rocket asked.

"We wait," The Spectrum said. "In this dangerous game of chess that we've been playing for the last five years, we have just taken our turn. We just moved our bishop. Now, it's Neon's turn to make a move."

"But, what move is he going to make?" Flare asked.

"Well… that's anyone's guess," The Spectrum replied in a stupidly calm tone.

"I've just thought of something. Something that could either be an asset to us or a threat," Gecko blurted out.

"Well? Out with it, boy," The Spectrum coaxed.

Gecko went over to Rocket who was still pacing.

"Remember Kevin's reaction when we said 'your rivals set Prismatic HQ on fire'?"

The gang near enough saw the light bulb over Rocket's head.

"Yeah… he was horrified. Scared, even."

"What if that was his plan with the drug scam? What if it wasn't The Lion's Den we were to be wary of, but this rival gang that we know nothing about?"

"Youth?" Rocket pleaded.

"Holding off on the tunnel exit and looking them up now," he said with no hesitation as he tapped incessantly on his tablet screen.

"So… is this a move he's made then?" Tide asked, confused at the brainstorm Gecko and Rocket just had.

"Or he's already made his move and now it's our turn," Youth chimed in.

His face was pale, as though he had seen a ghost.

"Youth?" Sparrow called over to him. "What is it?"

Without any mutter of a sound, Youth lay his tablet out flat on his hand and hit a button. A hologram of what he was reviewing morphed into the air above the screen.

"I literally just stumbled across this. It's made the headlines everywhere. And it's going viral."

A news report with subtitles.

Youth hit another button to allow sound to be heard over and above a picture of David Watt sitting side by side with a picture of Bullet in the top left-hand corner, while a middle-aged woman spoke directly to the camera.

"...and claims have been made that, in the anonymous phone call, the gentleman is said to have told the attendant: 'Miss Wells admitted to me that she killed Watt after she had tried to enlist my help. I refused, and we never spoke of it again. I never thought in a million years that this would happen.' I'm here now with the attendee that took the phone call, Angela Mitchell. Angela, did the man seem calm on the phone?"

"He seemed pretty anxious and maybe nervous, but it's hard to tell someone's demeanour over the phone."

"So, he accused Georgina Wells of killing David Watt. He accused her of asking him to help her do it. Did he say anything about how Mr Watt ended up on top of the monument?"

"Only that she had a friend who had a pilot's license, so he considered the possibility of him being involved. When I asked for details about this man, he said he couldn't remember his full name, but, his surname was definitely Marks. He gave a description of tall, medium build, dark brown hair that was usually well groomed... and, randomly, his favourite colour is silver..."

Youth shut down the report.

Slowly, all heads started turning to face Sparrow, who looked sick to his stomach. And completely mortified.

"Oh, my God..." Lab trailed off.

"Is this true?" Tide snapped, floating towards him threateningly.

"At this point, that doesn't matter," The Spectrum stepped in front of her, "he's most definitely just made his move. And now, we have to make plans."

"He's just flung her right in the shit!" Gecko howled with anguish. "Pasts... pasts are forbidden here. Now, we know her name and everything."

"And he's prodding slightly at Sparrow. That was a sly move... 'his favourite colour is silver'. Smooth... real smooth," Rocket said, anxiety getting the better of him.

"We need to make a plan. We defend our own, and we don't ask questions when we do. That's the one absolute rule of this organisation," The Spectrum announced, his authoritative tones returning quickly. "Youth, I want that report on a constant feed into every room, stat. Sparrow, my office, now."

He stormed out of the infirmary.

Terrified, Sparrow followed him a few seconds later.

Everyone was stunned.

That was one hell of a hand to play.

Neon was the only one that knew about the pasts of Flare, Rocket, Sparrow and Bullet.

No one ever really thought that he would have something he could use.

No one apart from Bullet, who lay awake and had tuned into the conversation they just had. Her breathing was sticky and she couldn't move, but her hearing and her sight were a lot more clear today.

While it was unknown to everyone else, she had been awake for a while.

The whole time, she had been staring at Sparrow who was blatantly holding her gaze, both of them with nothing but fear and anger between them.

Neon just handed her over.

When once Police Scotland were on their side, now they would be against them. Neon was a stone's throw away from starting a civil war between criminals and law enforcement; Colour Coded being at the forefront of it all.

Not only was he trying to scare them all, Neon was, moreover, trying to show just how much power he had over everything he wanted.

And he wanted the Black Bullet.

Chapter Thirty-Three

It was as though the world had tipped upside-down when Jack awoke from his deep and much-needed slumber.

He felt a lot more alert in amongst his aching limbs and nipping wounds, and he panicked when the infirmary was empty. He attempted to get up, but the tubes from the machines held him back, and he slumped back on to the mattress, agitated.

Bullet was as still as ever.

Jack rested his eyes on her, a wave of calmness flushing through him as he heard the sound of her heart monitor beeping at a regular pace. She was still okay.

Maybe not okay, but alive at least.

Lab entering the hospital wing encouraged him to perk up again as he attempted to sit up.

"Right, wriggler, take it easy."

She leaned across him and adjusted the pillows behind the back of his neck and shoulders, helping him to shuffle further upwards.

"Where is everybody?"

"They're in Youth's room. Try and relax."

Jack had spent enough time with Lab to learn what her tell was.

Her short responses and lack of light-heartedness was her way of trying to act normal when circumstances were anything but.

"What happened?"

Lab glanced at him.

She was going to tell him. But, changed her mind.

"How are you feeling? Hungry? Thirsty?"

"As a matter of fact, agitated. What's going on?"

"You need to relax, Jack."

"I will when you tell me what's going on."

"Believe me, you won't."

Jack tried to read her as she pulled away from him to check on Bullet. He watched her as she removed a syringe from a packet and penetrated the needle into a vial from a tray by Bullet's bedside. After sucking some of the solution from the bottle, she inserted the syringe into the valve in Bullet's arm and projected the substance through the needle.

As she finished, The Spectrum walked in to join them. He stood at the foot of Bullet's bed, eyeing her with concern as he acknowledged her condition beginning to visibly look a lot worse. Lab approached him and the pair mumbled in hushed tones.

Jack began to feel frustrated.

He was furious.

"Will someone just talk to me already?"

Both The Spectrum and the Lavender Lab spun to face him, stunned at his outburst. They shared a look between them.

Instantly, The Spectrum now knew that Jack hadn't been updated.

"What would you like to discuss, boy?"

"How about telling me what the hell is going on?"

Without saying a word, The Spectrum pulled a chair over to him and placed himself down on to it.

"Neon made his move."

Jack knew it.

And even though nothing specific had been mentioned, Jack knew it wasn't anything minuscular.

"How bad?"

"Bullet's face and birth name have been plastered all over the national news with the accusation that she murdered David Watt. The anonymous caller said that she asked him to help, but he refused."

"We both know that's not true. We know what really happened."

The Spectrum looked at Jack with much surprise in his expression.

"Well, clearly you know what really happened. I don't. No pasts. That's the rule."

"I think you're going to have to come around to the fact that pasts might *need* to be exposed to keep everyone safe."

"Over my dead body," The Spectrum stood with stubbornness and frustration as he turned to leave.

But, Jack wasn't done with him yet.

"It will be over your dead body if you don't think this through properly."

"I'm sorry?"

"You will be."

"Speak frankly, Jack. I don't have all day."

"If you keep trying to keep everyone's pasts hidden, they will eventually come out. And it will be over your dead body, as well as however many other people's."

"We have rules here!"

"And sometimes rules need to be changed! Neon's power over you guys is exposing the truth… take that power away from him! Expose it yourselves! On your own terms!"

Silence engulfed the room violently.

The Lavender Lab shuffled uncomfortably, her fidgetiness becoming increasingly unbearable.

"Maybe this is something that should be Colour Coded, sir?"

"We have too much to be Colour Coded already without throwing this ridiculousness into the furnace and causing an unnecessary inferno!"

"Well, it's a good thing the Fuschia Flare and the Teal Tide are here then, isn't it?" Jack stabbed.

The Spectrum yanked his glasses off his face and rubbed his eyes.

Stress was beginning to consume him.

There was a good chance everything Jack was saying was right, but he wasn't prepared to give in to it just yet.

"I would be asking a lot of my team if I declared that pasts were now going to be known. I ask a lot of them as it is; the fact that they don't have to reveal things about themselves that they're trying to get away from is a huge part of how I earned their respect. I don't want that to change."

"Sir, their respect for you wouldn't waver," Jack stated.

"And you know this for a fact?"

"I know them," Jack proclaimed as he shuffled his stiff body further up the pillows behind him, "and I know that they don't just respect you; they adore you."

"Which is wonderful. It is news to me, and it is news that I welcome with open arms as I, too, adore them like my own children…" He trailed off.

Something else was bothering this man. Jack could see it in his face.

The Spectrum was worried.

"What're you so scared of?"

"Jack, don't," Lab cut in.

"No, I think we deserve to know. It's not just the hand that Neon has played. There's something about people's pasts coming out that he's scared of. What is it? Do you know something about one of them that you don't think others will receive well?"

"In a sense, yes."

"Well, whose? I know about my own and Bullet's; hers is devastating to the point where I don't even know how she functions as well as she does. But, to be honest, I can't imagine how much worse anyone else's could possibly be. So, whose past are you worried about people finding out?"

"MY OWN!"

Jack stopped dead at The Spectrum's emotional response.

Him having a past, especially one that would be looked down upon, hadn't even occurred to him.

The Spectrum was worried about his own life coming out into the light.

"Well, then, keep yours off limits."

"That would hardly be fair, would it?"

"Can we just take a breath for a second?" Lab interjected once again. "I really don't think this is a conversation we should be having without everyone else here to hear it and wade in, so, let's just quit while we're ahead."

"Agreed," said The Spectrum, respectfully. "Jack, I had another purpose in visiting the infirmary. It was never to fight with you."

"No, it was to check up on Bullet."

"Yes, that was also one of the reasons, but the main one being to speak with you."

"What about?"

"You."

"Me?"

"Yes, you."

"What about me?"

"Well, since much time has been wasted, I will just rip off the band-aid, shall I? I'd like for you to join Colour Coded."

Any words that Jack could even think to say wouldn't form no matter how much he tried. He already felt like a member anyway.

But, this was making it official.

It also meant he would need to give up everything about himself to do so.

"So, I'd no longer be called Jack?"

"Correct."

"I can't do that."

"Why not?"

"Because that's my name. And as much as my past is full of many hiccups and many mistakes, I'm proud of it. It's made me who I am."

263

"Which is definitely something to be proud of, boy. I wholeheartedly agree. But, we need you with us to take down Neon."

"You have me," Jack assured him, "just not officially."

The Spectrum merely ushered a slight nod in his direction before abruptly leaving the infirmary, leaving a very stunned Jack and Lab staring after him.

"Well, I didn't expect that," Jack admitted.

"Neither did I," Lab followed, "I thought you'd say yes."

"What? You knew he was going to ask me?"

"Of course, I did. As soon as he said he respected you because you had values I knew he was going to ask."

"Oh... well, thanks for the heads up!"

"Well, another heads up I can give you is: in reporting Bullet to the police, Neon also dropped some hints that Sparrow is next."

"His next target?"

"No. His next revelation."

"Shit."

"Yep," Lab stopped all of a sudden, bracing herself as she listened to the room.

Jack couldn't hear a thing.

"Lab to Tide, I'm on my way," she announced as she stuck her finger into her ear. "I have to go. Don't do anything stupid before I get back."

"So, I've to do something stupid when you get here?"

"Yeah, that way I have an excuse to slap you," Lab left the infirmary chuckling to herself as Jack smiled at her.

He settled back into the big puffy pillows that supported him and shut his eyes. They wanted him to stay.

For good.

A big part of Jack felt exceedingly happy about that.

Another felt incredibly nervous.

Scared, even.

They wanted him so badly that he would have to give everything up.

He'd never find his sister if he did that.

Like his thoughts were heard, a voice surprised him.

"If you join Colour Coded, we could help you find Abby," Bullet croaked.

Jack's head snapped to the left.

Bullet hadn't moved.

Her eyes were still closed.

Was he hearing things?

"If they don't, I will."

Bullet's eyes fluttered open while her head dropped to the right so that she could look at him.

"You remember?"

"We made our way back together. How could I forget that?"

"How do you feel?"

"Like an overcooked turkey."

Jack laughed to the point he hurt himself in the process as he clutched at his broken ribs in frustration.

"How do you feel?" she breathed.

"A lot better now that you're here."

"I was always here."

"But, you were sleeping."

"Well, I'm tired."

"Yeah, no wonder."

They held each other's gaze.

A pin drop could have been heard in the infirmary, but neither of them cared. They were content with peace.

And each other's company.

"Join the team. We find your sister. We love you no matter what."

"You mean: no matter what my past is like?"

"Precisely."

Out of nowhere, noise flooded the infirmary.

It was coming from the corridor.

Footsteps. Lots of them.

The pair of them turned their attention to the door as the rest of the Colour Coded entered.

Seeing them both awake struck a much-awaited smile on each of their faces.

Flare ran to Bullet's bedside and hugged her; Bullet tried to reciprocate, but lifting her lower arm up to touch Flare's shoulder was all she could manage.

"Bullet, it's wonderful to see you smiling, child," The Spectrum said to her with a grin. "So, I brought you all down to the infirmary, but I didn't explain why, and that's because there was a heated discussion between Jack and myself earlier that Lab quite rightfully suggested should be broached to all of you."

Suddenly, Jack felt embarrassed.

He also felt realisation emerging from the depths of his mind.

They all gave up their pasts for a reason.

And that reason was personal to them.

If they found out that Jack thought their pasts should all come to light, it could cause a feud that could split Colour Coded right down the middle.

With what Neon was doing, and with none of them knowing what he was going to do next, a divide wasn't an option.

"Without beating around the bush, I wanted an answer to… "

"YES," Jack ruptured.

The Spectrum turned to him, confusion almost bursting at the seams.

"Yes?"

"Yes," Jack affirmed, "I'll join Colour Coded. If that's okay with everyone else?"

Rocket walked over without hesitation and held out his hand, a grin smacked across his face.

"Never thought of you in any other fashion, pal."

Jack struggled to take his hand, and, as quick as he made it reach Rocket's, he dropped it back down beside him.

It almost wore him out.

The Spectrum, however, had a smile on his face that was double the size of everyone else's put together.

Respect.

That's what it was all about.

"Ladies and gentlemen, with the expertise in electricity, wiring and other forms of power supply, I'm happy to introduce our newest recruit, Jack. All, if anything, you know about his past up to this point is all you will ever know from now on."

Colour Coded gave a wholehearted round of applause as they cheered in approval of this new-found information. It wasn't until he accepted The Spectrum's offer that he realised that if he didn't, he'd need to leave them. He'd need to leave Bullet.

And that really wasn't an option.

Furthermore, if he left, he would be on his own; no means of finding his sister, and, more importantly, no way of taking Neon down.

Finally, Jack had found a family.

But, had he made the right choice?

"After his full recovery, this young man will no longer be Jack Burns," The Spectrum continued after the celebratory antics simmered down a little, "but, instead, will live on with the title: The White Wire."

Jack caught Bullet's eye. That was all he needed.

Just that look.

The one that he loved the most.

The one that told him he had definitely made the right choice. That told him everything he needed to know.

He had most definitely made the right choice.